BEVAN G. ROBERTS

KINGDOM OF SPIES

This novel is entirely fiction. Characters, organisations, events and places are the products of the author's imagination or are used fictitiously. Any resemblance to actual locations, incidents, organisations or persons is coincidental.

First published in 2022 by Aussie Spook Press

Paperback ISBN 978-0-6454469-9-9
Ebook ISBN 978-0-6454469-4-4

Map design by Guy Holt
www.guyholt.com

Cover design by Design by Committee
www.designbycommittee.com.au

Independent authors thrive on word of mouth. If you enjoy this work, please consider posting a review on consumer and review websites, or tweet your thoughts: #kingdomofspies

For Serena, Ethan and Alec

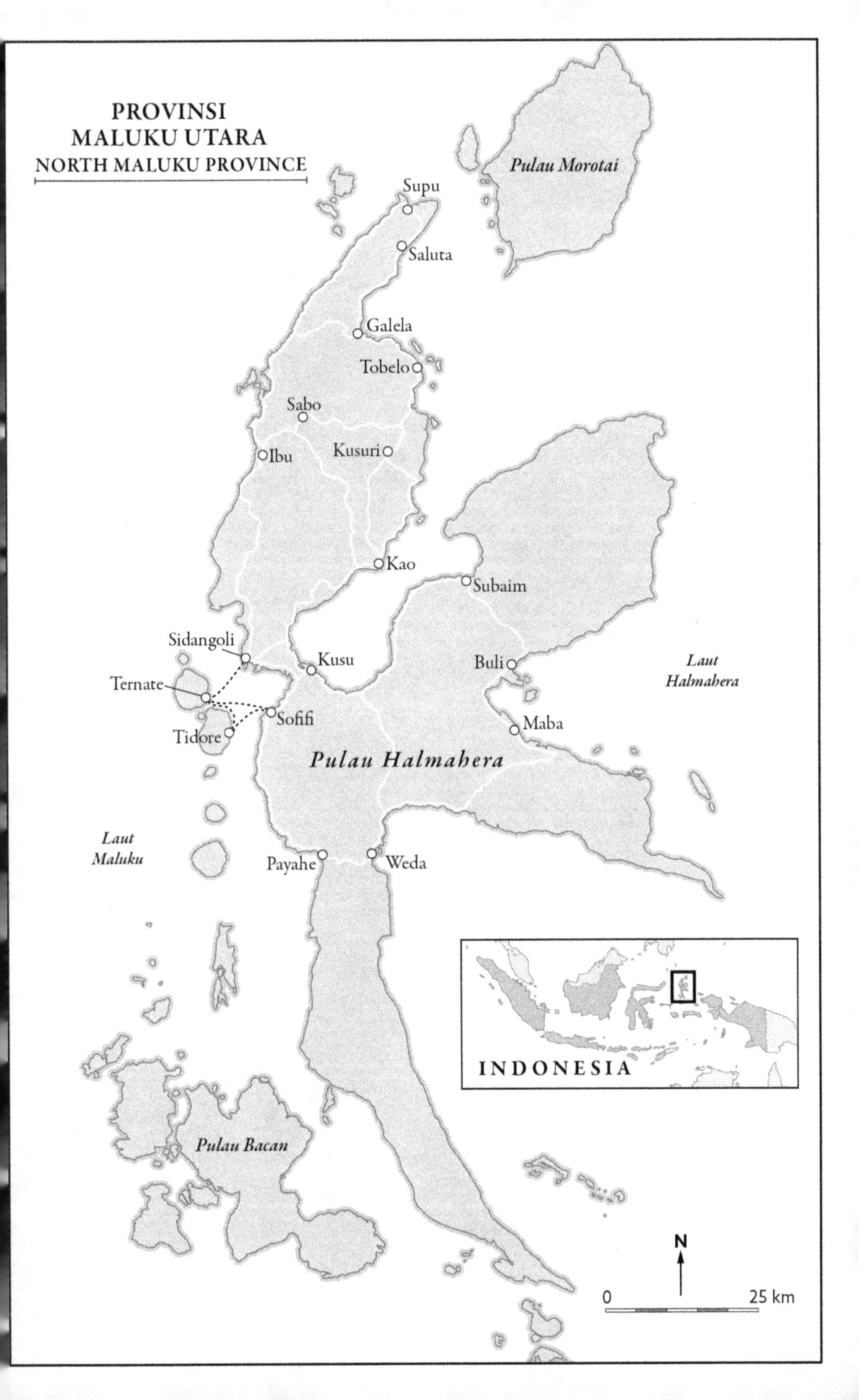
PROVINSI
MALUKU UTARA
NORTH MALUKU PROVINCE
Pulau Morotai
Supu
Saluta
Galela
Tobelo
Sabo
Ibu
Kusuri
Kao
Subaim
Sidangoli
Kusu
Buli
Laut
Halmahera
Ternate
Sofifi
Tidore
Maba
Pulau Halmahera
Laut
Maluku
Payahe
Weda
INDONESIA
Pulau Bacan
N
0
25 km

1

KAO, NORTH MALUKU, INDONESIA

Sugianto handed the camera through the driver's window and lit a cigarette. 'Eight of them so far,' he said, 'all male. Four motorcycles, two cars, nothing suspicious.' He took a sharp drag. 'No sign of Maqsood.'

Carter flicked through the images on the viewfinder. Eight faces he recognised, each photographed from a vantage point outside the mosque gates. Local license plates. He passed the camera to Yoyok.

'Watchers?'

'None, bos.' Sugianto rested a thick arm on the roof of the jeep and looked out over the airfield. Behind him, several of his soldiers checked equipment and weapons. 'Two of my boys took a tour past the mosque half an hour ago. No-one paid them any attention. There's nobody here.'

Yoyok scanned the last of the surveillance shots and returned the camera. Eight photos captured the façade of the so-called grand mosque of Kao, a shell of breeze blocks painted off-white and green topped with a rusted terrace roof. Hardly Mecca, but well-frequented and in neutral territory. Useful cover for the rendezvous.

'If you ask me,' Sugianto continued, 'your guy isn't coming.'

He took a long drag and exhaled skywards. 'There should be sign of him by now.'

Familiar streets and landmarks filled the viewfinder. Carter and Yoyok had arrived that morning with Sugianto's special-forces team and spent eight hours reconnoitring every egress route and observation point in town. There was no trace of surveillance. Kao was clean.

'Not if he comes alone,' said Carter.

A passenger turboprop spooled up at the southern end of the runway. Sugianto ignored it, flicked the cigarette and leaned into the window, eyes darting between the two spooks. 'Anyone with Maqsood's profile and half a brain would have sent a scouting party, Pak.' His gaze settled on Carter. 'Something's not right about this.'

The turboprop lurched forward and began its take-off roll. Carter returned the captain's stare.

'Leave the spy shit to me, Sugi. Worry about keeping your men far enough away to not fuck anything up.'

Sugianto took another drag as the aircraft lifted off and banked west towards the highlands. 'You got it, Pak,' he said. He ditched the smoke and ground it under his boot. 'But I'll stay nice and close.' His face broke to a sarcastic grin. 'In case you need me.'

Carter made a final check of the photos and held out the camera. 'We won't need you.'

Sugianto took the camera by the lens barrel. 'If you say so, bos,' he said with a smile. 'Just remember only your mother was Indonesian.' He smacked Carter's shoulder. 'A half-*bulè* stands out in a place like this.'

A shit-eating grin stretched across Yoyok's broad face. Carter smirked and responded in a thick Ternate creole: 'I blend in better than you think.'

Sugianto sniffed as if to say, 'all right,' and felt for another cigarette. He decided against it and shouted at his men to ready up. Then he made to leave, hesitated, and turned back to the window.

'Like I said, Pak. Here if you need me.' He patted the jeep roof and walked off.

Carter watched Sugianto return to his vehicle before retrieving his backpack from behind the seat. Inside was his own camera, laptop, satphone and a tactical radio. He placed the radio in the centre console and hooked up an earpiece.

Yoyok checked his own kit. 'He could be right, bos,' said the Indonesian. 'We know Maqsood is paranoid.'

Carter reached into the pack again and found the Glock. Loaded, round chambered. 'He's also desperate.'

'Hasan isn't.' Yoyok zipped his bag and stashed it between his feet. 'His message was a warning.'

Sugianto's voice crackled into the earpiece. *'Comms check.'*

Carter thumbed the push-to-talk. 'Check.'

Sugianto's Land Rover moved off.

'Maqsood will show,' said Carter. He replaced the backpack behind his seat and started the jeep. 'Hasan's just spooked.'

Hasan had cowered in the passenger seat while a midday rainstorm battered the Landcruiser. He had tried to light a cigarette, but his shaking hands fumbled the lighter. Yoyok lit it for him.

The agent took an anxious drag. 'I told them I would be back soon.'

Yoyok watched the mirrors. They had parked on a jungle track between two blocks of Tobelo suburb, concealed from the main road. Apart from an emaciated dog, nothing moved.

'This won't take long.' Carter leaned forward and handed a flash drive to Hasan. 'Give this to Abu Maqsood.'

Hasan examined the drive and frowned. A bead of water ran the length of his cheek. 'What is it?'

'Evidence the Indonesians will use when they try Maqsood for subversion if he walks back on his deal,' said Carter. 'We'd prefer they didn't do that, but the only way that happens is if Maqsood cooperates.'

Hasan turned to face Carter. 'What do you want from him?'

'A meeting.'

Hasan opened the window a crack and flicked a stick of ash. 'That will be difficult, Pak. It is not safe for him.' He fidgeted with the drive and finished his cigarette. 'It's not safe,' he repeated.

Carter reclined and rested an arm over the back of the seat. 'It will be less safe if he backs out of our agreement,' he said. 'Tell him if he meets me within ten days, I can prevent his arrest.'

Hasan stared at the flash drive, cheeks gaunt and sullen. A spy's exhaustion.

'Ten days,' said Carter. He signalled to Yoyok to start the Landcruiser. The engine roared to life and they crept along the track. 'Tell me you understood me.'

Hasan turned to face him. 'Ya, Pak,' he had said. 'I will arrange the meeting.'

'Two mikes.'

Sugianto's Land Rover made a right turn onto the highway that led to the centre of Kao. Two minutes until he was in place. The observation teams were in position.

Carter continued and turned right onto a gravel road that ran parallel to the highway. Unlit houses of breezeblocks and rusted corrugated iron lined the track, broken only by the occasional abandoned lot that gave way onto the sea. The cresting sun caught tendrils of rubbish smoke in faint gold and soaked the street in twilight. *Adhan* rippled across the sky from minarets a kilometre away. It was fifteen minutes before the start of *Maghreb* prayer, the designated time for the rendezvous with Maqsood.

The radio popped with surveillance calls from the obs teams. *'Lorry, single driver, no cargo. Heading north.'*

'Two, seen.'

The spies continued south. Women in body-length hijab meandered along the roadside towards the mosque. School children in white school uniforms played soccer amongst construction debris and refuse in an empty street. Men loitered pointlessly in clumps of three and four, smoking but not talking, looking but not watching.

'Alpha, set,' said Sugianto.

They stopped at an intersection. Fifty metres to their right was the mosque. To the left, a small street led to a decrepit jetty over the still grey sea. Reports from the surveillance teams filled Carter's earpiece. An elderly couple turned the corner for the mosque.

'Give me two minutes,' said Carter.

'Got it, bos.' Yoyok donned a white *taqiyah* and tucked his ponytail into the back of his tunic. Carter watched the mirror while the Indonesian intelligence officer climbed out and entered a corner store. He had recruited the owner that morning as an informant.

Carter grabbed the backpack and chucked it on the passenger seat. He clicked the push-to-talk on his radio as he moved off.

'Yankee's on foot.'

'Roger,' replied Sugianto.

The road reached the southern edge of town and turned west, then north, onto the main street that led past the mosque. Carter stopped fifty metres south by a row of low-set dwellings. Opposite, a stray dog picked at rubbish piled along a high concrete wall that ran the length of the street. Carter opened his window to the tinny sound of the minarets and the smell of rotting fish and felt for the push-to-talk on his radio.

Click.

'Charlie, set.'

A moment of static.

'Copy Charlie,' said Sugianto.

Carter propped the camera on the dash and examined the front gate of the mosque under the fading light. Worshippers filed into the forecourt through a funnel of double-parked cars and motorcycles, drawn to the call to Maghreb prayer. An elderly man pushed a *kaki lima* cart in vain search of a sale, malnourished dog in tow. A scooter arrived from a side street and two men dismounted. Carter adjusted the zoom and set the exposure to capture their faces: locals from Sugianto's surveillance report. Observation calls continued to ring in the earpiece. He checked his watch; Maqsood still had time.

Carter texted Yoyok to move in. The reply was immediate and confirmed the storekeeper had reported nothing suspect. A moment later the cool, stocky operative appeared in the viewfinder, weaved through the gathered crowd and disappeared into the mosque compound. Carter waited for a break in the surveillance traffic then reported on the radio:

'Yankee in place.'

'Roger.'

Seven minutes to Maghreb.

Hasan had stood at the sink, alone, eyes fixed on Carter in the cracked mirror. Carter ignored him and checked the cubicle. Empty; reeking of shit. He returned to the sink and started the tap.

'Anyone know you're here?'

'No.'

'Were you followed?'

'No.'

Carter left the tap running and watched the door that led back to the mall. 'What did Maqsood say?'

Hasan looked at his hands. 'He told me nothing, Pak. He will speak only with you.'

A door opened in the corridor outside. The room echoed with women's laughter. Hasan shuddered.

'Hasan.'

Hasan leaned against the sink. Sweat drained from his taqiyah. 'Something is not right,' he said. 'It wasn't like before. He was different.' His head fell. 'I'm sorry, Pak.'

Carter placed a hand on the agent's shoulder. 'This is important, Hasan.'

Hasan muttered something and said, 'I know.'

'Then you know I'll take care of you.'

Hasan inhaled deeply and nodded. 'He will meet you Thursday.'

'Where?'

'Same as last time,' Hasan had said. 'In Kao.'

Minarets sang over Kao. Townsfolk had descended on the mosque in response to the call, each man, woman and child captured in the telescopic lens of Carter's camera. He checked his watch; there were still three minutes to Maghreb. Three minutes to the rendezvous.

A radio call pierced the cries of the adhan. *'Tally bus, inbound on the mosque. Looks full.'*

'Acknowledged,' said Sugianto.

Carter trained the camera on the main road beyond the mosque. Headlights lit the frame as a blue tour bus arrived and parked in the intersection, half-obscured by the wall of the mosque compound. Carter adjusted the exposure and caught movement.

'They're coming out... eight of them.' A burst of static. *'...look like workers.'*

A group of men in blue overalls emerged from behind the bus.

'They're from the mines,' said Sugianto.

The *muezzin* was in full flight as the adhan approached its climax.

Carter checked his watch. 'Keep eyes on,' he said. 'This could be him.'

'Roger.'

A passing local blocked Carter's field of view. Carter swore under his breath and waited. When the view cleared, the miners had formed a single file and had begun to walk south towards the forecourt gate. The first man's face was youthful and shaven. The rest were obscured.

Carter reached for the radio. 'I can't get visual,' he shouted. 'Move someone in close.'

The muezzin reached a crescendo.

'One, do a tour,' said Sugianto.

'Wilco.'

Carter scanned faces in the crowd as more vehicles arrived and parked in front of the gates. A man with a stoop emerged from a small alley and turned for the mosque. Carter got a shot of his weathered face and ignored him. He checked his phone. Nothing from Yoyok.

A trailbike arrived at the intersection in front of the gates. *'Stand by,'* said Sugianto's rider.

Carter retrained on the miners. The procession bobbed and weaved towards him through the camera, halfway to the gates, faces still out of view. They took no notice of the bike.

'Do you have him?' called Sugianto.

'Wait.'

One by one, the men reached the gates, turned, and filed into the forecourt. One of the men paused and glanced in the rider's direction. Carter pivoted the camera as a frail figure in full Islamic dress emerged from a van and approached the remaining miners.

Carter reached for the push-to-talk. *Click.* 'Check the woman,' he called. 'Green hijab.'

'Say again, Charlie,' said Sugianto.

'Just do it.'

The woman turned for the gates.

'Copy.'

The trailbike engine roared over the prayer calls as Sugianto's rider accelerated. He reached the woman as she arrived at the gates and joined up with the miner, her face hidden in shadow. The rider crept past, eyes on the two figures, before coming to a stop.

Carter clicked the push-to-talk. 'Well?'

The woman disappeared into the forecourt. Carter turned his lens to the motorcycle as the rider brought a hand up to his lapel. Carter sat forward. The radio clicked.

'Negative contact,' was the call. *'It's not Uncle.'*

Carter smacked his hand on the steering wheel as the trailbike burst north through a slalom of parked cars and disappeared. Sugianto's voice crackled in the earpiece.

'He's not coming,' said the captain. *'We should stand down.'*

The adhan began to fade, replaced by the voice of the imam and the commencement of the Maghreb sermon. The plan gave Maqsood another fifteen minutes to show. If not: abort.

Carter picked up the radio and clicked the push-to-talk. 'Hold position.'

There was a short hiss.

'Roger,' said Sugianto. *'Holding.'*

Yoyok had rapped on Carter's front door at four a.m. They were due to rendezvous with Sugianto's team at seven for the flight to Kao.

Yoyok held up his phone. 'It's a warning.'

Carter took the phone and stared at the message: *'Nenekku sakit.'* My grandmother is unwell. Hasan's code for: *I think I'm blown.*

'Who else knows about this?' said Carter.

'No-one.'

Carter deleted the message and handed back the phone. 'Keep it that way.'

'He could be in danger, bos.'

Carter shook his head. 'We can't let Hasan fuck this up,' he said. 'Maqsood's too important.'

The voice echoed in the pauses between verses, indistinct and distant as it reverberated off the surrounding structures. Eleven minutes to cut-off; the street was still. Apart from the voices in the air, the only sounds were the occasional surveillance calls from Sugianto's teams. Carter gripped the wheel to steady his hands. His knuckles turned white.

The voice grew louder, off-cadence from the lines of verse.

Carter pressed to talk. 'Get eyes east of the mosque.'

'Eyes on what?' said Sugianto.

'Some sort of loudspeaker.'

'Could be an echo, bos.'

There was movement behind the jeep. Three men and two

women had emerged from one of the houses. Four others appeared further south.

'It's no echo. It's a chant.'

'Copy,' said Sugianto. *'One, get eyes on.'*

'Roger.'

The chants were audible now over the minarets. More onlookers had gathered in the street and were moving in the direction of the noise. A van arrived and parked fifty metres south of the jeep. A group of women climbed out.

'This is Two. Tally new group. Two hundred metres west.'

'How many?' said Sugianto.

'Wait.'

The radio hissed static. A group of bystanders had gathered near the jeep. Carter raised his window.

'Twenty-four.'

Sugianto shouted at One to report in.

More movement near the mosque. *'One's on the move. Thirty seconds.'* A woman in black burqa appeared from the side street carrying a red banner. Carter focused the camera and adjusted the exposure as the banner flicked in the wind. Eventually it unfolded to reveal the word GAMESHAR printed in black lettering.

'They're at the mosque,' said Carter. 'It's a rally.'

Eight minutes. Protesters gathered at the mosque gate. Each wore a red Gameshar shirt, their faces covered with bandanas. Carter strained to follow them through the crowd of onlookers.

'Eyes on,' said One. *'At least thirty of them.'*

The group's ringleader came into view and shouted into a loudspeaker:

'Allahu akbar! Maluku Utara merdeka! Masyarakat berdiri! Pemerintah larang di sini!'

God is great! North Maluku is free! People stand up! The government is prohibited here!

'Copy, One,' said Sugianto. *'Charlie, what are your instructions?'*

Carter scanned the protest crowd. Most of the faces were covered or obscured.

'This is Two. They are almost on us.'

'Stay in position,' said Carter. He adjusted the camera lens. Spectators gathered around the jeep and blocked a clear shot of the protest.

Sugianto shouted into the radio: *'We have to abort.'*

Carter sucked a deep breath and checked his watch. His hand was shaking. He braced it on the wheel.

'Seven minutes.'

The front gate came into focus as a line of worshippers emerged onto the street to confront the horde of protestors. The calls from the loudspeaker grew louder, faster.

'All teams, move back,' commanded Sugianto.

Carter's view was blocked. 'Negative,' he shouted. 'Get eyes on the mosque. Uncle can still make the rendezvous.'

A light flashed in the side mirror. A motorcycle, slow-moving through the crowd.

'Not possible,' said Sugianto. Someone in front of the jeep shouted at the protesters. At the gate, two miners shoved a Gameshar Red Shirt and were set upon. Red Shirts ran through the gates into the forecourt. *'It's too hot.'*

The motorcycle weaved among the onlookers and stopped at the van, fifty metres away. The passenger leaned towards it and looked inside.

'Hold position,' said Carter.

There was a flash and screams from the onlookers as a firebomb exploded beyond the mosque gates. Yellow light spilled from the forecourt onto the brawling crowd. The minarets fell silent.

'We must abort, Charlie.'

Six minutes.

'Negative,' shouted Carter. 'We can still—'

The phone vibrated on the dash. Smoke billowed skyward from the mosque.

'Say again, Charlie.'

Onlookers rushed towards the burning structure. Ahead of them, a lone figure, engulfed in flames, stumbled from the mosque gates and fell onto the street. Bodies lay prone under a black plume while Red Shirt protesters danced and chanted around them. Helpless bystanders gathered near the jeep, their shouts drowned out by the motorcycle as it crept behind them. Sugianto shouted something garbled over the radio as Carter opened Yoyok's message:

Out. On foot.

The motorcycle was ten metres away. Carter ignored it and grabbed the radio.

Click.

The op was over.

Breathe.

'All teams abort.'

Carter grabbed the backpack and replaced the camera. As a reflex, he felt for the Glock.

'All teams abort,' repeated Sugianto. *'Charlie, can you egress?'*

Carter threw the backpack onto the passenger seat and fumbled for the ignition. The starter motor wailed. The onlookers turned to look at the jeep. Then, the motorcycle.

The jeep started as the two Red Shirts skidded to a halt beside Carter's window. The passenger leaned up to the glass and peered in, eyes wide on sight of his target. For a moment, he stared into the glass as if unseeing, his bloodshot eyes narrowing above the line of the bandana before he recoiled and turned to the crowd.

'Mata-Mata!'

Spy.

The motorcycle blared its horn and accelerated away. A dozen onlookers fell into its wake and crowded the jeep. Carter hit the horn as they shouted. The gearbox complained as he engaged reverse. Someone smacked the bonnet. Carter dropped the clutch.

The jeep skidded rearwards over the gravel verge. The crowd came with him. Carter shouted again to move as he shifted into first.

A wall of bystanders stared at him under the headlights, their faces a mix of confusion and fear. He hit the horn and inched the jeep forward. Someone banged on the window. Another horn blast as he revved the engine. The motorcycle started up nearby. The crowd bashed the windows and bodywork as the jeep edged forward, then suddenly parted. Carter looked up as the motorcycle accelerated towards him, a point of yellow light cutting the darkness at its side.

'Charlie, what is your status?'

Carter gunned the engine and dropped the clutch. The motorcycle veered away as the point of light arced upwards into the night sky. The jeep lurched forward. Streetlights glinted off the sides of the glass bottle as it tumbled through the air – one turn, then two – before descending towards the jeep. Carter dived for the passenger seat as the firebomb bounced off the bonnet, broke into pieces and exploded in a wave of light and heat across the windshield. The cabin filled with smoke and noise. The radio fell into the passenger foot well and hissed with static. The jeep rolled to a halt and a woman screamed.

He covered his mouth and grasped the backpack with his spare hand. The door took two kicks to come free. The flames scorched his back as he pushed himself from the jeep and rolled from the inferno, coughing burning air as sirens wailed in the distance. Red and blue lights flashed on a column of white smoke that billowed from the mosque. Close by, stunned faces stared at him in the light of the burning jeep. He sat up and vomited.

'Mata-mata!'

Then there were Red Shirts.

One of the Gameshar men grabbed the backpack. Carter held onto it and rolled as the crowd shouted. Another man landed on his back and forced air and smoke from his lungs. An arm wrapped around his neck to pull him from the bag.

He kicked blindly to break the grip. His face was forced up towards the motorcycle spotter who was pulling at the backpack. Carter's right foot came free and struck something. Someone shouted in pain, and his other leg was freed. There was a blur of red to his left. Something struck him on the hip and forced the last of the burning smoke from his lungs. Carter rolled onto his back, then forced his head backwards into the mouth of the man beneath him. The grip loosened. Carter sucked for air while saliva and blood drained from his hair over his neck. Horns blared nearby. A Red Shirt stepped out of the crowd and launched a barrage of kicks into Carter's stomach. Carter convulsed forward, swung his head rearwards and crushed the nose of the man on his back. The chokehold gave way. The spotter released the bag.

Carter lunged on top of the backpack and gasped for air. The man who had kicked him landed on him and wrenched his neck. Carter held his chin to his chest and felt for the zipper of the backpack. His hand slipped from the zip. Someone kicked him again, the crack of his rib shuddering up his spine. His fingers reached the metal tab again, and he pulled. One of the attackers forced a hand under his arm and tried to lift him, but Carter had his hand inside the bag. Horns filled the air as he found metal. The man on top of him lifted again and they rolled. The crowd was now bathed in light. Steel glinted under a streetlamp as a Gameshar man stepped up, crowbar high above his head, ready to strike, then hesitated. The crowd parted as headlights saturated the scene. The light first caught the Red Shirt, frozen mid-swing, then the Glock that was pointed at his chest before revealing Carter's arms, extended upright to absorb the report, finger around the trigger at first pressure, ready to fire.

The Land Rover skidded to a halt three metres away. Neither Carter nor the Red Shirt moved. Soldiers shouted at the crowd. Boots landed on gravel. Sugianto's men pushed people back.

Yoyok pushed the Red Shirt away and turned to Carter. Carter lowered the Glock and wiped blood from his eyes. The kid ran off.

Yoyok gripped Carter by the arm and shouted, 'Get up.'

More sirens had reached the mosque. Sugianto and two of his men stood on the bonnet of the Land Rover, weapons up. Carter, right leg numb from the blow to his hip, limped with Yoyok to the waiting vehicle. Two soldiers followed them on board.

The crowd began to chant.

'Pemerintah dilarang di sini! Pemerintah dilarang di sini!'

Sugianto didn't flinch. 'Back it up.'

The driver engaged reverse and accelerated.

'Masyarakat berdiri! Masyarakat berdiri!'

The driver backed into a three-point turn. They drove south, then east, to box around the mosque. Light and sound faded behind them.

Sugianto turned to Carter as they reached the airport road. 'You should have aborted when I told you, Pak.'

A column of smoke rose over Kao. A helicopter orbited somewhere in the distance.

'It was a protest.' Carter grimaced and opened the backpack. There he found the satphone, still intact and with signal. 'Shit happens.'

Sugianto pointed back at Kao. 'That was an attack,' he said. 'Someone wanted you dead, bos.'

Carter spat blood. 'If they wanted me dead, I'd be dead.' He wiped his mouth and dialled a number. After ten seconds he got a dial tone. 'Like I told you, Sugi'—they reached the airport gate and the helicopter touched down—'leave the spy shit to me.'

2

CANBERRA, AUSTRALIA

Andy Gibson had never long contemplated the justification for Operation ANVIL. He had never needed to. ANVIL was a minnow of western intelligence, a limited operation in a remote corner of Indonesia that most Australians had never heard of and, by measure of success, never would. Justification was only required for catastrophic failure, and ANVIL had never come close. At least, that is, until the events in Kao the previous night that now threatened to blow the operation into public view. And so, at 7.28 a.m, slumped over his desk under the glare of the halogen lamps of his cramped, windowless office, ANVIL's justification was front of Gibson's mind: justification for the methods, the consequences, the sacrifices. Justification for why the Australian Secret Intelligence Service had conducted a secret campaign of subversion against Islamic radicals in North Maluku and, above all, justification for the cost in lives and property that had and would be paid for what was, at best, a lukewarm guarantee against the tide of Islamism rising at Australia's shore.

Not that he'd ever doubted the ends or means. Gibson had spent twenty years identifying, tracking, and dismantling terror organisations across Indonesia. He had seen countless groups proscribed and abolished, terror leaders imprisoned or executed, and training camps and weapons caches dismantled. But in all that time, down to the last suicide bomber and knife-wielding lone wolf, not once had he seen someone turn back from radicalism. Instead, those Indonesians who harboured extremist views had travelled abroad – first to the Philippines and Afghanistan, then Syria and Iraq – only to return as frustrated, inspired, and battle-hardened warriors, determined to continue the fight at home. Indonesia had responded with force and found it wanting. Densus 88, the police anti-terror unit, pursued countless suspects across Java and Sumatra but the bombings and stabbings had continued. The army, not subject to the same legal constraints the police were, had more success destroying budding militant groups in Sulawesi. But even they remained subject to the law of unintended consequences, and the toll of their operations on local communities drove as many recruits into terror pipelines as terrorists into custody and graves.

North Maluku demonstrated the alternative. Islamist-separatist undercurrents had long swirled in the province and, after decades of political and economic neglect, threatened to give way to extremism. The threat to Australia and Indonesia was obvious: an ungovernable Islamist hotbed of terror schools and bomb factories that could strike the glitzy shopping malls of Jakarta and the luxury resorts of Bali with ease and inspire, if not enable, direct attacks on the Australian homeland. Yet neither country could overcome the fear, shared by political masters in both countries, that outright military intervention would only fan the flames as it had everywhere else. It was Gibson who had proposed ANVIL: a joint operation between ASIS and *Badan Intelijen Negara,* the Indonesian State Intelligence Agency, to infiltrate Islamist organisations in the province, not to eradicate them but to harness them – turn each group on the others and let the threat to Indonesia's stability and Australia's security control itself. It was an achievement as much for breaking the handcuffs of ASIS's aversion to risk as for its success in the field. In twelve months, Jordan Carter had co-opted every Islamist organisation in the region with promises of covert funding, political autonomy and government protection, influence he used to provoke internecine conflicts that sapped the groups' morale and exhausted their resources. For years now, Operation ANVIL had succeeded in keeping the problem of Islamist extremism in North Maluku contained, controlled and secret until, seemingly out of nowhere and for reasons still unclear, two busloads of Gameshar protesters stormed the site of a secret rendezvous with Abu Maqsood, the high-profile Islamist leader of Barpemis and long-time Gameshar rival, and burned down a mosque, injured several-dozen civilians, and threatened Carter's life.

Carter's call had been taken by the ASIS duty officer by satellite phone at 7.34 p.m. Canberra time. The duty officer authenticated Carter using the cryptonym ANTLER and a seven-digit code, recorded and confirmed his coded message and dialled the first name on the call-card for ANTLER (Gibson) before passing on the message and ringing off – job well done, tea and medals to come, back to Spider Solitaire. Gibson, however, was in for a long night. It took him thirty minutes to reach the office and debrief Carter over the satphone; another thirty to staff an all-source intelligence request for anything related to Kao, Gameshar or Abu Maqsood to every branch of Australian intelligence, and two hours to reach every one of his contacts across Canberra and call in whatever favours he could. By then, it was after eleven, with an outside chance of hearing back by morning.

Only then did he call BIN.

Badan Intelijen Negara was an equal partner in ANVIL. Whereas the Australians provided access to the vast capabilities of western intelligence (or so claimed), BIN had the local knowledge, contacts and resources that were necessary for an operation of its kind. It was a partnership stronger in principle than practice. Gibson's calls that night were rebuffed, and Liam Ellis, ASIS's Jakarta-based liaison officer to Indonesian intelligence, had to camp in the empty foyer of BIN headquarters before some hapless intelligence staffer eventually came to see him. 'Midnight Jakarta time,' he'd confirmed to Gibson two hours later. 'They're in the ops room,' he said. 'Sounds bad.'

'Bad how?'

'Hartanto's got his back up,' said Ellis. 'Hope you're feeling charming.'

Gibson wasn't. 'Thanks. Book a flight to Ternate first thing. I need a full debrief with Jordan: psych, weapon, all the usual.'

Ellis sighed exhaustedly into the phone. 'Got it,' he said, and rang off.

Intelligence reports had filtered in through the night. Unsurprisingly, allied intelligence services contributed little other than open-source material; they weren't involved in eastern Indonesia and had little reason to divert resources from regions more relevant to their interests, i.e. China. Australian sources were no better. The Office of National Intelligence didn't consider North Maluku sufficiently strategic, which meant it offered no insight of value that they could trade with the Americans. Defence Intelligence were focused on the Middle East and the South China Sea; anything they had on the Indonesian archipelago was focused on people smuggling and naval movements. The Australian Geospatial-Intelligence Organisation, the *Google Maps* of Australian intelligence, only had satellite imagery from hours before the riots took place. A midnight update confirmed smoke emanating from the Kao mosque and several sites nearby but added nothing to Carter's version of events. Not even the eavesdroppers at the Australian Signals Directorate could penetrate the fog. Phone intercepts confirmed a spike in mobile traffic in Kao at the time of the riot, but nothing suspicious between known Gameshar or Barpemis contacts. Eventually one of Gibson's contacts called with the trace on Maqsood's phones:

'Seven mobiles,' she said. 'Most were active in or around Tobelo at the times you asked for.'

That only meant Maqsood left them behind. 'Are the rest off-grid?'

'Not quite. One showed up two days ago in the upper hinterland. A town called Sabo.'

'Sabo?'

'Thought you should know.'

Gibson thanked her and rang off. Sabo. He could point to it on a map but knew no obvious connection to Maqsood. It could have been nothing; the militants often shared, lost and sold phones, innocently as well as to confuse those watching. It was 2.40 a.m. now, and Gibson felt flat. There was no part of his job worse than pleading for BIN's help without anything to offer in return except, perhaps, doing so at three in the morning. But it had to be done, so, like the obedient-if-overaged spook he was, Gibson called the security officer, downed a double-shot instant espresso, and made his way to the SCIF.

International teleconferences at Top Secret were hard enough with close allies, let alone Indonesia. The encrypted link to Jakarta needed specialist facilities – in this case a Secure Compartmented Information Facility, or *skiff* – separate key material for the crypto, regular audits and expert operators. Probably deliberately, the link had been codenamed ANGINA. The setup had taken months for both countries to implement and approve for use, and the link was constantly plagued by keyloading issues and connectivity outages. This on top of the usual challenges of conference calls: people were busy, forgetful and, in the Indonesians' case, relaxed about time. It was well after three by the time the voice of Gibson's BIN counterpart Hartanto erupted from the speaker phone.

'Sorry for the delay, Pak Andy.' Hartanto's voice filled the narrow, padded conference room. 'We were busy cleaning up your mess.'

Gibson waved off a bemused look from the security officer beside him.

'With respect, Pak Hartanto, *our* mess,' said Gibson. He brought a hand up, raised his glasses, and squeezed the bridge of his nose. 'Let's focus on what happened.'

Hartanto scoffed. 'I will tell you what happened. An officer of your service failed to abort as instructed. Instead, he put one of my intelligence officers and six Kopassus soldiers at risk, not to mention the damage inflicted on Kao.'

'Who gave the instruction to abort?' said Gibson.

'Captain Sugianto.'

'No-one else?'

'He is sufficient.'

'Not when it comes to intelligence matters,' said Gibson. 'Jordan was in charge. Abort or no abort, it was his call.'

'And this is the result!' Hartanto's voice echoed around the SCIF. 'My officers should have control, Pak. We need stability in the lead up to elections.' Elections for North Maluku's *kabupaten* – regencies – were scheduled to be held in two months. 'Instead, we have a destroyed mosque and thirty-three Indonesians injured which, if not for our quick action, would have made the front page of tomorrow's *Koran.* If the media finds a link to ANVIL this will be a scandal, Pak.'

A scandal that would destroy everything they had worked for, Gibson was sure. 'Is there any risk of this reaching the press?'

'No, but take no comfort from that. This was not a random event, I'm sure you agree.'

Gibson did. The riot had all the marks of a calculated hit. 'Who instigated the riot?' he said.

There was a sound of shuffling paper across the line. 'We have several leads.'

Gibson took this to mean they didn't know, or weren't sharing, so he shut down the call and returned to his office, only to wake with a start a few hours later. Questions circled his mind like vultures, ready to pick at his corpse, so he lay there, half-asleep on his desk as the clock reached seven-thirty, and ruminated on Maqsood, the riots, Sabo, then Hasan, the intermediary to Maqsood who Carter hadn't mentioned – and Gibson hadn't asked about – yet held the keys to the entire rendezvous. But at that moment his door swung open, revealing Scarlett, fresh from a full night's sleep, coffee in hand and a mischievous smile on her face, and he lost the thought.

'You're alive,' she said as she stepped over a box from archive. 'I was about to call the coroner.' She placed the coffee on the desk and inspected Gibson's office: three metres square, devoid of natural light, a computer and three-drawer safe for company. 'You know, if we sealed the doors, they'd call this a tomb.'

Gibson lifted himself off the desk and peeled a report off his face. 'I'm only dead on the inside.'

'Call it an office, then.' Scarlett sat down in one of the guest chairs and smiled.

He enjoyed that smile. The lipstick matched the name, and the personality. Scarlett was in her third year with ASIS, assigned to support Gibson while she completed language training for her first three-year posting to Bangkok. She had an intelligence officer's gift for picking the moods and needs of people, which she used to good effect on Gibson. This included, as if summoned by the creaking of his forty-something year-old body after pulling his first all-nighter in a decade, bringing him coffee from the cafeteria. In today's case: burnt long black.

'Good coffee,' he lied.

At least the vultures had gone.

'Cute,' she said. 'You could be a spy.'

He wiped his glasses and put them on. 'I was, once. Would you believe it?'

Another smile. 'Not with that look.'

He checked his reflection in an old photo frame. The photograph, taken in Penang, showed his handsome former self arm-in-arm with an old friend from Malaysian intelligence. Better, younger days, unlike the reflection in the glass: day-old stubble and dishevelled, greying hair. God knows what he smelt like.

He slicked his hair back with his hand. 'Thanks.'

'Welcome.' She stood up and went to the door. 'By the way,' she said, 'they're almost ready in the DDG's office.'

The vultures returned. Gibson rubbed his face as if to shoo them away.

'Got it,' he said. 'What do I owe you?'

'A fiver for the coffee.'

'And the wakeup call?'

That only earned a smirk. 'I'll think of something.'

The Deputy Director-General's office was, for all intents and purposes, like that of the Director-General himself, except for the view. Instead of the lush surrounds of Parliament House, the DDG's windows looked out over the main carpark for the R.G. Casey building, the headquarters of the Department of Foreign Affairs and Trade where, for the sake of security and convenience, ASIS occupied half of the top floor. It was apt. The DG was an outsider, usually a former diplomat, drafted in to provide a public face to the service and keep Capital Hill at bay. The DDG, on the other hand, an ASIS veteran, actually ran the place. In theory, he cared who showed up to work.

The DDG's principal leadership team – the Director of Operations, the General Counsel, Director of Security, and Gibson's own boss, Gary Neill, Director of Collection – had arrived early and arranged themselves on the armchairs. There wasn't one spare for Gibson, so he brought in an office chair and sat in a corner.

The DDG's Executive Assistant placed a tray of tea on the coffee table. 'Terry will just be a moment,' she said. Neill helped himself, leaving a film of brown milk across the length of his tea-stained moustache while the rest, perhaps out of revulsion, abstained. Gibson, unaccustomed to the lofty environs of head office, studied the DDG's souvenir collection: an Israeli flag gifted from Mossad, a pair of leather shoes liberated from one of Saddam Hussein's palaces, and the defunct remains of a Pakistani car bomb. Fitting mementos to a thirty-year career that had earned the DDG an Order of Australia, countless secret accolades, and his service nickname, *Terrence of Arabia.*

The DDG arrived in lycra carrying a bicycle pump and spare tyre tube. 'Sorry to keep you waiting,' he said. He chucked the tube in the bin and put the pump in a desk drawer, then sat in his grand leather chair, put his feet on the desk, and looked out over his assembled flock. 'Well, let's get on with it. I'm with the DG in'—he checked his watch— 'fuck, make it quick.' He dropped his feet and sat upright.

Neill's eyes were closed as he sipped his tea. Director Ops, a Greek-Australian woman with a gaze like a scythe, leaned in with the force of a startled springbok. 'Terry—'

The DDG cut her off. 'Andy, it's with you. Your op, your flop. Own it.'

Ops scowled. Neill stared at his teacup and licked fluid off the tips of his moustache.

'Thanks, Terry.' Gibson opened a file marked *TOP SECRET // AUSTEO REL INDO // ANVIL,* indicating classified intelligence for Operation ANVIL, for Australian eyes only, with exceptions made for the Indonesians but only because they provided it to begin with. He took out a profile on Maqsood and handed it to Security. She rested it on the pressed skirt of her prim grey suit, set her featureless face in an expressionless gaze, and blended back into the patternless furniture.

Neill sipped.

'As we know,' said Gibson, 'last night one of our intelligence officers, Jordan Carter, was ambushed while attempting to rendezvous with one Abu Maqsood, founder and leader of *Barisan Pembebasan Islam North Maluku*. The North Maluku Islamic Liberation Front, otherwise known as Barpemis. Excuse me.'

The directors evacuated their teacups as Gibson stood up and unfolded a map of North Maluku over the coffee table. The large, K-shaped island of Halmahera dominated the view.

'The meeting was to take place at the city of Kao.' Gibson pointed at a town on the south-eastern coast of the northern peninsula. 'Maqsood chose the site for a degree of anonymity, since

Barpemis isn't active or well-known south of this town: Kusuri.' He moved his finger twenty kilometres north and inland. 'Jordan arrived in Kao yesterday morning along with his BIN counterpart, an intelligence officer by the name of Yoyok, and a Kopassus special forces detachment that was there to secure the meet. His plan was to rendezvous with Maqsood at a mosque under cover of evening prayer and debrief him at a secure site at the airport. It's been done before, in Kao and other locations, and we've never had an issue. So far, so good.'

The Maqsood profile had made it to Legal. He slicked his greasy black hair back to the collar of his four-thousand-dollar Savile Row suit and passed the file to Ops. She took it in a slender craw and frowned at it.

'At the planned RV time,' Gibson continued, employing the shorthand for rendezvous, 'two busloads of followers from a rival Islamist political group, *Garisan Merah Shariah* – or Gameshar, the Shariah Red Line – converged on the mosque waving banners and spouting separatist rhetoric. Protests are common in the region, especially with elections coming up, but Gameshar is based in Maba.' He pointed at a city on the south-eastern leg of the 'K'. 'They have no political presence in North Halmahera so, understandably, the citizens of Kao took exception. Given Gameshar brought firebombs, that was probably what they wanted.'

Security examined the map and frowned. 'Why would they target Kao?'

'Gameshar hates Barpemis,' said Neill into his cup.

'Which means they knew that Maqsood would be there,' said Security.

'Or that we would be,' said Ops.

Legal scribbled something on his pad, then brushed something off his trousers with a bejewelled finger.

'Does that mean Maqsood is blown?' said Security.

'There was always that risk,' said Gibson.

The directors turned to him.

'Usually,' he said, 'we interact with persons of interest via intermediaries; so-called cut-outs to provide deniability for both parties.' Gibson pushed away a thought of Hasan. 'However,'—he cleared his throat—'we keep open the option of direct contact in case a friend of ours misbehaves. In Maqsood's case, he had decided to field half a dozen separatist candidates in the upcoming regency elections. The Indonesians were livid, so we thought it only decent to remind him that we could only prevent his arrest for subversion if he remained cooperative. Given the gravity of the matter, we went direct.'

'And then he fucked us,' said Ops.

Neill's teacup crashed into the saucer.

'Oh, come on, Gary,' said Ops. 'Maqsood's as security conscious as they come. Even his own entourage wouldn't know if he met with us.' She gestured at the Maqsood profile, now on the lap of Security's grey skirt. 'He sold us out.'

'Sold us out to who?' said Neill. 'Gameshar? Al Ramah? They hate each other.'

'Sure,' said Ops. 'But they weren't threatening to charge him with subversion, were they?' She turned to the DDG. 'I say we bring him in. Bag him if we need to.'

'Typical,' said Neill. 'Blow the whole operation for us, why don't you.'

'Looks already blown to me,' shouted Ops. 'Chatter has it every jihadi and his child bride is still doing a victory lap for the Taliban, and Indonesia's no exception. Now we have Islamists ambushing an Australian intelligence officer in Kao. *In broad daylight,* thank you very much. It's as brazen as it is public.'

'Circumstantial,' said Neill. He licked his moustache. 'There's nothing suggesting this is linked to the wider political situation. ANVIL is fine.'

Ops scoffed. 'We can't ignore it, though, can we?' She turned to the DDG. 'The world has changed, Terry. So has North Maluku, by the looks of it. We need to stop mollycoddling these pricks or next thing we know, Maluku will be pumping martyrs and bomb vests into Bali, Jakarta and Melbourne. Then what?'

'Not sure, Hera, what's your suggestion?' said Neill. 'Make arrests? Raid a few villages? How would you ever find them all? Oh, that's right. ANVIL. Except not after pissing off the Indonesians.'

'Our fault for being dependent on them,' said Ops. 'When it comes to protecting this country, the Indonesians, or any other nation for that matter, shouldn't get a say.'

'Thank you both,' said the DDG. He wore half a smirk, as if savouring the spectacle. 'Andy?'

Gibson was lost in thought, scouring his memory for mention of Hasan in Carter's reports leading up to the ambush and since, more convinced with each passing second of the cut-out's role in what had panned out.

'Liam Ellis is on a flight to Ternate as we speak,' he said. 'He'll debrief Jordan, dig into what happened and why. We'll have his report over the embassy link tomorrow.'

'We might have a flap by then,' said the DDG.

'BIN has that under control,' said Gibson. 'Today's papers barely mention what happened.'

'Let's see how long that lasts,' said the DDG. He looked around the room, then at his watch. 'Speaking of time.'

The directors scrambled out of their seats and headed for the door. Gibson followed them out, returned to his office and called Scarlett. 'It's me,' he said.

'What do you need?'

A scotch would do.

'A trace report on Hasan.'

3

TERNATE, NORTH MALUKU

'Nice digs,' said Ellis as Carter let him into the apartment. It was an executive condo, part of a small enclave built on high ground with a clear view over most of Ternate, the jungle peaks of Maitara and Tidore, and the distant coast of Halmahera.

'Stayed in worse,' said Carter. He double locked the oversized front door and turned for the kitchen, an open-plan setup of white tile and stainless steel that glistened under the morning sun of a full-length skylight. He hobbled over to it, his right leg stiff at the knee, then glanced at Ellis. 'You look like shit.'

Ellis knew it. It had been midnight by the time he arrived home from BIN headquarters, and by four he was in a taxi to the airport for the six-hour flight to Ternate. That, and he was below average height, above average weight, and had the fashion sense of a debating society secretary with a *Target* gift card. He loosened his grammar school tie and threw his jacket on the sofa, one of three arranged around a wall-mounted television and a pair of ten-foot-high bookcases. 'Speak for yourself.'

Carter had a black eye, a red rash across his cheek and a bloodied bandage over his left hand, like he'd been a bar fight. He ignored the comment and opened the refrigerator.

'Remind me why you're here.'

Ellis dumped his travel bag and admired the expanse of the apartment. The grand kitchen occupied the centre of the cavernous space and gave way to a raised outdoor dining area overlooking the steep incline of Mount Gamalama. Elaborate Indonesian artwork adorned the sandstone walls and set off the white tiled floor. 'Usual deal,' he said. 'Check you're not sleeping with the enemy, having suicidal thoughts, *et cetera.*' His eyes fell on the bookshelves either side of the television, each lined with assorted birdwatching books and Indonesian memorabilia, but seemingly untouched. He figured Carter spent little of his time here. 'Or worse, suddenly want to come home.'

Carter smirked as he returned, one step at a time, with two tumblers of iced tea. Ellis took one with a thanks as he planted himself on a sofa and retrieved a manila folder from his travel case. Inside were two questionnaires. The first, a psychological evaluation, was an exquisite token of institutional duty-of-care, each question designed to probe the subject's mental and physical wellbeing, the answers to no doubt be poured over by an ASIS psychologist in the too-distant future to be of any help. A second form examined recent contacts, adherence to security protocols and any suspicious activity: fodder for the overzealous counter-intelligence wonks back in Canberra for whom no-one was more suspicious than an ASIS intelligence officer doing his job. Ellis gave Carter an apologetic glance and said, 'You know I have to do this.'

Carter shrugged his shoulders, eased himself opposite, and swept his hair into a man-bun. Apart from the visible injuries he gave no sign he had almost been murdered the night before. He rested his injured leg on the coffee table and draped a long, tanned arm over the sofa.

'Shoot.'

Ellis cleared his throat and read out questions from the form. He skipped what he already knew from Carter's file: born '88 in Jakarta; mother Indonesian, father an expat with one of the Australian miners; money around but not for long, same for the mother, who fled when Carter was fourteen to leave him at the mercy of Sydney's inner-western suburbs and the arbitrary torments of her abusive ex-husband. Despite the hardship, Carter went on to complete an Asian Studies degree with honours and attract the attention of ASIS. Ellis could see why: Carter was tenacious, resilient and persuasive bordering on manipulative – indispensable qualities for an intelligence officer, not to mention invaluable for the task of subverting armed Islamists in some hideaway hellhole few had ever heard of.

The questions Ellis did ask soon became ridiculous: *Any problematic changes in alcohol or drug consumption? Disruptions to sleep patterns? Unusual or compromising sexual habits? Any fantasies of harming self or others?* So it went on without raising any flags: Carter was a force of nature, as likely to complain of hardship in a place like Ternate as he was a headache. Ellis knew no other person as determined to control his own environment, and certainly no-one as effective at doing so. Carter's success in bringing North Maluku's would-be terrorists to heel was ASIS legend, as was his reputation for recklessness, a fact the questionnaire, strangely, didn't contemplate. The second form was no more helpful. Carter's job required extensive contact with foreign intelligence officials and suspected terrorists and made him a potential target for countless Islamist radicals across Indonesia; the stuff of a security assessor's wet dream but an utter waste of time. Carter, to his credit, gave serious and succinct answers, but by the end of the five pages, Ellis had learned nothing he didn't already know and both men were bored, tired, and fed up with ASIS bureaucracy.

'You could've asked me that shit over the phone,' said Carter.

'And miss your pretty face?' Ellis dumped the form in his bag and took out another piece of paper. 'Actually, I need to see the weapon.'

Carter groaned and pushed himself off the sofa. He limped to the bedroom, where he opened the wardrobe and dialled a code into the safe to reveal the Glock and a loaded clip of nine-millimetre rounds. Ellis checked the pistol and counted the ammunition against what was written on his form: all checked out, another tick in the box for the regulators back home. He followed Carter back to the living room.

'All done then,' said Carter.

'The fun's just getting started,' said Ellis with a grin.

Carter rolled his eyes. 'Fuck me.'

Seated, Ellis debriefed Carter on the operation. He took his time, first asking for Carter's retelling of the events leading up to the abort, then poking and prodding at details, times and identities of persons sighted at the mosque while he typed into a secure laptop. Carter was forthcoming about the decision to abort, and Ellis dutifully recorded there was no way anyone could have known the protest would turn violent, even if he didn't believe it himself. He knew Carter had held on to the op as long as he could, disregarding the risk to himself or others. It was part of who he was, and in his own way, Ellis respected him for it. Ellis backtracked further, exploring the activities of the Kopassus team in Kao and the original setup with Maqsood himself in search of clues for how the operation went wrong, all the while watching Carter but detecting no reaction. Ellis frowned. He felt no closer to explaining how a clandestine intelligence operation, conducted by the best Australian and Indonesian intelligence could offer, had been ambushed by a random flash mob of Islamists.

He looked up from the laptop and said, 'So what do you think happened?'

'Election season,' said Carter. 'Gameshar thinks they can intimidate the vote.'

'In Kao, you mean? Not Maba?'

'These guys are hardliners,' said Carter, 'but they won't shit in their own nest. This way, they can claim credit without pissing off their own people.'

Ellis stared at the screen and nodded slowly. 'I guess shit happens, then.'

'Shit happens.'

Ellis tapped notes into the laptop as if to hide his disappointment. Unlike some in the service, Ellis believed in Carter. Carter proved that ASIS could still get things done in a complex world, despite lacking the resources of its American and British counterparts and being tied at the wrist by red tape. His lies, infrequent but deliberate, shattered that illusion and made it impossible to help him. Ellis looked up. Carter was picking grit from under a fingernail.

'Any word on our boy Hasan?' said Ellis.

Carter lowered his hand and shot back a glance. 'Should there be?'

'He's the one link to Maqsood in all this. I'm surprised he didn't come up.'

'Hasan's not relevant.'

'Yet, his phone was active until a few hours before the RV and now it's gone. I'd call that relevant.'

Carter shrugged. 'Not if you worked here.'

Ellis ignored the jab. 'Headshed's going to need better than that, mate. They reckon he turned.'

'Is that so?' Carter's voice echoed around the apartment. 'Nice of them to take this shit seriously, for once. I thought I'd have to report the rioters were from Guangzhou.'

Ellis matched his volume. 'What happened to Hasan, Jordan?'

Both men were still. For a time, the only sound in the apartment was the ticking of a wall clock that echoed the pulse in Ellis's neck, each second passing louder than the last. Suddenly, Carter stood up and walked to the kitchen. He filled a glass of water from a bottle, drank a mouthful then stood there, swirling the glass.

Ellis waited. The clock ticked louder.

'He went to ground,' said Carter. He drained the glass, placed it on the counter and remained still, contemplating its newfound emptiness. 'Must have heard about the riot and fled.' His eyes flicked to Ellis. 'He came to us. Yoyok's arranged to bring him in.'

Ellis shook his head in disbelief. 'You didn't think that was something we should know?'

'Fuck would I?'

Ellis stood and walked to the kitchen counter. 'Because if anyone knew the RV was blown, it would be Hasan.'

Carter took a step towards him. Six-foot-two and built like an Australian Rules footballer, he had little trouble imposing himself. 'What if he did?'

'Then he might have sent a warning,' said Ellis, standing his ground. 'In which case, it would've been stupid to go ahead with the RV.'

'Or imperative.' Carter leaned against the counter and folded his arms. 'For all we knew, Maqsood was in the shit.'

'Maybe he'd turned on you.'

'Or someone turned against him,' said Carter. He unfolded his arms and held the edge of the benchtop. 'Either way, last night was a warning. What matters is who had the balls to send it.'

A cloud passed overhead, blocking the sun and shrouding the apartment in grey.

'I guess you're right,' said Ellis.

'Yeah, I'm right. Which is why you sit in a windowless box in Jakarta writing cables and dreaming up stupid questions for bureaucrats back home while I'm here dealing with the world as it is.'

And getting people killed, Ellis thought unkindly, a reaction prompted more by frustration at Carter's ingratitude than empathy for those that suffered. Ellis would never claim to be a top intelligence officer, but he worked hard to push his side of the cart. It was unglamorous, tiring, and thankless enough already.

'We've all got a job to do, Jordan.'

'Exactly,' said Carter. 'So keep out of my way.' He raised his arm and thrust a finger in the direction of the enormous door. 'Tell that to Andy.'

Nothing moved in the apartment. The ticking clock had subsided, as had Ellis's pulse, replaced with the croak of a wandering gecko. Ellis had what he had come for, so he broke off and collected his belongings. Carter didn't move.

'When do you debrief Hasan?' said Ellis as he donned the jacket.

Carter watched him. 'Tomorrow,' he said. 'I'll tell you all about it.' Then, as a sudden movement, he stepped up to Ellis, took his hand, and shook it.

Ellis squeezed his colleague's hand, if only to counter the overwhelming pressure, and held Carter's stare. The taller man's eyes watched with calm intensity, tinged with something approaching fondness. Ellis knew it was part of the spell, one that Carter had used on countless others before: assets, women, anyone who held something he wanted. Ellis could only nod.

Carter's face softened to a grin. He released Ellis's hand and gripped his shoulder.

'Now fuck off back to J-town.'

4

JAKARTA

Ana Kovacevic took a breath and dialled. There was silence while the phone connected, then the long tones that signalled the international call. *Come on.* She suppressed a tap of her foot.

The tones were cut. She cleared her throat, waiting for the voicemail introduction that didn't come. Instead:

'Tanner.'

'Michael, hi,' she said. 'It's Ana. I have something for you.'

'Make it quick.'

She sat upright to make the pitch. She had already made it four times that day since catching sight of the story of a mosque fire in the far-eastern city of Kao, part of her daily trawl of the Indonesian media for a scrap of a story some other reporter had left behind. For once, she had something more, a shard of something precious, not left over as much as covered up: *The Jakarta Post* had given it two paragraphs and no details, as if burning mosques were an everyday nuisance. Ana wasn't buying the 'nothing to see here' line. Wherever Kao was lay a story.

'It's a piece about an arson attack on a North Maluku mosque,' she said. 'Media's tight-lipped. The government's towing a ridiculous line about—'

'Where the fuck?'

'North Maluku,' she said. 'About a thousand kays east of Makassar—'

'No-one cares about some local bullshit in North... fuck it. Indonesia.'

'Think of it this way.' Her speech was fast, too fast. Slow it down. 'A Muslim-dominated province on Australia's doorstep.' Breathe. 'Someone firebombs a mosque and the media says nothing – a *mosque,* Michael, in *Indonesia* – yet it's the third violent incident in that province this year. Don't forget, a month ago police killed yet another terrorist in a central Sulawesi jungle, like it's hunting season. Australians want to know if Indonesia's about to explode, Mick.'

Nailed it.

'Don't call me Mick.'

Fuck.

'Sorry.' Ana checked the clock. 'Look, I'll let you have it at a dollar a word for a thousand words,' she said. 'Another grand for expenses.'

'I won't pay you half that.'

Ana shook her head. 'This is a bargain, Michael.'

'And find your own way,' he added. 'Or get lost. What do I care?'

Her heart sank. As a freelance journalist, Ana had been forced to live on a never-ending shoestring, one of the unhelpful facts of life pummelled into her since she abandoned the comforts of suburban Melbourne for the naked insecurity of South-east Asia. Were she to fund her own tickets for the three-thousand-kilometre journey to Ternate, not to mention necessary 'sundries' that would facilitate her passage, she would return to Jakarta and promptly starve. That, or face a relentless barrage of resentment for borrowing money from her mother.

'Help me out,' she said. 'It's a good story, you know it.'

'I get that you're broke,' said Tanner. 'But so is *The Age.* Get a loan or something.'

She remembered to breathe. On the back of the door to her tiny single-room apartment hung the cocktail dress she'd bought at the Jatinegara market, a little black thing to complement her pale skin and match the only set of heels she had. Soon she would be in Menteng amongst Jakarta's expansive cadre of correspondents and stringers, maybe even enjoying herself.

Breathe in.

'Last chance, Michael.'

Breathe out.

'Maybe next time.'

She cursed under her breath as he rang off, and again out loud once the line was clear. Only the prospect of a night out kept her from ruminating on the lost story and the lost day, and even that promise was suspect. The previous two events had fizzled out for lack of attendance. Most journalists in the city, time and cash poor, couldn't afford a night out in central Jakarta. But Zoe had insisted, with a wink, that she would 'make it worth your while,' and Ana agreed to give it another go. So she showered, dressed and did her make up to the audiobook of *The Taliban Shuffle,* and within thirty minutes, her grit-stained blonde hair tied back and black Jimmy Choos on the dusty pavement, she forgot all about North Maluku.

Ah, Jakarta.

The intoxication had never faded. Her nostrils filled with the aroma of the city: exhaust fumes, street saté and a trace of sulphur. Every corner of the *kampung* was in motion. The air was alive with the calls of the dozen minarets in a hundred-metre radius and the shouts of hawkers from every street corner, and the setting sun cast the smog-filled sky in hazy bronze. She treaded carefully along the potholed street, inches from collision with a torrent of passing motorcycles and the cracked concrete covers of the open sewers, stopping only to say a quick *Selamat Sorè* to the old man selling newspapers from a blue tarp laid over the muddy red bricks of the sidewalk. Ana had become his best customer by far, lapping up copies of all the city's mastheads each morning and now on first name terms. She turned from his warm smile towards a shopping mall that promised air conditioning, western cuisine, and a generous supply of taxis. Ten minutes later, she was cold in the back seat of a *Bluebird,* stuck in evening traffic, overwhelmed to be alive.

It was a far cry from Melbourne, where instead she'd been overwhelmed by the stifling captivity of family. Since her father died, Ana had become benefactor to her mother's emotional dependence and a condescending parade of overbearing uncles, aunts and cousins that lasted until the life insurance ran out. Whatever resilience she had left had been eroded further by the tedium of metropolitan journalism: deadlines, political spin and an Australian obsession with first-world problems. There had to be stories *out there,* and sure enough, she had found them in Jakarta. Within throwing distance of her cab was ten-thousand words-worth for the *Herald Sun* were she in Melbourne, be it the crumbling busway, the flooded sewers-cum-stormwater canals, or the three school-aged girls that now approached Ana's taxi window, pleading for money, while pervasive government corruption simply stole it from everyone in sight. But she wasn't in Melbourne, so no-one cared – especially Michael Tanner. She hurriedly opened the window and handed the girls some old notes without even counting, frustrated to have fed their dependence without improving anything for them. It had become a recurring feeling these past few weeks, along with the sense of hopelessness for her career, her profile, her prospects. The girls reached the far side of the road and started pointing in Ana's direction, and in moments half a dozen other desperate souls descended on the taxi and the gullible bulè. A gap appeared in traffic and the taxi lurched forward before they reached her. Helpless, Ana could only return their stares in hope they could see she was at least *trying.*

Forty minutes and five kilometres later it was dark in Menteng. The Camden, a retro-styled bar purpose-designed for the city's expats, was packed. Ana paid off the driver and pushed her way into a thicket of cashed-up westerners and well-to-do locals, finally breaking through to the beer garden to find Zoe, in her element, holding court for a group of dazed Europeans.

'Hope I'm not interrupting,' said Ana.

'There you are!' cried Zoe. 'I was about to send a search party.' Zoe leaned in from a great height and kissed Ana on the cheek before turning to her audience. 'Gentlemen,' she said with an exaggerated motion of her hands, 'this is Ana.'

The three men, each in their twenties, nodded without expression. It wasn't clear they understood what she'd said.

'Pleasure,' said Ana.

'In from Riga, of all places, barely speak English. Not that I mind.' Zoe winked. 'So good to see you.'

'And you,' said Ana. 'How's the *Guardian?*'

Zoe was a stringer. Technically a freelancer, but with the sure thing of a contracted editor and a steady stream of work, even if the demands eclipsed the pay.

'Great!' said Zoe. 'But, you know, shit.'

They both laughed.

'We'll be back,' Zoe said to the Latvians. She took Ana by the arm and led her to the bar, where Zoe ordered two Mojitos. When the drinks arrived, Zoe whispered conspiratorially in Ana's ear. 'There's someone here I want you to meet.' Zoe's eyes flicked somewhere behind Ana. 'Don't look now,' she said. 'Come.'

She took Ana's hand and led her to a high-set table outside surrounded by a group of western media professionals. Zoe introduced Ana to each of them in turn; two of them had just flown in from Sydney, a third was in Jakarta for two weeks with the *Financial Times.* The other three were all en route to a holiday in Bali. Eventually Zoe came to the last of the group, a man Ana recognised as one of the more renowned freelance journalists in South-east Asia.

'Jerome Elliott,' he said as he held out his hand. The accent was all London. Cologne was splashed somewhere across his tanned neck. He looked even more handsome in person.

'Ana Kovacevic.' She smiled and shook his hand, wondering if the wet touch was his sweat or her own. Her mind raced at the sudden opportunity, but she was lost for words. Suddenly she blurted, 'I loved your work on Islamic State returnees a few years ago.'

Elliott had been one of the first to report on returning Indonesian fighters after the collapse of Islamic State. The Indonesian government had neither the will nor facilities to take them into custody, so they had been released into the community with little more than a courtesy interview, a policy condemned by most of Elliott's readers at the time. They spilled their lattés again a few years later when Indonesia banned returnees outright, thus condemning them to statelessness, but not before most had disappeared throughout the Indonesian archipelago and given rise to a wave of violent attacks nationwide.

Elliott swayed on his feet. 'Glad you enjoyed it.' He grinned.

Say something.

'I always wondered what happened to them,' said Ana. She gulped a mouthful of Mojito. 'Those that returned.'

Elliott made a puzzled look.

'Ana's freelance, too,' said Zoe with a wink.

His puzzlement gave way to a sly grin. 'They're out there,' he said, but he didn't seem to know where, much less care. Instead, his eyes scanned downwards to her shoes and flicked back. Ana glanced at Zoe.

'I'll let you both get acquainted,' said Zoe, then beat a retreat to the Latvians.

Elliott watched her leave and flashed a grin. 'Write anything I'd know, or what?'

'Maybe.' Probably not, Ana thought. 'I write about social issues, mainly. Try to raise awareness of what goes on in the world. I'll send you my portfolio sometime.'

'I'd like that.' His eyes bounced off her chest. She tried not to notice. 'But first, tell me: how does a girl like you end up in a sinking tip like Jakarta?'

There was no point telling him what she really felt. She was enchanted by Indonesia, it was true, but equally true was that she'd been naïve and foolish, chasing a moonshot story when she should be plugging away back home, patiently building a career and working towards a marriage, house, kids, all those things a middle-class, second-generation immigrant girl was supposed to want. It wouldn't be such a problem if she could leave, but she was too broke to move on and too proud to go home.

'I've wanted to come here since I was a girl.' It wasn't entirely a lie. Since reading *The Year of Living Dangerously* for a high school assignment, she had harboured a romantic if misguided fascination with Jakarta, but in truth she had ended up here for economic reasons. Qantas tickets to the city were on sale that month, and Indonesian visas were cheap for a country none of her relatives would dare set foot in. 'No-one was going to hire me as a correspondent,' she said, 'so I went my own way.'

'Right,' said Elliott as he took another swig of what could have been vodka, only cloudier. Ana had hoped for a shared professional interest, to bond over common ambition, maybe some guidance for the road ahead. Instead, he swayed slightly, stole a glance at her dress and squinted. 'Been here long, have you?'

She thought about it. 'Six months.'

More like eight, actually, but it made no difference. Elliott peered at her, as if pondering a question of profound insight.

'You met anyone, like?'

Fuck, really? Ana almost laughed. She had come out for a night with fellow professionals, been introduced to a would-be dream mentor, and ended up with a creep.

'There's someone back home,' she said. Easy lie, unless he checked. It'd been two years since she'd set her Facebook status to 'single'. She was no longer sure how to change it.

'Shame, innit,' said Elliott, but it wasn't clear if it was his shame or hers. He checked her out again and drained his glass. 'Another, what?'

She held up her Mojito, still half-full. He shrugged and walked off to the bar.

Zoe came over. 'Hot, don't you think?'

'Drunk, you mean.'

'Oh, come on. He knows everyone who's anyone in journalism, dear.' Zoe gave her a gentle smack on the shoulder and whispered in her ear. 'He could be very, uh,' she looked for the right word. 'Helpful.' She winked. 'Believe you me.'

After her day spent failing to pitch what she thought was a sure bet, Ana wished it were true. Her mind drifted back to Kao with a pang of frustration.

Elliott returned holding another glass of opaque fluid. Almost automatically his spare hand found its way to Zoe's waist. 'You girls having fun?' His glass was already half-empty.

'I was just telling Ana you had the best contacts in the industry.' Zoe smiled at Ana, then released herself.

Elliott seemed oblivious. 'Maybe you and I could meet up, like,' he said to Ana. He suppressed a burp. 'I could introduce you to some people.'

She doubted he was any more likely to help her career than she was to let him sleep with her. 'Sure,' she said with a smile. Somewhere, in a dark recess of her mind, an idea formed for how to land the Kao story after all. 'Let me and my girl dance, first.' She took Zoe's hand and led her to the dance floor. Zoe blew Elliott a kiss.

The two of them chatted as they danced to a series of '70s disco tracks while Elliott watched on from the bar. After half an hour, Zoe was trance-like, so Ana left her and headed for the bathroom. She returned to the high crescendo of 'Stayin' Alive'. Elliott was gone. The dance floor was packed now, and Zoe was dancing with her Latvians. Ana decided on another drink, then Elliott grabbed her.

'I wondered where you went,' he said. He pushed her up against the wall next to the bar.

Ana squirmed, but his grip was tight. 'I wanted space to think about your, uh, contacts,' she said.

He leaned in close and tried to kiss her neck. The cologne was overpowered by gin. She pushed his face away.

'Maybe I could introduce you to them.' His wet lips slid up towards her ear. 'If you're nice.'

An Indonesian girl emerged from the bathroom and gave them a sideways look.

'I need all the help I can get,' said Ana.

'Yeah?' He raised his head and smiled. 'Why's that?'

'Because I have this story to pitch, but it really needs the right editor.'

'What's the story?' He began to lean in, but she grabbed him by the hair and held his head back.

'It's about a sleazebag freelancer in Jakarta exploiting women with the promise of helping their journalism careers.'

He pulled back. She held him close.

'I've got witnesses, Jerome.'

Zoe appeared beside him. Elliott glanced at her, then back to Ana.

'Fucking bitch,' he said. 'You publish that, you're finished.'

'I won't,' she said. 'Not if you help me.'

His gaze locked onto hers. He suddenly seemed sober again.

'I need three thousand dollars for a story about Islamic extremists in North Maluku,' she said. 'Pitch it to one of your editors and get me the deal.'

He scoffed. 'They'd never take you on, like. You're a nobody.'

She squeezed his hair harder. He winced and pulled back. 'Shh,' she said. Two Americans moved past, headed for the men's.

'They'll take your word for it,' she said. 'You've got until tomorrow midday before my other story hits VICE. Deal?'

He pushed back again, and this time she let him go. He looked at them both and swore. 'Fine, it's a deal,' he said. He spat something as he pushed past Zoe and walked off.

Zoe turned to Ana. 'You okay?'

'Perfect,' said Ana. She took Zoe by the hand and realised she was shaking. 'Let's get another drink.'

5

TERNATE

The powerboat pulled alongside the dock under fading twilight. Three men hovered on board: Raf, Jaja, and Hasan. Only Raf moved, his black mohawk flicking in the wind as he prepared the rope. Jaja cut the engine and steered the hull to a stop. Raf moored the craft, took Hasan by the arm, and led him onto the platform.

'Good to see you,' said Carter.

Hasan adjusted his taqiyah and stared at his feet. '*Salam,* Pak.'

Raf shoved him forward with a sinewy, tattoo-covered arm and walked him to the Landcruiser. Jaja's bald, giant silhouette loomed from the boat. Carter returned his wave and followed Raf along the dock.

'Any trouble?'

Raf stood back and lit a cigarette.

'None, bos.' Raf exhaled a stream of smoke and flicked his nose with a long finger emblazoned with the word *'hati'*. 'Nothing suspicious. Nobody followed us. The imam said the same.'

The imam of the Kusu mosque worked for Carter as part of an escape network for agents across Halmahera. Hasan had arrived at the mosque the day after the riots.

'How is he?'

'He is fine, but he didn't know who we were. We had to force him.'

Carter thanked him and climbed into the Landcruiser. Yoyok helped Hasan into the rear seat. The agent stared at Carter in the rear-view mirror.

'You're safe now,' said Carter. He started the Landcruiser and moved off.

'So long as you talk.'

Mount Gamalama cast a deep shadow over the steep lanes of Ternate in the late afternoon. Hasan stared wide-eyed at the lights and motion of the city as they progressed uphill, like he had entered another world. It was the same look he wore the day he met Carter, the first foreigner he had ever laid eyes on. A man of his kind, but not.

Hasan's recruitment had been slower than the others. Maqsood had been quick to understand the need to distance himself from Carter for the sake of security and had volunteered Hasan as his intermediary almost immediately. The role called for a delicate combination of trustworthiness and naïveté; for everyone's sake, the intermediary operated in secret, known only to Maqsood, the intelligence services, and Hasan himself. By virtue of family ties, Hasan was close enough to Maqsood that regular contact with the Barpemis leader would raise no questions, and he was young enough for Maqsood to exclude from his most sensitive matters. Maqsood trusted him, but Hasan fulfilled a purpose. Maqsood understood that; Hasan understood it.

Carter sought to change it.

For a year, Hasan diligently passed messages to and from Carter on Maqsood's behalf without taking instruction from Carter nor showing undue interest in his boss's affairs. Part of it was the fear of knowing too much if he were to be discovered, and part of it was duty. Carter was in no hurry. He needed his conduit to Maqsood more than an agent in the Islamist's camp and was happy to wait for Hasan to warm to him. In the meantime, Carter plied him with gifts and luxuries a devout boy from a remote Islamic village could never conceive – chocolate, Coca-Cola, a Nintendo Switch – and taught him basic English, anything to allay Hasan's fears of this immense foreigner and his motives towards Maqsood. The eventual breakthrough came during a routine pickup in Kusuri, the moment Carter started the car and *Smells Like Teen Spirit* erupted from every speaker. Carter reached for the volume but hesitated when he saw the look of mesmerisation on the boy's face. He let the song play, and for the next fifteen minutes they did nothing but listen.

'Maksud liriknya apa, Pak?' Hasan had asked. What do the lyrics mean?

Carter laughed. 'It's Nirvana,' he said. 'The words don't mean anything.'

The strain nevertheless began to show in Hasan. A carton of cigarettes no longer sustained him between monthly meetings. His juvenile arthritis, an affliction passed down from his mother, flared in every joint and bone of his feeble body. His skin and hair began to grey like a man twice his age. Lapses in protocol began to threaten his security: in one case, he had been tailed by a group of Barpemis heavies to Tobelo and forced a last-second abort. The shrinks in Canberra insisted these were the symptoms of an agent unfit for clandestine work and demanded Hasan be retired, but fuck that. Carter abducted him instead.

Hasan had writhed and screamed into Jaja's arm as the giant wrestled him into the Landcruiser from the side of a Galela street. 'Calm down, it's us,' Carter shouted to no effect. 'Go,' he said, and Yoyok sped off into the darkness. Fifteen minutes later, they had parked in a darkened alley behind a mosque in central Tobelo and Hasan had stopped panicking. Carter offered him water; he declined and demanded a cigarette.

'Did someone get to you, Hasan?'

The glowing tip of the cigarette danced in the darkness of the cabin. Hasan stared at it, then pulled another drag.

'We're all friends here,' said Carter. 'You can tell us, and we can help you.'

Hasan let out a long stream of smoke. 'You cannot help me.'

Carter glanced at Jaja. The big man shrugged.

'I can help your family.'

Hasan's eyes betrayed the slightest hint of bewilderment.

Carter produced a photograph from his satchel and handed it to Hasan. The young man stared at it.

'That's an AK-47 in his hands, Hasan. He's big enough to fire it now. Not a bad shot, from what I hear.'

Hasan was still, except for his hands. The paper fluttered in his fingertips. The burning ember reached his fingers, and he dropped the cigarette.

'Where did you get this?'

'Does it matter?'

A tear had formed under Hasan's left eye.

'You are spying on my brother!'

'Why do you think that is?'

The tear fell. Hasan wiped his face and lit another cigarette, eyes locked on the photograph of his brother, barely fourteen, arms wrapped around the Russian assault rifle like a surfboard while he received instruction from a Barpemis militant at a makeshift shooting range. It was an image that would put the boy on shoot-to-kill lists around the country, innocent or not. Hasan's mouth twisted in despair.

'He always wished to join the militia,' he said eventually. 'There was nothing more I could do.'

But there was, Carter had assured him. There was plenty he could do, and in exchange, it was only reasonable Carter would do right by his family. The arrangements were already in place in Jakarta: specialist treatment for Hasan's mother and a real education for his brother away from the perils of militant separatism. Hasan's family would be safe there, Carter said. Hasan just had to give the word.

For a while, they had listened to the roaring cicadas while the night darkened. *'Okeh,'* Hasan said eventually. 'I will do it. I will be your agent.'

From that point, Maqsood belonged to Carter.

They reached the safehouse. It was a free-standing bungalow at the end of a short street that cut into the mountain jungle high above Ternate. BIN had purchased it through a front company years earlier and filled it with overpriced furniture that made it feel like a Bali hotel. Yoyok led Hasan inside and sat him on a bamboo sofa under the dim glow of a wall lamp.

'Rokok?' said Carter. Hasan took a cigarette and lit up. Yoyok watched from the kitchen while a kettle boiled.

Carter sat opposite Hasan and tied his hair. His leg was still corked from the fight in Kao, so he lifted it onto the coffee table. The agent looked away from it, then flicked ash into a tray on the arm of his chair.

'I didn't know about the riots,' said Hasan. 'I saw them on the news.'

Yoyok arrived with tea. He placed the tray next to Carter's foot and opened a jar of *tempé.* Hasan ignored it.

'You knew something when you warned us,' said Carter.

'I was scared, Pak. Abu Maqsood's men used me to trap you. They must have known about us.'

'That's not possible.'

Hasan finished his cigarette and stubbed it repeatedly on the ashtray. 'There is no other explanation, Pak.'

Carter waited for him to light another, then said, 'Tell us what happened after our last meeting.'

Hasan blew a stream of smoke towards the ceiling.

'An old friend came to see me when I returned to Supu. I don't see him often anymore, but we studied together at the *madrassah.* He told me some men came to see him.' He took another puff. 'About me.'

'Abu Maqsood's men?' said Yoyok.

Hasan hummed agreement. 'It happens sometimes, when people need me to work for them, or if Pak Maqsood needs help. But my friend was frightened. He didn't know what they wanted, but it was not for work. I was nervous, so I went to see Abu Maqsood for guidance. He was gone.'

Another drag. The tip glowed bright at his fingertips.

'I spoke to one of the muezzin. Sometimes he works for Abu Maqsood, like me. I asked him where Maqsood was, but he would not say. But he is boastful, this boy. He said Abu Maqsood had asked him to carry a lot of money to Sabo.'

'Sabo near Ibu?'

Hasan nodded. 'This is an important task. It means Abu Maqsood trusted him. I told him he was making up stories, but he insisted it was true. He said the money was for an important meeting in a few days' time and I realised it was the same night Abu Maqsood was meant to meet you.'

'Is that when you tried to warn us?'

'No,' said Hasan, staring into the middle distance. 'My first duty was to Abu Maqsood. I was worried someone had discovered he was in contact with the government.' He examined the half-smoked cigarette in his fingertips and deposited it on the ashtray, then said, 'I have a secret phone I use to contact him in emergencies, but when I returned home to get it, his men were there. That's when I knew I had been betrayed, so I sent you the message. When you didn't respond, I was—'

Hasan wept. Yoyok sat beside him and placed an arm across his shoulders. Carter said nothing.

'That is why I fled,' said Hasan. 'I am sorry, Pak.'

A car approached along the street. Yoyok left Hasan's side and looked out through a gap in the boards. 'It's them,' he said.

'Let's take a break,' Carter said to Hasan.

Raf and Jaja entered. Raf had changed into a singlet, revealing the oriental dragon that coiled his arms, one wrist to the other, its red-ink claws grasping the circumference of his neck. Jaja carried bags of *bakso,* fried chicken and rice in two gigantic hands, his shaved head casting glare from the overhead lamp as he ducked through the door. The two men laid the food on the dining table and arranged places for three. In the sitting room, Hasan had laid down on the sofa and appeared to be asleep. Raf woke him and instructed him to eat.

Carter and Yoyok left them and went to the kitchen.

'What's in Sabo?' said Carter.

'Maqsood has property there,' said Yoyok. They watched Hasan pick at a meatball. 'Could still be bullshit, bos.'

Carter watched the men eat. Hasan slumped over his bowl, pausing to wipe his eyes or massage his shoulders. He had panicked, and he could have been lying his way out of his double-life, but the trace of Maqsood's phone to Sabo suggested otherwise.

'I believe him,' said Carter.

The men had finished eating. Raf left Hasan in the sitting room and joined Jaja outside.

Yoyok stood by the door while Carter sat opposite Hasan. The agent watched him closely, cigarette in hand, which he swayed in the air to trace a thin orange line in front of him.

'I'm told your mother walked on her own a few days ago,' said Carter. Hasan's hand stopped mid-swing. 'The first time in three months.'

'She is better?'

'Much better.'

Hasan whispered *'alhamdulillah'* as he exhaled smoke. 'And my brother?'

Carter let out a sigh. 'Not as good. He wants to come back.'

'No,' said Hasan. 'They will kill him!'

Carter shrugged. 'He's a grown man now, Hasan, and this is his home.'

'It is not safe!' shouted Hasan.

'Calm down.'

'You promised to protect him.'

'How can I keep him safe if you leave, Hasan?'

Hasan hesitated, and the fury in his face gave way to resignation. 'You want me to return to Supu.'

Carter got up and sat next to Hasan. 'I'm counting on you,' he said. 'I just got my arse kicked in Kao, and I need to know why.' He placed an arm around the agent's shoulder. 'I need someone I can trust to find out why Maqsood went to Sabo that night. Who he met with, what they discussed, what the money was for.'

'They will kill me, Mister Carter.'

'Listen,' said Carter. 'No-one knows you're here. No-one knows you work with us, except Maqsood. Would he ever betray you?'

Hasan thought for a moment, then shook his head.

'If they come for you, stick to the story like you always have.' He squeezed Hasan's shoulder. The agent nodded.

'Your secrets keep you safe, Hasan. *I* keep you safe. Always remember that.'

6

The Lion Air red eye touched down at Ternate's Sultan Babullah airport forty-five minutes late. The conditioned air and gleaming floors of the arrivals terminal belied the cramped, clove-scented disarray of the city beyond, where Ana entered a serpentine warren of convoluted narrow streets lined with mosques, houses, spice traders and the occasional colonial relic.

Ternate was a tapestry of pinks, yellows and blues that clung for life at the nape of Mount Gamalama, one of a half-dozen volcanic peaks visible from street level. Gamalama climbed sharply from the shoreline and stretched the city the full length of its eastern flank for Ana's inspection from the back seat of a thirty-year-old Toyota taxi. For an hour she watched Ternate pass by in the heat: rickshaws by the dozen, street peddlers on every corner, stray pets with amputated tails – not unlike anywhere else in Indonesia, yet somehow less refined, as if it were the original article. She checked into a hotel near the southern port precinct of the city and slept until sundown, when it would be cooler, before venturing out in search of food. A hundred eyes followed her every move as she roamed streetside food stalls, *warungs* selling cuisine from across the archipelago, and countless seafood vendors. This part of town was a hub for tourists, but she could have been the only foreigner on the island. Not that she minded it: Jakarta offered the security, as well as the isolation, of anonymity, but the real Indonesia was curious and unguarded, waiting to be reported, and now she was here to report it, with the scent of a story thick in her nostrils where it mixed with the open sewers and sea. She found a small restaurant where she ordered *Ikan Woku Belanga*, an elaborate dish of white-fleshed Maluku snapper topped with a sambal of spiced tomatoes and herbs, and watched the ferries land at Bastiong while she chatted to a teenage girl who had asked to join her in a selfie. Fed, Ana returned to her hotel and relayed the day's experience in a four-sentence tweet before collapsing in exhaustion on the squeaky, king-sized spring bed.

She woke to the piercing shrill of her phone before dawn. She scrambled out of bed and ripped it from its charger.

'Hello?'

'*Mbak* Ana,' said a man's voice. 'This is Rimbo?'

The fixer. Ana took the phone from her ear and checked the time: six-fifteen in the morning.

'Mbak?'

'I'll be right down,' she said.

She checked her backpack for her passport and packed her laptop, camera and belongings. She took an envelope of cash from her travel case and placed it in her jeans pocket. She left the case in the room. She had booked the hotel for four nights, enough for a few days in Kao if the story led somewhere. She made one last check of the room and hung a 'Do not disturb' sign on the door handle as she left.

Rimbo was a brittle-looking man in his mid-forties that wore a stained white prayer cap that couldn't hide his receding hairline. With exaggerated courtesy he took Ana's bag, opened the passenger door and showed her to the rear seat of his ten-year-old Toyota Corolla. He smiled as he accepted the envelope of cash – the agreed fee of two-million rupiah for the first day, around two-hundred dollars' worth – and drove swiftly to Bastiong port where Ana ate a bowl of bakso and Rimbo arranged ferry tickets. Half an hour later they were underway. Ana stood at the bow with wind in her hair while the Halmahera ridgeline spread across the horizon.

They wasted no time in Sofifi. In the ten years since the small town became provincial capital, none of the charm of its historic neighbours seemed to have drifted across the strait. The highway north was in good condition and almost empty. Occasionally they passed a bus or lorry that had slowed for the twisting, two-way roads across the highlands, but otherwise the run was smooth until the large town of Malifut a few kilometres west of their destination. Rimbo drove efficiently and they reached the outskirts of Kao by eleven, soon breaking through a line of trees to arrive in the town proper, where the rusted peak of the Kao Mosque protruded from the ragged skyline.

The mosque looked unaffected. Ana checked her phone map to be sure they were at the right place and told Rimbo to stop. Rimbo slowed and pulled onto the grass verge opposite two roads that led south from the highway, one each side of the mosque. The first was blockaded with a police barrier. The other was blocked by lorries and a long line of old scooters.

'We can walk,' she said.

Rimbo climbed out, adjusted his prayer cap and followed her to the main gate. Ana told him to wait as she took out her camera and captured the carnage. The southern corner of the iron roof had collapsed, leaving a scorched hole over what remained of the breezeblock walls. Windows had shattered across the paved balconies that lined the hall, and the frames that once held them were blackened and blistered. The stench of smoke hung in the air. Workers emerged from the doors carrying debris which they offloaded into one of the lorries. Locals gathered amongst the charred shells of cars that had been parked here when the riots struck, where they prayed and sang to relieve their grief and shock. A group of children played soccer on the remnants of the forecourt lawn under the watch of a group of elderly women who offered food and water to the workmen. One of them gestured at Ana and the rest turned to look at her.

Rimbo stood awkwardly by the gate and smoked a cigarette.

'Come,' said Ana, and walked towards the group of women. Rimbo stubbed his cigarette and followed her into the compound.

The women stopped speaking as Ana approached.

'Selamat Pagi,' said Ana.

The women ignored her. One of them spoke to Rimbo.

'They want know where you from,' he said.

'Tell them I'm an Australian journalist. I want to report what happened here.'

He turned and spoke to the women. As he did so, she showed them her camera and photographed them, then the mosque. They seemed to debate the details of events, pointing in various directions and talking over one another, the word 'Gameshar' repeating itself as they spoke.

Eventually Rimbo turned to Ana. 'They say there was big fight,' he said. 'Some political people from far away start shouting in front of the mosque during evening prayer. The worshippers tell them to leave, so they attack.'

Ana recalled the original report in the *Jakarta Post*. There'd been no mention of a political dimension to the fire.

'What does Gameshar mean?'

'I don't know, mbak.'

'Ask them.'

He put the question to the women, but they turned away. Two men in Islamic clothing had approached from the mosque. They spoke to the women, then looked at Ana.

'I think we should go,' said Rimbo.

One of the men spoke to him.

'What's going on?' said Ana. 'We have a right to be here.'

The man shouted and pointed to the street. The workers stopped and looked at them. The soccer ball rolled away between a pair of scooters.

'They say it is disrespectful.'

Ana held up her hands as a gesture of compliance. The men stared at her as she backed away. Rimbo followed her as she turned south in search of more evidence of the violence. Rubbish lay across the scorched road. Fifty metres from the mosque, she found a jeep that had mounted the curb and been torched. Beyond, she could see nothing more of interest.

'Head back to the car,' she said, after a half-hour photographing the damage. Rimbo looked relieved. 'Take me to the nearest hospital.'

Rimbo hesitated; Ana waited. Eventually, he adjusted his prayer cap and set off.

Ana took out her phone as they walked and looked up the word 'Gameshar'. She found nothing in the dictionary, and the first Google results linked to defunct social-media profiles and a website that was no longer hosted. Beneath a long list of search results was a two-year-old news article that confirmed Gameshar was an abbreviation for 'Garisan Merah Shariah', a provincial Islamist political party. She clicked the link as Rimbo stopped abruptly.

Ana looked up to see a police car by the Corolla. A police officer circled around the far side while the another wrote something in a notebook.

'What do they want?' she said to Rimbo.

'I don't know.'

'Go find out. You're supposed to be a fixer.'

He cleared his throat and crossed the road. The officers ignored him. One of them looked at Ana and made a gesture. Rimbo beckoned her to come over.

'They want to speak to you,' said Rimbo.

Ana shook her head in frustration. 'It's your car, Rimbo.'

'Not about the car.'

'Bagasi,' said the officer. He put the notepad away and pointed at her backpack. 'Open please.'

'Tell him not without a warrant.'

Rimbo blinked, then translated. The officer stood still for a moment, then grabbed Ana by the arm and thrust her towards the police car.

'Let go of me!' she said. The second officer opened the door. They pushed her into the rear seat and snatched her bag.

The officer shut the door. Rimbo loitered helplessly while the officer searched the handbag and flicked through the pages of her passport. When he found her visa, he gave her a look, then threw the passport into the bag. He ignored the laptop. Eventually he found her phone and held it up to the window. 'Open.'

'Not without a warrant.'

He stared at her a moment, then pocketed it. He shouted something at his colleague, who ushered Rimbo back to the Corolla. Rimbo complied without complaint. He gave Ana an apologetic look as he climbed inside and started the car. Ten seconds later, he had disappeared along the road back to Sofifi.

Some fixer.

They drove north. After an hour, they reached Tobelo and the police headquarters for North Halmahera. The policemen led her from the car and through a grand lobby that gave way to a long passageway. Another police officer stood outside an interview room halfway along and gestured inside. In rudimentary English, he questioned her on who she was, where she was from and her contact details. She refused to open her laptop and phone. Whether they needed a warrant was irrelevant; it was a matter of professional pride that she would never volunteer her material. 'Am I under arrest?' she asked him.

'No.'

'Am I free to go?'

'No.'

'Why not?'

'We will have more questions.' He left the room.

She knew better than to argue. If they were serious, they would have cuffed her. This was intimidation. She lay down on the metal desk and let the story turn over in her mind.

The clang of the iron door handle jolted her from her thoughts. An overweight man in elaborate uniform entered and sat down opposite her. He moved slowly due to his size and the chair groaned under his weight. A bead of sweat ran the length of his cheek and collected in his groomed moustache.

The door closed behind him.

The man placed a file on the desk and opened it. Inside were reports and a photocopy of her passport. Ana sat upright.

'I am Inspector Rachmann.'

'Why have you brought me here?'

'For your safety. Please, what you were doing in Kao?'

'My job.'

'I see,' he said. 'Are you a journalist, Miss Kovacevic?'

'Yes.'

'For which paper?'

'Freelance.'

'I see,' he repeated. He flicked through the pages of his file. 'It appears you reside in this country on a limited stay visa, is that correct?'

'Yes.'

'Not a journalism visa.'

'Like I said, I'm a freelancer. There was no-one to sponsor me. The consulate said it would be easier this way.'

He licked the front of his teeth and made a short sucking noise. 'It's an anomaly,' he said.

'Is that why I've been detained?' she said. 'An *anomaly?*'

He rearranged the documents and laid them on the desk. 'Your activities were reported by people who take special notice of foreigners on their territory.' He wiped sweat from his moustache. 'My only concern is for your safety, Miss Kovacevic.'

'Spare me, inspector. This is about making sure I don't report what really happened in Kao.'

He stared at her for a moment, then closed the folder.

'The papers already reported it,' he said. 'An arson attack, nothing more.'

He drummed his fingers on the desk.

'Have you found the culprits?'

'We are still making enquiries.'

'Perhaps you should enquire with Gameshar.'

The drumming stopped.

'After all,' she said, 'they did bring firebombs all the way from Maba.'

He clicked his tongue.

'Do you want to make a comment, inspector?'

'No.'

'That's disappointing. The people of North Maluku would be interested in the police's view of why an Islamist group turned on an innocent community. Until now, the groups have only fought amongst themselves.'

He shifted his seat back and stood up. 'Good evening, Miss Kovacevic.'

'Why did a gang of Islamists from Maba attack an innocent mosque in Kao?'

He picked up the folder and stepped from the table. 'Door!'

She stood and shouted across the table. 'Why are you covering it up?'

The door swung open to reveal another police officer. He carried a pillow and prison blanket.

Rachmann turned back to face her. 'As I said, Miss Kovacevic, good evening.' He bowed his head. 'One of my officers will return you to Sofifi in the morning. In the meantime,'—he waved at nothing in particular—'enjoy the hospitality.'

The officer led her to a cell and made the bed. Ana lay down and let her mind swirl as rusted springs skewered her through the thin mattress. Eventually dawn broke on a new day and she resigned to return to Jakarta broke, tired and still looking for a story. She would submit an article to fill the obvious void left by the *Post*, but that would be it. For a second article, a mere hint at political unrest simply wasn't going to cut it.

In Tanner's words: no-one gave a shit.

7

TOBELO, NORTH MALUKU

The *Pasar Modern* shopping mall was set back twenty metres from a congested Tobelo street. There was nothing modern about it. Behind its silver façade was a gigantic warehouse lined with aisles of bespoke shopping stalls lit by plastic-panel skylights and halogen lamps strung from red iron trusses. The only brand names in sight were counterfeit, and there were no iPhones or Galaxies to be found at the mobile phone store where Carter searched for a new case while he watched the mall entrance. The foyer and carpark were almost empty in the mid-afternoon, the crowds drawn away to the resonant calls of *Asr* prayer. The time made it easier to sight Hasan and anyone who followed him. If Hasan had not made contact by the end of Asr, Carter would exit through the front doors, depart the scene with Yoyok, and reattempt twenty-four hours later. He checked his watch. Hasan had fifteen minutes.

He tried phone cases of various colours and designs while the shop clerk, a young Christian woman, stared at him, interested only by the fact he was a foreigner, not a potential customer. The din of the mall went on around him. The aroma of *satè* and grilled fish wafted in from the adjacent food court. Bored shop staff stared quietly into their phones. Schoolchildren chased each other around a cluster of clothing racks. An old man swept the floors of a row of ATMs by the front entrance. He didn't so much as glance in Carter's direction, but paused for a teenage boy who entered, forgot what he was looking for, and walked out again to the forecourt. In the distance, Yoyok posed as an overpriced *ojek* driver and kept watch along the street, ready to clock Hasan's arrival. Carter had planned for fifteen minutes to debrief Hasan on developments within Barpemis, after which time Yoyok would start up the Landcruiser, collect Carter by the emergency exit and egress from the area.

With seven minutes to go, the mall began to crowd again. A mother and three children emerged from the farmer's market and entered one of the aisles. The old man finished sweeping the foyer and made way for another group of school children who entered from the main entrance, uniforms bright under the skylights, voices deafening in the cavernous hall. A group of men in Islamic tunics appeared in the carpark and meandered up the steps into the entry. They debated where to go next before disappearing into the food court. The foyer filled with noise and movement. Carter scanned the faces. Hasan still had three minutes.

Then he saw the boy.

He entered the same way he had left nine minutes earlier, mind now made up, and walked directly to a rack of shoes next to the phone store. He wore cut-off jeans and a black Nike t-shirt that was too large for him. His hair was slicked against his scalp, like he'd worn a helmet, but Carter hadn't seen a motorcycle arrive. The boy ignored the clerk and stared at a pair of shoes that were too small. There was a shout near the doorway and Carter turned to look. When he turned back, the boy was staring at him, eyes wide, like Carter might punish him for some misdemeanour. Carter broke eye contact, reached for the shop rack, and replaced the case he was holding.

Then he walked.

It took five seconds to cross the foyer and descend the steps that led to the forecourt. Seven seconds later, he reached the street. Yoyok ignored Carter to watch whoever followed him, ready to fall in trail in case the pursuer tried anything. Carter pushed through the pain of his injured leg and headed east to reach an intersection. A taxi slowed for him. He crossed in front of it, then looked back to see the boy search for a gap in the traffic. A road led north along an arcade of supermarkets and electronics stores. Halfway along, Carter crossed the street and entered an alley. Garbage bags leaned against a wall. He tore one open and scattered the contents across the alley, then waited in the niche of a doorway. A plastic bottle crunched underfoot. Carter launched himself, grabbed the boy's arm and threw him into the opposite wall.

The boy screamed but didn't resist. Carter twisted his arm behind his back and threw him onto the ground. He checked the boy for weapons and found an old mobile phone and a roll of bubble wrap. He lifted the boy face first to the wall and pulled one of his hands between his shoulder blades.

'Are you alone?' he said in Indonesian.

'Y—yes.'

'Who sent you?'

'I don't—'

Carter lifted the arm again. The boy moaned.

'I was told to meet you at Pasar Modern.'

'Who told you?'

'They didn't say, Pak. They offered money to give you the package.'

The plastic bundle was at Carter's feet. He shoved the boy into the wall. 'Don't move.' The boy shivered against the wall.

He released the boy and picked up the roll of bubble wrap. It was three or four layers deep with the ends taped over. He tore at it until it came apart, then retched.

There was a noise from the entrance to the alley. 'What's going on?' said Yoyok.

The finger had been severed at the base, fingernail removed.

Underneath was a piece of paper with a handwritten address in northern Tobelo.

The boy scrambled to his feet and ran off. Yoyok moved to chase him.

'Leave him,' said Carter. 'Get the car.'

'What is it?' said Yoyok.

Carter fought back the revulsion and guilt.

'It's Hasan.'

The four Kopassus *Komodos* sliced through northern Tobelo in the night gloom, each armoured vehicle reaching eighty kilometres an hour along the narrow streets. The local government had cut power to leave the city in darkness, and in the blackout the roads were clear of traffic.

Carter and Yoyok followed the convoy in the Landcruiser. After calling in the address, they had driven twenty kilometres north to Galela airport, where Sugianto's team had flown in by C-130 to set up for the raid.

The convoy reached a small suburb on the fringe of town that looked out over the sea. The Komodos turned right, continued for two hundred metres and stopped. The gunners on each vehicle trained their fifty-cals on a housing compound while thirty-two troopers disembarked and moved up on the walls. Carter arrived as they breached the main gates. Ten seconds later, they were gone.

The two intelligence officers climbed out and walked to the compound. They were stopped by Sugianto.

'Wait here.'

There was shouting, and the occasional scream, as the Kopassus teams cleared each townhouse on their way through to the target building. They all knew the layout by heart; within ten minutes of receiving the call from BIN, they had acquired detailed satellite imagery of the complex and pinpointed the room where Hasan was likely held.

The complex fell silent.

'They're at the target,' said Sugianto. 'Stand by.'

There was movement in the street. Confused neighbours emerged from houses, torches and phones in hand, drawn to the shouts and vehicles.

'Deal with them,' said Carter.

Sugianto walked towards the onlookers, M4 raised, and shouted for them to leave. Two of his men ran to them and repeated the order until the crowd backed off.

Flashbangs ripped through the night as the Kopassus men stormed the final building. More shouting, but no screams this time. And no shots fired. Sugianto's radio burst with chatter. Two medics moved in. Sugianto listened to a transmission from his fire team and called Carter and Yoyok over.

'The complex is clear. Stick to the main paths; there could still be boobytraps.'

They checked their pistols and jogged through the gates. Troopers guarded people at gunpoint; others lay face down on muddy courtyards. Troopers stood guard at a standalone townhouse and waved them through. Faint smoke rose from the door. Someone rigged a light as the intelligence officers arrived. It flickered on to reveal Hasan's corpse, upright on a wooden chair, partly burnt, throat cut, right ring finger removed at the base.

A medic was at Hasan's side, inspecting the wounds and searching his pockets. He walked over to Sugianto.

'He's been dead for hours, sir. There is no bleeding around the finger. He was dead before they took it.'

Carter took a knee beside the remains of his agent.

'Some comfort, at least,' said Sugianto. 'He suffered enough.'

Hasan's face said it all. His bloodshot eyes remained half-open over blackened cheeks and a mouth contorted by an unending scream. His nose, once almost Caucasian with its high ridge, was now flattened and bloodied. The injuries extended the length of his body. The skin of his neck was torn and reddened where the rope had been tied. Several of the remaining fingers hung at unnatural angles. His feet were blue and black from the ties at his ankles that had cut off circulation long before his death. Based on the dry stab wounds in Hasan's chest, the violence had continued post-mortem.

'I found this in his pocket,' said the medic. He handed a piece of paper to Sugianto.

Sugianto held it up to the light.

'What is it?' said Yoyok.

Sugianto handed him the paper. 'Looks like Hasan gave up a name.'

Yoyok inspected it and gave it to Carter. 'How did Hasan know about Taufik?'

Carter glanced at the paper and shook his head. 'He didn't know,' he said. '*They* do.' He wiped his face and gave the paper to Sugianto. 'Get it to forensics,' he said, 'along with the rest of it. Interrogate everyone.'

Sugianto frowned. 'Forensics won't find anything, Pak. These guys were smart. They probably came here for the first time today.'

Carter stood and turned to the Kopassus officer. Sugianto was unmoved.

'We could be blown, Sugi,' said Carter. 'All of us. Everything we've worked for might have just died in that chair, so whatever you need to do to find out how, just do it.'

'Sure, bos,' said Sugianto. 'Then what?'

Carter stared at Hasan's corpse. Whoever had done this didn't want information; they wanted to send a message. Carter would reply.

He turned back to Sugianto.

'You'll see.'

CANBERRA

The DDG joined the rest of the leadership team on the sofas in deference to Hasan. There was no lycra. He had come in early and changed into his trademark safari jacket, navy blue trousers and white shirt.

'Do we know who did it?'

Gibson rubbed his eyes. 'Not yet,' he said. 'Forensics will be a few more days.'

'Leaves Maqsood as the most likely culprit,' said Ops. She folded her arms and frowned.

Neill grunted. 'Maqsood couldn't know about Taufik. Taufik works for Ibrahim.'

'The leader of Gameshar,' said Security, as if to remind everyone she was still present. 'Is this connected to the riots?'

The group was silent.

'If it is,' said the DDG, 'we'll soon find out.' He turned to Gibson. 'What are we doing about Taufik?'

'Jordan will check on him,' said Gibson, but it was probably Carter that needed checking on. 'Remind him to be vigilant.'

'And that's it?' said Legal.

Neill's moustache twitched. 'We don't want to confirm he's involved with us by evacuating him,' he said.

Legal pulled his hair back.

'His cover's that good?' said the DDG.

'Watertight, Terry. Apart from us, no-one is aware of the connection.'

'Ibrahim knows,' said Ops.

'Of course he bloody does. Taufik is Ibrahim's cut-out, for Christ's sake.'

'Precisely.'

'Fucking hell, Hera. If Ibrahim blabs about Taufik, he admits to working with the government. Hasan's treatment would compare nicely to what they would do to him.'

No-one spoke. Neill ploughed on.

'Look, we knew our guys would come under suspicion from time to time. It was always part of the risk assessment.'

'Then explain how Taufik's name was found on Hasan's body,' said Ops.

'Easy.' Neill raised his voice. 'The heads of these groups hate one another, but the worker bees still mix. That's how information moves around between the groups. We report on it. In some cases, we depend on it. Someone caught a rumour about Taufik and decided to shake the tree. It's—'

'Enough, you two,' said the DDG, terminating the contest. He looked at Gibson.

'You know my next question.'

'The Indonesians have kept quiet,' said Gibson. He had called Hartanto three times that morning while he reviewed reports of the raid. All he'd received back was a two-sentence email via Liam Ellis at the Australian embassy, and only after Ellis had hounded the staff at BIN headquarters. 'They've called a meeting for ANVIL principals tomorrow.'

'Fair enough,' said the DDG. He brought his hands up to form a steeple in front of his face.

'I'll look forward to it.'

8

TERNATE

Ana woke from a dream about dental surgery. She had been tied down to the chair, mouth clamped open while vibrations of a hand drill reverberated through her head, and now she was on a hotel bed, disoriented in the half light of the early morning while the buzzing continued. A car horn sounded outside her room as if to remind her she was still in Ternate. She sat up with a start. The vibrating sound was muted. She lifted her pillow to reveal her phone.

'Fuck,' she whispered as she looked at the screen. She answered. 'Mum?'

'Ana. What's the matter with you?'

'Nothing.' She rubbed sleep from her eyes. 'Why?'

'Haven't you read the paper? It says you're in a place called Ternate.' She pronounced it *'Turn-Eight'*.

Ana squeezed the bridge of her nose. 'It's called *tur-nah-tay.*' She looked around for her laptop and found it in her backpack, resting neatly by her travel case that she'd packed for the afternoon flight back to Jakarta.

'You never told me you were off on some adventure.'

She fought one-handed with the zip and retrieved the laptop. 'Sorry Mama, I forgot.'

'Like you forgot how to answer the phone? I was worried sick.'

Ana took the phone from her ear and checked the screen. Seven missed calls and too many social media notifications to view.

'I'm fine, Mum. Really. I've been meaning to call.'

The laptop booted and she navigated to the website for *The Australian.*

'You always say that. You know your uncle's wife had her forty-fifth birthday last weekend?'

Yeah, she knew, she just didn't care. She scrolled the headlines until she found her story: *'Indonesia Mosque Fire Linked to Resurgent Islamism.'*

She clicked. Her mother continued to tell her about the birthday party and some hapless cousin who had found her husband in bed with the cleaner.

'Sounds awful,' said Ana, but her mind was on the article. Five-hundred words, mostly unscathed by the editor's pen, that led the reader to a far-off corner of South-east Asia – a light year and one stone's throw from Australia's shores – to an innocent town attacked by Islamic extremists and shrouded in secrecy by the Indonesian Government. By Ana Kovacevic, reporting from Ternate, Indonesia.

'Sorry?' she said.

'I said you should come home, Ana.'

Ana took a drink from a half-empty bottle of water. 'I will. Soon.'

'I mean it. It is dangerous there. This article says so.'

'I know what I wrote, Mum.'

'It's a warzone now that the army is involved. It was like this before your Papa and I came to Australia.'

Ana stared across the strait to Maitara and shook her head. 'Where did you get that idea?'

'I saw it on the Twitter. It says the army raided some house in a place called Tobylow.'

Ana rolled her eyes and opened Twitter. 'It's pronounced—' She cut herself off. At the top of her feed was a photograph posted by someone named Henra that showed two army vehicles parked by a street. In the background, armed soldiers were emerging from an alleyway.

'Ana?'

The caption described, in English, the extent of the military operation the night before. Henra had mentioned Ana's article, which was how her mother had seen it. Ana scrolled and found a retweet that showed the location on Google Maps in northwestern Tobelo.

'Are you there?'

Ana realised her mother had been speaking.

'Sorry, it cut out. Look, Mum, I have to go.'

'I miss you, *mileni.* Come home.'

'I miss you too, Mama.'

She rang off, stunned by a series of tweets describing the aftermath of what could only have been a terror raid. She browsed a list of news websites and found nothing. Her luggage waited obediently next to the door. She was due to leave for Jakarta in three hours.

She opened her phone and dialled. It was answered on the fourth ring.

'Tanner.'

'It's me.'

Tanner sighed. 'What do you want?'

'I've got something for you.'

'Shop it to Murdoch like last time.'

'So you read my story?'

'No.'

'Well, this one's even better. Something just went down in Tobelo.'

'Below what?'

'*Toh-beh-loh.* Forget it. Look, the army raided a house there overnight. It could be connected to my article, and I'm the only journalist in this part of the country.'

'So what?'

'So today's article has been retweeted a hundred times. I could've pitched this straight back to *The Australian,* but I didn't. I'm offering it to you.'

He grunted. 'Okay,' he said. 'Say it.'

'Three grand plus expenses.'

'You are taking the fucking piss.'

'This is a bargain. Everyone else will have to fly someone in.'

The line went quiet.

'Michael?'

'Yeah, yeah, I'm thinking.'

She stared at the ceiling while she waited. *Come on, come on.*

'Fine. Two-point-five and expenses. Due Thursday. Don't send me any tripe.'

Ana smiled and blew him a kiss. 'I won't. Thanks Mick.'

'Don't fucking call me—'

She rang off.

CANBERRA

'We're on with BIN in fifteen,' said Scarlett. She entered Gibson's office and placed a coffee tray on the desk. A macchiato for her, long black for him.

Gibson was reading the Kovacevic article in *The Australian.* He lay the paper on his desk.

Scarlett glanced at the page. 'I wonder who put her up to it?'

'All her own work, apparently.' He took a sip. For once, it wasn't burnt.

'Do you think it'll be a problem?'

'Shouldn't think so. Says nothing about the operation or our involvement.'

'I meant with the Indonesians.'

Gibson smiled at her. 'They'll be fine.'

He wasn't so sure.

◆

The six ASIS staff took up every available seat in the SCIF. Scarlett joined the DDG, Gibson, Neill and the security officer. A contract Indonesian translator completed the group. She wasn't necessary, since the Indonesians spoke near-perfect English, but customary, since the DDG didn't speak a word of Indonesian.

They had already set up the ANGINA link, so they waited on mute for the Indonesians.

The DDG rubbed his hands together and beamed at his staff. 'Show some excitement, team.'

Neill yawned.

'I know Hartanto can be a pain sometimes,' continued the DDG. 'Just be glad you don't have to deal with the Americans.'

'Bullshit,' said Neill. 'The Singaporeans are the worst.'

Scarlett looked at Gibson and raised an eyebrow. Gibson smiled back.

'Outside Five Eyes, sure,' said the DDG. 'But it depends on who you get up there. Some Singaporeans actually care about Australia.'

'Better than the pricks across the lake,' said Neill. He meant ASIO. 'They'll invent the self-licking ice-cream machine soon.'

'And then tell the world about it,' said Gibson.

Scarlett suppressed a laugh and glanced at Gibson again. ASIS's domestic cousin was unique amongst Australia's spy agencies in that it both collected and analysed intelligence, a conflict of interest that had more than paid for its grand, shiny castle on the north shore of Lake Burley-Griffin. To add insult, in recent years, ASIO had enjoyed lifting the veil on its capabilities and methods, a deviance from the usual culture of secrecy that was universally resented by almost the entire intelligence community.

The Wireline cracked into life. 'Uh, hello? Jakarta is on the line.' The voice belonged to Anas, one of Hartanto's deputies.

'Hello Anas,' said the DDG. 'Who have we got there?'

'Pak Hartanto, sir. And me, Anas.'

Scarlett scribbled the names.

The DDG hit mute and looked at Gibson. 'Small crowd?'

BIN usually brought a full complement from ops, analysis, personnel and security. Gibson shrugged.

The DDG unmuted himself. 'Okay then. I thought we could begin with the facts of Hasan's murder and next-stage plans for Operation ANVIL.'

Mute.

No-one said anything. The DDG stared at the Wireline as if he might conjure a response.

It was Hartanto who broke the silence. 'There is no time for that, Pak Terry,' he said. 'We must suspend ANVIL immediately.'

The DDG leaned back in his chair. 'That's a new one.'

Scarlett made a face in confusion. Neill opened his eyes and made a gesture that meant, 'Allow me.'

The DDG waved him on.

Unmute.

'Seems a little premature to me,' said Neill.

'It is necessary, Pak Gary. Hasan's death proves that our cut-out network is compromised. We cannot guarantee the safety of our agents. Therefore, we must suspend cooperation.'

Neill wiped his hands down his cheeks and leaned to the microphone. 'Now listen here, Pak. Someone is targeting our agents and our intelligence officers. This is exactly why we should continue.'

'These are not targeted attacks. They are the consequences of poor decision-making.'

'Jordan Carter has operational control.'

'Tell it to the newspapers.'

'Is that what this is about?' said Neill. 'The Kovacevic article?'

A pause.

'BIN has worked hard to suppress reports of the riots to prevent matters escalating,' said Hartanto. His voice rose with irritation. 'Thanks to you, it is now public knowledge.'

Scarlett gave Gibson a look as if to say, 'Are they joking?'

'It's a free press,' said Neill. 'Nothing to do with us.'

There was another pause.

Gibson reached over and hit mute. 'They think we leaked it.'

The DDG rolled his eyes. The line came back.

'As you may appreciate, Pak Gary and Pak Terry, my government is concerned about North Maluku's stability in the lead up to regency elections. We cannot afford any more incidents like the one in Kao. We certainly cannot afford to lose any more agents. The Indonesian Government's position is clear.'

'As is ours,' shouted Neill. 'We can't have a new wave of Islamist extremism crash across North Maluku—'

The DDG gestured at the phone. It was muted.

Neill swore and stroked his moustache.

'Therefore,' continued Hartanto, 'we have decided to suspend our cooperation at this time.'

The SCIF fell silent. Scarlett glanced at Gibson as if he might respond, but there was nothing he could say without inflaming things. Gibson had worked on-and-off with Hartanto for two decades and knew the Indonesian spymaster would have backstopped this decision two, probably three levels up in his own hierarchy and kicked the ball out of the field of play. There was nothing to be done.

Unmute.

The DDG was leaned over the mic, half a smirk on his face.

'Let's take a step back, shall we?' he said.

Neill raised an eyebrow.

'As you wish,' said Hartanto.

'And let's stick to facts, if we can. Fact one'—the DDG held up a finger, as if the BIN staff were in the room—'is that any decision to suspend or terminate operation ANVIL must be agreed jointly by the foreign ministers of both countries.'

Scarlett looked to Gibson for confirmation.

He nodded.

Two fingers now: 'Fact two is that my minister informed me of her warm and productive discussion with your own minister this very morning, and she was kind enough to confirm that your minister was *very* supportive of continuing Operation ANVIL, especially in light of the evolving security situation in West Asia and the middle East. In fact, he was eager to explore further cooperative security actions along the same lines. "A template for broader security engagement across the Republic" seemed to be his words.'

There was brief silence, then:

'Such enthusiasm only extends so far, Pak Terry.' Hartanto's voice was quieter, but no less stern. 'We both know that.'

'Indeed,' said the DDG, but his smirk held. 'So let me offer a compromise.'

Gibson looked over at the DDG, searching the man's face for a sign of what was about to be sacrificed.

The DDG ignored him. 'Recognising that we do not want the rest of our cut-outs to be subject to what poor Hasan encountered, I will instruct Jordan Carter to evacuate them at the earliest. What that means for the operation, I will leave to Gary and Andy. However, and let me be absolutely crystal clear on this, for the benefit of you and those you work for, ANVIL remains a significant counterterrorism priority for this government. We cannot – I repeat, *cannot* – allow extremist groups to gain a foothold within our closest neighbour from where they might spill over into this country. Nor can you, so I expect BIN's full cooperation, as before.'

The room was silent apart from the hiss of the open line. Gibson suppressed an urge to bang his head on the table. Neill reached forward and muted the mic.

'Terry, how the fuck can we run ANVIL without any bloody agents?'

The DDG held up his hand. 'Find a way,' he said, 'or explain it to the minister yourself.'

Neill sat back and folded his arms, as if finally resigned to what Gibson could see had been inevitable. For his bravado, bordering on arrogance, the DDG was often dismissed as a rogue operator who had charmed his way to the top, yet in a single move he had neutered BIN's resistance to ANVIL and eliminated a brewing political problem that threatened Australian Government support for the operation. But whatever sense could be made of the DDG's capitulation couldn't overcome Gibson's sense of shock. Worse, it would fall to him to explain it to Carter.

The DDG unmuted. 'Do we have an agreement?'

He looked around the room, like he was talking to his own staff.

Hartanto exhaled into the microphone.

'For now.'

9

TOBELO

The highway meandered through twenty kilometres of residential districts before a large green sign welcomed Ana to Tobelo. It was eleven-thirty, and Rimbo had driven non-stop from Sofifi as she had told him to. She was eager to capitalise on her proximity to the army raid that had taken place two nights earlier and find out what – and who – they had been looking for.

Ana recognised landmarks and buildings from her first journey to Tobelo three days earlier at the pleasure of the North Halmahera police. The police had turned off the highway not far from the outskirts and headed for the government quarter inland, but Rimbo continued north through the centre of town to the northern reaches of the city, where the highway passed through a knot of suburbs that skirted the sea.

'Left here,' said Ana.

Rimbo turned into a narrow street. Low-set houses lined both sides, but there was little sign of life. Ahead they heard the wailing of a minaret. The street turned ninety degrees to reach their destination.

A police officer leaned against a high concrete wall and played with a smartphone. Next to him, yellow police tape was strewn across the opening of a wide gate that led into a housing compound. The officer looked up at them and went back to his phone. Rimbo continued past while Ana took photos inside. The compound seemed empty.

'Up there,' said Ana. Rimbo parked near the mosque as the minarets died down and fanned himself with his prayer cap. It was a small community building painted yellow and green. A dozen worshippers filed out and disappeared into the surrounding village. Ana watched them walk past the police officer. Some pointed at the police tape and muttered to one-another, but none went inside.

Ana typed another address into her phone. The destination was behind them. She tapped out a short message and climbed out of the car under the gaze of the imam, who watched from the veranda of the mosque with placid curiosity. Rimbo locked the car and they walked towards the compound.

'Find a way inside,' said Ana as they reached the compound. Rimbo clicked his tongue and crossed the street to the police officer. The officer stood to attention as Rimbo approached. Ana took photos of the compound gates. Small houses lined up either side of a long alley. At the end was a T-junction and more police tape, but no sign of activity.

Rimbo returned. 'Sorry, mbak. He not let us in.'

The officer stared at them from across the street.

Ana quelled her frustration. 'Why not?'

'He makes sure no-one sees the crime scene.'

'Crime scene?'

Rimbo's face twisted with confusion. 'The murder, mbak.'

'Murder of who?'

'A boy,' said Rimbo. He looked like he had said something stupid. 'The policeman told me.'

Ana smiled. 'At least you're good for something,' she said under her breath.

'Permisi?'

Ana's phone sounded.

'Never mind,' she said. 'Let's go.'

Henra, the woman who had revealed the Army raid, turned out to be a twenty-something year-old housewife. She wore a blue headscarf that clung tight around her pale, acne-marked face, but there were no other obvious displays of religion in her three-metre square sitting room. *'Assalamu alaikum,'* she said timidly.

'Mualaikum assalam,' replied Rimbo. Ana shook Henra's hand.

'Please, sit,' said Henra. Ana and Rimbo sat next to each other on the small sofa. Henra offered tea and a jar of baked tempè. Rimbo helped himself as a toddler wandered into the room and sidled up to his mother. Henra kissed him and ushered him back to the bedroom.

'Thank you for seeing us,' said Ana.

'It is okay,' said Henra. 'You must have come very far.'

They made idle conversation. Out of politeness Ana held back from direct questioning. Most people were more talkative when relaxed, and Henra, who sat upright on the corner of her stool, was more anxious than most. Ana humoured her with anecdotes of life as a foreigner in Jakarta, and Henra explained she had trained as a nurse there before she married, which was where she learned English. Eventually, it was Henra who broached the topic of the raid.

'It was dark,' she said. 'They cut out the lights before they came.'

'The army?'

'I think so. It was nine o'clock, I think. My husband had just put our son to sleep and the electricity went out. It was nothing unusual until the trucks came.'

Ana had laid her phone on the small coffee table. She checked it was recording.

'They stopped outside,' Henra continued. 'We went to see what happened and saw soldiers run into the compound. That's when I took the photo. They yelled at us to go back inside the house. They threatened to arrest anyone who didn't.'

'Did you see or hear anything after that?'

Henra pondered. 'There was shouting, some loud noises. Like doors slamming.'

'Any gunshots? Explosions?'

'I don't know,' she said. Her eyes fell. 'I am sorry.'

Ana placed her hand on Henra's. Henra looked up.

'Why did you decide to contact me?' said Ana.

'I couldn't sleep,' said Henra. 'I looked on the internet in case someone knew what had happened. I saw your article and wondered if it had something to do with the Islamists.' She shook her head in frustration. 'They are always causing trouble with their politics. They push for the mosques to promote independence. Then they send children into the schools to bully anyone who doesn't support them. My husband tries hard to keep them away from our boy, but it is difficult.'

'How long has this gone on?'

Henra frowned. 'A few years, at least. But they have become more aggressive recently.'

'How recently?'

'In the past few months.'

There was a banging sound from the bedroom. Henra appeared anxious to return to her child.

'Can you tell me any more about who the Islamists are?'

Henra straightened and shook her head. 'I don't know,' she said, but she couldn't hold Ana's eye contact.

They said their goodbyes and walked back to the street. The police officer had sat down by the wall, unable to find shade. Ana stared beyond him to the small house lined with police tape.

'You okay, mbak?' said Rimbo.

'How long would it take to find out who owned the house?'

He looked over at the gate. 'A few days, maybe.'

At a hundred dollars per day, no doubt. Even if he was up to it, Ana suspected he'd find nothing of value.

'I will call some friends,' he said.

The imam had reappeared at the mosque. He leaned against a pillar and smoked.

'Forget it,' she said.

'He say he know nothing more about it,' said Rimbo.

Ana adjusted the muslin wrap she had draped over her head. The three of them sat on cushions in the centre of the main hall. The imam sipped his tea while he brushed dust off his white tunic. His face affected a look of serene superiority.

'Isn't he curious about a murder fifty metres from his mosque?'

Rimbo relayed the question. The imam's response was terse.

'He ask why you think it is important.'

Ana watched the imam. His eyes dropped to the tea.

'Tell him I know there has been escalating violence between Islamist factions in North Maluku for years. Everything about what happened the other night points to counterterrorism. There must be a link.'

The imam smiled as Rimbo spoke, then responded without breaking eye contact.

'He say you are very clever,' said Rimbo. The imam continued speaking. 'He say the dead boy is from Barpemis.'

'Barpemis?'

'Barisan Pembebasan Islam, mbak.'

'I know who they are.'

Rimbo swallowed. 'The imam say everyone knows this but is too afraid to say it.'

Ana glanced at the imam, then back to Rimbo. 'Why isn't he afraid?'

Rimbo translated. The imam responded with venom.

'Barpemis is a stain on Islam and the community, he say, but it is not Barpemis that causes these problems, it is the government. They make trouble and make division in this place. It is good that Barpemis has finally turned against them. The good Muslims of Maluku are victims. They deserve justice.'

Ana took this in, her mind turning with the imam's revelation, her own arrest, the cover up of the Kao mosque riot. One point stood out.

She turned to Rimbo. 'What did he mean when he said Barpemis finally turned against the government? What changed?'

The imam raised his voice in response.

'People say for a long time the boy work for the government. Everyone believe he was a spy, but Barpemis never do anything until two nights ago.'

The imam's face had sharpened.

'Why two nights ago?' said Ana.

'Mashallah,' said the imam.

Ana looked at Rimbo. He cleared his throat and said, 'God was willing.'

Rimbo climbed into the car with an air of finality, first replacing his prayer cap with a fresh one from the glove box, then undoing the top button of his tunic. It was almost three o'clock. If they headed back now, they could catch the last ferry to Ternate.

'Change of plan,' said Ana.

Rimbo looked at her expectantly.

'Take me to police headquarters.'

Rimbo clicked his tongue and started the car.

Half an hour and several wrong turns later, they reached the grand building that housed the regional headquarters of the North Halmahera police. It had been four days, but it felt like a month since Ana had spent a night here. As a free woman, she noticed the patched asphalt of the front carpark, the fresh paint and the deafening silence. Her ears were tuned to the constant din of Jakarta. Here, they rang for lack of noise.

'Find a hotel,' she said to Rimbo. He nodded and drove off. She walked inside and approached the reception desk. A young female officer sat stoically. Ana thought she recognised her from her previous visit.

'I'd like to speak to Inspector Rachmann.'

'Do you have an appointment?'

'No.'

The woman smiled. 'You must make an appointment, mbak.'

'Tell him I have information about the murder two nights ago. I'll only speak to him.'

'Murder?'

'Yes, a murder. It's vital I speak to him.'

The woman eyed her quizzically. 'One moment, please.'

Ana sat down and waited. The officer glanced at Ana as she spoke at length on the phone. She eventually hung up and went back to her duties. It was a good sign. If Rachmann wasn't going to see her, the officer would have asked her to leave.

Half an hour passed before the rotund figure of Rachmann entered the lobby. 'Miss Kovacevic,' he said with false excitement. 'We don't usually expect return visitors.'

'I got so much value out of our last conversation. Perhaps you read about it.'

Rachmann's smile faded. 'Come,' he said.

He led her up a flight of stairs – groaning with each step – and along a corridor. At the northern end he ushered her into an office and sat down behind a large wooden desk made small by the enormity of his waist. Ana noticed a line of photos on the shelf behind him, where he posed with all number of political officials, none of whom she recognised.

He wiped a finger across his moustache. 'It seems you have information for me.'

'I do,' said Ana. 'I've discovered that a member of Barpemis was murdered for acting as an informant.'

Rachmann stiffened. His eyes scanned the items scattered on his desk – files, a stained coffee mug, a brass engraving of his name and rank – but couldn't find whatever he was looking for.

'Perhaps you knew already,' she said. 'It was an open secret the victim had been in contact with the government for years.'

'If you say so.'

'Do you have any comment?'

Rachman smiled. 'Only that it would explain his murder.'

'He survived too long to be a known informant, Inspector. It's more likely he was a go-between for the police.'

The smile vanished. He moved a folder out of the way and rested his elbows on the desk.

'Why are the Indonesian police secretly in contact with known extremists?' said Ana.

'They are not.'

'So you deny it.'

He slammed his hand on the table. Ana flinched. The hand came back up and he pointed his finger at her face.

'The police had nothing to do with this,' he said. 'Not now, not ever. If it were up to me, they would all be in jail.'

Ana was still. Rachmann's head dropped, and he put his hand down. 'I warned them this would happen eventually. You cannot trust these…' he searched for the word, 'extremists.'

'Warned who?' said Ana.

He looked up at her. 'None of your business. What matters is that this boy did not work for the police. Write that.'

Rimbo was waiting outside. He drove her to a hotel near the centre of town, where she spent the evening drafting her next piece. When she had her draft, she called Tanner.

'Fucking what now?'

'I'm about to submit. You'll like it.'

'I don't like anything, especially calls after deadline.'

'I know, Michael, but it's important. The government has been in secret contact with Islamist groups here for years.'

'So what? You gonna tell me the whole place is corrupt, too? It's Indonesia, sweetie.'

Ana tried not to smile. 'This isn't Java or Sulawesi, Michael. The police aren't involved. This is all undercover.'

'It's no different here, so, show me the story.'

'The story is that one of the cut-outs turned up dead five nights after an innocent mosque was burnt down. Whatever operation the Indonesians are running, it's coming apart. I want to find out why.'

'Money's what you want.'

'And you want to tell the world that Australia's largest neighbour has an extremism problem it can't control. This could be Mindanao all over again.'

'"Now" what?'

'The Philippines—forget it. Fund me for another month and I'll give you an exclusive. There's no-one else here, but that will change.'

He gave a long sigh. 'You don't know where this rabbit hole leads, Alice.'

'When have my instincts ever let you down?' she said. 'Wasn't I right about the Kao story?'

'I get it,' he said. He sounded defeated. Ana pictured him at his desk, after dark, hacking at yet another story without the usual army of sub-editors to help, pushed to the brink by endless budget cuts and the ever-increasing demands of profit-driven backers.

'Is it a deal?'

'Yeah, it's a deal.'

Ana closed her eyes and exhaled, long and deep, into the darkness of the room. She finally had her story.

'Thank you, Michael.'

She was about to ring off when he spoke again.

'Don't fuck this up, Ana.'

10

SUBAIM, NORTH MALUKU

The adhan started softly. Four repetitions of *Allahu akbar,* each more intense than the last, until the muezzin's voice soared across Subaim to recount the remainder of the *Fajr* call to prayer. It was 4.59 a.m., still and dark, *God is the greatest* the first thing the villagers would hear that morning, like every morning before and all those to come; just as it had been the final thing they had thought of the night before.

Taufik had been awake for hours. He lay still, staring into the darkness, his mind still at war with the consequences of his decision. Whether or not he had slept at all, he felt no fatigue, only the adrenaline that accompanied his sense of duty. Duty to his faith; duty to his country. To his family.

His wife stirred next to him. He rolled off the mattress, dressed and left her in privacy. In the next room the children were still asleep. 'Come quick,' he said to his daughter. She pushed his hand away and he shook her until she sat up. Outside, a car came to a stop on the gravel. 'Wake your brother,' he told her. She rubbed her eyes.

He left the children to dress. He took two schoolbags from the sitting room, checked their contents and returned. 'Take these,' he said to them. His daughter, only six, frowned at the bag.

'Why aren't we praying?' she said.

He took her gently by her shoulders. 'There is something more important we must do.'

'What is more important than *salah?*'

'Family. Come.'

The children waited in the sitting room while he took another bag into the bedroom. His wife was only half dressed. He held out the bag.

'Take this.'

'What is going on, Taufik?'

'You must go,' he said. 'There is no time to explain. If you go now, we will be safe.'

The expression of annoyance on her face gave way to concern.

'In the bag is money and documents for you and the children,' he said. 'Do not take your own.'

She stared at the bag in her hand. 'Taufik, what have you done?'

He left her to dress and led the children out to the street where a blue van waited. A black SUV was parked fifty metres away, where Taufik expected it. A man climbed out of the van.

'Cousin,' said Taufik. They embraced.

'Where are we going?' asked his daughter.

He squatted beside her. 'On an adventure. I know you like adventures.'

He turned to his wife. She stood silent, shaking, eyes glazed with tears.

'He will drive you west,' he told her. 'Take the ferry to Tidore, find a hotel and stay there. If anyone stops you, give them money. Do not tell anyone where you are going.'

'You are not coming?'

'There is something I must do first, then I will come.' Taufik turned. 'Stay on the main roads, cousin,' he said. 'Do not stop.'

'I know.' The man smiled at him. 'You can trust me.'

Taufik hugged his wife and children as they climbed aboard and watched as they drove away. The SUV didn't follow them. It was possible others would, but Taufik trusted his cousin to evade Ibrahim's men. Trusted him to protect his family.

Taufik returned to the sitting room and checked his shoulder bag: a roll of US currency, another of Rupiah; a change of clothes, shaving kit, duct tape, bottled water and tempè. In the flap pocket was a fresh Indonesian identity card with his photo and a false name. He returned to the children's room and lifted a mattress. He scratched at one of the floor tiles until it came loose, and inside found an old pistol he had stolen from Ibrahim's armoury two days earlier. He checked it was clean, loaded and safe, then placed it in the bag.

He left by the front door at the usual time, as though headed to work. He rode his motorcycle to the centre of town and stopped at a supermarket. Inside were several customers, but none paid him attention. The SUV arrived. Taufik found the bottled-water aisle and walked towards the rear of the store.

A man stood at the end of the aisle. He was of a similar build and complexion to Taufik, and dressed the same: pale slacks, white shirt, faded taqiyah, black shoulder bag. Taufik held the bike key and moved towards him. When he was two steps away, he lifted his hand.

The man looked past Taufik's shoulder, then at the key. He reached up with his left hand and took it, then handed over another key with his right hand before he picked up a bottle of water and walked to the front counter. Taufik left by a rear door and entered a bathroom. He took the shaving kit from the bag and shaved his beard, then changed into the spare clothes. He checked outside. His colleague was gone; so was the SUV.

The motorcycle was parked in an alley at the rear of the supermarket, behind a delivery truck where it was invisible from the street. Taufik had provided the money for it, a second-hand trailbike in impressive condition. It started first time. He donned the helmet and rode onto the street. After two-hundred metres, he reached an intersection and turned left, uphill, then stopped where the road reached the jungle and became a steep trail. He lit a cigarette and watched, but there was no sign of anyone. After fifteen minutes, he flicked the cigarette, started the trailbike and rode into the jungle.

An unsealed road followed the treeline behind a large kampung. Taufik waited behind a fallen tree, out of sight of the houses and anyone that followed the track. The track stretched a hundred metres in both directions, lit by needles of sunlight that penetrated the jungle canopy.

His decision to evacuate had been easy, in retrospect. God knew he had thought about it almost every day that he spied on Ibrahim; the Australian had warned him to prepare to flee at any moment, since any delay would endanger his own life as well as others. But it had not been his discovery of Ibrahim's surveillance that had prompted it, nor his lack of foreknowledge of the Gameshar riots in Kao. As Ibrahim's designated go-between to the government, he had long faced suspicion and excommunication. Only the Australian's message confirmed he was compromised, and now, thanks to his preparation, and to God, his family was safe. But it was not enough: he had been careful; he had made no mistakes.

So he needed to know what had happened.

He heard the two-stroke motor before it rounded the curve. Agus rode alone. Taufik checked the pistol was cocked and flicked off the safety catch. The bike was fifty metres away, twenty. Taufik took a breath and stepped onto the track.

Agus didn't react, at first, then turned the handlebars in panic. The bike flipped and speared into the verge. Taufik followed Agus as he was thrown onto the track beside him.

Agus was stunned. 'You fool!' he shouted. His pitted face held nothing but scorn for Taufik, his nicotine-stained teeth bared like a rabid dog.

Then he saw the pistol.

'Come,' said Taufik.

He gripped Agus's spindly bicep through his loose tunic and

dragged him through the undergrowth to a tall sapling. Taufik's backpack lay next to it alongside a roll of duct tape. He kicked Agus's leg so that he fell, then he pulled his arms behind the tree and taped them together. Agus swore at him. Taufik ignored him and aimed the pistol. Agus shook his head and took deep, rapid breaths. His taqiyah had fallen, revealing a patchwork of black and grey hair.

'Ibrahim's men have been following me since last Friday,' said Taufik. 'Why?'

Agus recovered his breath and laughed. 'Because Ibrahim wants you dead.'

Taufik picked up Agus's bag. Inside he found what he was looking for.

'So why not kill me?'

Agus's face twisted in pain. 'Did you do all this just to ask me that?'

'No,' said Taufik. He knew the answer: they wanted the rest of his network. That at least meant they were safe.

Agus struggled against the tree.

'Last Wednesday Ibrahim met with Abu Maqsood,' said Taufik. 'What did they meet about?'

Agus spat at him. His tongue crept out and flicked across the front of his yellow teeth.

Taufik walked over and stepped on his left thigh. Agus screamed.

'You know better than anyone that Ibrahim does not tolerate traitors.' Taufik lifted his foot.

Agus let out a laugh. 'I know as well as you. Ibrahim knows you are a spy for the government.'

'Of course he does,' said Taufik. 'He told me to do it.'

'You are a liar,' said Agus, but he wasn't sure.

Taufik took a hardback notebook from Agus's bag and flicked through the pages.

'Does Ibrahim know his personal assistant keeps a secret ledger of his affairs?'

Agus strained at the tree. 'You dog!'

Taufik held up the notebook. 'It is all here, Agus.'

Agus slumped back.

'Why did Ibrahim meet with Maqsood?'

Agus shook his narrow head. With his unkempt hair and sullen cheeks, he looked naked and ill.

'Was it the riots?' Taufik demanded.

Agus's head fell.

'Speak!'

His voice echoed back from the forest.

'They will kill me, Taufik.'

'Ibrahim will kill you himself when he sees this ledger.'

Agus stared at his feet. Taufik left him and opened his backpack. He took out the tempè and water and began to eat.

Agus licked his teeth and stared at him. His eyes hardened for a moment, then fell to Taufik's feet.

'They are negotiating a pact.'

'That's not possible,' said Taufik. 'They hate each other.'

'They hate the government more.'

'What changed, Agus?'

Agus groaned. The adrenaline of the crash and his capture had worn off.

'I don't know, brother.' Agus rested his head against the sapling. 'I only know it is a good thing.'

'There must be a reason. These two men are sworn enemies. Barpemis killed Ibrahim's son.'

Agus scoffed. 'Only because the spies told them to.'

Taufik scanned the ledger. It was nothing but endless names, dates and places that meant nothing to him. He needed to get going. He placed the notebook in his bag and left the rest of the food and water for Agus. 'In case you break free, or if someone rescues you,' he said.

'Filthy dog!'

He gestured at Agus with the pistol. Agus stiffened.

Taufik kneeled next to him and spoke quietly. 'If you tell anyone of this, or if anything happens to my family, I will send this'—he gestured at the backpack—'to Ibrahim himself.'

The motorcycle was hidden fifty metres away. Taufik left Agus and returned to Subaim just before nightfall. He bought new clothes from a street seller and changed behind an empty building. The precaution seemed pointless now. Even if Agus had escaped and raised the alarm, the danger to Taufik's life was now insignificant. Ibrahim and Maqsood, had they had joined forces, would control most of northern Halmahera. Both were fanatical in their pursuit of independence from the central government and prepared to do anything to obtain it. Until now, the only thing that had stopped them was the mutual antipathy Taufik had stoked on behalf of the Australian.

Opposite was a bus station where a coach bound for Sofifi was loading passengers. He sent a text message to an emergency number the Australian had given him, made a final check of the street, crossed it and boarded. He would tell Mister Carter what he had learned.

God willing, the Australian would know what to do.

TIDORE, NORTH MALUKU

The lights of the ferry appeared at nine p.m. The ferry pulled slowly up to the dock, rocking on the swell until it came to rest at the pier. A coxswain jumped onto the platform and shouted something at the dock worker. A floodlight came on and a ramp was lowered, inch-by-inch, before a single vehicle drove off the ferry and along the access road. Carter watched it through a windscreen streaked with rain. There was more movement at the top of the ramp, then a line of shadows descended onto the platform, passing one by one under the floodlight.

Yoyok examined each one through a pair of binoculars. 'It's him,' he said. 'Fourth from the end.'

Ten passengers descended the ramp. Five went straight for taxis while the others ran for shelter by the ferry, the screens of their smartphones dancing in the darkness. The seventh in line reached the dock and walked straight on into the rain.

'He's clear,' said Yoyok. He lowered his window.

Taufik hurried over. 'Is my family safe?'

'Yes,' said Carter. 'Get in.'

Carter gave Taufik a pack of cigarettes once he was seated. Yoyok drove the Landcruiser off the docks and into Tidore.

'When can I see them?' said Taufik.

Yoyok glanced up at the mirror. 'Soon, Pak.'

Yoyok stopped the car by a row of two-storey buildings. Taufik followed Carter inside and sat down as Yoyok shut the door. Carter brought a tray from the kitchen loaded with tea, cigarettes and Tim Tams, and placed it on a coffee table.

'Your favourite,' said Carter. 'Straight from Aus.'

Yoyok brought towels and a blanket. The rainstorm had been unusually cold, and the agent was shaking. Taufik dried himself then washed down a Tim Tam with hot tea. When he was ready, he lit a cigarette and leaned back on the sofa. He watched Carter sit down and tie his hair into a bun.

'Are you injured, Pak?'

Most of Carter's injuries from the Kao riots had healed except for the red rash across his cheek.

'Birdwatching accident,' said Carter.

Taufik exhaled smoke sharply from his nose.

Carter opened the video recorder on his phone and placed it on the table so it had a clear view of Taufik. He made a short recording, checked the audio and image quality, then set the phone down again. 'Let's begin,' he said.

Taufik took a drag, flicked the ash and kicked off the debrief. He recounted the five days of surveillance and his decision to evacuate, stopping every so often to light another cigarette. He outlined his plan to uncover how he was compromised, then described his interrogation of Agus and his discovery of Maqsood's negotiations with

Ibrahim. He told of his fears a separatist union that would come to dominate North Maluku, but could offer no further detail. 'It must be there in the ledger,' he said.

Yoyok took the ledger and photographed the pages. Carter stayed with Taufik and clarified details of Agus's testimony and the safety of his remaining agents.

'They are safe,' said Taufik. 'I had not met any of them other than my cousin since the surveillance began, Pak, and he is family.'

'Could anyone have followed your family here?'

'My cousin is too good for that.'

Yoyok returned and handed the ledger to Carter. 'Here,' he said. He pointed at a single entry dated the night of the riots in Kao. The word 'Sabo' was written next to the name Maqsood. It corroborated the phone intercept and Taufik's testimony.

'Anything else?' said Carter.

Yoyok shrugged. 'Needs more time.'

'I hope you stop them,' said Taufik through smoke. 'If what Agus said is true, it will be a disaster for North Maluku. For everything we have worked for.'

'I understand,' said Carter.

Taufik sat upright. 'Do you, Mister Carter? Do you know Ibrahim like I do?' He looked Carter in the eye. 'Please promise me you will stop this man.'

Carter held the stare. His fist clenched white on the arm of the sofa.

'I promise.'

They arrived at the hotel after eleven-thirty. Two floors of rooms were arranged around three sides of a central carpark.

'Your family's inside,' said Carter.

'Thank you.'

Carter turned in his seat and shook Taufik's hand. Yoyok did the same.

'Someone will meet you in the morning. His name is Anas. He

will ask if you ordered a tour to the volcano at ten o'clock. When you say you would prefer the snorkelling, Anas will take you to Ternate, then to Bandung, where the government will prepare your family for a new life.'

Taufik reached for the door handle and hesitated. 'Will I see you again, Mister Carter? Mister Yoyok?'

'It wouldn't be safe,' said Carter.

Taufik nodded. 'I understand.'

'You served well, Taufik.'

Taufik looked at both men. 'Thank you, Pak.' He climbed out and disappeared into a stairwell, appearing a moment later at the door of room 203. His family emerged and he embraced them. They returned inside but he lingered, eyes on the Landcruiser, before he followed them. Carter watched the illuminated doorway for a moment, in case of catching one more sight of Taufik, the last of Carter's active agents that were all now retired or dead. There'd been no commemorations and no funerals to mark their demise at the hands of the self-interested bureaucrats who would forever benefit from yet never comprehend their sacrifice. All that was left for them now was a quiet life in hope they would never be found by those they had betrayed, but for Carter, the mission went on. It fell to him to ensure their work wasn't in vain. So that's what he'd do.

Yoyok started the Cruiser and backed out of the parking lot. 'What do you think is going on?' he said once they reached the street. The rain had cleared, leaving the empty streets to glisten under the streetlights.

'Pak?'

'Unsure,' said Carter. His gaze didn't shift from the twinkling lights of Sofifi, ten kilometres across the strait. 'Maqsood and Ibrahim made a deal in Sabo. Money changed hands, so it's big. We need to find out who else is involved.'

Yoyok accelerated and shifted gear. 'Not safe without the cut-outs, Pak. The bosses will never let us.'

'I won't give them the choice.'

◆

CANBERRA

It took two days to pouch the ledger to Canberra. Gibson let Scarlett lead the task of mapping Ibrahim's patterns and routines and identifying any connections as-yet unknown to ANVIL. It was gruelling work, and Gibson was unsuited to it. He had no mind for paper and data, the raw byproducts of his work that were used to generate insight for ASIS customers, and he'd only waste time getting involved. Gibson was a field man, a recruiter. A *handler.* And everyone knew it.

He himself had recruited Taufik, one of the first acquisitions as part of Operation ANVIL. The former police officer had been talent-spotted by a Maba imam, who had learned of Taufik's reservations about the cleric Ibrahim and his desire to pressure the Indonesian Government to grant autonomy, and eventual independence, to North Maluku. The imam, who had trained in Java and been a casual informant for Gibson in the wake of the Bali bombings, had reached out to his former runner with news of the new prospect. Taufik needed little convincing, and over the years tirelessly worked his way into Ibrahim's inner circle while secretly running the firebrand's dreams aground. With Gameshar on the ropes, loyal Taufik proposed to Ibrahim an answer: accept a secret offer of assistance from the government in return for silence on the prospect of North Maluku's independence. It was that or face annihilation, and no-one would have to know. Except loyal Taufik.

The other half-dozen cut-outs placed throughout North Maluku's Islamist-separatist movement had shared a similar story: conscientious volunteers for the intelligence services prepared to place themselves and their families at extreme risk in hope of saving lives. Now, like Taufik, they had all been retired. Carter had acted on the instruction with typical muted fury. Gibson could hardly blame him, which was why he'd ignored his suspicion that Carter had put Taufik up to the task of obtaining Ibrahim's ledger. It was reckless and insubordinate, but like so often with Carter, it worked. Hell, Gibson hoped he would have done the same. The ledger was a gold mine, the opening they desperately needed; a chance to regain the initiative.

Thanks to Carter, they were in.

Scarlett still looked fresh despite pulling an all-nighter on the ledger. Gibson wondered how she did it. Feeling his age, he had set up a sleeping bag and pillow in the narrow space behind his desk for those moments he could no longer hold his head up after working through the night. It'd been days since he was home and he'd begun to miss it, not that there was anyone there to miss him. A far cry from his marriage, where most nights there had been a woman waiting for him – just not always the same woman, and seldom his wife. So it was only fair when she bought him out of the house, leaving him with his cherished '96 Saab 900, a fistful of cash that got him most of the way to a one-bedder in Canberra's inner south, and a determination to clean up his act. The apartment, like his new life, was almost empty, leaving room for what remained of his career as a spy.

'I think I have most of it,' said Scarlett.

Gibson came to, eyes fixed on her collarbone. She hadn't noticed or didn't mind. Instead, her finger traced a series of rows on a typed report of dates, names, and locations. Gibson forced himself to concentrate.

'Ibrahim met with Maqsood three times in the past five weeks,' she continued. 'Makes sense if they were hashing out a deal.'

Gibson wiped his face. 'And burying the hatchet.'

'There was something else.' She opened a purple file on the desk and flicked to one of the pages. 'A name appears twice in the weeks leading up to the first meeting with Maqsood: El-Akhtar. It means "most dangerous" in Arabic.'

'A code?'

'Maybe,' she said. 'Or a *nomme de guerre.* Islamic State recruits were known to give them to each other or themselves. *Abdul the*

Fierce. Sadiq the Sorcerer, that sort of thing. They'd use it to hide their identities and to gee each other up whenever they were fighting, raping, whatever.'

'A returnee.'

'Just a theory.'

Gibson puffed his cheeks. Countless Islamic State veterans still roamed free in Indonesia, emboldened by the collapse of Western resolve in Afghanistan, and the threat they posed remained a high intelligence priority for government. If IS was behind events in North Maluku, it would mean they had found the foothold they'd long sought. They would grow bolder by the day, and so would their legions of secret followers across Asia and Australia, where twenty years of undivided attention on terrorism had still failed to eradicate jihadi aspiration.

'Someone like that is going to carry credibility among the likes of Maqsood and Ibrahim,' continued Scarlett. 'If he exists, maybe he brokered the deal.'

Maybe, thought Gibson. 'Not everyone's a fan of IS.'

'I know. Like I said, just a theory.'

'What do you need?'

'Your blessing for coded access to the files. I'll dig up candidate names for our guy.'

'Done,' he said without thought. 'Get me the forms.'

She smiled, collected the file and reached for the door.

For once, Gibson didn't watch her leave.

11

TERNATE

The street was a single lane of asphalt that led through a dense Ternate neighbourhood to a large mosque by the sea. Ana stopped the taxi at the western end and climbed out into a midday breeze of sea and cloves. She checked the address she'd been given, took her bearings and swore to herself when she realised the buildings weren't numbered. It was going to be a long afternoon, but that was what she'd signed up for when she'd promised Tanner an exposé on a potential Islamist uprising, so she drank some water, slung her backpack over one shoulder, and set off in search of the *advokat.*

Her second article had revealed the death of a long-time intermediary between the Indonesian government and Barpemis, an Islamist political faction based in northern Halmahera. It had generated all the attention she had hoped for and propelled her into the national spotlight, an outcome she had long coveted yet now struggled to comprehend. She had struck a nerve with suburban Australians who, despite most foreign affairs coverage focusing on China and Europe, remained anxious to avoid a re-emergence of Islamic extremism in South-east Asia. The national media had latched on to her story, as had their platoons of commentators, each happy to cast their judgement on the Australian or Indonesian governments depending which way they leaned. Tanner was ecstatic, but had reminded Ana she still owed him for the next month's expenses. She reassured him with the promise of a new lead, something that would dredge up whatever was occurring in the province and scatter it for a closer inspection.

'How sure are you?' he'd said.

'One-hundred per cent,' she'd lied.

In contrast, the Indonesian press had directed their attention at Ana. Some pointed out her claims were circumstantial, while others criticised her lack of understanding of Indonesian society and insensitivity to everyday Muslims. A government spokesman downplayed non-existent rumours Ana was a visa cheat, then repeated claims that economic and social development in North Maluku was progressing well and would inevitably extinguish any lingering prospect of Islamist unrest. Not that the government would comment to her. After two days, her calls to the Indonesian Ministries of Home Affairs, Defence, Religious Affairs, and Law and Human Rights remained unanswered. She had reached out to politicians from the national parliament, most of whom had declined an interview, and the rest, anxious for any press at all, had no awareness of the issues she was writing about, or, if they did, quoted the government line. She wasn't concerned; she had sought comment out of professional courtesy, not curiosity, so they could take it or leave it.

She walked casually along the street, checking each building and doorway for signs of a number or nameplate. Ahead, Ana saw two boys begging by a doorway, and only when she got close did she realise one of the boys had no arms. He held up a bowl with his feet to reveal a few coins and a ten-thousand Rupiah note. It was a confronting sight: there were two pitted craters where his arms had been, and his torso, ungirded by muscle tension, had contorted in on itself. Ana deposited fifty-thousand rupiah into the bowl. It was more than any other donation he had received, but not enough to assuage her shock and guilt. She adjusted her handbag and hurried on along the street, chased by the sound of the boy's helpless screeches.

An *angkot* motor buzzed somewhere behind her and she stepped off the pavement. Two patches of cloves had been laid out to dry under the sun, watched over by an elderly couple who stared at her from a doorway. She looked the way she'd come as the angkot sped past and saw her taxi pull away from the end of the street. She was suddenly conscious of those watching her. Children giggled at her from an upstairs window. A family rode past on a scooter, eyes fixed on the lonely white girl. Two women, each dressed head-to-toe in hijab, glanced as they walked past, then hurried on to reach another alley. She told herself it was normal Indonesian inquisitiveness, but she had a profile now. A reason to be here, but a reason for people to want to know what she was doing.

For once, she didn't want them to know.

The only others who could comment on operations against Islamist groups were the Islamists themselves. Her web searches had uncovered spokesmen for half a dozen groups, but she'd ignored them once she discovered Sayeed. An English speaker, Sayeed had been quoted five years ago in a series of news articles about the arson murder of the family of a mosque owner in Maba. The mosque had been attacked by three teenage members of Al Ramah, an Islamist group led by Sayeed. One of the reports had quoted Sayeed as claiming the attack had been sponsored and organised by government spies. Ana hadn't been able to find Sayeed through the internet, so she tracked down the reporter who had interviewed him.

'He had no evidence,' the reporter had said, after she had failed to dissuade Ana with claims of longstanding retirement. 'But he was convinced the government had recruited the boys and incited them to perform the attack. He said the boys had been coached by a government agent, but there was no such person. I searched.'

'Did you speak to the boys?' said Ana.

'They were murdered in custody by Sayeed's rivals. Sayeed

claimed it was more evidence of government meddling. It was a far-fetched claim, and by then people had lost interest.'

'Do you still know how to contact Sayeed?'

'Why, mbak?'

'I'd prefer not to say,' said Ana. 'But it's important. You'd be doing a favour for people here.'

The reporter took an anxious breath. 'Sayeed was extremely security conscious. He would only communicate through a trusted intermediary, a solicitor in Ternate. He may still be there.'

'Thank you,' said Ana. 'This means a lot.'

'Be careful, mbak,' the reporter had said. 'Sayeed is dangerous and paranoid. He is not someone you can trust.'

Ana was near the end of the street when she found the small brass plate mounted next to the front door that read: ADVOKAT. Solicitor. The ground-floor windows were boarded. A rider on a scooter called out 'Hey bulè!' as he rode past. Ana ignored him and knocked on the door.

No response.

Ana knocked again. This time she heard something that sounded like a scrape.

She crossed the street to look at the upper windows. The shutters were open, but the rooms were dark. There were no vehicles in front of the house, and there was no access to the back.

This time she knocked louder. Two men in business shirts walked past.

'Permisi?' she called out.

The men turned to look, then continued on.

She reached up to knock one more time, then heard footsteps. She heard the lock turn and stepped back from the door as it opened, revealing a man's face shrouded in gloom. Two decrepit eyes looked her up and down, then to the street behind her.

'Ada apa?'

'I am looking for Sayeed.'

He cocked his head. 'No Sayeed here.' He tried to close the door.

Ana put her hand up to stop him. 'Wait,' she said. She took two pieces of paper from her handbag and gave them to him. 'Give him this.' One was a message, printed in English, that gave her contact details and an offer to report on his claims of government interference. The other was a copy of her article on the Tobelo raids. Finally, she held up an envelope. 'This is two-million Rupiah,' she said. 'There's another two-million if Sayeed makes contact.'

The advokat stared at the cash, then checked the street. He held out his hand.

She gave him the envelope. The hand disappeared and the door closed.

It took an hour to find a cab and reach the air-conditioned sanctuary of her hotel lobby. A single receptionist was on duty while a janitor swept the polished tiles near the elevator. A tall man sat on one of the sofas, side on to the entrance, a large birdwatching camera on his lap and a heavy hiker's backpack by his feet. His skin had the deep tan of a local, but his chiselled features, longish wavy black hair and Swiss watch gave him away as a westerner. He looked up from the camera and gave her a slight nod as she passed, in that way fellow expats do in remote places, and she realised he was the first foreigner she'd seen since she left Jakarta.

The girl at reception gave her a sideways look as she crossed the desk to the lifts. At the fourth floor, she walked to her room, went straight to the bathroom, took two Panadol tablets and stripped off. The shower helped, but she needed to lie down. She put on a bathrobe and wrapped a towel around her hair.

She stepped into the sitting room and froze. After hundreds of hotel stays in her life she was attuned to the appearance of a tidy room: bed made, towels stacked, belongings untouched. Instead she was confronted with disarray. The bed had been pulled from the wall. It was covered in the contents of her suitcase, which lay open on top, as well as the shopping bags of clothes she had bought to support her month-long tenure. The sofa cushions had been lifted, and one lay half on top of the other. Her bedside drawers had been searched, and the papers and books she had been researching had been sifted on the desk.

Her brain struggled to take it in. She ran to the wardrobe and checked the safe. After three failed attempts, she tried the default code and it opened. Someone had reset it. She had left a stack of cash inside and it was still there, stacked loosely as though the searchers had left in a hurry. She performed a check of what she had left in the room. Apart from the cash, she had taken her valuables with her: passport, laptop, phone, keys. Nothing was missing from the stack on her desk, but if the intruders were trying to find out what she was working on, now they knew. She sifted the debris for clothes and got dressed as rage and fear consumed her. Finally, she packed the rest of her belongings and headed to the lobby.

The girl at reception smiled nervously as Ana approached.

'Someone has been in my room,' said Ana.

The smile turned to a frown.

'You let them in there,' said Ana. 'You opened the safe.'

'I'm sorry, mbak, I—'

'Who was in my room?'

'Something the matter?' The accent was Australian.

Ana turned and looked up to see the foreigner. He had tied his hair into a ponytail since she went upstairs, and she saw now that he was half-Indonesian. A faded red rash across his left cheek was the only blemish on his otherwise flawless face.

'I'm fine,' she said quickly. She cleared her throat. 'I'm just checking out.'

'Don't blame you,' he said. 'I've heard the cleaning service here is terrible.' He smiled at the girl and said something in effortless Indonesian.

The girl glanced at Ana and retreated to the back office.

'You don't have to go to any trouble,' said Ana.

'Not at all,' he said. He lifted his wrist and looked at his watch. 'Driver's late, as usual.' He held out his hand. 'I'm Jonah.'

She shook it. 'Ana.'

'Ana Kovacevic, right? You wrote about Kao last week.'

She suppressed her surprise. 'That's me.'

'Rare to see a foreign face around here,' he said. 'Let alone a famous journo.'

'Infamous, more like it.'

'That why you're checking out?'

She bit her lip. 'In a way.'

The girl returned, followed closely by a middle-aged man in a grey vest and white shirt. The receptionist said something and pointed at Ana.

The manager adjusted his taqiyah and glanced at them both. 'Yes, mbak? You would like to check out?'

'I'd like my money back.'

His smile registered confusion. 'Is there a problem?'

'Not if room searches are part of the service,' she said.

He had no idea what she had just said.

Jonah made a gesture of 'May I?'. She nodded. He conversed with the man in Indonesian and asked what sounded like probing questions. The manager seemed defensive at first, but eventually opened the till and, with a gracious bow, handed Ana five-hundred thousand Rupiah.

'The hotel gives its apologies,' said Jonah. 'The police demanded to search your room this morning. The staff couldn't stop them.' He shrugged. 'It's probably true.'

She pocketed the cash and said, 'Thanks.'

'Are you okay?'

'They're just trying to scare me off.'

'You must be onto something, then. Here.' He took a card from his wallet and wrote something on the back. 'This is a place where they won't register your passport. The police will leave you alone if they have to do any work to find you.'

It was an address for a guesthouse.

'You don't have to,' said Ana.

'Don't mention it,' he said. 'Foreigners are rare here. Better if we look out for one another.' He stepped to the sofa, collected his bag and flashed a grin. 'I'll see you round, Ana Kovacevic.'

She turned over the card: *Jonah Somerville. Avian Photographer at large.* His phone number and social media handles were listed across the bottom. When she looked up again, he was gone.

12

Imam Aayid will see you on the third of the month.

The message would appear innocuous to anyone not meant to see it. If they investigated, they would find that Aayid was a real imam in the town of Buli, who, if contacted, would confirm that he was indeed planning to meet a client on the third for private consultation, as he often did. If asked, he would not reveal the identity of the client for the sake of confidentiality. In truth, he had never met him. It didn't matter, because Aayid worked for Yoyok.

For the intended recipient, ANARCHY, the message carried a coded instruction to meet his handler. 'The third' meant three days from now at five p.m, the prescribed time. 'The month' referred to the Qimalaha mosque, in Maba. ANARCHY knew the protocol: he was to arrive alone and wear a red turban to signal he was safe; any other headwear would signal duress. If he detected surveillance he was to abort and reattempt contact twenty-four hours later, and if anyone asked, he was to deny all knowledge of his handler and proclaim his interest in the mosque.

Carter addressed the message to a seldom-used phone in Weda that had been procured for ANARCHY for the sole purpose of receiving it. Intelligence confirmed the phone remained connected to a cellular tower near Weda and hadn't been used for any other purpose in the past three months. It was impossible to know if the phone had been compromised, but it was worth the risk. ANVIL needed a breakthrough.

Hartanto gave only half-hearted agreement to the operation and withheld Kopassus support. Gibson saw this as a cynical gesture and warned that the Australians would abort without it. Hartanto relented, but only as far as placing Captain Sugianto's team on standby. Gibson's frustration receded when Carter received ANARCHY's response: *I must delay until the seventeenth.* It was the correct date for the rendezvous, plus five days to indicate ANARCHY wasn't under duress.

Everything was in place. Gibson called the DDG's EA and made an appointment to brief the leadership team.

The DDG stared at the photo for a long time. It was a mugshot of a bearded Indonesian in his fifties. He had one black eye and scabs on the side of his face, his hair wet and knotted.

'Nadeer Eko Sanjana,' said Gibson. 'To anyone who asks: ANARCHY. He's a sitting representative for South Halmahera, up for re-election in a couple months' time. On the side, leader of the Maluku Independent Militia, or MIM. Been on our books since 2016.'

'I thought we'd lost all our access to these individuals?' said Security. Her inscrutable face, for once, expressed something resembling surprise.

'Only the intermediaries. We've always kept the means to reach high-level contacts. The cut-outs came later to give both sides deniability.'

'What makes you think he'll show?' said Ops.

'Nadeer's got form. The photo is from his arrest at a brothel in Manila, one of many secret sins his colleagues would never acquit him for. He needs religious cred to get anywhere in his game, so would prefer we held our tongues.'

The DDG smiled and handed the photo to Legal. Security

stroked fluff from her skirt. 'It's a big risk,' she said. 'Let's hope he has something.'

'More of a risk not to do anything,' said Ops. 'Get on with it.'

'I can't give a guarantee,' said Gibson. 'But ANVIL has moved to a new phase. Everything just got harder and more important.'

Gibson felt the room get colder. There were risks in approaching Nadeer, especially with Indonesian pressure to suspend Operation ANVIL. But Nadeer remained the best option for penetrating whatever Ibrahim and Maqsood were up to. If the two militants had put aside their feud, it was possible others were aware of it, jealous of it, or fearful of it, if not involved. Gibson needed this. ANVIL needed it. Indonesia needed it, whether or not it wanted it. So ASIS would carry on, and Carter would have an opportunity to redeem himself.

The DDG sat forward. 'What's the setup?'

'Carter and Yoyok arrive in Maba tomorrow. They'll spend two days checking for surveillance before the rendezvous with Nadeer.'

'They good on their own?'

The directors turned to face Gibson.

'Jordan and Yoyok have operated in the region for years,' said Gibson. 'Without Kopassus, they can at least keep a low profile.'

The DDG scanned the faces of his team and nodded in satisfaction. 'Proceed.'

BULI, NORTH MALUKU

Carter and Yoyok landed by chartered turboprop at sunrise, two days before the meet. Raf and Jaja had sourced a couple of SUVs, in which the four intelligence officers drove the final fifty kilometres along the eastern Halmahera coast to Maba. There they met a team of private security contractors that Raf had hired for countersurveillance.

Raf had organized a six-room villa on the outskirts of Maba. It was close enough to support surveillance patrols throughout town; remote enough to pass as a staging point for a team of birdwatchers and provide easy egress in an emergency. The plan was to debrief Nadeer in the comforts of a three-star sitting room with a view over a nearby hillside to play on his vanity. The intelligence officers arranged themselves two to a bedroom, Raf and Jaja closest to the sitting room from where they could supervise Nadeer overnight if his debriefing required a second day.

It took three hours for Jaja to arrange the communications gear in the study and test the radios the team would use for Nadeer's rendezvous and extraction. Raf ensured the villa was well-stocked for the debrief and that nothing looked out of order. Meanwhile, Yoyok and Carter plotted and catalogued ingress and egress routes to the Qimalaha mosque, potential observation and rendezvous sites and points of interest on a large paper map of Maba spread over the kitchen table.

Raf's crew arranged themselves in pairs and set off to reconnoitre the town. The meet was simple in theory: Raf, Jaja and four watchers would pre-position in the vicinity of the mosque before Asr prayer an hour before the scheduled meeting time, five p.m. Other observers would monitor both potential egress routes. Once Nadeer showed at the mosque, and provided he was clear of surveillance, Carter would arrive on scene and make contact. From there, the agent would be loaded into one of the SUVs and driven to the villa. Raf and Jaja made quick work of the initial reconnaissance, and by late afternoon had visited and recorded the highest priority sites on Carter's list. They repeated their tours after dark and retired for the night.

Despite its simplicity, the plan entailed risks. Security demanded multiple egress routes in case of compromise, in which case the teams needed secure, easily identifiable locations to extract to and rendezvous. There was the possibility of sites and routes becoming unsafe or inaccessible, which necessitated backups. On the second day, Raf, Jaja and their team of contractors set out on foot and by vehicle and by midday had toured most of the city and examined every backup route and emergency point. That was how, when they returned to debrief Carter at the villa, Raf and Jaja were certain they had detected hostile surveillance.

Raf inserted a flash drive and brought up a series of surveillance photos on a laptop. 'We counted seven, Pak,' he said, pointing at the screen. 'Three more, maybe.' He scrolled through photos of repeat faces at various locations; the angle of the shadows suggesting they had been taken at different times throughout the day.

Yoyok watched on as Carter scrolled through the images. He reached a photograph of two men, each dressed in a long white tunic and matching taqiyah. One of them held a phone to his ear and stared down the barrel of the camera, eyes wide. His colleague's face was blurred as he turned to the photographer.

'You were sighted?' said Carter.

Raf rubbed his neck, as if the tattoo dragon's claw had literally hooked his skin. 'If they knew we were coming, it was easy, Pak.'

'Gameshar's all over this town,' said Yoyok. 'One of their spotters could have called you in if they noticed outsiders.'

'They were not Gameshar,' said Jaja from the edge of the room. His bulging eyes, nestled deep in his round, bald head, glanced at each spook. 'Two of them'—he gestured at the screen—'tried to follow us on their own, like amateurs, bos. Gameshar would have played dumb. Tried to lure us all out.'

'It makes no sense, Pak,' said Raf. 'Why Gameshar let these guys on their turf?'

Carter and Yoyok exchanged a glance. Carter nodded at Raf. Jaja retrieved the flash drive and the two of them left the room.

'Gameshar must know what Nadeer's up to,' said Yoyok. 'He's blown.'

Carter stared at the photograph and shook his head. 'He's turned on us.'

'You think Nadeer has joined Maqsood?'

'Only one way to be sure.'

Yoyok stared at him for a moment, then nodded. 'I'll call Hartanto.'

13

WEDA

Nadeer Eko Sanjaya prayed alone. He had prayed more often lately, and for longer. He needed solitude. Time to think.

He cursed his men. They said the Australian had never arrived in Maba, but these were face-saving lies. They were too eager and had been detected. Nadeer had wanted to force the Australian to leave Maluku altogether and claim the credit, and they had failed him.

The prayer refreshed him, but the disappointment remained. He made one final request of his God – that he bless his journey to Payahe – and left the villa. His Range Rover idled in the courtyard, driver at the wheel and ready to depart. His bodyguard opened the passenger door.

'When will we arrive at Payahe?' said Nadeer.

The bodyguard climbed into the front passenger seat with a grunt. 'Half-to-ten, Pak.'

They drove through the villa gates onto the highway that led inland from Weda. Nadeer was due to speak at a political rally at ten o'clock. Afterwards, he would spend two hours with voters and town officials, eat and pray alone, then return to Weda. His mistress was due at two o'clock. He reclined his seat and thought about what he would do to her.

The road climbed steeply through thick jungle to reach a wide plateau where the forest gave way to large areas of deforestation and an occasional quarry. The air was cooler at altitude, so Nadeer opened the window to feel the breeze on his face. Then he sat up.

'What is that noise?' he said to his men.

A distant thump echoed across a large clearing.

His guard looked around. 'What noise, Pak?'

The thumping grew stronger.

'The window, you fool.'

The guard lowered the glass and listened. 'Helicopter,' he said.

Nadeer scanned the distant treetops. The thumping dissipated.

'Miners,' said the driver. He eased the Range Rover into a ninety-degree bend that turned west. The thump was still there, in the distance.

The bodyguard turned suddenly. 'Army!' he shouted.

Nadeer followed his gaze. Through the trees, he saw a large helicopter flying parallel to the road.

'Drive faster,' shouted Nadeer. 'Take the next turn.'

The driver continued for five-hundred metres then turned south. The helicopter vanished behind the trees.

'Go!' screamed Nadeer. The road twisted up a hill then flattened out. The thumping of the helicopter blades followed them.

'What do they want?' said Nadeer.

The guard swivelled his head on the lookout. 'Maybe they are practicing.'

They turned west onto a road concealed by the jungle canopy. The sound of the helicopter dissipated. The driver's knuckles were white on the steering wheel.

'Relax,' Nadeer told him. 'We lost them.'

'Yes, Pak.'

'Do you know the way from here?'

The driver gave a rigid nod. 'It's not far.'

Nadeer reclined his seat. The road snaked through the forest and he soon dozed off, only to be woken by sun on his face. The jungle to the right of the road had been cleared for several hundred metres. He sat upright.

'Where are—'

The cabin filled with the scream of rotors as the helicopter swooped a hundred feet overhead and across the clearing. Nadeer and his bodyguard ducked while the driver fought to keep the Range Rover on the road.

'Where did they go?' said Nadeer.

The bodyguard strained to scan the clearing. 'I lost them, Pak.'

The car slowed as they rounded a curve.

'Speed up!' shouted Nadeer.

'Bos?' said the driver.

Nadeer looked through the windscreen to see movement on the road ahead. The helicopter had landed in the clearing, its rotors still turning as soldiers dismounted and ran for the road.

The driver slowed to a crawl. 'What should I do?'

'Shut up,' said Nadeer. Three soldiers reached the road and took up firing positions. They were two-hundred metres away.

'Behind us,' said the guard.

Nadeer turned to see an armoured vehicle emerge from the treeline. When it was within fifty metres, it slowed. On top, a soldier trained a fifty-calibre machine gun on them.

The guard reached between his legs and pulled out an Uzi.

'Wait,' said Nadeer. He tapped the driver. 'Stop here.'

The driver hit the brakes. The army vehicle screeched to a halt behind them. A soldier at the roadblock called out to them through a loudspeaker.

'Nadeer Eko Sanjaya. Shut down your vehicle. All occupants show hands. If you resist arrest, you will be shot.'

The guard checked his Uzi. The driver took short, rapid breaths.

'Calm down,' said Nadeer. He placed a hand on the driver's shoulder and leaned to his ear. 'When I say so, drive straight at the roadblock.'

'But bos—'

'Listen to me! You cannot let them arrest me. Look.' He thrust a finger past the driver's face. 'Up ahead is a turnoff. It is too narrow for their vehicle. We will drive through the roadblock, follow that road, and escape. Do you understand?'

The driver tried to compose his breathing. Eventually, he nodded.

'They will shoot,' said the guard.

'Nadeer Eko Sanjaya. Shut down your vehicle. All occupants show hands. If you resist arrest, you will be shot.'

'They will not shoot at civilians.' Nadeer gripped the driver's shoulder. 'Get ready.'

The driver gulped. 'Okay.'

'Bos,' said the guard. His eyes were on the mirror.

Nadeer turned. Two soldiers had climbed out of the armoured vehicle. They approached slowly, one each side of the road, weapons up.

'Get ready,' Nadeer repeated. The driver held tight.

'Nadeer Eko Sanjaya. Shut down your vehicle. All occupants show hands. If you resist arrest, you will be shot.'

The soldiers behind were ten metres away.

'Nadeer Eko—'

'Go!'

The Range Rover lurched forward. The windshield shattered and the air cracked as the driver's head exploded. Fragments of bone and brain ricocheted off upholstery and window glass. The bodyguard screamed.

Nadeer dived for cover. He held his hands over his head and felt warm fluid and shards of windscreen. The Range Rover coasted.

The guard smashed his side window with the Uzi, then reached out and fired. The burst of gunfire was cut by another crack. The guard groaned.

The Rover rolled off the edge of the road and beached itself. Nadeer looked up. His guard writhed in his seat, one hand on his neck, unable to stop the bleeding.

Nadeer reached for the doorhandle. The door opened and a soldier appeared, rifle up. 'Don't move!' he shouted. The other door opened and the other soldier dragged Nadeer from the Rover, feet first.

'Let me go!' shouted Nadeer as he landed. He rolled on his back to see a rifle in his face. More soldiers reached them from the roadblock. They dragged him to the verge and turned him over, face down. He screamed and kicked until someone struck him in the kidney and he capitulated. They cuffed his wrists and ankles. Someone said, 'Hood him,' and then his world went black.

Sugianto's men had helped Yoyok set up a new safehouse. It was a small disused bungalow, rented from one of Yoyok's informants, at the end of a long jungle track off the main highway north of Payahe. Two soldiers cleaned out the sitting room and bolted a metal chair to the floor. The bedroom stank of mould, but they didn't clean it; instead, they boarded up the windows, cut a peep hole in the door, and rigged a stereo system in the ceiling that they powered from a small generator. Outside they set up tents and stretchers to house the security detail while Yoyok drove to the nearest town and bought gas for the kitchen burner and food and water to last seven days. This was no Maba villa; Nadeer was confirmed hostile and would get no three-star treatment.

Carter joined two Kopassus teams to rendezvous with Sugianto. The Russian transport helicopter hovered uneasily over a jungle clearing, like it might pitch into the Earth at any moment, before it settled at the centre, its gigantic rotors almost clipping the trees. Soldiers alighted as soon as it touched down. They carried a suited man, hands and feet bound, his head under a hood. Sugianto supervised while soldiers loaded two body bags into one of the Kopassus Land Rovers.

Sugianto walked over to Carter and gestured to Nadeer. 'Didn't come peacefully,' he said. 'Guard and driver are dead.'

Nadeer stumbled and swore at his captors.

'Has he talked?'

'Not a word.'

Sugianto shouted at his men to load Nadeer into one of the Land Rovers. Sugianto joined Carter in his Landcruiser. The three vehicles departed in convoy as the helicopter took off.

'His men will know we took him,' said Sugianto over the noise.

'Fine,' said Carter. The lumbering helicopter disappeared beyond the trees. 'I want them to know they can't run from us.'

'I thought you preferred to be discreet, Pak.'

Carter steered the Landcruiser through a deep gully in pursuit of the Kopassus vehicles.

'Situation's changed, Sugi.' The convoy descended a long slope and turned west onto a highway without stopping. 'I was happy to let the Islamists exist so long as they stayed obedient. They always knew that if they turned, that would be it.'

The convoy accelerated to over a hundred kilometres an hour. Sugianto had to shout over the roar of the engine.

'Is that why you do this?' he asked. He braced against the door as Carter steered through a bend. 'Because they're insubordinate?'

The convoy was slowing. Eventually it turned into another jungle track that led up a forested slope. A large conic mountain loomed over them. The track steepened and slowed until they reached a terraced clearing. The vehicles parked up near the safehouse and Sugianto's men carried Nadeer inside.

Carter shut off the engine and turned to face Sugianto. 'The world is coming apart, Sugi,' he said. 'Piece by piece falling under the control of Islamist maniacs. This place'—he gestured at the treeline—'will be next. You want that? Bomb factories and terror training camps a ferry ride from Bali, Jakarta, Darwin? All-out war to stop them?' He turned away and drummed his fingers on the steering wheel. 'I don't pretend to be the good guy. But I'll stop more people from dying.'

Sugianto stared. 'Like Hasan, you mean?'

'This isn't about vengeance.'

'I agree, bos,' said Sugianto. 'It's about control. And you don't care who gets in your way or who pays the price.'

Carter broke off and scanned the clearing. Soldiers had erected a large tent complex up slope from the bungalow. One had taken guard at the front door. Two men climbed in one of the Land Rovers and headed for the track. Sugianto waved as they passed. It wasn't true that Carter didn't care. He derived no pleasure from what was about to happen to Nadeer, but his motives were absolute. He was protecting people. *His* people. A society he was born into. He wouldn't apologise for it.

'Where will your men be?' he said. The clearing was quiet now. The fresh air of the mountainside carried a faint scent of cloves.

Sugianto sighed and pulled a cigarette from his chest pocket. 'Two out on the highway to watch each direction,' he said as he lit up. 'Four to guard the house; four resting. Twenty-four-seven.'

Carter left him and walked to the bungalow. Two armed soldiers in combat fatigues stood guard over Nadeer, who was cuffed to a chair at the centre of the room, hood on, head on his chest. Yoyok stood by the window, arms crossed.

A soldier turned on a camping light in front of Nadeer. One side was covered so that it only illuminated the prisoner.

'Unhood him,' said Carter.

One of the soldiers stowed his rifle and ripped off the prisoner's hood to reveal a face stained with blood. Carter moved closer to flick a chunk of flesh from Nadeer's cheek. Nadeer lifted his face and blinked his eyes to adjust to the light. When he saw Carter, he groaned.

'Sorry to miss you in Maba,' said Carter.

Nadeer looked around. 'Release me,' he said.

'After all this trouble?'

Nadeer struggled at his restraints.

Carter leaned into the light, inches from Nadeer's face. Nadeer's cheek twitched. 'We just want to ask a few questions, nothing more. Then you can go back to playing politics.'

'I will not tell you anything, no matter what you do.' Nadeer stared at Carter. 'And I will make sure the world knows your men murdered my guard and my driver. Innocent men.'

'You can tell your friends anything you like,' said Carter. He smiled. 'As soon as you get out of this house.'

Nadeer struggled at his restraints. 'Like I said, *bulè.*' He spat the word. 'I will not talk.'

'Fair enough,' said Carter. He stood up and looked at Yoyok.

The Indonesian shrugged.

'Bedroom.'

Nadeer cried out as one of the soldiers stepped in, uncuffed him from the chair and dragged him to the bedroom. Another brought the camplight and hung it from the ceiling, then bound Nadeer's wrists to his ankles.

The soldiers left the room, and Carter knelt by Nadeer. 'We'll chat again when you're ready,' he said. 'Get some sleep.'

He shut the door. Yoyok pressed play on the stereo and filled the bungalow with the sound of trance music. Nadeer shouted something but was inaudible over the noise.

'No-one in or out,' Carter said to Sugianto as he walked to the Landcruiser.

The captain inserted a set of earplugs. 'You got it.'

14

TERNATE

'What is this shit?' shouted Tanner. 'I pay you half a fortune and you send me a *Wikipedia* article.'

Ana had submitted the piece less than an hour ago. Four-hundred words on the present economic conditions in North Maluku inspired by the boy with no arms in the clove-scented lane in central Ternate. It was all she had. It had been two days since she had approached the advokat in hope of finding Sayeed, and with each passing day it seemed less likely she would hear from either of them.

'It's relevant,' she said. 'Extremist movements don't spring up for no reason. North Maluku has been left behind.'

'It's tripe, Ana.'

She knew he was right. No-one cared. That had been the point of the article.

'I'm still chasing a big lead,' she said. 'It needs time.'

'Yeah? Who?'

She checked the clock. She moved from the desk to the long sofa in the sitting room. Her new room had more space than she was used to in Indonesia, and the novelty hadn't worn off.

'I can't say, obviously. It's a big fish, very hush-hush.'

He breathed into the phone.

'Look,' she said. 'He could be one of the Islamists. I'm not sure yet.'

'If he is, then you're stupid.'

'Not if he confirms what the government has been up to and for how long.'

'Then what's the hold up?'

'If it were easy, you wouldn't get your money's worth,' she said. 'I've got to go. Will you print?'

He rang off.

At least her profile had grown. The Australian media had taken an active interest in Islamist developments in Indonesia, linking her stories to the threat of lone wolf attacks at Australian schools, bombs targeting westerners in Jakarta and Bali, and the prospect of a regional Islamic State or Al-Qaeda offshoot targeting Singapore, Auckland and Brisbane. Now here was Ana Kovacevic, the courageous Aussie girl taking them on like a true battler. It was satisfying to finally be at the centre of something, even if it felt premature. She hadn't found the bottom of the story yet, and was already distracted by a social media barrage, media coverage and countless messages of concern and encouragement from friends and family. ABC News 24 had been first to offer an interview: a ten-minute segment with veteran journalist Anthony Brenner that was scheduled for five p.m. She reached for her phone, anxious for contact from Sayeed or the advokat, but she turned it over. Time to calm down; time to compose. The story would come, she told herself. This moment was about her.

The ABC production assistant called her with ten minutes to go. 'Are you comfortable, free of distractions?'

Ana looked around and felt silly for it. 'Ready.'

'I understand you'll only be joining by audio, is that correct?'

The girl's voice was measured and professional, trained for the mic. She was part of the media clan, but aspired to spend a career in the studio, not in the field. Ana resented her ignorance. 'The connection isn't great out here,' she said.

Minutes of silence followed. Eventually the girl came back. 'You're on in thirty seconds. Stand by.'

Ana's pulse quickened and her throat became taut. Apart from her media training, she had never done a live interview before. She unscrewed a bottle of water as the voice of Anthony Brenner arrived through her headset to announce the interview.

'Ana Kovacevic joins us tonight from Ternate, Indonesia. Ms Kovacevic, how are you?'

'Well thanks, Anthony.'

She concentrated for the first question. It never came.

'I'm also joined by Indonesia's ambassador to Australia, Sukiman Cahyadi. Ambassador Cahyadi, thank you for joining us.'

Ana scrambled for her laptop and opened the email invitation for the interview. There was no mention of a televised debate.

'Thank you for having me,' said Cahyadi.

'I'll start with you, Mister Ambassador. Ms Kovacevic writes that the situation in North Maluku appears volatile. What is the Indonesian Government's view?'

There was a brief cut of the line, then: '...need to be careful about jumping to conclusions. There has been Islamist activity in North Maluku for many years, but it is a fringe minority and poses no threat to security. The people of North Maluku are overwhelmingly peace-loving and hard-working, and they have been misrepresented by this sensationalist and fear-mongering reporting.'

'Ms Kovacevic,' said Brenner. 'It is true, isn't it, that the majority of Indonesians are not extremists.'

'Of course that's true,' she said. 'It's only a minority torching mosques and murdering informants.'

'This is what I mean by sensationalist reporting,' said Cahyadi. 'Look in any country, including Australia, and you will find problems. All Ms Kovacevic has done is extrapolate from a biased selection of facts to portray a menace. It is wrong, and it is a betrayal of the country that has welcomed Ms Kovacevic for more than half a year.'

Ana bit down on her bottom lip.

'Ms Kovacevic?'

'These aren't everyday problems, Tony,' she said. 'The cases fit a recent pattern of brewing Islamism in this country. What's troubling is there are signs of government interference in Islamic affairs in North Maluku that is contributing to the instability.'

Cahyadi cut in. 'This is speculation.'

'I've quoted a source inside the Indonesian Government.'

'An anonymous source,' scoffed Cahyadi. 'If Ms Kovacevic wants to be taken seriously as a professional journalist, she should do real research.'

Ana fought to control her temper. This was an ambush; the ambassador knew it. She closed her eyes and inhaled.

'I'm impressed the ambassador knows my trade so well,' she said. Her eyes opened as she found clarity. 'Perhaps he could turn his attention to his own country's governance.'

'Really, I must protest—'

'The reality is that development in North Maluku still lags that of the rest of the country,' she continued. 'Just yesterday I met a woman, a widow, begging for money in Ternate so she could send her child to a doctor, even though she qualifies for free medical care under the social security support program. This is just one example of systemic failures all over the province. Is it any wonder people turn to independence movements?'

'Mister Ambassador, what do you think? Is your government doing enough?'

'The government knows all too well there are issues, as there are in any developing country. I would also note that the Australian Government continues to reduce its aid budget to Indonesia.'

He paused for effect. You arrogant bastard, thought Ana.

'But in any case, you cannot equate poverty with extremism. I know Ms Kovacevic means well, but these issues are very complex. Ms Kovacevic does not have the necessary experience as a journalist and the understanding of Indonesia, let alone the complexities of North Maluku, to do them justice.'

Ana was about to reply. Brenner got in first.

'Mister Ambassador, is it not true that Indonesia has had a long-standing issue with religious extremism?'

Her phone vibrated.

'I am not here to comment on the past,' said Cahyadi. 'Ms Kovacevic's article is negligent slander against North Maluku and Indonesia.'

She lifted the phone and saw a WhatsApp message. The number was unknown.

'It is irresponsible and hurtful,' continued Cahyadi.

She opened it.

'Fuck.'

'Ms Kovacevic?'

She stared at the message while her mind raced. The interview became irrelevant.

'We appear to be having some difficulty reaching—'

She hung up the call. *Fuckfuckfuck.* She collected her belongings and ran for the door.

She waited by the main gates of the football stadium as instructed. The sun had almost set, and she had trouble making out faces and shapes in the twilight. A cheer erupted from the stadium behind her; otherwise, apart from the occasional scooter, the street was quiet. Taxis and ojeks lined up to wait for fleeing spectators. The offices opposite were dark. A final whistle signalled the end of the match.

She checked the message and confirmed she was in the right place. The advokat's instructions had been clear, the tone urgent, and she had arrived on time. Spectators began to file out of the stadium and within minutes the sidewalk was full of *Persiter Ternate* jerseys and cheery voices. She lost sight of her surroundings in the crowd and checked the time: fifteen minutes overdue. Her heart sank, then someone gripped her arm and thrust her into the flow of the crowd.

The advokat said nothing as they followed the swarm. He kept her close and in the centre of the crowd as dozens of football fans meandered and chanted in celebration. When they reached the northern edge of the stadium, he diverted her into an alley. The crowd continued towards a row of restaurants.

'Money,' he said. He pushed her against the wall.

She watched him. His eyes scanned each end of the alley.

'Quick,' he said.

She opened her bag and removed the second envelope. He snatched it and placed it in his pocket. He made another check of the alley and gave her a phone. He grabbed her again and led her away from the crowd.

Cars floated by on the main road at the end of the alley. They were ten metres away.

'Pak Sayeed will call you at seven.'

He let go and she checked her watch. Forty-five minutes.

'Thank you,' she said, but when she turned, the advokat was already gone.

15

NORTH OF PAYAHE

Nadeer broke on the morning of the third day. By that time, Carter had returned to Ternate to collect a package from Gibson. When he reached the safehouse, it was after five p.m. and the jungle was shrouded in shadow.

Carter parked next to one of the Land Rovers. There was a faint glow in the window of the safehouse. Beyond it, Kopassus special forces soldiers loitered at the tents and cleaned their weapons. Sugianto walked over to greet him.

Carter shook his hand. 'Where's Yoyok?'

Sugianto gestured towards the house. 'Waiting for you.'

The soldier at the front door signalled to stop. He knocked gently, then the door was opened from inside. The room stank of mould and piss. Nadeer was tied to the chair, asleep, the camping light casting his face in black and gold. One of Sugianto's troopers stood against the wall and suppressed a yawn.

Yoyok sat in front of Nadeer on a plastic stool. He stood up and greeted Carter. Nadeer stirred.

'What's he said?' said Carter.

'Nothing,' said Yoyok. 'I made him wait until you got here.'

Carter nodded.

Yoyok returned to his seat. 'Pak Nadeer,' he said. He clicked his fingers in Nadeer's face. Nadeer's eyes opened, then looked at Yoyok. Yoyok held up a bottle of water. 'Here.'

They waited for him to drink. Carter pulled another chair beside Yoyok and sat down. Nadeer's eyes widened.

Yoyok spoke. 'We will ask you some questions now, okay?'

Nadeer's head teetered. He muttered something.

'Louder!' said Yoyok.

Nadeer flinched. His head lolled forward again before it came back up. 'I said I am ready.'

Carter inched his chair forward. 'Thank you,' he said. He gave Nadeer a comforting smile.

Nadeer lowered his head but kept his eyes on Carter.

'Tell me about Barpemis.'

A flicker of anger crossed Nadeer's face. 'They are in the north,' he said. 'I don't care.'

'Yet you signed an alliance with them. With Maqsood.'

Nadeer held a defiant look.

'Your people were sloppy, Nadeer. We have the phone intercepts.'

'So what?' Nadeer snapped. 'We are free to cooperate with who we wish.'

Carter watched him. Yoyok opened a bottle of water and drank.

'I wonder what your nephew thinks.'

'Leave him out of this.'

'Perhaps he's recovered enough to forgive them.'

Nadeer glared.

'But you, well, I thought it would take a lot to forgive the torture of a family member.'

Nadeer sucked air sharply, then spat on the floor.

'What about the weapons they stole? Paid for with your money, only to be used against you by Barpemis thugs.'

Nadeer looked up. 'Only because of you and your dogs,' he sneered. 'It was your agent who sold me the weapons, Pak, then told Maqsood's men. It was all a trick.'

'Is that what El-Akhtar told you?'

Nadeer's nose twitched. He glanced at the two men, then the soldier by the wall.

'Did he convince you that you were fighting the wrong war? That if you joined with Barpemis you could take revenge against us?'

Nadeer's breathing was rapid and shallow. He stared at the floor.

Carter let out a frustrated sigh. 'Bedroom,' he said.

The soldier stepped away from the wall.

'Wait!' said Nadeer.

Yoyok held up his hand. The soldier halted.

Carter folded his arms and leaned back on the chair. 'Got something to say, Nadeer?'

Nadeer's breathing slowed and his face relaxed. Yoyok waved the soldier off.

Nadeer glanced at each spy. 'He told us we were fools,' he said. 'He said we were spoiled brothers fighting over toys while a pot of gold lay before us, that we had lost perspective. We have money, weapons, fighters. He said that if we worked together, we could achieve independence. No more humiliation. No more oppression.'

Nadeer looked anxiously at Carter and Yoyok, then the doorway to the bedroom. He let out a shivery breath.

'What were the terms of the alliance?' said Carter.

'We settled our disputes and agreed to not compete against each other in the elections. I would control political strategy; Abu Maqsood would command my militia.' He looked Carter in the eye. 'And we agreed to cut all ties with the government. Instead, we would wage jihad.'

'Wage it how?'

Nadeer hesitated. His eyes fell to the doorway again. 'Disrupt the elections. El-Akhtar said if people were scared to vote, we could claim it was Allah's will.'

Yoyok glanced at Carter. The Kopassus soldier, lamenting the lack of action, cleared his throat.

'How will you attack them?'

'He did not say. Not even Maqsood knows this.'

Carter nodded. Yoyok held up a bottle of water and let Nadeer drink.

Carter produced an envelope from his shoulderbag and placed eight sheets of paper on the floor. Eight faces stared up at them under the glare of the camplight. Two were classic mugshots, another had been taken for a passport. One was grainy, taken from a distance. The others looked like stills from a video.

'What is this?' said Nadeer.

'I need to know you're telling the truth,' said Carter. 'Point to El-Akhtar.'

Nadeer looked at Yoyok, as if for guidance. The Indonesian folded his arms.

Nadeer looked at the photographs and shook his head. 'He is not any of these men.'

'Try harder,' said Carter. 'It'll make it easier for me not to tell Maqsood everything you have said tonight.'

'I swear, Pak!'

Carter glared at him, then softened his face to a grin. Nadeer watched him collect the photos and stash them in the bag. 'My mistake,' said Carter. He removed another set and laid them out as before.

Nadeer's eyes settled on one quickly. 'This one.' He breathed relief. 'Third from the right.'

Carter picked it up and held it closer. 'Be sure.'

'I am sure, Pak. This is El-Akhtar.'

Carter examined the photo and shook his head.

'Please.' Nadeer shifted in his chair. 'It is true.'

'Bedroom.'

The soldier's boots thudded on the floorboards as he gripped Nadeer under the shoulders.

'No!' Nadeer screamed.

'Lift him.'

The Kopassus trooper lifted Nadeer along with the chair that was still tied to him. Nadeer cried. 'It is him, Pak, I swear.'

Carter stood in front him. Their faces were inches apart.

'Prove it.' He gripped Nadeer by the jaw. 'Where is he, Nadeer?'

Nadeer sobbed. 'North. Past Galela.'

'I need more than that.'

Nadeer blew mucus from his nose. 'He moves around. I heard of a camp.'

Carter glanced at Yoyok.

'What's the camp for?'

'It must be for the election.'

Carter held him for a while, then released. He nodded to the soldier to sit Nadeer down.

Nadeer struggled to control his breathing. 'Do you believe me?' he said.

Carter repacked the photos and stood up.

'Pak?'

'Stay here while we figure out what to do with you.'

Nadeer's face changed to despair. 'Pak!'

Carter gripped Nadeer's collar. The prisoner gasped.

'Do not underestimate the shit you are in. You've admitted to conspiracy to commit a terrorist act and to breaching your agreement with the Indonesian authorities. We will let you rest, but you are not a free man. Do you understand?'

A tear emerged from one of Nadeer's bloodshot eyes and fell down his cheek.

Carter spoke forcefully: 'Do you understand?'

Nadeer nodded. Carter released him and walked out.

Sugianto watched Carter quizzically.

'He talked enough to earn some sleep,' said Carter. 'Feed him, water him, keep him under watch at all times. If he misbehaves, do what you need to do.'

Sugianto frowned. 'For how long, bos?'

Carter opened the door to the Landcruiser and threw his bag inside. 'Long enough to make sure ANVIL doesn't fuck this up.'

Sugianto gave a mock salute. 'Take your time, Pak Carter. We love it out here.'

16

CANBERRA

'Zaid Uthmaa Saabiq Sudirman,' said Gibson. He held out a printed mugshot. 'Age thirty-seven. Native to North Maluku, which helped narrow the search. Known as El-Akhtar within Islamic State.'

The directors craned their necks to get a view of the printed sheet. A withered twenty-seven year-old Indonesian stared back at them, eyes ablaze amongst a sunbeaten face lined with a corona of wispy hair, a mugshot for countless Islamists across the country.

'Any idea when he returned to Indonesia?' said the DDG.

'Not yet.'

The DDG raised an eyebrow.

'We've held off notifying BIN of his identity,' said Gibson. 'Due to the sensitivities.'

Ops leaned forward and glared at Gibson. 'What about the camp?' she said.

'Satellite coverage over that area is patchy,' said Gibson. 'AGO's working it.'

The directors let out a collective groan. The Australian Geospatial-Intelligence Organisation, responsible for satellite imagery and *geospatial data* – otherwise known as maps – was slow in proportion to the syllables of its name. Those in the intelligence community said that if you wanted to know where something was, use Google Maps. If you wanted to know where it was six months ago, call AGO, and be prepared to wait.

The DDG leaned over his desk. 'So how bad is it?'

Gibson lifted his glasses and squeezed the bridge of his nose. The threat of Islamic State gaining a foothold in Indonesia had kept the intelligence community awake at night for years, and ASIS was now, literally, staring it in the face.

'Based on his record,' he said, lowering his hand, 'and with Maqsood, Ibrahim and Nadeer in his pocket, it could be bad.'

Ops leaned back in her sofa and thrust her pointed jaw forward. 'Don't say I didn't warn you.'

'Something to say, Gary?' said the DDG.

Neill was staring into his cup. Tea dripped onto the saucer from his moustache, and for once he didn't lick it.

'I'm not so sure,' he said. 'These guys are hardliners, but they're not psychopaths. They've always been suspicious of Islamic State. Especially Maqsood.'

Ops rolled her eyes. 'Who cares? They're pragmatists, is what they are. Who they like won't count much when North Maluku becomes a caliphate.'

The DDG contemplated his hands. 'How seriously should we take the election threat?'

The directors turned to face Gibson.

'It's an obvious target,' said Gibson. 'But without clear intelligence on what El-Akhtar has planned, it will be hard for Indonesia to justify new security measures.'

'They'll need to do something,' said the DDG. 'Make the call to Hartanto. I'll speak to the minister and get you top cover.'

'What's the plan for Nadeer?' said Neill.

'Send him back,' said Ops. 'We need eyes on this IS whacko.'

'We'll need to follow BIN's lead on that point,' said the DDG. He looked at Gibson. 'Find out what they want to do.'

Gibson braced himself for what that would entail. 'Will do.'

◆

Hartanto's voice boomed through the Wireline. 'There is no evidence of IS fighters in North Maluku,' he said. 'You are mistaken, Pak.'

'We're quite certain,' Gibson said coolly.

'A disgraced jihadi points at a photograph and you blame us for losing track of this... El-Akhtar?'

'There's no suggestion of blame,' said Gibson. A wave of exhaustion crashed over him. 'We need to focus our attention on El-Akhtar. The intelligence is credible and consistent.'

Hartanto breathed loudly into the phone before the hiss of the line returned.

'It is far-fetched.'

'Not if you look into El-Akhtar's background,' said Gibson. 'In Syria, he led two-thousand men in the Battle of Raqqa. He had grown his battalion from a platoon of thirty by being ruthless, not to mention charismatic, and in Maluku he has found a fertile group of potential followers. He's brokered alliances with three of the major Islamist factions so far, there may be others.'

'Only if you believe Nadeer,' said Hartanto. 'He is a fraud and a traitor.'

'His testimony aligns with other intel. It explains everything that has occurred since Kao, if not before. The alliance deals include turning in or eliminating covert links to us, which explains why our cut-outs were targeted.'

Hartanto grunted. 'And yet, there is no sign of any "camp" in northern Halmahera.'

Gibson had to concede that point. He'd received two sets of high-resolution satellite photographs of the northern tip of Halmahera, one night, one day, in visible and infra-red light. They revealed nothing to back Nadeer's claims of training camps in the region.

'The imagery isn't conclusive,' said Gibson. 'We need to survey the area from the ground before we can rule anything out.'

'You mean troops.'

'Yes.'

'Out of the question.'

Gibson squeezed his nose. 'We should still take Nadeer's testimony seriously,' he said. 'The low-level Islamist violence we have seen over the past ten years will look tame if El-Akhtar has succeeded in uniting the groups.'

'Fine,' said Hartanto. 'What do you propose?'

'We propose to recruit Nadeer to return to Weda and have him resume his role with the Maluku Independent Militia. From there he can report on, if not disrupt, El-Akhtar's operation.'

'No,' said Hartanto. 'Nadeer has served his purpose and the risk is too great. We have seen the consequences of trying to run agents close to the Islamists.'

Gibson pictured Hasan's broken body and shuddered. 'With respect, Pak, we have been forced to dismantle most of our network in North Maluku. Without Nadeer we will be blind.'

Hartanto made some sort of growling noise. 'Remind me, Andy, why Australia is a partner in this operation. You have your spy satellites, your signals collection. If the only way to keep track of these thugs is through criminals and fraudsters like Nadeer, Indonesia can continue the operation on its own.'

Gibson rubbed his forehead, unsure how to respond.

Hartanto continued. 'If you have specific intelligence of an attack being planned by El-Akhtar, or anyone, bring it to my attention. Until that time, we will manage this operation our way. I will arrange for secure accommodation and immunity for Pak Nadeer and debrief him personally. Turn him over to BIN custody immediately.'

Gibson shook his head in frustration. He had expected the call to be difficult, but not a disaster. They rang off and Gibson returned to his office.

Scarlett was waiting for him. 'Looks like it went well.'

'As well as any other case of ANGINA.'

She gave him a mock pout. 'Anything I can do?'

A touch of lipstick had trailed at the corner of her lips. Chlorine lined the scent of her perfume. She'd been swimming.

Gibson pushed the image from his mind. 'Draft a cable for Jordan,' he said. 'Tell him to bring Nadeer in.'

'Goodie,' she said. 'But I'll let you send it.'

Gibson didn't blame her.

'That is,' she continued, 'if you can work that thing.' She pointed at the computer.

He glanced at the computer, then at her. 'Perhaps you can show me how.'

She arched an eyebrow. 'Then you'll really owe me.'

17

TERNATE

Four rings and the phone finally answered. 'Hello?'

Rimbo's voice was tense.

'It's Ana. Don't hang up.'

She heard breathing, then, 'Okay.'

'Why won't you answer my calls?'

She'd borrowed a phone from her new landlord. True to Jonah's word, the elderly proprietor-cum-tourguide had let her book a long-stay apartment on the cheap and without reporting her to the police. He also had a phone. This was useful, because Rimbo, her less-than-trustworthy fixer, had blocked Ana's number.

'I cannot work for you anymore, mbak. They said…' His voice trailed off.

'They said what? Rimbo?'

Rimbo made a sniffing sound. He was sobbing.

'Don't let them scare you. You've done nothing wrong.'

'I know, but…'

'I need your help,' she said. 'You know how important this work is, Rimbo.'

'I'm sorry, mbak.'

He cut the call. She tried again but he cancelled it. She needed transport, quick. Rimbo was the only fixer her friend Zoe had been able to dredge up east of Bali. The guesthouse offered various day tours around Ternate and the surrounding islands, but they were expensive and inflexible. Driving herself was an option, but it was a last resort she couldn't afford. Only when she got back to her room did the solution come to her.

She retrieved Jonah Somerville's card and typed out a message:

Hi, this is Ana K. You said I could call you for help. I need transport. A

The message disappeared into the ether and she lay on the sofa. The beep of her phone startled her, and she realised she'd been dozing.

Where to?

Sabo.

Ten minutes passed.

Why?

Because the reclusive English-speaking Islamist leader Sayeed had promised she would find the next part of her story there, but that was none of his business. She didn't bother hiding her frustration:

Can you help or not?

After five minutes without a reply, she searched in vain for a private driver. A search for 'rental car Ternate' turned up a dozen dodgy results. Jonah replied as she clicked on the first link.

Someone will contact you in the morning. His name is Raf. Stay out of trouble. J

Raf turned out to be a fit man in his twenties adorned with a long, red dragon tattoo that wrapped around each arm and seemed to strangle him with pointed talons. He had contacted her as Jonah had promised and quoted a token fee for the return trip to Sabo. 'For my friend,' he explained. He had arrived with Jaja – his 'cousin', albeit twice Raf's size, shaved-headed, and with none of Raf's gleam – who packed her travel case into the brand-new Nissan Patrol then helped her into the rear seat. The two men agreed something in Indonesian before Raf started the Patrol and manoeuvred into the morning traffic.

Ana watched Ternate come to life as they drove to the ferry docks. Raf directed Jaja along a warren of backstreets to avoid the jammed streets, but it still took half an hour to reach the seaside. By then, the ferry had started boarding.

Jaja paid off the attendant, drove on board and parked so that they would be first off the boat at the destination. It was a three-decked ship, painted white, and almost empty for the voyage to Sidangoli. Ana left Raf and Jaja at the car and roamed the decks, ignoring, as best she could, the usual attention from fellow passengers. She settled at the bow of the ship and photographed the approaching coastline of Halmahera, different compared to her previous arrivals further south, and a looming cold front. By the time they reached Sidangoli, the sky had darkened, and the sea had become choppy.

Raf appeared beside her. 'We are ready, mbak.'

Ana gripped the railing as she followed him back to the Patrol. Jaja flicked the remains of a cigarette overboard and lumbered into the driver's seat. The other passengers migrated to their own vehicles as the engines of the ferry reversed and the deck began to vibrate. Eventually, the ramp lowered and they drove off the ferry into faint drizzle.

Sidangoli was larger than she'd expected. It was an old seaside town from colonial times, though it remained a patchwork of crumbling roads and breezeblock houses. The streets were almost deserted. After ten minutes, the urban sprawl subsided and they reached rice fields. They crossed a small bridge and Jaja pulled over. The road ahead of them led to wilderness.

'Why are we stopping?' said Ana.

Jaja seemed preoccupied with the rear-view mirrors.

Raf turned to her and smiled. 'We check map,' he said. He took out an old folded-up paper map from the glove box and oriented it, then turned it and checked something else, almost for show. He said something to Jaja, who acknowledged him and restarted the car.

'Everything okay,' said Raf. Another smile. 'We go now.'

They drove for an hour on gravel roads. The raised suspension of the Patrol made short work of the ruts and potholes left from tropical rain and lack of maintenance. Jaja drove fast – too fast – overtaking scooters and trucks with abandon as the rain cleared. Ana braced herself against the door and tried not to think of potential catastrophe.

The Patrol slowed. Ana looked through the windscreen to see a queue of vehicles that led to a police checkpoint. A four-wheel drive was parked on the opposite verge, and three figures loitered in green raincoats.

Raf turned to her. *'Cap tikus,'* he said. 'Moonshine. They look.'

Ana reclined her seat. She knew illegal alcohol distribution had long been a problem in the province so gave it no more thought, instead passing the time on Twitter while they waited. Jaja inched the Patrol forward every few minutes as the vehicles ahead cleared the inspectors, then the line of cars halted while drivers and passengers poured out to perform the midday prayer. Raf and Jaja left to join them, and Ana drifted off in the heat and silence before waking to Raf's voice. She sat upright and saw they had reached the head of the queue.

The policemen had retreated to the shadow of a tent, where they drank water and smoked in full view of the waiting motorists. One of them noticed Ana and said something to the others. They laughed. A larger man, whom she assumed was the senior officer, barked something at them.

Two policemen walked over from the tent. One carried a long pole with a mirror attached and inspected the underside of the Patrol. The other made one orbit and recorded their registration. He glared at Ana as he passed. Jaja popped the rear doors. The officer checked the boot and shut it again.

'Sudah,' he called out. Done.

The police commander walked over from the tent.

Ana noticed Raf roll a hundred-thou note into the tattooed palm of his left hand. He turned and gave Ana a reassuring smile. The money seemed petty if they were searching for alcohol.

The commander asked Jaja a question and looked at Ana. Jaja responded politely and efficiently. The commander asked something he couldn't answer, so Raf chimed in. Ana watched Raf's hands, waiting for the handshake that would make the bribe, but it never came.

'Mbak?'

Raf had spoken. She looked up to see the commander staring at her.

'Passport,' said Raf.

She hesitated before handing it over. To her relief, Raf handed it to the officer without the hundred-thou note. The officer flicked the pages.

'They're not looking for alcohol,' said Ana.

Jaja drummed his fingers on the steering wheel.

'It is normal,' said Raf. 'Trust me.'

The commander said something to Jaja but held onto the passport. Jaja responded with something about Sabo. The commander looked at Ana, then replied to Jaja with what sounded like concern. Raf spoke calmly and slowly. The commander tapped the passport in his hand a few times, then handed it back to Raf and waved them through.

'What did he want?' said Ana.

Jaja shifted the Patrol into gear and accelerated from the checkpoint.

'He say it is dangerous. Too dangerous for bulè. Especially girl.'

Ana rolled her eyes. 'Dangerous how?'

Raf and Jaja shared a glance.

'You want to go back?' said Raf, half in hope.

'No,' she said. 'I want to know what he said.'

'He say there is bad people up here. No police.' He turned to face forward again. 'He worry too much. We keep you safe.'

Ana watched a woman in burqa cross the street in front of them. The garment obscured her features and the movement of her limbs so that she appeared shapeless and unnatural. Ana had only seen a burqa once before, at a suburban mosque in Melbourne, and despite her sympathy for Islam she felt as confronted by it then as she did now. She could believe a woman would choose to wear a hijab, the traditional veil seen the world over that covered the head and chest, but the burqa stripped a woman of her form, her identity, as if she was something to be ashamed of.

Raf returned with three bottles of water. They had arrived at the town of Ibu, north of Mount Gamkonora. Ibu was the largest town in the area, clutching a small inlet at the western base of a large volcano that shared its name. The tone of the place was different to Sidangoli. Everyone wore some form of Islamic dress: women in long hijab, the men in dark smocks, their heads adorned with skullcaps or turbans. There were no laughing children and no curious onlookers, the whole place was intensely concentrated on its religious devotion. She drank half the bottle of water and ate an apple. Despite the long morning, she wasn't hungry.

The woman in burqa had disappeared. Ana's mind replayed the events of that morning while the men ate. They had brought lunch with them and ate in the car. Ana was grateful not to have to get out. She had dressed modestly in camping trousers and a cotton, buttoned shirt, but without a veil she felt naked and obscene.

They finished lunch and continued north. The road turned inland, and they passed through a succession of small towns, each identical in their constructions of breezeblocks and iron roofs, dotted along the highway like rusted pearls on a string. The road climbed sharply, and the cloud dissipated to reveal the volcanic peak of Mount Ibu as they rounded its northern side. The air began to cool. Ana noticed they hadn't passed a car or motorcycle since Ibu.

'How far to Sabo?' she said.

'Not far,' said Raf. 'Ten minutes.'

Sabo was the largest town in the jungle valley and could have been in a different country. The men wore black tunics and turbans like uniforms, and stood, or squatted, in groups. There were no women in hijab; the burqa was the norm. They moved swiftly from place to place, avoiding the men like pigeons unsure where to perch.

For the first time, Raf and Jaja seemed apprehensive. Jaja slowed to avoid the flow of pedestrians and motorcycles near the centre of town while Raf put on a white long-sleeved shirt, flicked the collar over his tattoos and removed his cap to reveal a mohawk. Minarets loomed over the rooftops ahead. 'Stop by the mosque,' said Ana.

Jaja did so. A prayer emanated from the minarets. People passed back and forth on bicycles and scooters. A man shouted something and a woman, in burqa, shuffled off and disappeared. Ana grabbed her pack and took out a long cotton dress that she wrapped around her head as a veil. She made sure her shirt was buttoned up and sleeves rolled down all the way.

'Let's go,' she said.

She stepped out into noise and heat. Her guides followed her, each now wearing grey prayer caps they must have packed for the ride. The sky had cleared, and despite the altitude, the town was scorched and humid. The mosque stood diagonally opposite the Patrol, surrounded by low houses. Further along the street was a row of stores: a grocer, a workshop and a private clinic. A large warehouse that sold Islamic clothing stood opposite.

She photographed each structure and as many of the townsfolk as she could. One frame caught the piercing eyes of a young woman through the mailbox-like opening of her *niqab.* The woman's daughter pulled at her arm in disobedience. Ana photographed two boys playing soccer before they were admonished for soiling their silken tunics. A group of men watched Ana from the veranda of a house two doors up from the mosque. She photographed them and they moved inside. The stares began to feel menacing, not curious. She tried to ignore them. Raf and Jaja moved cautiously; it felt strange to see a man of Jaja's bulk appear so jittery. Ana caught her breath, checked her camera and forced herself on.

A street seller had set up by the mosque. The man, in his sixties or seventies, squatted by a collection of Quranic magazines and political pamphlets, each adorned with photographs of religious leaders, some of which she recognised as running for election. He stood as she reached him.

'*Assalamu alaikum,*' she said.

He ignored her.

Ana turned to Raf. 'Could you ask him what he is selling?'

Raf translated the question. The man didn't say anything at first, then spoke in a harsh tone.

'He say he not talk to woman.'

'Tell him I am a journalist.'

Raf explained. The man grew more agitated. Raf tried to calm him, but he shouted back, then shouted something at Ana and walked off, leaving his goods on the roadside. She shook her head, then took photos of the man's stock.

'Sorry, Miss,' said Raf.

'Forget it.'

She continued along the front wall of the mosque compound, Raf and Jaja in tow. The gate was halfway along. She stopped next to the opening and checked the settings of her camera. Across the street, a group of young boys in Islamic robes stared at her and laughed. The wind picked up and she had to adjust her veil. The camera was set.

She stepped through the gate.

The mosque stood at the centre of the compound behind a forecourt of trampled dirt and concrete ten metres square. The mosque itself was simple enough, though unlike many regional mosques it was adorned with elaborate minarets and a gold-painted *qubba*. Above the main door, strung from rope attached to the top corners of the facade, was a single Black Standard, two metres across, obscured from view as it flapped in the breeze.

Someone called out as she raised her camera for a photo of the mosque. The zoom was off. She lowered the camera and twisted the lens barrel. As she prepared to raise it again, the wind fell, and the Black Standard unfolded before her.

Raf appeared beside her. 'We must go, mbak,' he said.

Ana ignored him, transfixed by the sight.

'Mbak?'

It was no Black Standard. Instead, the primitive, hand-drawn shapes that stared out at her, caught bright white in the sun against the deep black of the flag, revealed to her a fearsome, eternal symbol of pure hatred, an image forever etched into her mind as the flag of Islamic State.

'We must go.'

She broke her stare and turned to him. 'Go where?'

Then she saw the men.

Six of them. They watched her with intent from twenty metres away. One of them carried a large cane; he began to walk towards them.

Jaja had already started moving to the Patrol.

'Ignore them,' she said.

The man had crossed the street. The others followed a few metres behind.

'Mbak,' said Raf.

'Wait.'

Ana lifted her camera, focused it on the flag and adjusted for the light. It folded again in the breeze.

The man shouted something at her.

Ana ignored him. 'Come on,' she said to herself.

The man stopped a few metres away. The text was still obscured. 'Damn it.' She looked to see Raf standing in front of the men. They pointed at her and shouted.

'What do they want?' said Ana.

'We must go!'

She looked up in time to see the flag drop again. She raised her camera, felt for the shoot button, and pressed.

One of the men shoved Raf. He stood his ground. 'Mbak!'

She checked the photo. Out of focus. *Fuck.* She made the adjustment and took more shots.

An engine approached from behind. It was Jaja.

'Go!'

She checked the shot. This time she had got it.

'Okay,' she said.

Raf tried to step away from the men. One of them grabbed him by the arm and shoved him. His prayer cap fell, and hair fell over his face.

'Give them the camera,' said Raf.

She held the camera away from him. 'I won't.'

More shouting. She looked at their faces. They weren't thieves; they were afraid. She took a step towards them and raised the camera.

Click.

They released Raf and shouted at her. He rushed forward and grabbed her by the arm. Ana yelled out with pain as he dragged her to the Patrol and pushed her inside. He closed the door as the men reached him. He pushed them off and climbed into the front passenger seat. Jaja threw the Patrol into gear. The men slammed their hands on the windows while they accelerated away.

Raf caught his breath. 'You okay, mbak?'

'Yeah.' She rubbed her arm and looked at the two men. Raf was leaned against the door. Jaja drove in silence. 'I'm sorry,' she said.

The two men exchanged a glance before Raf turned to her. 'No problem, mbak,' he said. The sleeve of his shirt had torn from the shoulder to reveal the trunk of the red dragon and a bruise from his assailants' grip. 'Everything okay.'

◆

The police checkpoint was larger than the one they passed that morning. There were two small huts either side, each occupied by policemen. Boom gates spanned the narrow road that had led them over the mountains.

'Where are we?' said Ana.

Raf handed her a map and pointed. Despite the time, they were only ten kilometres east of Sabo, halfway to the sea.

A lorry was stopped at the gate. A police officer approached the driver's side window while another checked the chassis and climbed into the trailer. He reappeared a moment later and shouted at his comrade. The gates opened, and the lorry passed through.

'Get your passport,' said Raf.

She did so. Jaja pulled up to the gate beside the waiting officer. He said something to Jaja, and Raf handed over the passport and their IDs. The officer looked at Ana and checked the documents while the second man performed the underbody check. Ana was relieved. These men were more professional than the police en route to Sabo. She checked her watch; almost four. It was probably another hour and a half back to Sofifi. They could still make the last ferry to Ternate.

'Step out please, Miss,' said the officer in perfect English.

Ana looked at Raf. He looked surprised.

She did as she was told. The officer led her to one of the huts. Raf said something and climbed out, but the second officer told him to wait.

'What's going on?' she said to the officer.

He ignored her and dialled something on a telephone. He spoke to someone in Indonesian and read off the details of her passport.

'Wait here, please,' he said. He gestured to a wooden chair in the corner. 'Would you like tea, coffee?'

Raf argued with the other police officer outside.

'How long will this take?' said Ana.

'Tobelo is an hour away.'

Which meant Rachmann, she thought, and a night in a cell.

She rested her head against the wall while traffic backed up behind the Patrol. Raf argued with the other police officer over the sound of truck engines and horns before giving up and rejoining Jaja in the Patrol. The police officer watched the Patrol take off in a cloud of yellow dust, then pointed at the table and a stack of cups, drink supplies and a kettle.

‘Please,’ he said, ‘help yourself.’

18

TERNATE

'They were three cousins from Buli,' Sayeed had said to her, referring to the three young men at the centre of the arson story that had led Ana to him. 'The imam that managed the madrassah spoke highly of them, which is how they joined Al Ramah.' He coughed. 'Then they were led from my flock.'

Ana had transcribed one-handed into her laptop. The advokat's phone she'd received outside Ternate stadium had no headset and no recording app, and she was too scared to use a speakerphone in the guesthouse.

'You were quoted saying they were recruited by a government agent,' she said. 'Do you still stand by that?'

'As long as I stand by Allah,' he said. Despite the weak phone connection, he had sounded like a father in mourning. 'Al Ramah has no capacity for violence, no desire to impose our will.'

'How could you know he worked for the government?'

'Because he told us.' Sayeed pulled the phone away and spat something. 'He offered us information and security. It was like this for everyone, an open secret. In exchange, we were required to disavow calls for independence and inform on our brothers.'

Ana paused to relieve her typing hand. 'You mean rival groups?'

'United under Islam.'

'And did you agree to the agent's offer?'

'We had no choice,' said Sayeed. 'Arifin proved this.'

She shuffled through her notes and found the reference. Arifin, a former Gameshar figurehead, was six years into a thirty-year sentence for conspiracy to commit terrorism.

'How does this relate to the arson attack?'

'The government was greedy. It was not enough that we submitted to them. They taught the boys things we could not: shooting, self-defence, survival skills. Told them it was to help protect Al Ramah, but that it was secret. They believed him, this'—he hissed the word—'spy.'

Ana scrambled to keep up while Sayeed coughed violently into the phone. Eventually, he continued.

'He taught them about the imam in Maba; that he was planning to betray Al Ramah's deal with the government. By then they were so convinced of their importance to the cause that they agreed to destroy this man and his family without question. They planned the whole thing themselves. The spies only had to supply the bombs.'

Ana took a sip of water and loosened her hands.

'Do you believe me, mbak Ana?'

She considered her answer. 'It's not my job to believe you. I'm here to report.'

'Are you not afraid?'

'It's not my job to be afraid, either.'

Sayeed laughed, a raspy sound that became another cough. 'When the media reported the Maba bombing, the government began to intimidate reporters. The articles stopped, and reporters stopped coming. I'm surprised they have not come for you.'

She recalled her false arrest, the room search, Rimbo's intimidation. 'Perhaps because I'm a foreigner.'

'I mean your own government.'

Ana's hand paused above the laptop. 'The *Australian* Government? What would they have to do with this?'

Sayeed sneered into the phone. 'The Australians have always enjoyed dominating Muslims. Witness Afghanistan, Iraq, Syria. In the Philippines your spies support the army to crush righteous Islamic rebellion. Innocent Muslim refugees are caged like animals on faraway islands pleading for mercy, only to be exported to distant corners of the globe. Now, they send their spies here, in league with our own government, to join in the oppression of North Maluku.'

Ana thought back to the reporter's advice not to trust Sayeed. She could tell Sayeed enjoyed the sound of his own voice, and he was yet to give away anything of substance. 'Is there any evidence to back that claim?'

He coughed something, which she took as a 'No'. She returned to the core thread.

'I don't understand something,' she said. 'You said the government openly undermined Islamist groups. Why did you allow it?'

'Fear and greed,' he said. 'By the time we knew we had been tricked, we were divided. No-one believed in unity for fear of showing weakness. We were foolish and naïve, but not anymore.'

She stopped typing. 'What's changed?'

'We have newfound clarity, Miss Ana. Our conflicts were petty and doctored, but we know, as one, we can fight back against the oppressors. You wrote of Kao and Tobelo, and there will be more. They cannot divide us any longer. We will destroy them if they try.'

'What else have you planned?'

'It is not important what we have planned, but what we have achieved. An independent, Islamic dominion in North Maluku. See it for yourself, mbak, and you will believe it.'

'I don't understand. Where?'

He breathed heavily into the phone, then said, 'Sabo.'

TOBELO

Ana woke with a start to the sound of footsteps along the hall. She wiped saliva from her cheek and checked her watch. It was six hours since she'd been apprehended at the police checkpoint, two hours since she was offloaded at Tobelo police headquarters, and a week since she'd last been left to herself in the same exact interview room.

Keys were inserted; locks unlatched. The bulk of Inspector Rachmann entered the interview room. He pulled out his chair, took a pen and notepad from his pocket, and sat down.

'We meet again, Miss Kovacevic.'

'I want to go.'

He made a soft grunt.

'Why were you waiting for me?' she said.

'Our friends in Sidangoli were kind enough to let us know of your travels. I warned them to apprehend you if you returned, but you turned up at my checkpoint instead.'

'Why did they let us through in the first place?'

'They could not explain.'

He took off his peak cap and placed it on the desk. The belt of the cap had left a mark around the circumference of his balding head.

'It is very dangerous up there, Ana.'

'So you do know what is happening in Sabo?'

Rachmann twitched his cheek. 'I know they are hostile to outsiders.'

'And police, it seems. Not one of you was there.'

He looked at his notepad, then his cap, then back to her.

She leaned forward. 'People have a right to know.'

'Fine,' he said. He stroked his moustache. 'It's not my problem anymore.'

'What's that supposed to mean?'

He waved his hand coolly at the door. 'My men will be here in a moment. In the morning, they will take you back to Ternate to collect your things, then escort you to the airport.'

'I won't go. You'll have to arrest me.'

He placed the cap back on his head. 'I'm sorry you feel that way. Guard!'

Two officers walked in. One held a baton, the other a set of handcuffs. They took her by the arms and forced her to stand. She held Rachmann's gaze as they cuffed her, then she was pushed out, down the hall and into a cell.

It was after four a.m. when they came for her. Three officers, including the woman she had seen at reception. She carried Ana's handbag.

'Please come,' said the woman.

Ana stood up. She expected to be cuffed, but instead the woman gestured to the hall. Ana followed her through a side exit that led to a small alley alongside the station lit by the red glow of dawn. The Patrol idled a few metres from the entrance. Next to the vehicle, a small, wiry man pulled at a long, black mohawk as he puffed a cigarette. Raf. Rachmann was shouting at someone on his phone as he paced the alley. When he saw Ana, he muted the phone on his chest.

'I was trying to protect you,' he said. He nodded in Raf's direction. 'I hope your friends share my concern.'

Ana took her handbag from the woman and walked to the Patrol. Raf flicked the cigarette and opened the door for her but didn't look her in the eye. She climbed in to see the large frame of Jaja in the driver's seat.

'What just happened?' she said once Raf was inside.

Jaja put the Patrol in gear and drove out of the alley.

'Raf?'

'Like I say,' he said. He turned and smiled. 'We keep you safe.'

19

NORTH OF PAYAHE

It was raining when Carter returned to the safehouse. He parked next to a small river of stormwater that led from the tents where the burly, raincoated figure of Sugianto watched on. He climbed out, jumped the crevasse, and joined Yoyok at the front door.

They went inside. Nadeer slept on an army stretcher rigged in a corner of the room. A guard stood opposite. The interrogation chair was gone.

Yoyok signalled to the guard. The soldier walked up to Nadeer, barked something at him and turned on the camping light. Nadeer groaned and sat up.

Carter placed a chair beside Nadeer and lit him a cigarette. The prisoner blinked at him in the light, relieved to see him. He savoured the smoke and exhaled in long, white trails.

'The government wants me to take you into custody,' said Carter. 'Immunity, new identity, everything.'

Nadeer coughed smoke. 'I don't understand,' he said. 'You said I was a terrorist.'

'Obviously, you would have to disavow any association with separatist or Islamist movements.'

Nadeer flicked ash onto the floor.

'And you would need to promise never to reveal you had spied on them for us.'

Nadeer's eyes widened at Carter. 'I am no spy!'

'Of course you are,' said Carter. 'You're invaluable. Besides'—Carter shifted off the chair so they were face-to-face—'it's hardly your most damning secret.'

Nadeer threw the cigarette and stood up. The Kopassus man was on him instantly. He threw Nadeer onto the floor, turned him over and held his arm behind his back. Nadeer screamed.

Carter removed a folder from his backpack.

Nadeer groaned with pain. 'Please, Pak.'

'Sign this confession.' Carter placed the folder on the ground next to Nadeer's head. Nadeer thrashed against the soldier and the wall. 'Sign it, and you can live out your days in peace.'

Nadeer winced, then spat at the document. Carter nodded. The special forces man lifted Nadeer and shoved him against the wall. Nadeer fell to a sitting position and choked for breath.

Carter picked up the document and shook his head. Blood and saliva trailed across the page. 'What am I going to tell the Indonesians?' he said. He kneeled next to Nadeer. 'I can hardly let a terrorist go free.'

Nadeer spoke through gritted teeth. 'I would prefer death than prison.'

'You're too useful to go to prison.'

'I am no spy.' Nadeer grunted. 'I will not work for you.'

'Don't be so sure.' Carter watched for a moment, then tapped the soldier. The Kopassus man eased his pressure and stood aside.

Carter placed his hand on the back of Nadeer's neck and pulled him close. 'Listen carefully,' he said. 'The Indonesians want to destroy the Maluku Independent Militia along with every other separatist group in the region. And they will unless you help me.'

A tear fell from Nadeer's cheek. His breathing slowed; the rasps of each breath filled the bungalow.

'However, if you return,' said Carter, 'I can say MIM is on our side and they will leave you alone. You can go back to your politics, keep your alliance with Maqsood, whatever you like, as long as you cooperate.'

Carter let him go. Nadeer crouched against the wall, shaking.

'But they will kill me, Pak. I am discredited. This man, this—El-Akhtar. He promised to kill anyone who speaks to the government.' Nadeer inhaled deeply. 'He said there is no mercy for spies.'

Carter sucked air through his teeth and nodded to Yoyok. Yoyok lit a cigarette and offered it to Nadeer, who took it with a shaking hand.

'How much do you know about El-Akhtar?' said Carter.

Nadeer stared blankly as he flicked the lighter.

'Did you know he served for Islamic State?'

Nadeer looked away. For a moment, he stared at the floor before fumbling to light his cigarette. His hand was shaking so much he could barely find his mouth.

'It's not possible, Pak.'

Carter placed a stool next to Nadeer. He sat down, elbows on his knees, so that he loomed over the prisoner. Nadeer avoided eye contact.

'Turns out he was a platoon commander in Syria.' Carter gripped Nadeer's hand and guided the cigarette to the man's mouth. 'Responsible for a suburb in the south of Raqqa. Bit of a shithole. El-Akhtar ruled the place without mercy but, from all accounts, he was loved by his people until the coalition eventually arrived and bombed them back to the stone age. El-Akhtar survived and spent a few years in a Turkish prison before he was released for lack of evidence, since no-one was brave enough to testify against him. Two years ago, he returned to Indonesia and we lost track of him. We think he grew up in Sabo, so it's only natural he turned up here. There's more.'

Nadeer exhaled smoke and watched Carter.

'Your deal with Maqsood isn't the only one. El-Akhtar brokered an agreement with Ibrahim as well. We think other groups are involved, or will be. Like you, they all believe they are joined in a campaign against the Republic, but autonomy for Islamist groups in eastern Indonesia is only half of what El-Akhtar is planning. The truth is they will be junior partners in a future Islamic caliphate under El-Akhtar's control. They—*you*—will have replaced one oppressor with another.'

Nadeer finished the cigarette. Yoyok took out another one, but he refused.

'Why do you tell me this?' said Nadeer.

'I didn't tell you,' said Carter. 'Your cousin in the police told you.'

Nadeer frowned. 'I have no such cousin.'

'El-Akhtar doesn't know that.'

Nadeer started shaking again. His eyes darted to Yoyok, then back to Carter.

'Tell El-Akhtar what we know about him,' Carter continued. 'Tell him you can find out more and that you can turn this to his advantage. He will never find your cousin, so he will need to keep you alive.'

Nadeer shook his head. 'They will believe it is a trick.'

Carter moved in close again. 'Nadeer, you must trust me. If you do not, the government will imprison you, and eventually kill you. You will forever be known as a terrorist, and the lives of everyone you have ever loved will be destroyed for being associated with you. Is that what you want?'

Nadeer suddenly remembered his cigarette and took a belated lungful. He wheezed as he exhaled. 'No.'

Carter smiled. 'Then we have a deal.'

Nadeer hadn't left the house in a week. The rain had cleared and he had to shield his eyes. Carter guided him over the eroded clearing to a waiting Land Rover. Yoyok followed.

A waiting soldier cuffed Nadeer and helped him on board.

The agent stared at the trees and said nothing. Sugianto's men had dismantled the tents and packed them into the vehicles.

'Take him back to Weda,' said Carter.

Sugianto chucked his cigarette. 'My instructions were to return him to custody, Pak.'

'We cut a deal. Take him back. Be discreet.'

Sugianto looked at Yoyok. Yoyok nodded.

'And then what? Organise his funeral?' Sugianto stepped in close. 'How many more need to die, Pak Jordan?'

'Good question,' said Carter, unmoved. He stepped close to the Kopassus man and spoke quietly. 'Could be a lot, if this El-Akhtar guy is anything like we fear. You want that on your conscience?'

Sugianto hissed.

'What happens to Nadeer is irrelevant now,' Carter continued. 'Finding and stopping El-Akhtar is all that matters, so just do it.' He leaned closer. *'Kapten.'*

Sugianto was still, then stepped away. *'Okelah,'* he said. 'Anything you say.' He made a circle motion with his hand and the Land Rovers started up. A minute later, the convoy had left the clearing.

Yoyok turned to Carter. 'How will you explain this?' he said.

Carter opened his phone. 'Here's how.' An image showed the black flag of IS draped across the main entrance of a mosque, its hand-drawn letters gleaming under a midday sun. 'This was taken in Sabo yesterday.'

Yoyok's eyes widened as he examined it. 'Where did you get this?'

'It's not important,' said Carter. 'What's important is we're behind, mate. ANVIL is holding us back. This'—he held up the phone—'shows what El-Akhtar is capable of, and we're blind. We need someone in there – now – and it doesn't matter who.'

'You think Nadeer can do it?'

Carter gripped the doorhandle of the Landcruiser and opened. 'Nadeer will be fine once the others learn the truth about El-Akhtar.'

Yoyok scratched his chin. 'What makes you so sure?'

Carter scanned the treetops as the sun broke the clouds and cast the clearing in deep orange. He turned back to Yoyok. 'Because I know Maqsood. He's old Jemaah Islamiyah from way back. He disappeared in Pakistan in the late nineties, we think to find his way to an Al-Qaeda training camp, but we could never prove it.' He closed down the phone and returned it to his pocket. 'Al-Qaeda hates IS. Maqsood will think El-Akhtar's an apostate.'

Yoyok nodded. 'Then, bos?'

'Then we turn him. Split El-Akhtar's coalition in two, before he strikes.' He climbed into the driver's seat. 'And before ANVIL stops us.'

CANBERRA

'I don't understand.' Hartanto's voice crackled through the phone speaker and echoed around the SCIF. 'Why did he refuse the offer?'

Gibson leaned over the mic. 'He seemed convinced he was better off on his own.'

'Then he should have been arrested. He is a terrorist.'

Gibson looked across at the DDG. The DDG gestured to continue.

'The charges may not stick,' said Gibson, 'and if he goes to trial, he will claim he was a government informant acting on instructions. He'll go free, we will all be embarrassed, and we will lose ANVIL.'

Hartanto cursed something into the phone. 'So be it,' he said. 'But if anything happens to Nadeer, I will hold you responsible.'

The line went dead.

'Fine fellow,' said the DDG. He looked at Gibson. 'You have doubts about Jordan.'

Gibson rubbed the bridge of his nose. It wasn't doubt, it was certainty. The knowledge that his man would stop at nothing, not even a man's life, and there was nothing ASIS could do about it. Now, with photos circulating of the black flag of IS flying in Sabo, a scene that confirmed ASIS's worst fears, he was sure Carter would go even further.

'This was reckless,' he said.

'But you understand why he did it.'

Gibson nodded, but the understanding remained unspoken, buried amongst the files from Carter's recruitment. The vetting process for intelligence officers was unrelentingly invasive, designed to explore every hidden facet of the candidate's character and expose his or her loyalties, values, and weaknesses, both to assess their merits and filter out those at risk of betrayal. In Carter, ASIS had found a man not only of above average intelligence, resilience, and capacity for persuasion, but a man haunted by his failure to protect his own mother, an innocent girl from West Java whose only sin had been to seek a better life. For years, Carter's father had beaten and dominated her, and by the time Carter was old enough to confront him, she had fled, abandoning Carter to the mercy of an aggrieved tyrant. The experience had made him headstrong and resentful of authority, qualities ASIS had been only too happy to hone before firing Carter like an unguided missile at the North Maluku problem.

'ANVIL is his life,' said Gibson. 'North Maluku is his kingdom.' He let out a deep sigh. 'Now this El-Akhtar character has invaded and turned his barons against him, and his allies'— Gibson gestured to himself and the DDG— 'aren't there for him.' He rubbed his nose. 'Yeah, I understand why he did it, but damn it, Terry, he crossed a line.'

The DDG shrugged. 'We can be glad he did,' he said. 'That's why you hired him, isn't it?'

Gibson acknowledged it was. Carter was his creation, making him a witting accomplice in whatever happened. He looked up and said, 'You don't seem concerned.'

The DDG locked eyes with him. 'No,' he said. He adjusted his jacket. 'I take a different view entirely.' He stood up and walked to the front of the SCIF, where a large flat-screen television hung from the ceiling, connected by transparent pipes to allow easy inspection of cabling for signs of tampering. He checked something in his reflection, turned, and rested his arms on the back of one of the conference chairs.

'Our Lady the minister has been concerned about an IS presence in Indonesia for some time.' He brushed something off his lapel. 'It's up to you and me to help her sleep at night, Andy, however and whenever we can. Whatever Jordan's faults, whatever's eating at him, I've never known an officer of this service more dedicated to the cause, let alone as prepared to make the tough calls. I say good on him.' He stepped around the chair and placed a hand on Gibson's shoulder, his cologne overpowering.

'So worry not about Nadeer or Hartanto, least of all Jordan,' said the DDG. He had that twinkle in his eye again, the spark of the adventurer.

'Imagine if he wasn't on our side.'

20

TERNATE

Ana had spent two days researching and drafting her article since her release from Rachmann's custody. When she had returned to Ternate, she called Tanner, who had agreed to two-thousand words alongside a copy of her photograph of the IS flag above the Sabo mosque which, coupled with Sayeed's testimony, would serve as a wake-up call to anyone who thought the threat of Islamic radicalism had faded in Asia. Islamic State had long been eradicated as an organisation, but the idea of it lived on like a virus, ready to infect a viable host, and from North Maluku it was only a matter of time before it spread across the Indonesian archipelago and dominated the region. She blamed the Indonesians for the failure to inoculate North Maluku against it, whatever their methods, a sentiment that ran strong throughout the article.

'Tone it down,' Tanner had told her after he read her first draft. He wanted a series of articles, something to generate revenue over days, if not a week.

'Your readers need to know why this happened,' she said.

'I know, Ana, but bleed it slowly. For now, focus on what you saw.'

She was exhausted and wanted it over with. She put off rework to tomorrow and collapsed on her desk to a call of Maghreb prayer a block away. She woke after what felt like a long sleep, then realised the same prayer was being called. Her phone glowed on the desk. She opened it to find a message from Jonah.

Heard you made it back. Dinner?

She stared at it for a long time and wondered why she hadn't made the offer herself.

Jonah's driver arrived half an hour later. He didn't speak as he sped through the Ternate streets. Ana tried to keep track of where they were but lost her bearings in the darkness. Eventually he stopped at a nondescript warung, refused payment and drove away the moment she climbed out.

The warung was almost empty. Jonah sat at a table near the back. In the opposite corner, a stocky Indonesian man with his hair tied in a ponytail ate with his back to the room. Apart from the staff, there was no-one else there.

Jonah stood up as she approached. 'Good to see you again,' he said. He helped her to her chair.

'Thank you,' she said. Kitchen staff shouted at each other behind a doorway at the rear of the room. 'What is this place?'

'Anonymous.' He flashed a smile as he sat down. 'Figured you wouldn't want too much attention.'

She didn't mind this attention. At least it validated her fashion choice: a white silk blouse with floral print that she'd bought for the equivalent of five dollars at a market near the Ternate ferry terminal.

'I was always told to judge Indonesian restaurants by how many people ate there,' she said.

'Good advice.' Jonah glanced around the empty room. A lock of wavy black hair fell over his face. He pulled it back over his ear. 'I guess this place wouldn't rate a mention.'

'Quality over quantity, let's hope.'

He glanced at her blouse and smiled. 'The quality seems fine to me.'

He had said it in half-jest, but Ana felt her cheeks blush

anyway. The waitress arrived before she could respond. Jonah said something and she walked off. His Indonesian was as fluent as any local.

'You must have lived here a long time to speak like that,' said Ana.

He smiled. 'My mother was a good teacher.'

Ana studied the list of options while she contemplated her own lack of Croatian. She'd grown up immersed in it, yet barely spoke a word. Then her dad died, and the sound of the language became forever intolerable. She ordered chicken saté and thought of her mother.

'Must help to get around,' she said.

'It helps with unexpected situations.' He picked up a menu. 'I'm sure you'd agree.'

She looked at him over the menu. His eyes scanned the page, then flicked to catch hers.

'Is that why we're here?' she said. 'To talk about Sabo?'

'I heard it was a new experience for you.'

'As for most people,' she said. 'Not often you get busted out of jail by your driver.' She cocked her head. 'I wonder how Raf did it?'

Jonah grinned. 'He's a persuasive guy. Part of the service.'

She leaned over at him. 'Who are you, Jonah, really?'

'Not sure what you mean.' He waved his hand. The waitress arrived and took their orders.

Ana waited for the girl to leave.

'You know exactly what I mean.'

He watched her without expression. 'You got what you wanted, didn't you? No-one else would have taken you.'

She thumped her hand on the table. 'You have no right to interfere with my work.'

'Without me you would have no work. You might not have all your limbs.' He leaned forward and spoke quietly. 'So you'll think twice about telling the world what you saw up there, won't you, Ana Kovacevic.'

She shook her head. 'I won't be censored by you.'

'I'm protecting you.'

Ana held his gaze. 'Don't.'

Jonah unfolded his arms. Their faces were inches apart, and for the first time, she saw the menace in his eyes.

'Information is dangerous, Ana,' he said, his voice barely above a whisper. 'It gets out, it spreads, then distorts and amplifies as it goes. Unfortunately, some people just can't help but act on it. Sometimes, the wrong people.'

'Information isn't dangerous,' she said. '*Secrets* are dangerous. The only protection is to shine light on them. So that's what I'm going to do. Whatever is going on in Sabo, people deserve to know about it.'

'Thanks to you, I know about it.'

'You being the Australian Government.'

He was still. Inches from her face, a bead of sweat formed at his brow and traced the outer contour of his eye before the kitchen door opened and cast him in white light. He hadn't expected her to join the dots. The waitress arrived with their meals, and he pushed himself away. The long-haired man hadn't moved.

Jonah watched the waitress leave. 'I know you don't trust me,' he said finally, 'but believe it or not, I want the same as you. Peace, stability, prosperity for Indonesia and her citizens. All that shit.'

She shook her head in disgust. 'I want truth.'

'You tell yourself that, but it's half the answer.' He leaned towards her again. 'In case you hadn't noticed,' he said, 'the situation here is delicate. North Maluku has long been a hotbed of violence: Muslim, Christian, official, separatist, whatever. Those forces need to be kept in equilibrium, and for all your good intentions, a few words out of place could upset that balance.' He leaned back and wiped his hand with a cloth. 'Some people won't appreciate that.'

'You can't intimidate me, Jonah.'

'This is not about intimidation. It's about the everyday people of North Maluku just going about their lives. They don't need to know about Sabo, and they'll never care. What good will it do to tell them?'

'You make me sick.' She pushed her chair out and stood up. Jonah didn't move. She turned for the entrance, then turned back. 'Who are you to decide they can't make that judgement for themselves?'

He shook his head like he was disappointed.

She left him to find an empty street. Headlights appeared fifty metres away and Jonah's driver rolled to a stop in front of her. The window lowered and the driver called out to her.

She ignored him and reached for her phone.

'You'd better go with him,' said Jonah.

She turned to see him in the doorway to the restaurant, leaning against the doorframe.

She opened the phone and found Maps. 'I don't need your help.'

She took her bearings. The road curved after fifty metres in either direction. Maps told her she was a kilometre from the nearest main road, but it wasn't clear which direction.

Jonah walked past her and opened the passenger door.

Ana looked at him, then the street, then the map. It'd take an hour to find her way home. She swore under her breath and climbed in.

He closed the door and leaned through the window. 'Just think of me as another editor,' he said. 'All you have to do is tell me what you know, what you write about and when. That way, you'll always find a safe ride on dark streets.'

He tapped the car and they moved off. Only then did she realise how hungry she was.

21

WEDA

For two days Nadeer tried to wash away the stench of his betrayal. It was deep in the pores of every inch of his skin. His bones ached with guilt and shame, yet it was the fear that hurt most. He hadn't left the villa since his return, no-one had visited, and he had avoided contact. Anyone who saw him would see him for what he was: nothing but a dog. A traitor.

A spy.

He prayed. God would see through even this sin, as He had done before, and rebuild him from his soul. Nadeer had prayed ceaselessly during his captivity, first to numb the pain of the music, then to relieve the boredom; finally, to seek salvation from his tormentors. Now he prayed in fits and starts, unsure what to plead for. God would not assist him to lie to his comrades, and he had made his own choice not to flee. All he could ask for was forgiveness; from God, from family, his friends and, most importantly, his brothers within the Maluku Independent Militia.

He washed and resolved to call Jihaad. His deputy might still be searching for him and would be relieved to hear from him. Nadeer trusted Jihaad like a brother, and wanted to reveal the Australian's plot, eliminate any suspicion of his disappearance, and rebuild his command of the militia. The militia was his strength. It would protect him from the spies and from El-Akhtar. He dialled Jihaad's phone. It rang for a time until Jihaad picked up.

'Brother,' said Nadeer. 'It's me. I need your help.'

'Abu Nadeer?' said Jihaad. He sounded surprised. 'Are you okay, Pak?'

'It is urgent, Jihaad. You must come now.'

Nadeer heard road traffic in the background.

'Now, you fool.'

'Okay, Pak.'

Nadeer rang off and relaxed. Jihaad would understand. Jihaad would help explain.

He dozed. He heard a car in the distance. Half an hour had passed. He lay still and watched the ceiling while he waited. The engine noise increased, and the note changed. It was moving uphill, along the only road to the compound from Weda, but it wasn't Jihaad. Jihaad's car had made the journey many times and Nadeer was familiar with the sound. The engine approached within fifty metres of the villa and stopped. Nadeer listened, but the only sounds were the cicadas and the ceiling fan.

Another engine arrived, this one a motorcycle. He heard shouts and a door slam from where the car had stopped. The whine of the two-stroke engine cut through the din and continued past the front gate of the villa. It stopped five seconds later. More shouts, then silence.

He listened from the rear door. For ten minutes there was no other sound apart from the jungle beyond the walls. He checked the time: Jihaad should have been here by now. Something snapped at the front of the house as he returned inside. He moved through the house and saw the front gate move on its bolts. Someone called out to him.

Nadeer tensed. His hand gripped the doorhandle tight.

'Dear God,' he choked.

'Nadeer, you infidel bastard! We know you are there.'

He ran through the hall, to the bedroom, to the wardrobe. His fingers slipped on the dial of the safe. The combination deserted him. He turned it left, then right, but couldn't make it open. He swore, then heard the bang. He turned and saw them. He ran for the window and fell. One of them landed on him. He shouted and the other man covered his mouth. They tried to pull him but he convulsed and loosened their grip. His legs were free and he pushed for the window. A hand gripped his ankle and his face struck the concrete floor. He moaned. Blood flowed over the polished white tiles.

'Take him,' said a voice.

One of them lifted him by the shoulders and dragged him outside. A man watched on from the front gate. Through his blurred vision, Nadeer recognised him.

'Jihaad!' he shouted.

Someone pulled a hood over his head.

'Jihaad!'

They carried him along the road and loaded him into a van. They tied his hands to a seat and left him on the floor. The door closed, and he passed out.

They drove for hours. He vomited twice: once for nausea, again for the stench in his hood that was soiled with blood and vomit. They stopped and dragged him into a building where he cried out for Jihaad, desperate to explain what had happened and earn his forgiveness. Eventually, his pleas became curses. He denounced his brothers for their treachery and demanded his release.

He woke in darkness to the stench of the hood. The room was silent except for the echoes of his short, panicked breaths. He told himself to wait. They would eventually interrogate him, and he would tell them what the Australian had told him. He rehearsed his responses. They would believe it if he believed it himself.

The door shrieked on its hinges and crashed into the wall. He sat up with a start. Through the hood he saw the light and dark of figures as they moved into the room. 'Jihaad!' he shouted. 'Take me to Jihaad!' The men lifted him to his feet. They walked him along a tiled floor and through a doorway. The sun was on his neck. He heard truck engines. Someone opened a door and the men pushed him into the middle seat. He sat forward in the seat to take weight off his hands, but someone pushed him back. There were four of them. The vehicle accelerated, and he moaned for the pain in his wrists.

They stopped after a few minutes and pulled him from the vehicle. There was a loud call of adhan nearby, and in the distance, chanting. Someone shouted at him and shoved him forward, but he tripped and fell. More shouting. They kicked him, and he rolled to blunt further blows. 'Stand!' said a voice. He pushed his feet into the ground but his legs couldn't take his weight. Someone pulled him up by the base of the hood. He choked and kicked at the ground. Another man pushed him forward. The hood went dark, then light again.

They were in a courtyard. The chanting was louder now. The adhan had subsided, replaced now by a loudspeaker that echoed off the walls. He was propelled forward again. The voice grew louder.

'Ashhadu anna Muhammadan rasul-ullah. Ashhadu anna Muhammadan rasul-ullah!'

The loudspeaker was next to him now, then behind him. The crowd in front chanted in repeat.

'Hayya 'alas-salah. Hayya 'alas-salah.

'Hayya 'alal-falah. Hayya 'alal-falah.'

A boot struck his leg and he fell to his knees. The hood was ripped off to reveal a crowd of two dozen people that shouted their hatred for him.

'Allahu akbar!' shouted the speaker. *'Allahu akbar!'*

The crowd repeated after him.

Nadeer turned to see the speaker. He wore a balaclava, but the voice was unmistakable. 'Jihaad.'

Someone kicked him. 'Look forward!'

He lay on the ground to wait for the second kick, but it never came. He turned and saw the mosque behind him. Draped across it was *al-rayat*. A large man in black stood next to Jihaad bearing a sword. Nadeer began to panic. Someone lifted him and he screamed.

'We bear witness,' shouted Jihaad, *'to the destruction of our enemies, to the slaughter of the infidels, to the salvation of this promised land in the name of Allah, the one and only God.'*

The crowd chanted *'Allahu akbar!'*

'Jihaad, please!' shouted Nadeer. 'I will tell you everything, brother. I will bring you the spies. I love you, brother! Please—'

The next kick struck his kidney, and for an instant he thought he had been impaled with the blade. Another hand gripped him to hold him upright.

'We, the pure and pious citizens of North Maluku, pledge our allegiance to Islamic State and our fidelity to the prophet!'

Nadeer strained to follow the words, unable to believe they were from Jihaad's own mouth.

'We will wipe this land of those who fail to accept Allah into their hearts and who fail to follow the words of Mohammad, his one true prophet.'

The words rang in Nadeer's ears. He lost sense of hearing and balance. The crowd's chant faded to the background. He knew now that he would perish. For salvation he turned to his one true God, the one he had communed with in secret while he sought favour with the devils that now commanded him to die. He let his head fall forward and felt the blade against his neck.

'O Father,' he whispered. 'Into your hands I commend my spirit.'

Jihaad shouted again. *'Allah commands this sacred glory! Allahu akbar! Allahu akbar!'*

Nadeer barely heard him. The world fell away and he was one with God. 'Into your hands I commend my spirit. Into your hands I commend my spirit.'

He felt a hand on his head. It could have been Jesus, commanding his return to heaven. He felt his throat stretch taut, and the warmth of the sun on his face.

'See this before you!' shouted Jihaad. The crowd jeered in unison.

The blade felt cool on his neck.

'Death for those who oppose us,' shouted Jihaad. Another jeer from the crowd. Nadeer opened his eyes to see bright shapes flutter in the sky.

They might have been angels.

'Death to infidels!'

And he felt elation. Like blessed homecoming after a treacherous voyage.

'Into your hands I—'

22

CANBERRA

The old Saab wouldn't start. The engine turned over, the choke was out, but it didn't fire. It had been a mild day in Canberra, not cold enough for anything to seize, and the car had started without trouble that morning after Gibson's first night at his apartment in four days. It was nearly ten p.m. and there were no other cars in the lot. Just what Gibson needed.

He got out and checked the engine. It took ten minutes to discover the loose spark plug and hook it back on. He hoped he hadn't flooded the poor thing. One more crank. The engine turned and he massaged the accelerator – ignition, relief. Then the phone rang.

What now.

He nearly fumbled the phone as he took it from his trouser pocket. The screen showed a Jakarta number. The Australian embassy.

Gibson answered the call.

'You're not in,' said Ellis.

Obviously.

'I'm just leaving.'

'I need to call you on the secure line. It's urgent.'

The revs wavered as the Saab idled.

'What's this—never mind. Call me in ten.'

Ellis rang off.

Gibson let the Saab idle, not sure it would ever start again. He only needed five minutes to get upstairs. The rest went to charging the car.

The phone rang as he got to his office. He dumped his bag and picked up. 'Gibson.'

Ellis cleared his throat. 'Look, you remember how I told you I was working on Anas? Works for Hartanto. One of his underlings.'

Gibson remembered. He hadn't explicitly authorised Ellis to cultivate the BIN officer, but Ellis had a strong instinct for a good source, and Anas was close to Hartanto. So Gibson hadn't stopped him, either.

'Anyway, I got him talking. Took him out for a drink, splashed a bit of cash. Nice guy, just a bit lonely. Works for a prick.'

Gibson turned his computer on and thought of Hartanto. 'I know too well.'

'Then I baited him by airing some frustration around our handling of ANVIL. Said you guys were rushing things, pushing too hard; more people might get killed, that sort of thing, expecting him to just nod and chink my glass.'

'He didn't?'

'He went further,' said Ellis. 'Off the deep end, if you ask me. Started telling me all about problems inside BIN. Hartanto's fights with his bosses, enquiries from the ministry, usual bureaucratic shit.'

Footsteps approached. Scarlett appeared in the doorway. Gibson stared blankly, surprised she was back so late.

'Then he told me they've shut down ANVIL. As of today.'

Scarlett smiled briefly and continued on.

'Say that again?' said Gibson.

Ellis took an audible breath.

'Nadeer's dead, mate.'

Gibson sat up. 'How?'

'You can guess. Body delivered to a police station in Tobelo, head sold separately.'

'Christ,' said Gibson. He lifted his glasses and squeezed the bridge of his nose.

'Hartanto's pissed, as you'd expect,' said Ellis. 'The whole lot of them are.'

Gibson's computer finally came up with a login screen. He typed in his details and brought up an antiquated version of Outlook.

'You there?' said Ellis.

'Hang on,' said Gibson. He scanned the contents of his inbox, nothing but contact reports, expenditure forms and meeting requests – the administrative detritus of modern-day espionage, most of which remained unread. At the top, an emailed message from Ellis, but nothing else of note. 'We haven't received anything from them.'

'There might still be time to push it up the chain.'

Gibson let the events play out in his head. If he got to the DDG tonight there was a chance the minister could reach her counterpart by close of play. It would have to be indirect, to not expose Ellis's contact.

'Have you spoken to Jordan?' said Gibson.

There was a pause. 'No.'

'Liam?'

Ellis exhaled loudly into the phone. 'I think Jordan's up to something with that journo bird. Kovacevic or whatever.'

'Why would you think that?'

'Just a hunch,' said Ellis. 'Anas said BIN was done doing favours for him, so I asked what he meant. He said the girl was picked up by the cops up near Sabo. They had to bust her out of jail.'

'What's that got to do with Jordan?'

'He arranged her guides. Two BIN guys.'

Gibson squeezed his nose again. 'Jordan knows he can't collect on Australians. It doesn't make sense.'

Oh, but it did.

'They're more concerned he's leaking stuff to her,' said Ellis. 'It's all in the cable.'

Gibson double-clicked Ellis's message and scanned it. 'Thank you, Liam.'

'Cheers.'

Gibson cut the call, lifted the unclassified phone and dialled Carter's mobile. It went to Jonah Somerville's voicemail.

Gibson threw the phone down and let out an almighty *Fuck.* He scanned the confines of his tiny office in search of an explanation. 'Fuck,' he repeated while he thought through his options. After deciding, he read through Ellis's cable to double-check key facts, then rang the DDG.

Scarlett had reappeared. 'Everything okay?'

The call connected.

'Andy,' said the DDG.

Gibson took in the sight of her, then gave a brisk nod.

'Sorry to bother you late, Terry. We might have a situation—'

'It's fine, the minister called me an hour ago.' The DDG sounded weary. 'You didn't answer your mobile.'

'I'm at the office.'

'Sure. Well, go home and rest. Be in my office at seven.'

Gibson wanted to ask if he should prepare anything, but the DDG closed the call. Gibson knew he wouldn't sleep that night. He wasn't even sure the Saab would get him home. His sleeping kit lay at the foot of his desk, unwashed and uninviting, the smell of it only softened by a fine trace of perfume.

Suddenly, he had another idea.

'Thank you all for joining,' said the DDG. He resumed his throne behind the desk. His EA poured tea for the leadership team in court around the coffee table.

'Wish it could be under better circumstances.' The DDG held up a printed letter marked with the seal of Indonesian intelligence.

'This is formal notification that BIN has suspended all cooperation on Operation ANVIL until further notice.'

Gibson bowed in despair. Neill stroked his moustache and shook his head solemnly. The rest of the directors stared at the letter in stunned silence.

'Their minister called ours yesterday afternoon to give the good news. Our lady reminded him that confronting the threat of IS was of paramount importance to both nations, but he was adamant it was now an internal issue for Indonesia and wouldn't budge.'

'That's it?' said Neill, his face reddened. 'She just bent over and took that?'

'Watch it,' said Ops.

Neill was undeterred. 'North Maluku means more to us than to them. How can we stand by and let them turn the place into a bloody terror haven?'

'That's more like it.'

'They've lost confidence in us, Gary,' shouted the DDG. It was the first time Gibson could remember that he'd done so. 'We lost the bloody cut-out networks, Hasan was brutally bloody murdered, and now Nadeer has been delivered in pieces to their very own *bloody* police, postage paid. The situation is out of control, folks, and the Indonesians blame us. They have every right to.'

'Hold on, Terry,' said Gibson. 'Nadeer chose to go back.'

'Did he, Andy?'

There was silence. The room turned to look at Gibson as though expecting insight; more likely, to warn him off responding.

Gibson looked at his hands, then at the DDG. 'What do I tell Jordan?'

'Tell him to lay low while we sort things out. Maybe a week, maybe a few.'

'This could end badly for us,' said Gibson. 'We're taking our eyes off the ball.'

The DDG sighed. 'I'll speak with the DG and the minister. We'll come up with a plan.' He leaned over the desk and clasped his hands. 'You know how it works, Andy, it's always a negotiation. For now, make sure Jordan does what he's told.'

Carter finally answered on the fourth ring. Gibson had already placed seven calls.

'Where have you been?' said Gibson.

'Working.'

'Call me on your secure phone.'

They rang off. A minute later a call came thorough on Gibson's desk phone.

Gibson took in a long breath. 'What did Nadeer say to you when you offered him protection?'

'Not sure what you mean.'

'What did he say?' Gibson shouted.

'Like I told you, he wanted to go back. He hates us. Either way, it's not important. He gave us El-Akhtar, we need to act on that.'

'They beheaded him, Jordan.'

'That's his own fault.'

'You—*we* let him go back. That makes it our fault. Australia's. ANVIL is dead.'

'On who's say?'

'The minister's. The Indonesians went to her direct.'

'Fuck's sake, Andy, I don't have time for politics. A year from now this place won't even be part of Indonesia.'

'That's what they're afraid of,' said Gibson. 'It's over, Jordan. I need you to stand down. Remain in Ternate and keep your head down until we resolve this.'

Carter let out a frustrated sigh.

'And stay away from Kovacevic,' said Gibson.

Carter paused. 'Mind your own business.'

'You don't deny it.'

'Why would I?'

'Cut the crap, Jordan. You know full-well it's illegal to spy on Australians. And private or not, it's unprofessional.'

'Sure,' said Carter. 'I guess it is unprofessional. By the way, how's Scarlett?'

Bastard.

'She's fine. Goodbye, Jordan.'

23

TERNATE

Ana had wanted to write from a young age. Her father, an immigrant labourer, had encouraged at her at every turn, whether stories, poetry, or descriptions of flowers, aeroplanes, or strange people they encountered on the tram, and passed on whatever he learned from his night school English classes after his shifts on site each day. She developed quickly, and by her fifth birthday, their roles had reversed. She showed him the finer points of English grammar and taught him the new words she learned in school – some from the classroom, others from the playground – only to watch him rinse them away with his three nightly glasses of whisky that he insisted on like therapy for the self-declared failure of his life. Ana and her mother watched helplessly as melancholy and alcohol propelled his descent until finally, after the love had worn thin and the tears no longer flowed, he hit the bottom.

She started her cadetship the week after his suicide. Even then, she hadn't suffered writer's block. That first week she wrote a two-paragraph obituary for him that was printed in the following Sunday's *Age*, that on top of separate articles covering lost pets, a school fete and the election of a new chairperson to the Malvern High Parent's and Citizen's committee. Whatever the issue, words came to her freely and danced to whatever choreography she set for them in her mind, but now, in the dim light of her apartment, they retreated backstage, safe from the unseen hands that had manipulated her since her arrival in Ternate. Jonah was right: if not for his leads and his protection, she would have no story, even if he was wrong to think she would cower from him. She could afford to tolerate censorship for a few weeks at least, enough to compile what she knew would blow the lid on the social tragedy unfolding in Halmahera, and then she would return home, free to publish whatever she wanted. Home. Melbourne: the cleanliness and order of it, the casual conversations with strangers where she could think less about choices of words and turns of phrase and let her consciousness run free. It seemed light years away now, and she longed to bring a piece of it just a little closer, so she opened her phone, lay on her bed, and dialled a number she hadn't in months.

'Ana?'

'Mama.'

There was a hissing noise in the background.

'What's that?'

'I'm cooking.'

Ana wiped away a tear. 'Cooking what?'

'Dinner, dear. What time is it there?'

Ana pictured her mum in her tiny kitchen with the oversized cooktop her uncle had bought for her, so large that the door couldn't fully open. Then she pictured the backyard swing set amongst the overgrown grass and rusted bicycle frames, and her childhood bedroom, where the childhood teddy bear she left behind when she'd joined *The Age* still waited for her. 'It's dinner time, too,' she said.

'Is this urgent, dear?'

Ana's handset vibrated in her hand. 'No, Mama.'

'Your cousin Rita's family is here. I must go. I will call you soon.'

Ana wiped a tear. 'Okay.'

There was a rustling sound. Ana said a final 'I miss you,' but the line was silent. She took the phone from her ear and saw a WhatsApp notification. She opened it to find a blurry video thumbnail and single text message: *Your government did this.* Ana pressed play. The video was upside-down, and when she rotated her phone, she saw it was taken from the front gate to a mosque compound. In the distance, a black flag with scrawled white text hung across the facade of the main hall—

She bolted upright. The apartment was silent apart from the road noise and her own heartbeat. She took deep breaths to calm down and forced herself out of the bed to check the windows and doors were locked. Safe again in the bedroom, she stared at the phone, knowing what it now contained but praying it could not be true. She connected her earphones and hovered her thumb over the icon on the screen. She held her breath and counted to three.

Then she pressed play.

It took three attempts before Jonah picked up.

'I have something to show you,' said Ana.

'Not sure I follow.'

'I won't explain over the phone. If you want to see this before I go live with it, you need to come, now.'

The line went silent, like it had been cut. Ana gripped a lock of her hair and squeezed, anxious for his reply. Everything counted on it.

'Okay,' he said eventually. 'Thirty minutes.'

The footage was sharp, blurred only by the motion of whoever was filming. Based on the angle and movements of the camera, they had held the phone in their hand to hide the act. Bodies moved past in either direction until a man in fatigues stepped into frame to give a greeting that was drowned out by the sound of a loudspeaker. As the photographer moved into the courtyard, another man came into view and revealed the source of the noise, a hand-held public address speaker into which he shouted incomprehensible epithets and strict commands.

The camera panned to reveal several dozen townsfolk crowded into the forecourt of the Sabo mosque. The announcer shouted and they began to chant. It was obvious that the photographer was male by the way he jostled with men to reach the front of the crowd that began to chant. The camera went dark for a few seconds before the mosque appeared. The crowd shouted again: *'Allahu akbar!'* The camera stabilised on the front entrance. The announcer shouted and pointed at a man who knelt on the concrete beside a black-clad figure holding something in his right hand. Only when it was raised to the back of the kneeling man's neck did the horror become apparent. Seconds went by, then the camera was deafened as the crowd cheered the falling head and cried for glory.

The picture smeared with motion and the video cut to black.

'Anyone else seen this?' said Jonah. He sat at the desk holding the phone. Ana hovered over his shoulder.

'Not this copy. I searched online and no-one's posted it.'

He played the video again, pausing at critical points to study details.

'Why did you want me to see this?' he said.

'To find out what it was worth to you.'

He turned to her and made a quizzical look.

She sat down on the sofa. 'I want a comment, Jonah. I want to know what the Australian Government is doing in North Maluku before I tell every voter and commentator that you're responsible for what happened in that video.'

He drummed his hands on his knees, then stood up. 'I can't help you with that.'

'I know you're involved.' She got up and stood in front of him. 'You were the one who arranged my release from Tobelo. Raf and Jaja were intelligence officers and they put in the call. It wasn't part of your plan, was it, but you needed me.'

His face twitched, and he turned from her. 'Got any other theories?'

'Maybe the inspector-general will if I tell her you were spying on an Australian journalist.'

He gave no reaction. Instead, he stepped to the desk and put down the phone.

'What are you doing in North Maluku, Jonah?'

He leaned on the edge of the desk. The wooden top groaned under his weight.

'Answer me!'

He turned around, rested against the desk and folded his arms. 'I'm not the story,' he said.

'You will be if you don't tell me.'

He raised one hand and scratched his eye. 'Who sent you the video, Ana?'

'Answer my question!'

His hand returned to hold his arm. His face showed only a mixture of anger and concern.

'Listen,' he said. 'Whoever sent this to you'—he lifted his hand again and gestured at the phone—'took steps to conceal it, which means he's working against the fanatics you see in the video. It won't take them long to find him.'

'How?' she said. 'No-one even knows about it.'

He seemed amused. Not for the first time, Ana felt like a child. She resented him for it, just like his secrecy.

'You ask me what I do here,' he said. He stepped forward and spoke in her ear. 'All I do is get people to talk. It's easy. No-one here can keep a secret. Chances are that someone involved in the production of this'—he waved at the phone—'has spoken to someone they shouldn't, everyone in Sabo knows about the video, and some wannabe Al-Baghdadi is making casting calls for the next one. Follow?' He sat against the desk again. 'The only way your source gets out alive is if you tell me who he is.'

'I can't do that,' she said.

'Will you publish his beheading, too?'

'Fuck you.'

'You might make front page.'

'Fuck you,' she repeated. She fell to the sofa as the weight of responsibility for a man's life began to crush her. She brought her hands to her face and began to cry. Cry for the mess she had created. Cry for the man at the end of the sword. Cry for her naivete.

Jonah sat beside her and placed his arm around her. 'This'—he waved a hand to signal the world—'is the truth that you seek,' he said. 'Bad people do bad things. Good people do them, too.'

She sobbed into her hands and thought of her father. His despair, his numbness. Nothing he did ever made a difference. She wondered why that would drive a man to kill himself, when the alternative – to feel responsible for what happened – was so much worse.

She let out a shivery breath and composed herself. She lowered her hands and peered at the network of lines strung across her palms, deeper now than they had been in Jakarta.

'His name is Sayeed,' she said. 'He's a leader of one of the Islamist groups. Al Ramah.' She looked up.

Jonah gave no reaction.

'Do you know him?' she said.

'No.'

She shook her head in dismay. 'Can you find him?'

He stood up.

'Jonah?'

He walked to the front door, then turned to her and said, 'Stay here for now.'

She thought of places she might go.

'Okay.'

24

CENTRAL HALMAHERA

Sayeed had almost completed morning prayer when Reza came for him. He was bowed, arms outstretched towards Mecca, arthritic fingers squeezed tightly around a battered Quran. He filled his lungs with the still morning air, coughed the final line of the *rak'ah*, then turned to his security chief.

'Speak.'

Reza knelt close to him. 'You must come, Abu Sayeed.' His voice was low and calm. 'It is a matter of security. It is urgent.'

The tent was dark except for a small lantern by his bed that lit the corners of Reza's face. Sayeed rose to a seated position, his head bowed, and recited the *tashahhud*. He would not be hurried.

'What kind of security matter?' he said eventually.

'I cannot say here,' said Reza. 'Please, Abu.'

Sayeed pocketed the Quran in the lapel of his tunic and donned a green overcoat. Reza stood by the door and checked outside was clear. When he was satisfied, he gestured to Sayeed to go.

The camp was quiet. For security reasons, there were no prayer calls here, so most of the inhabitants prayed privately inside their tents. Sayeed suspected they did not pray at all, but they were loyal, which mattered more. The two men moved quietly among haphazard rows of shelters erected deep amongst the foliage, each adorned with the black flag of Islamic State, that formed the accommodation and storage areas of the militant headquarters of Al Ramah. Reza's four-wheel-drive pinged in the cool air at the end of the path. He had arrived recently.

Reza opened a rear door. 'Please.'

Sayeed climbed in and lit a cigarette. Reza checked something in the rear hold before he joined him and started the vehicle. Sayeed held tightly as Reza negotiated the rutted mountain track.

'Tell me what is going on,' said Sayeed. Reza held up his hand to indicate silence.

Sayeed lit another cigarette.

They reached a highway and turned east. The sky above the hilltops was deep red with the dawn. Apart from the sound of the Landcruiser, the jungle was silent.

'We found the traitor, Pak,' said Reza.

Sayeed flicked his cigarette and smiled. A week ago, his men had discovered one of the fighters collecting details of Al Ramah weapons caches. To his frustration, his men had failed to catch him, but it was only a matter of time. Yet, he hadn't known Reza was involved in the case.

He held a breath of smoke and let it out as he spoke. 'Where?'

Reza scanned the road ahead, then his mirrors. 'In Subaim, last night. I have an informant there.'

Ibrahim. The dog of Subaim had long worked to sabotage Al Ramah. It made no difference if they had signed a pact, the distrust coursed through Sayeed and Ibrahim like blood. Then again, Ibrahim already knew of the weapon caches.

Sayeed threw his cigarette from the window and lit another. 'Did you recover the files?'

Reza glanced in the mirror and hesitated. 'I'm sorry, Abu.' He shifted down a gear as the road steepened. 'He must have sold them.'

There were no files.

'Sold them to who?'

'I do not know. We have not yet forced him to speak. We thought you would want to be there.'

He did. If only it were true.

'Where is he now?'

'Somewhere secret, Abu. No-one will disturb us. It is not far.'

Sayeed looked at his phone. 'Pull over.'

'Abu?'

'I need to make a phone call. There is signal here.'

Reza's hands gripped tight on the wheel, then he pulled over into a small gap in the trees.

'Stay in the car, please, Pak.'

'Ya, ya, okeh.'

Sayeed's call was picked up straight away. 'Pak,' said a voice.

'I will not make our meeting at ten,' said Sayeed.

The man on the other end scrambled. 'Where are they taking you?'

'I don't know. Puffed Rice. Tea.' *Mountains. Jungle.*

'Wait.' There was a whipping sound, like flicking through pages of a notebook.

'Which direction?' said the man.

'Three o'clock.' *East.*

'How far?'

Reza watched him in the mirror.

'One hundred.' *Far.* 'I must go.'

'We will find you.'

Sayeed rang off.

They drove in silence. Sayeed savoured his cigarette and the sunrise. After an hour they stopped again. Reza waited for five minutes to check for anyone following, then turned onto a track that led uphill into the jungle.

Reza put the Landcruiser into high gear and climbed the track. The engine roared with the strain. The road flattened out and they entered a long clearing that stretched north along a ridgeline.

Halfway along the western edge was a cabin. Another Landcruiser was parked outside. Otherwise, the clearing was empty.

Reza parked next to the other Landcruiser and they climbed out. The morning was bright now, the sky cloudless. Apart from the songs of birds, it was silent. The air smelled of cloves.

Reza retrieved a bag from the back of the vehicle then joined Sayeed. 'They are inside,' he said.

Sayeed walked up to the house. It was a newer construction, built with reinforced concrete, but the jungle had already claimed it. The walls were cracked and covered in moss. The windows were dusty and opaque. The paint, once green, had long faded. Something scraped on the floor as he approached. Reza moved past him and opened the door.

Sayeed stood at the threshold and waited for his eyes to adjust to the darkness. A chair stood at the centre of a sitting room, but the cabin was unfurnished. He heard a noise, something like a footstep. He stepped inside for a closer look. A figure appeared and moved into the sitting room, then, to his right, another. The taller man stepped forward into the light. Sayeed recognised him as the Australian. The other man he knew as Yoyok.

Reza pushed him forward. Sayeed turned and saw the barrel of a rifle aimed at his chest. The bag lay on the ground.

'Kneel,' said Reza.

'You're a dead man.'

'Kneel!'

'Better do as he says,' said the Australian.

Sayeed lowered himself onto one knee. Reza kept the rifle pointed at his head.

'You dog,' hissed Sayeed. He lowered the other leg.

'Hands on head,' said Reza.

Sayeed brought his hands up and placed them on his taqiyah. One of the other men pulled them down behind his back and the taqiyah fell. Plasticuffs tightened around his wrists. Reza lowered the weapon and patted him down with one hand. He reached inside Sayeed's overcoat and took out the Quran. From the opposite lapel he retrieved the phone. He handed both items to the Australian. 'Clean.'

The Australian stood in front of him and tapped the Quran in his hand. 'Put him on the chair.'

Sayeed's breath echoed in the empty room as Reza forced him, at gunpoint, to sit down. Yoyok forced his ankles to the base of the chair and cuffed them tight, then tied his hands to it. Sayeed pulled against the restraints.

'Watch him,' said the Australian. Yoyok moved behind Sayeed. Reza followed the Australian outside.

Sayeed strained at the cuffs. 'Dogs!'

25

The sun had cleared the treetops to illuminate the clearing. The access track cut into the jungle at the southern end. The house was bordered by a gravel escarpment that ran north for fifty metres along the western edge of the clearing. Apart from the singing of the birds and Reza's cooling Landcruiser, there was no sound.

'Anyone know we're here?' said Carter.

Reza stood upright, shoulders back, M4 in his arms across his chest. He had served ten years in the infantry before joining Al Ramah's security arm. Unbeknownst to them, Reza had been discharged for selling weapons to militants in Sulawesi. Carter saved him from military prison and offered to plant him in Sayeed's organisation. BIN and ASIS would never allow it, so Carter ran him off-books.

'Nobody saw us leave,' said Reza.

'What about your brother-in-law?'

'He thinks I am alone. I stay here sometimes to hike in the forest.'

Carter looked at the two Landcruisers. 'It won't look like you're alone.'

Reza shrugged.

'Stay out here,' said Carter. 'We need a few hours alone with him.'

Reza leaned his rifle against one of the vehicles and offered Carter a cigarette. Carter declined and he lit up.

'Fine by me, Pak.'

Sayeed stared as Carter entered the sitting room. He was a long, skeletal man, and his skin, where it was taut, exposed jagged edges of bones that seemed bent and crooked from overuse. Yet by reputation he was anything but fragile, so Yoyok hovered over his shoulder, armed with a pistol.

'What do you want?' hissed Sayeed.

Carter kneeled in front of him. 'I want you to tell me about El-Akhtar.'

Sayeed scoffed. 'I know no such man.' His emaciated wrists strained at the plasticuffs. 'Release me.'

'Save it,' said Carter. 'We know about the deal.'

Sayeed glared at him.

Yoyok stepped away and brought a cardboard folder. Carter opened it and held up a page. 'Recognise this?'

Sayeed spat at him. 'I will tell you nothing.'

Carter wiped his face with his shirt. 'This document says you agree to hand over operational control of all Al Ramah militia, weapons, encampments, businesses and places of worship to Barpemis.'

Sayeed said nothing.

'It goes on to say that you agree to terminate all conduct with the government and purge Al Ramah of any "secret agents". I guess that's why we haven't heard from you.'

Sayeed strained at his cuffs. 'Fuck you!' he screamed. *'Pis off shet.'*

Carter placed a gentle hand behind Sayeed's neck. 'This'—he held the contract in front of Sayeed's face—'is a humiliation.'

Sayeed's breaths became short and rapid.

Carter squeezed Sayeed's neck just enough to be felt. 'Listen carefully.'

Sayeed winced.

'We know El-Akhtar brokered this agreement,' said Carter, 'which makes you an accessory to terrorism. I can protect you from arrest, prosecution and near-certain execution, but only if you talk.'

Sayeed gave a derisive sniff. 'Your protection is worthless.'

Carter cocked his head. 'This is tiresome, Sayeed.' He squeezed.

Sayeed groaned. Carter released him and sat down.

'You think you are so powerful,' said Sayeed. He took a long, sharp breath and spat on the floor. 'It is you who is the humiliation, Pak. For too long you have played us for fools, turned brother against brother, like a game. No more.'

Yoyok leaned against the wall and folded his arms.

'El-Akhtar united us,' Sayeed continued. 'Turned our energy away from one another to liberate us from you and the oppressors. He will lead us to a united, free, Islamic North Maluku. I would give my family again just to see this.'

'Would Nadeer have said the same thing?'

Sayeed exhaled through his nose.

Carter stood up and handed the file to Yoyok. Sayeed watched him closely.

'I need you to tell me about El-Akhtar's plans,' said Carter as he sat down. 'Who he has united to his cause, where he gets his resources, what he plans for the elections. I can keep you from harm's way, Sayeed.'

Sayeed grinned. 'Just like Nadeer.'

'This is no joke,' said Carter. 'People could die. You could die.'

'I will die with honour. I will never betray El-Akhtar.'

'But you already have.'

Sayeed gave the slightest reaction, a brief widening of the eyes before he looked up at Yoyok for explanation.

Carter opened his phone to a video app and held the phone so that Sayeed could see what played. Islamic chants filled the sitting room as Nadeer was executed. Sayeed leaned to one side and spat on the floor. Spittle clung to his chin.

'It was you who told Ana Kovacevic about Sabo, wasn't it?'

The hiss of Sayeed's breathing filled the room.

'You wanted her to see this.'

Sayeed looked at the floor, then up again, flicking to each spy.

'El-Akhtar told me to film it,' he said. 'Like *Da'esh.*'

'Bullshit,' said Carter. 'This was filmed in secret.'

Sayeed's head slumped forward.

'Perhaps you're not as loyal as you say.'

Sayeed stared at the floor.

'Maybe you were up to your old tricks. You knew El-Akhtar would suspect betrayal if this was ever published. He'd have no choice but to investigate everyone that was close to him. Maqsood, Ibrahim, all your old rivals.'

Carter gripped Sayeed's hair and lifted his face. 'Which means there was something he would find. Something you couldn't admit to knowing.'

Sayeed's eyes were bloodshot. His breath smelled of digested tempè.

'What was it?' Carter squeezed Sayeed's jaw. Sayeed moaned. 'Tell me!'

Sayeed let out a gasp.

Carter released him. Sayeed's head fell and he coughed for breath.

'Say that again.'

'You—' Sayeed coughed a ball of phlegm onto the floor. 'Your deal with Maqsood.'

Yoyok frowned.

'Explain,' said Carter.

A long trail of spit hung from the corner of Sayeed's mouth and swayed as he heaved for breath. 'I found out Maqsood was negotiating with you—the government,' he said quietly. 'One of my men heard about it.'

The two spies shared a glance.

'I watched Maqsood. Who he met, where he went. I always

knew he was a traitor to the caliphate. We all knew, except El-Akhtar.' Sayeed coughed again. 'So I proved it.'

Yoyok opened a bottle of water and let Sayeed drink.

'Proved it how?' said Carter.

Sayeed swallowed with discomfort. Water dripped on the ball of mucus to form a green pool on the floor.

'He travelled to Kusuri five nights ago. I know because I followed him.'

Yoyok gave Carter a bemused look. Kusuri was a highway town in the hinterland, half-way between Tobelo and Kao. Neither man had been there recently.

'This was not unusual, except that there were police.' His breathing slowed. He looked at Carter. 'At first, we thought he had been tricked and that they would arrest him, but they did not. They were there to secure the meeting. *Your* meeting.'

He cleared his throat and smirked. More phlegm dribbled from his bottom lip. 'Do you deny it?'

Carter ignored the question. 'Why didn't you tell El-Akhtar?'

Sayeed laughed. 'He would assume I was disloyal to Maqsood and that I had broken my agreement.' His face straightened. 'El-Akhtar demands absolute loyalty. It is his weakness and his strength.'

'So El-Akhtar had to discover Maqsood's betrayal for himself.'

Sayeed nodded and looked at the water. Yoyok let him drink again.

'What if he already knew? What if he had instructed it?'

Sayeed scoffed. 'You know nothing of this man.'

Carter stood up. Yoyok let Sayeed drink again, then followed Carter to the rear bedroom. A window looked south over the clearing. Another door faced the escarpment. Yoyok closed the door to the sitting room. An engine droned in the distance.

Carter kept his voice low. 'What the fuck are your guys doing?'

'Nothing, bos. I swear.'

'Is Hartanto up to something?'

'Why would he tell me?'

Carter watched him. 'You better not be lying, mate.'

'Trust me. I'm here helping you, no? Not even Hartanto knows.'

The engine grew louder. Carter turned his ear to the noise.

'What is that?'

Yoyok stepped to the window. 'Fuck,' he said. 'Bos, look.'

A white Honda motorcycle emerged from the treeline, one hundred metres away. There were two on board. Reza was by the Landcruisers. He stubbed a cigarette with his foot and walked towards them as they approached.

Carter pointed to the next room. 'Keep him quiet.'

Yoyok nodded and left.

The motorcycle pulled to a stop and Reza spoke to the rider. The passenger dismounted and peered at the house. The two men wore cargo pants and long-sleeved shirts, no helmets. Fighting kit.

Carter unholstered his Glock and chambered a round.

Reza was still speaking to the driver. He offered the men cigarettes, then pointed at the surrounding jungle. The rider turned around and the passenger climbed aboard. A few seconds later, they disappeared into the trees. Reza ran for the house.

Carter moved to the sitting room to meet him. Yoyok had one arm around Sayeed's neck, the other hand over the man's mouth. Reza appeared at the front door.

'Who were they?' said Carter.

Reza glanced at both spies. 'Al Ramah,' he said. 'They will be back.'

Yoyok swore under his breath.

'What did they want?' said Carter.

'They said they were looking for him.' Reza pointed at Sayeed. 'I told them he wasn't here. I said I was here to visit my brother-in-law.'

Carter grabbed Reza by the arm. 'Why would they be looking for him? It's only been a few hours.'

'I don't know, bos.'

Sayeed groaned. Yoyok tightened his grip.

'Got something to say, Sayeed?' said Carter.

Sayeed groaned again. Yoyok released him and he fell forward. Carter caught him and pushed him upright. The Islamist fought a moment for breath, then laughed. 'You are a fool, Reza.'

'What the fuck does that mean?' said Carter.

Sayeed nodded towards Reza. 'Ask him.'

Reza stared at Sayeed.

'Reza!'

Reza's gaze returned to Carter. He blinked. 'He said he had to call someone,' he said. 'I didn't want him to become suspicious, so I let him.'

Yoyok's head sank.

'He tricked me.' Reza slouched against the wall.

Carter turned to Sayeed. 'Who did you call?'

Sayeed's face broke into a grin. 'You still have time to escape.'

'He tricked me,' repeated Reza.

'Who did you call?' shouted Carter.

'Listen.'

Yoyok had his hand up to signal silence. The sound of the motorcycle engine had returned. Other engines followed, lower in pitch. Vehicles.

'Get him out,' shouted Carter.

'It's too late, bos,' said Yoyok. 'Leave—'

Yoyok's gaze shifted to something behind Carter.

'Reza, no!'

Carter turned. Reza had his rifle at his shoulder, finger on the trigger, aimed at Sayeed.

He fired.

Carter was knocked over by the shock of the muzzle blast and landed facing the room. Sayeed's head had exploded over the sitting room wall. Yoyok writhed on the ground, covered in chunks of red flesh. Reza was still. Carter checked himself for injury. His ears rang. He could no longer hear the engines.

He got to his feet and grabbed Reza. 'What the fuck!'

Reza pushed him off. 'It's done, bos.' He wiped blood from his face. 'He would have killed my family.'

The vehicles had entered the clearing. Carter left Reza and watched from the window. The motorcycle was followed by two utility vehicles, two men on each tray, each armed with an AK-47. The utes pulled off the track and the men jumped off. Two men climbed out of each cab.

Yoyok rubbed his ear.

'Can you walk?' said Carter.

Yoyok stood up, panting for breath, and wiped a blood-soaked chunk of bone from his face. 'Ya, bos.' He spat blood.

The Al Ramah fighters assembled at the vehicles. One of them called out, checked his weapon and began to walk towards the house.

'From the rear door it's ten metres to the treeline,' said Carter.

'There's no time,' said Reza. His eyes were on the scene outside.

The lead fighter called something out.

'Got a better idea?'

Reza turned to face them. 'I will go out the front,' he said. 'When I start shooting, you go.'

'They'll fucking kill you.'

Reza shrugged.

'Reza!' called the voice. The leader was twenty metres from the house. The others loitered by the vehicles, smokes in hand.

Reza stepped to the front door and checked his weapon. 'Go,' he said.

The leader called out again.

Reza cracked the door, peeked, then stepped outside. The door closed.

Carter crouched and looked at Yoyok. Yoyok nodded.

They had barely moved when Reza fired a three-round burst from the balcony. The walls did nothing to absorb the shock. Carter stumbled after Yoyok to the back door. Men screamed in the distance.

Carter opened the door wide enough to see the Al Ramah vehicles. Reza fired another burst. Rounds ricocheted off one of the utilities. The fighters scrambled for cover. Carter could only see four of them.

'You set?' said Carter.

The scene erupted as the fighters returned fire at Reza. Carter took cover.

Reza followed up with another burst, this time from near the Landcruisers.

'He's drawing them away,' said Yoyok.

The edge of the jungle was uphill from the house. The excavated ground was uneven and covered in gravel.

Another round cracked over the house, followed by shouts.

'Get to the trees. I'll cover you.'

Reza fired again. Two bursts this time.

The fighters returned fire.

Yoyok stepped to the threshold. He glanced at Carter and nodded.

Then he ran.

As he crossed the threshold, there was a shout. Something moved to his left. Carter looked up as a fighter broke cover from a tree, weapon raised.

Yoyok shielded his face as the first round exploded in the gravel. He had taken three steps, four, then he stumbled as the second bullet struck him in the thigh. Carter raised the Glock, foresight in focus over the shooter. Yoyok pushed himself onto his hands and knees and tried to kick forward. Carter took up first trigger pressure and tensed his arms. Second pressure. *Pop.* The pistol jerked back. The shooter fired again. A round exploded through Yoyok's shoulder blade and he fell. Carter aimed again. *Pop.* The shooter had disappeared. Carter watched and waited. Nothing.

'Yoyok!'

Yoyok lay four metres from the house. Carter scrambled to reach him. There was more gunfire from the front of the house.

Carter lifted Yoyok under the arms and dragged him inside. The Indonesian's head lolled as Carter sat him up against the wall and searched desperately for sign of life. No pulse and no breath. He was gone.

Silence. No sign of the shooter. Carter stumbled backwards to the wall opposite his dead comrade. A shout from the clearing broke his trance.

Reza shouted something, then fired a series of single shots.

Carter checked the escarpment and forced himself to run. His feet slipped as he climbed the gravel. There was more shooting, but no cracks overhead. They were still shooting at Reza.

The treeline was three metres away. Two. One. No-one shot at him. He broke through the first layer of foliage and collapsed behind a tree. He gasped for breath and looked around. He could see no more than a few metres into the jungle. He heard shouts from the clearing and turned to see them drag Reza's body from behind one of the Landcruisers. One of the men shouted and pointed towards the treeline.

Carter took one more look at the house. Yoyok's body was slumped in the doorway, helpless and lifeless. Somewhere beyond the green wall of the jungle was the man who had killed him, but so was freedom. There was no other option, so Carter said a quiet farewell to Yoyok, turned, and ran.

26

CANBERRA

It was standing room only inside the SCIF. Only the DDG, Security and the translator had secured seats. The rest stood facing the far wall. A video, filmed with a mobile phone, played on the television. The cameraman adjusted his grip on the phone and stepped out of a vehicle. A gunman greeted him with the usual *'assalamu alaikum'* and beckoned him to follow. The cameraman began to commentate.

'He says this is where the great leader Sayeed perished at the hands of the infidels,' said the translator. 'Praise be to God.'

The camera panned over the scene. Someone rendered care to a man sitting against a utility in the middle of the clearing. Beyond were two Landcruisers, and up the slope a small house sat near the treeline. The cameraman followed the gunman and spoke to the wounded man, blood trickling from his abdomen, but received no reply. They continued to the Landcruisers. The camera swept to a body.

'This man is a traitor to Al Ramah,' said the translator. She could have been reading a weather report. 'May God punish him and his family for eternity.' The cameraman spat on the corpse.

Scarlett paused the video. 'This man is Reza,' she said. 'Head of Sayeed's personal security detail. He's not on our books, but we think he was working with Jordan and Yoyok. Based on the location of his body, he might have been trying to draw the attackers from the house.'

'Poor bastard,' whispered Ops.

The video continued. The camera panned to the house. The door was open. Two gunmen smoked on a small balcony, AKs in hand. The cameraman called out to them. 'He asks where the body is,' was the translation. The gunmen waved him up and directed him inside the darkened room. It took a second for the exposure to adjust and reveal a body lying on the floor, still strapped to a chair.

'Y'allah, y'allah,' said the cameraman.

The phone shook as he spoke to himself. The translator continued: 'He says the infidels executed this great man. They will pay the ultimate price, God willing.'

The camera panned over Sayeed's legs and chest before settling on his mangled face. Scarlett paused. Security and Neill looked away from the screen.

There was a black dot slightly above the left eye, the size of a five-cent piece. The head appeared flattened where the cranium had exploded. Blood pooled on the floor.

'The gunshot wound is consistent with an assault rifle fired from close range,' said Scarlett. 'Too devastating to be from a pistol. It rules Jordan out.'

'Not as far as the Indonesians are concerned,' said the DDG. 'Carry on.'

The cameraman continued through the house to the rear door. A body was visible next to it. There was a collective groan as Yoyok's face came into view. The cameraman held his face up to the camera and spoke. 'He says death to government spies.' The camera panned out the door and adjusted to the light. A streak of blood ran along the ground from the threshold.

'He was shot outside,' said Scarlett. 'He either crawled back inside, or someone moved him.'

Legal held his hand to his mouth, ready to kiss his half-dozen gold rings. The camera panned up a small escarpment to the jungle. More Al Ramah men paced the edge of the clearing.

The cameraman walked up to the fighters. Two more emerged from the jungle, one carrying a body over his shoulders. The audience stiffened. The cameraman insisted the body be put down. Only once it was clear the victim was Al Ramah did anyone relax. The footage focused on a gunshot wound in the left thigh where the man had bled out. 'Praise be to God,' said the translator.

The video ended.

The DDG turned to face the room. 'So where does that leave Jordan?'

'Assuming he was there, we think he managed to get to the treeline,' said Scarlett. 'It's consistent with where Yoyok was found and the dead guy in the jungle. From there he had a chance of escape. Unfortunately, his mobile and satphone are disconnected.'

The DDG turned to Gibson. 'Any idea what he was doing out there after you'd told him to stand down?'

Gibson realised he was frowning. 'We don't know for sure he was there.'

The DDG held his gaze. Gibson returned the stare, then broke eye contact.

'The Indonesians are pretty sure he was,' said the DDG. He spoke to the room. 'He's wanted for questioning, of course, and they'll go to town on him. *Persona non grata,* international scandal, and humiliation for this service, guilty or not.'

The SCIF fell silent except for the hum of the air conditioner. Each person stared at their own patch of wall.

To everyone's surprise, it was Security who finally spoke. 'So how do we find him?'

The DDG's gaze returned to Gibson. The rest of the room followed suit.

'I'll get Liam on a plane to Ternate,' said Gibson. From Jakarta, Ellis was still the better part of a day away from Ternate, but closer than anyone else.

'Send the whole bloody station,' said Ops.

Gibson shook his head. 'If the Indonesians know we've lost him, we'll lose whatever influence we have left. Liam is solid; he knows the region.'

The DDG raised an eyebrow. 'You don't need him in Jakarta?'

It was a fair question. Ellis had made headway with Anas, a valuable source within Hartanto's inner circle; sending him to Ternate meant ASIS would lose insight into Hartanto's next move.

'It's more important we protect Jordan.'

The DDG gazed at him before nodding. 'Fine, make it happen,' he said. 'Updates daily.'

The group filed out. As soon as Gibson got to his office, he picked up the secure phone.

'Ellis.'

'Liam, it's me. How soon can you get to Ternate?'

Ellis suppressed a curse. 'Tomorrow. Why?'

'Jordan's missing.'

'Missing how?'

'Missing missing. I need you to get over there and track him down.'

'How the hell am I supposed to do that?'

Gibson tried not to think of the rules he was about to break.

'Find Kovacevic.'

CENTRAL HALMAHERA

The beat of helicopter blades danced across distant treetops and echoed off the mountainside. The pitch and volume oscillated while noise advanced and retreated from all directions like an apparition, rising to a high shrill before fading below the din of the protesting cicadas. For ten minutes this continued as the pilot and crew searched for Carter, while he waited for them at the edge of a logging clearing that extended over a large mountain spur. He had only given them rough coordinates to find him. It kept his options open.

He had trekked for hours through jungle to make his escape. He hadn't planned to lose the Landcruiser but knew that the mountain contours would lead him north to a highway logging village. It was a risk: Al Ramah controlled most of the region and would have put the word out. But a town meant phones, vehicles and people, all of which could be useful.

He had reached the town after dark. Apart from the occasional bus or lorry along the highway, the streets were deserted. At the centre of the village was a row of shuttered commercial buildings – only a small grocer remained open. The young girl at the counter wore no hijab and played with a smartphone. She watched him curiously as he entered.

'I'm a tourist,' he said to her in deliberately broken Indonesian. 'I got lost in the mountains. Has anyone been searching for me?'

She studied his face, then shook her head.

Al Ramah hadn't got to her.

'Can I use your phone?' said Carter. He held out a hundred-thousand Rupiah note.

She looked at the cash, then at him, then put the phone on the counter. He thanked her, walked outside and watched the street while he made a call. Thirty minutes later, he reached the end of a track that led uphill from the centre of town. It was another two hours before the utility turned off the highway and climbed towards him.

The headlights bobbed and weaved over the rutted track. Carter stepped in front of them as the utility came to a halt in a cloud of dust. The lights went out. Carter climbed into the passenger seat and shook Raf's tattooed hand. The Indonesian smiled and handed over a six-pack of bottled water.

'I came as fast as I could,' he said. His tattoos gleamed under the moonlight as he grabbed a bottle of his own and drank. 'It's bad, bos. Al Ramah sent some video to Hartanto. I never seen him so pissed off. They must know BIN is involved.' The mohawk fell across his face as he removed his cap. 'Bos?'

'They got Yoyok, that's why,' said Carter.

Raf clicked his tongue. 'How?'

'Shot,' said Carter. He rubbed a hand over his face. 'It was quick.'

Raf bowed his head. *'Mashallah.'*

The two men sat in silence to remember their mate. Raf, because he had long looked up to his elder colleague; Carter, for being responsible for his death. He alone had organised Sayeed's interrogation and obliged when Yoyok insisted he not do it alone. Yoyok should be the one sitting here, he thought. It was Yoyok who had earned the vindication of what they had learned.

'You brought it?' Carter said eventually.

Raf sniffed and reached behind his seat. He produced a mud-stained satchel bag and handed it to Carter. Inside was a phone, map and a set of keys. 'Bike's on the back tray.'

Carter unfolded the map and held it under the moonlight. 'Where is BIN searching?'

Raf sat up and cleared his throat. 'South, mostly,' he said. 'They think you went downhill. Kopassus is not so sure.'

'Sugianto?'

'Ya, bos.'

Carter studied the map. When he'd picked out his route, he refolded it and placed it in the bag. 'Give me a hand.'

They climbed out and slid the bike off the tray. Carter inserted the key and turned the ignition. The motorcycle started without hesitation.

He killed the engine and turned to Raf. 'I need you to get a message to Sugianto.'

'Sure, bos.'

Carter took out the map again and indicated a valley deep in central Halmahera. 'Tell him he can find me here.'

Raf examined the location on the map, as if to memorise it. 'When?'

'Tomorrow, after sunrise.' He gave the map to Raf and slung the bag over his shoulder. 'One more thing.'

'Bos?' Raf's eyes glistened.

'Take care of Yoyok's family. I don't trust Hartanto not to fuck them over.'

Raf placed his hand on his heart. 'I will, bos.'

Carter watched the Indonesian climb into the truck and reverse to the highway. Once the truck had gone, he started the motorcycle.

The clearing filled with the sound of rotors. Carter scanned the treetops and saw movement to the east. The sound receded, only to re-emerge as the light special forces helicopter climbed above the lip of the spur. The motorcycle lay on the grass, fifty metres from the treeline and directly beneath the chopper's path as it swooped over the clearing. Carter drank the remains of a bottle of water, reclined against a tree, and waited.

The helicopter returned low over the trees. Carter walked into the clearing, hands above his head, and waited by the motorcycle, the satchel bag at his feet. The chopper entered a hover twenty metres away. It tilted and drifted towards Carter until he could see the whites in the eyes of the Kopassus soldiers as they trained their rifles on him. Sugianto, one arm braced on the bulkhead, guided the pilot through an intercom headset.

The downwash kicked dust and leaves as the helicopter touched down. Two troopers jumped off, rifles up, and moved directly towards Carter. 'Get down!' they shouted. Carter dropped to his knees and kept his arms up. Four more troopers filed out of the helicopter and encircled him.

The first trooper stopped three metres away and trained his rifle on Carter's chest while his buddy stepped behind Carter and searched him. The Glock came out, then the phone. Carter felt a boot between his shoulder blades, then, a kick. He lay where he fell, arms outstretched, as the downwash of the helicopter blades swept over his back.

The soldiers sifted Carter's bag then shouted back to the helicopter. The helicopter turbines whined as they shut down.

'Get him up,' said Sugianto.

Two hands went under Carter's arms and lifted him. He kicked his legs forward so he could stand.

'Enough.'

Sugianto stood hands on hips, dressed in clean-cut cams and the maroon beret of the Kopassus regiment.

The soldiers released Carter. One of them walked to Sugianto and spoke in his ear, then showed him the pistol and satchel bag. Sugianto grunted.

Carter brushed dirt from his clothes. 'Warm welcome.'

'You know how much I like you.' Sugianto took two steps forward. 'Which is why you have two minutes to convince me not to arrest you. Or shoot you. I'll decide later.'

'I know why they shut down ANVIL.'

The captain snorted.

'Don't pretend you don't want to know,' said Carter.

'I know you were out of line,' said Sugianto. 'You got Nadeer killed. After I warned you.'

'Hartanto had him killed,' said Carter.

'Fuck you.'

'He did it to protect Maqsood.'

Sugianto looked at him like he'd said the Earth was flat.

'Hartanto's been negotiating with Maqsood. Behind El-Akhtar's back, as well as ours. Turning Nadeer wasn't part of his plan.'

The whine of the helicopter engines began to slow.

Sugianto shrugged his shoulders and looked out over the valley. 'If Maqsood helps take down El-Akhtar, why should I care?'

'What makes you think Hartanto wants that?'

Sugianto squinted.

'Hartanto's not playing the same game as us, Sugi. He has no interest in taking anyone down if El-Akhtar keeps quiet about secession. That's Hartanto's deal; Maqsood's just the intermediary. In return, Hartanto kills ANVIL hoping for stability before the elections while you'—he thrust his finger at the special forces man—'sit back and watch. Eventually, everyone lives unhappily ever after under El-Akhtar in a murderous, Wahhabist caliphate.'

The rotors came to a stop. The hillside fell silent. The troopers remained still, weapons fixed on Carter's chest.

The captain let out a long exhale from his nose. 'Why should I believe you?'

'Wrong question.' Carter took a half-step forward. 'What are you going to do about it?'

Sugianto shrugged. 'I'm a soldier, Pak. I just follow orders.'

'Really, now,' said Carter. 'Anyone order you to come here?' He looked around the clearing. A bird of paradise lifted off from a tree top and flew across the valley.

Sugianto sighed. 'Nope.'

'How about give up the fight while Hartanto gives a jihadi psychopath a free ride?'

'Can't say they did.'

'Then no-one needs to tell you what to do next.'

Sugianto sucked through his teeth.

'You can arrest me if you want, Sugi, or you can help me take these guys down. Maqsood, El-Akhtar, Hartanto, all of them.'

Sugianto's laughter rang out across the valley. He gestured at his six men and the helicopter. 'What, with this?'

'Got anything better to do?'

The captain's face hardened. 'Matter of fact, Pak, I do: stay out of prison. You should try it.'

Carter walked up to him. A soldier flinched. Sugianto waved him down.

Carter stopped two paces away. 'No-one has to know, Sugi.'

Sugianto put his hands on his hips. He looked out at the clearing, to the trees, then the sky, then each of his men.

'Fine,' he said. His gaze returned to Carter. He made a gesture with his hand. 'But I'm taking no chances.'

Two soldiers sprung forward and took Carter by the arms.

'Get him on the chopper,' shouted Sugianto.

The helicopter began to spool up. Carter was loaded on board and strapped into a jumpseat. Sugianto climbed in once the engines were running.

'I missed you,' shouted Carter over the sound of the downdraft.

'Shut the fuck up,' said Sugianto as they lifted off.

There was only the trace of a grin on his lips.

27

TERNATE

Ana woke to the humid afterglow of Legu Gam, the Ternate festival held each year in celebration of religious plurality and tolerance; a cleansing ritual for the province after the sectarian violence that had gripped North Maluku at the turn of the century. The festivities had culminated the night before in a crescendo of music, traditional dance and street parades, and despite Ana's fatigue, the city seemed refreshed for it.

The Gamalama hillside was quiet now, and the air clear enough to see across the strait to Halmahera and the jungle hilltops above its broad coastline. Ana had always enjoyed this view, but since receiving the video from Sabo it had never been so vivid as it was now. Nor had it been as clear to her that, regardless of what Jonah had said to her, if she was to report what was happening to the people of North Maluku, she needed to get across that strait and not merely orbit from the safety of Ternate. The sun cleared the horizon and brought the sea into shimmery relief; it was time to go. She took one last look, packed her passport, laptop and phone, and navigated the festival debris outside the guesthouse to hail a taxi to Bastiong port.

The speedboat was crowded. Half those on board were civil

servants in trim business clothes; the others, weary but content, were returning home after celebrating Legu Gam. Ana found a space at the bow and enjoyed a view of the conical island of Tidore, rival to Ternate in sultanate times and, more recently, a competitor for North Maluku's limited tourist market. It was a mystery to her how a region so steeped in history and natural beauty could remain hidden from the world for so long. She had never heard of Maluku before she saw reports of the violence in Kao, and only later realised they were the same Spice Islands she learned about in primary school, where rival sultans had grown wealthy from sales of cloves to Europeans, then wasted their fortunes fighting one another until in their weakness they became dominated by the very foreigners that had enriched them. Sayeed had described internecine conflict raging amongst contemporary Islamists, but he could have been talking about any time in Maluku's history.

A shift in engine note broke her daydream. The ferry slowed, then drifted over choppy waves and up to the Sofifi docks.

The passengers alighted quickly and disappeared into Sofifi, eager to get the day's work over with and return to the beating heart across the strait. Ana took her time to catch her bearings, then walked along the platform to the street that bordered the port. She had made the journey to Sofifi twice before, but in the disorientation of her first week she never noticed how dull and featureless this artificial city was. A rickshaw called out to her as she left the gates, and to his delight, she accepted.

'*Ke mana,* Miss?' Where to?

'Polisi,' she said.

The driver nodded as if lone western women routinely paid visits on the police here. Ana climbed on board and he wrestled the rickshaw into the traffic. Five minutes later, they pulled into a wide asphalt parking lot. On the far side was a long, two-storey building marked with the letters POLDA – the Indonesian mnemonic for the provincial police force. Apart from a few parked cars, there seemed to be no-one around. Ana paid the driver and he disappeared. She went inside to a large reception area of pale walls and polished white tiles.

Ahead of her were three reception desks, each staffed by a police officer. They seemed preoccupied with their computers. She walked up to the youngest one.

'Permisi,' she said. 'English?'

'Yes?' said the officer. He sat up straight. He looked early twenties, fresh-faced. A fraction eager.

One of the other officers mentioned something to him. He smiled and waved them away.

'My name is Ana,' she said. 'I'm a journalist. I've just come from Tobelo where I interviewed Inspector Rachmann. Do you know him?'

A flicker of concern crossed the boy's face. 'I know him.'

'Oh, that's good,' she said. 'I'm sorry to trouble you, but Inspector Rachmann offered to provide some police reports for my investigation. Unfortunately, the computer system was down. He told me to come here to obtain them. Did he call?'

The officer frowned. 'I don't think so.'

'I see,' she said. She made a sad face.

The officer shifted uncomfortably in his seat.

'Perhaps you could call him for me?' she said. 'To check?'

He looked at her in near-shock.

'It was very important to him.'

He licked the corner of his mouth. 'What did you want again, Miss?'

'Homicide reports from Halmahera Utara for the past month.' She held up her phone. 'I can call him myself, if you like, and he could speak to you? Only, he insisted it would be no problem.'

He stared at the phone. 'It is no problem. Please wait.'

'Thank you so much,' she said.

He typed something into the computer. Ana looked around. At the other end of the lobby were two men in brown leather jackets. One of them averted her gaze. They paid no attention to the police.

'Here,' said the officer.

He turned the monitor so she could see. It was a tabulated list of names, dates and locations. There were eight reports listed. The last one showed only a case number alongside the label 'DIREDAKSI'.

She checked the list of dates. None of them were in the past week.

'What does that mean?' she said. She raised a hand to the redacted entry.

'I don't know,' he said. 'Maybe the details are sensitive.'

'Is there anything at all? Inspector Rachmann promised me full access.'

He looked sheepish. 'I'm sorry, miss, I cannot access it. You must ask the chief of police.'

She stared at the list for a while. She'd hoped it wouldn't come to this.

'Miss?'

She wrote down the case number. 'That's okay,' she said. 'I just have one more question: who are those men?'

He looked past her at the men in leather jackets, then shrugged.

She gave him a smile. 'Thank you so much. You've been most helpful.'

He smiled back, relieved to be off the hook.

Ana crossed the parking lot to hunt for a taxi. She took out her phone and searched for the Tobelo police headquarters. She dialled the reception number.

A woman greeted her in Indonesian.

'Hello,' said Ana. 'I wish to speak with Inspector Rachmann.'

The woman didn't respond.

'Inspector Rachmann,' Ana repeated. 'It is urgent.'

'Who is speaking?'

'Tell him it is Ana Kovacevic. He knows me.'

The woman asked her to spell it, so she did.

'Okay,' said the woman. 'Please wait.'

Ana listened to hold music while she waved down a taxi. She climbed in and directed the driver to the port. One of the men in leather jackets emerged from the station entrance as the taxi sped off.

The woman came back online. 'Miss Ana?'

'Yes?'

'I will transfer you now.'

Ana waited while the call was put through. The taxi weaved through traffic. The twin peaks of Ternate and Tidore loomed in the distance.

'What do you want?' said Rachmann.

'Good to speak with you too,' said Ana, shouting over the noise of the taxi. 'I want your comment for an article. It goes to print tonight.'

'What article?'

'I've obtained a police report on a recent murder.' She read out the number. 'It says the victim was beheaded by Islamic fundamentalists in Sabo.'

'Wait,' he said.

She heard him typing.

'How did you get this?' he said.

'Not telling.'

He grunted. 'I suggest you contact the right authorities.'

'Why is it suppressed?'

'I can't comment. What could I add anyway? I did not investigate this.'

'That's comment, Inspector Rachmann.'

'Whatever.'

The taxi pulled up at the dockside.

'Perhaps you can explain why it doesn't mention the video.'

Ana paid the driver and climbed out.

'What video?'

She walked along the pavement. 'The video I have showing this man's execution.'

'You should provide it to the police,' he said.

'I will hand it to you personally,' she said. 'But if you want me to do it before I publish, I need your comment.' A bus pulled up ahead of her, destined for Tobelo. 'Today.'

For a while all she heard was his breathing.

'Inspector, this doesn't have to be difficult.'

'Where are you?'

She had reached the bus. 'I'm on my way to Tobelo. I'll be at your office in three hours.'

'No,' he said. 'I will send you an address.'

She handed a fifty-thousand note to the bus driver. 'Okay.'

'Make sure you're alone.'

28

TERNATE

Liam Ellis sat at the wheel of his rented Pajero and flipped a padlock in his hands. He was thirty metres from Kovacevic's guesthouse complex, with a clear view of her second-floor apartment and the driveway entrance below. There had been almost no activity since he had arrived. Only the landlord had left the complex in that time, not long after Ellis had introduced himself as a consular officer of the Australian embassy in search of the 'blonde Australian girl' who had broken contact with her distraught parents back in Melbourne, a routine he'd employed at more than a dozen hotels and guesthouses across Ternate before this one. The landlord had confirmed the girl in the photo had moved in but professed no knowledge of her whereabouts. Maybe she was on another one of her daytrips, he'd said, before offering Ellis several package deals to visit Tidore, Mount Gamalama, or, if he was adventurous, the diving resorts of Weda. Ellis had thanked him, taken his leave and spent the next hour in his car thinking of a plan. Not that the plan was anything but obvious. He just needed the balls to go through with it.

The mosques sang; the light faded. 'Fuck it,' he said to himself. He grabbed his bag and climbed out of the Pajero. He dodged a passing motorcycle as he crossed the street. Reaching the front gate he turned in, close to the wall, out of view from the front office. He reached the stairs that led to the upper balcony and waited. There was no noise apart from the road. He took the stairs two at a time and walked directly to Kovacevic's door. The two large windows either side were dark and shrouded by mesh curtains. He looked out over the complex – no movement. He sucked in a breath.

Now or never.

He opened the bag and removed the lockpicking kit he had brought from the ASIS station at the embassy. Lockpicking was one of those obscure skills they taught intelligence officers on initial training, along with parachuting and tactical driving, that was more to build confidence and test mettle than leave any lasting competence. Three hours of practice on the padlock in the car proved unnecessary for the vintage door lock; the tension wrench and pick rake fit easily into the wide-bore keyway and the pins moved freely. One-by-one they locked into place above the sheer line, then the final pin freed and the lock turned.

He opened the door an inch and waited. The apartment was silent. He packed the tool set and checked the balcony. The front office light was still on, no sign of movement.

He closed the door behind him and let his eyes adjust. A dining table and chairs loomed in the foreground. Clothes hung over the back of a sofa; a tower of books cast a shadow along the kitchen bench. She hadn't left for long.

He waited for his pulse to settle before he moved across the sitting room. His knee clipped a dining chair which squealed over the tiled floor. 'Fuck,' he whispered. He listened for a reaction anywhere in the complex. Nothing but the pulse in his neck. He hobbled into the bedroom.

He scanned the small room under the light of his phone. The bed had been made in a hurry. A phone cable led under the covers but there was nothing attached. He searched the chest of drawers and bedside tables and found only clothes and a dog-eared

Lonely Planet guide. He flicked through it, but there were too many notations to narrow his search. There was no sign of her passport, purse or money. He turned for the bathroom.

A small halogen light flickered to life over a soap-stained mirror and a small shelf that held a stick of toothpaste and a toothbrush. The brush was still wet from that morning. In a corner of the bathroom was a modern-style toilet beneath a ceiling vent. A stainless-steel shower head dripped onto a small shelf that held half-empty bottles of shampoo and conditioner and a near-new block of soap. He checked the sink cabinet and found a toilet brush and cleaning fluid. Out of curiosity, he lifted the cover of the cistern. Nothing.

'She's gone, mate.'

'Fuck!' shouted Ellis as he turned and fell. He landed in the basin of the shower and his head struck the wall.

'Nice to see you too,' said Carter.

Ellis groaned. The back of his head was wet, but it was water. He pushed himself upright. 'What the fuck are you doing here?'

'You first,' said Carter. 'You're the one sniffing underwear.'

Ellis caught his breath. 'It's you I'm after.'

'Hm.' Carter stepped into the bathroom and looked around. 'Wonder why that is.'

'It's over, Jordan.' Ellis winced at the pain in his chest. 'You're on the most wanted list. Be happy you've got immunity.'

Carter squatted down and looked Ellis in the eye.

'Yoyok's dead, mate. I'm far from happy.'

'I know,' said Ellis. 'I'm sorry. We're all sorry.'

Carter studied him.

'Look,' said Ellis, 'things have gotten out of hand, Andy knows that. Come back in, mate, let's sort it out.'

'Don't be a pussy, Liam.'

'I want El-Akhtar as much as you do.'

A motorcycle started up outside and rode off.

'Yet here you are in Ternate.'

'You can fucking talk.'

Carter smiled. 'Fuck would you know?'

Ellis shook his head. 'Come on, Jordan. We can get ANVIL going again if we do it right. You just need to come in.'

Carter stood up and inspected a bruise in the mirror. 'What's Andy offering?'

'I...' Ellis climbed to his feet. He felt exhausted. 'I don't know, mate.'

Carter watched him in the mirror. 'So nothing, then.' He turned. 'We're just going to let the Indonesians run off with all the work we put in, watch North Maluku become a terror haven, pretend it doesn't matter?'

'What the fuck else can we do?'

'You've been in that embassy too long.'

'Trying to keep you out of trouble, Jordan. Trying to keep ANVIL on the rails. We're all trying to help you. Me, Andy, everybody. Stop pushing us away.'

Carter turned and put a hand on Ellis's shoulder. 'Forget Andy, forget ASIS.' He leaned down so their faces were level. 'You want to help?'

'Sure.'

'So help.'

'How?'

Carter looked out into Kovacevic's bedroom, then back to Ellis. 'All you have to do is help her if she comes to you.'

Ellis frowned.

'I won't explain,' said Carter. 'Just do it and good things will happen.'

'You know where she is?'

Carter let him go. Ellis followed him to the sitting room.

'Jordan?'

Carter reached the front door and turned back. 'Stay in Ternate,' he said. 'It won't be for long.'

Ellis rubbed his head. 'Where will you be?'

Carter opened the door. Streetlight cast an orange glow around his silhouette.

'Just do what I asked.'

Then he left.

29

TOBELO

Ana waited at the dock of a row of Tobelo shopfronts. It was dark, and for twenty minutes, apart from a stray cat, there had been no activity nearby. She hoped she had the address right. Rachmann had given her a landmark, a bright red steeple above one of the retail buildings, but she'd seen several like it on the journey and it was possible, in the dark and in a hurry, she'd found the wrong one. Only when the car entered the service road did she feel some relief.

The car extinguished its headlights as it approached. It was a rental. She could see the silhouette of the driver, a large frame that weaved and bobbed as he searched for her. Eventually it pulled into the dock and stopped. She stepped out of the alcove and into the moonlight, then to the passenger door.

Rachmann reached across and unlocked it. She climbed in.

He hushed her before she could speak, then drove.

He was almost unrecognisable in civilian clothes. His thin hair was uncombed and flicked in the wind from his open window. His posture was slouched. His gut, released from the burdens of his uniform, overflowed from his jeans.

They reached a main road. Rachmann breathed relief.

'Where are you taking me?' said Ana.

'Somewhere safe to talk,' he said. He checked his mirrors.

She looked but saw no-one behind them. 'Why all the cloak and dagger?'

He looked at her with a mixture of fear and annoyance. 'This is dangerous for me. It would be a scandal.'

They pulled into a laneway that led into a kampung. Rachmann made a series of turns before parking by a darkened house. Ana saw a stray dog in the headlights before he cut them.

'Come.'

She got out and followed him into the house. 'Sit,' he said, and pointed at a small table with two chairs placed by the wall. She did so. He went to the rear door and unlocked it, then returned to the front and checked outside again.

He turned on a light and took the seat opposite. His face was covered in sweat, and he stank of body odour.

'You got the video?' he said. 'Show me.'

Ana recoiled. 'You're scaring me,' she said.

He wiped his brow. 'Don't be scared of me,' he said. 'Be scared when fifty armed commandos storm us and throw us in prison.'

He held out his hand and made a 'gimme' gesture.

She unlocked the phone and showed him the beheading video. He stared at it intently. Only when the video hit a crescendo and the blade was inserted did he react. He placed the back of his hand to his mouth.

He whispered something and handed back the phone. 'Who gave this to you?'

'What does it matter? I want to know why the police aren't investigating.'

He pointed at the phone. 'Someone took a big risk with this. Whoever he is, he is close to the extremists. One wrong move and he ends up like the video, okay?'

'He—' She cleared her throat. 'Whoever it is knows I'm a journalist. They want me to publish it, and I will, alongside a piece where I highlight that the police report on the man's murder has been marked for suppression.'

Rachmann said nothing.

'The government knows this happened,' she continued. 'Just think how this is going to look. Not just in Indonesia.'

He rubbed his nose with the tip of his thumb and stared at the table. One of the halogen lamps flickered above them.

'Inspector Rachmann, you promised to comment.'

He mumbled something.

'I can't hear you.'

He slapped his palm on the table. 'I said it's out of my hands!'

'What is?'

He stared at something on the floor and drummed his fingers. 'This is all off the record, okay?'

'Of course.'

His eyes met hers. 'It is a national security matter,' he said. 'All of it is handled by the security services.'

'The security services.'

'Yes.'

'I'll need evidence of that, inspector. This looks like a police matter to me and will to my readers.'

He looked away. His head shook slightly, then he brought his hand to his eyes and rubbed them.

Ana watched him carefully. In all their interactions, Rachmann had seemed so stoic, so righteous. Now, here he was, alone, afraid, and a shell of his professional self. She felt a kind of pity for him now. She reminded herself this man had worked so actively to obstruct her investigations for the past few weeks.

'It's their fault, you know.' He lowered his hand and looked at her. His eyes glistened in the pale blue light.

'Whose?'

'The spies'.' He sat up straight and released a long breath. 'For years they have worked against the Islamist groups of the province, but it never stops. All they do is run informants which they use to encourage one group to attack another and spread lies. It just causes more violence. Now it's spinning out of control.'

Ana thought of the sultans and her interview with Sayeed. 'So you knew the government was in contact with the Islamists?'

'Yes.'

'Is that what happened in Kao?'

'Kao was different. The beginning of something new.'

The light flickered again.

'I do not know why,' he said, 'but the groups had turned on the intelligence services. Gameshar knew they would be there that night and staged a rally. They hoped the agents would be caught by surprise, maybe killed. Either way, they wanted to scare the government.'

'What was the government's response?'

He scoffed. 'You saw Sabo,' he said. 'They have lost control. It will only get worse. These people have been humiliated for so long, and now they have turned to evil to bring them hope.'

Ana reflected on the women in burqa, and the fear in the men's eyes.

'Tell this story, Ana, so that Jakarta will take this problem seriously.' He gestured at the phone. 'This is the beginning.'

He stared at her with large, black eyes. His cheeks had a sheen of sweat. She felt bad for what she was about to do.

'I can't publish this,' she said. 'Yet.'

He clicked his tongue. 'You must, mbak Ana.' His bulk shifted awkwardly as he leaned across the desk. 'I have risked my life for you to tell you this!'

'I know.' She placed her free hand on his. 'But I need proof that the government was in touch with the extremists. Without it, my editor will never publish. Do you understand?'

Tears formed in Rachmann's eyes. She worded her next question with care.

'Is there anything else you can give me?'

'Like what?'

'I'm no expert, inspector, but I would have thought that if government agents were meeting with members of the Islamist groups, they would sometimes notify the police, would they not? Maybe for security, or just to avoid being arrested.'

'Maybe,' he said. His expression changed as the penny dropped. 'Yes.'

'Perhaps it would confirm the meetings took place.'

Rachmann cleared his throat with a harsh grunt. He glanced around the room, then back to her. 'I need twenty-four hours.'

'My editor will be upset,' she said.

'It will prove what I told you,' he said. 'There is no other way.'

30

GALELA, NORTH MALUKU

Kuwat eased himself into a plastic chair by the entrance to the workshop. He had earned a rest. It had taken the morning to replace the chain on his motorcycle, a task made more oppressive by the unobstructed sun that pummelled the workshop forecourt. He still had a delivery to make that afternoon, one that would involve four hours of riding up and down the coast to and from Supu, but for now, he just needed a cigarette.

He lit up and watched the traffic pass by on the highway. Lorries carried goods into Tobelo from the airport ten kilometres to the northwest. Entire families passed on single scooters; others carried animals and fresh produce. An old man carried caged turkeys on a small wooden beam balanced across his shoulders. Kuwat was soothed by the sight and sound of it. It reminded him he was free.

'Two-hundred for the chain,' said the mechanic. He held out a blackened, wrinkled hand.

Kuwat held his cigarette in his mouth and reached for the cash in his shirt pocket. 'Here,' he said.

The mechanic snatched the money. 'Rain is coming this afternoon,' he said as he counted it. 'I heard on the radio.'

Kuwat nodded but didn't believe it. He had ridden these roads for years and knew it would be dry as a bone. At least it would be cooler. 'Thank you, Pak,' he said.

The mechanic returned to his hammock at the back of the workshop.

Kuwat leaned back and dozed. He tugged on the brim of his cap and let his mind wander until the descending pitch of a motorcycle engine made him look up. The motorcycle slowed and turned off the highway, then parked next to the workshop.

The rider was fit, but small. Javanese, Kuwat thought. His hair was cut into a mohawk that hung across one side of his face, and he wore a black singlet that revealed an ornate red dragon that climbed from one sinewy wrist, gripped the man's neck with enormous talons, and laid its head along the length of the other arm. The man dismounted and admired Kuwat's Honda over his aviator sunglasses.

'Nice bike,' said the man. 'Vintage.'

Kuwat breathed out a lungful of smoke. 'Reliable.'

'Looks like it's done some miles. Where do you ride?'

'All over.'

'Courier?'

Kuwat nodded.

The man smiled and held out his hand. 'I'm Raf.'

Kuwat shook it. In a show of politeness, Raf placed his hand over his heart.

'Boss here?' Raf lifted his sunglasses and peered into the garage.

'Out back,' said Kuwat. 'Sleeping.'

'That's okay,' said Raf. 'Maybe you can help me.'

'I don't work here.'

'I'm not here to buy anything.' Raf smiled. 'I'm looking for a man named Hamzah. He was a courier, too. Know him?'

Kuwat gulped, then shook his head. His pulse quickened.

'I'm helping his mother,' said Raf. 'She's very worried about him.'

Kuwat glanced away. Traffic continued past on the highway. The mechanic snored at the back of the workshop.

'Wh—why should she be worried?'

Raf stepped towards him then squatted down so that their faces were level. He spoke quietly, eyes on the sleeping mechanic in the back.

'Well, it's like this.' Raf took off his sunglasses and brushed the mohawk from his face. 'Hamzah's mother lives in a secret location in Sulawesi, under the protection of the government.' His eyes fixed on Kuwat's. 'Turns out Hamzah was involved with... certain people.'

Kuwat's chest began to ache. He took a deep drag and wiped sweat from his brow.

'You can imagine what might happen to poor Hamzah if those people discovered he had done a deal with the government, can't you?'

Kuwat looked around. There was no-one else near the workshop. The mechanic was still asleep. Traffic flowed obliviously on the highway.

'Or if they discovered his real name,' Raf added.

'What do you want?' said Kuwat, true name Hamzah. A secret he thought would die with him.

Raf placed a hand on Kuwat's shoulder. His face was cold now, serious. The grip was firm, just short of painful. With his other hand he took out a phone.

'Take this,' he said. 'Keep it secret. Answer it if it rings and follow whatever instructions I give you.'

Kuwat took the phone and stared at it. 'Okay,' he said. His hand shook.

Raf smiled. He stood up and turned for the motorcycle.

'Is my mother safe?' called Kuwat.

Raf paused. 'Make sure you answer the phone,' he said over his shoulder. He climbed on his motorcycle and started it.

'Nice bike,' he said again. Then he rode off.

◆

'How'd you find this guy?' said Sugianto.

They were in the sitting room of a small house west of Tobelo that Sugianto had rented as a makeshift command post. Several photos of Kuwat were scattered across a large map that was spread over the dining table.

'I recruited him a few years ago,' said Carter. 'He runs messages for the groups, one of the few people they all trust.'

Sugianto grunted understanding. 'Strange to let him go.'

'He'd kept his end of the bargain, and we no longer needed him. Now he's our only way to Maqsood.'

'You think Maqsood will just answer this guy's call and give El-Akhtar up?'

'Maqsood will do whatever it takes to survive.'

Sugianto crossed his arms and frowned.

'Got a better plan?' said Carter.

The captain shrugged. 'Nup.'

31

TOBELO

Ana spent a restless night in a cheap hostel near the centre of town. Rachmann had dropped her a block away and told her to lay low until the following evening. There was a Circle K supermarket two hundred metres away. He would meet her there.

The wait was tedious. She hacked at a draft of her article, but it did nothing for her anxiety. Instead, she binge-watched an Indonesian reality show and mentally rehearsed the route to the Circle K as if her ability to walk might falter at the last minute.

At eight o'clock, she packed, showered and changed. Rachmann had told her to meet at nine p.m. sharp and she planned on a ten-minute walk. At twenty-to-nine, she left the room and checked out.

Gusts blew from the sea a hundred metres east. Motorcycles and cars flew past as she walked along the uneven pavement to the intersection near the hotel. Through the glare of headlights, she could see the bright white logo of the supermarket across the road a hundred metres away. She looked the other way. A man stood beside an SUV talking on his phone, while across from him, workers unloaded a goods truck into a rusted warehouse. She walked to the supermarket.

It was five-to when she arrived, but she didn't have to wait.

Rachmann's rental car pulled to a stop on the gravel verge as soon as she stepped into the light of the supermarket. His face was visible in the windscreen. She walked to him and climbed in.

She knew not to speak. She braced as Rachmann sped through a long sequence of turns, by the end of which she was disoriented. He crossed a bridge that ran over a small creek and stopped. She remembered Jaja's manoeuvre on the way to Sabo.

'If I tell you to get out, run,' he said, eyes on the mirrors. 'You can't be seen with me.'

'Okay.'

They waited in silence for what felt like ten minutes. No vehicles followed them across the bridge. Rachmann relaxed and resumed the journey.

He turned into another kampung. Ana recognised the house from the night before.

He led her inside. The routine was the same. With the lights on, he sat down. He reached inside his shoulder bag and produced a flash drive.

'This is all of it,' he said.

She turned on her laptop and waited for it to boot. Rachmann tapped his feet.

'Sorry,' she said. 'Old laptop.'

He grunted.

Eventually she reached the login prompt.

She logged in and inserted the drive. It contained seven exported files from the police database, each with elaborate coded titles consisting of officer names, locations and unique identifiers. She recognised the last eight digits as dates. All of them were from the past three weeks.

'These are reports for operations where my officers supported meetings with the Islamists,' said Rachmann.

She looked at the list. There were towns she recognised all over North Halmahera, others she didn't. She opened one that was from the town of Kusuri. It had been recorded seven days ago.

'Is it enough?' he said.

The report was written in Indonesian, but provided a list of officers involved, timings, and what she assumed were observations.

'It's perfect,' she said.

He gestured to the drive. 'Give it back.'

'Wait.'

Neither spoke while she copied the files onto her laptop. Ana thought she heard a car nearby. Rachmann paid no notice.

'Done,' she said.

He ripped the drive from the laptop and dropped it on the floor. Then he placed the leg of his chair on top of it and kicked it down with his heel. The sound of the impact echoed through the house. The flash drive was still intact. He did it again and it cracked apart. He picked up the pieces and disappeared into the bathroom. Ana heard the toilet flush, then a scrape. The latter sounded like it was from outside.

She powered down the laptop and placed it in its bag. Rachmann re-emerged.

'You have what you need,' he said. 'Don't let me down.'

She stood up. 'I won't. Thank you.'

There was another noise, like a burst of static. Rachmann froze.

Ana whispered, 'What was—'

He held up his hand to stop her talking. 'Wait.'

The lights were cut. Silence. In the darkness, Ana heard Rachmann's strained breathing, the pulse in her neck, then a thud against the front door.

'Go!' shouted Rachmann. There was a loud crash from behind them as the front door was kicked in. Torch lights sliced through darkness, followed by soldiers.

'Police! Get down!'

Rachmann pushed her towards the rear hall. There was another crash. The hallway filled with soldiers and torchbeams. Rachmann screamed as more troopers appeared, weapons raised, aimed at them both.

Rachmann let go of her arm and she fell. The house filled with light and shouting. She rolled onto her stomach, arms outstretched. She gripped her bag with both hands.

'Let me go!' screamed Rachmann. 'No!' Ana looked up to see him dragged by his feet into the sitting room. A soldier shouted 'Clear!' as he checked the bathroom. They were on top of her now. She felt the gloved hands on her arms and legs, then she was dragged.

'I'm a journalist!' she screamed.

'Shut up!' yelled a soldier.

Rachmann struggled to stand up. A soldier slapped his face. She watched him fall, then they kicked him.

A soldier ripped the bag from her hands and pulled her arms behind her back. 'Don't move,' said one of them.

She didn't struggle as the plasticuffs were tightened around her wrists. Her eyes were on Rachmann.

One of them gripped his head under the jaw and lifted it. He looked directly at her as they cuffed him. His eyes were swollen; blood poured from his nose. It took three soldiers to lift him. He groaned, but never cut eye contact with Ana, his face cast in dread, sadness and defeat.

A soldier blocked Ana's view and lifted her to her feet. When she was upright, Rachmann was gone.

'Don't let me down,' he had said.

32

Her feet dragged along the concrete as they carried her, one soldier holding her under each arm. Military vehicles were parked where the alley joined the main street that led through the kampung. One moved off as they approached. The soldiers shouted something and the rear hatch of the second vehicle opened. She was lifted by her ankles and loaded in before someone tied her to a seat and shut the hatch. The engine started and she was thrust against the bulkhead.

She soon lost track of time. Her seat was mounted sideways and she retched with nausea. She called out for water but was ignored. The vehicle climbed a gradient and the turns became more frequent. When they stopped, someone thrust a bottle of water into her mouth. She choked on it, and the best she could do was rinse the taste of vomit from her mouth. They removed her from the vehicle and cuffed her to a steel chair at one end of a long, white-painted room. Her belongings had been laid out on a wooden table at the other end, each item tagged with an evidence number as if it had already given up her secrets. Minutes passed until a woman dressed in hiking pants and a grey business shirt entered. She walked directly to the table without making eye contact, opened the laptop and turned to Ana.

'Password.'

Ana strained to focus. The room was still spinning. 'No.'

The woman leaned against the table and folded her arms. Under a halogen lamp, Ana saw the scar of a cleft palate. 'We will open it anyway,' said the woman. 'The password will save time.'

'I won't give it to you.'

The woman uncrossed her arms and inspected the rest of Ana's belongings. Ana's chest tightened as the woman checked each page through her notebook. She had been careful never to write down source names or contact details, but under the glare of inquisition she couldn't know what they would find useful. The woman held up Ana's phone as if she presumed non-compliance. Ana shook her head and the woman put it back down. Ana had binned the memory card of her camera before leaving Ternate, so the woman found nothing. The woman threw the camera onto the table with finality. She placed a wooden stool in front of Ana and sat down.

'Am I under arrest?' said Ana.

'We will arrest you when we're done.'

'I'm a journalist,' said Ana. 'I've committed no crime.'

The woman licked her bottom lip. 'You are a foreign agent.'

'That's not true.' Ana strained at her cuffs.

'You were apprehended in the process of obtaining state secrets from a senior officer of Indonesian Police, an officer whom you conspired with ahead of the fact. Is that not true?'

'I was investigating malfeasance. It was my job.'

'This is espionage, not journalism.'

'Then arrest me.'

The woman licked her lip again. 'In time.'

Ana's hands were numb. The adrenaline had worn off and she was cold and lethargic.

'What have you done to Rachmann?'

The woman stood up and replaced the stool. 'You have your own problems,' she said. She walked to the door.

'He's a good man,' said Ana. 'He did the right thing.'

The woman gripped the door handle and pulled.

'There are people who say that about all traitors.'

A thin arc of sunlight cut the cell in two above where she had slept. The white blade penetrated through an elongated window, barely a fist wide and above head height, at an angle that suggested early morning. The rest of the room was dark and smelled of mould. She lay motionless on the cold concrete and listened to her own breath until she was interrupted by the sound of a vehicle outside, then voices. A door slammed, and she heard boots upon gravel.

For a while there was silence. The footsteps arrived quickly, and she had barely sat up before the door was opened in an outburst of metal clangs and creaks. Two men entered the room. 'Come,' said the taller of the two. She nursed her aching wrists as she stood. There was no sign of the woman who had interrogated her.

They didn't cuff her this time, but the grip on her arms had no less force than her arrest. They led her down a corridor lit by a single naked globe. At the end was a door. One of them released her arm and fumbled with a set of keys. The door opened to bathe her in sunlight and the fragrance of cloves. Ahead of her was a view across treetops to a wide mountain valley. In the foreground were two Landcruisers parked in a clearing. Beyond, a gravel road descended into the trees, and she realised she was in the middle of nowhere.

'Sit.'

An Indonesian man sat alone by a small circular table on a veranda that overlooked the clearing. He looked in his sixties, gaunt but upright. He tapped a cigarette on a steel ashtray placed next to two bottles of iced tea, then glared at her with dark, intense eyes, each ringed with fatigue and menace.

She sat down. The man's gaunt cheeks stretched taut over the ridges of his face as he took a final drag of the cigarette and stubbed it.

He took two more out of a packet. 'Smoke?'

She shook her head and he replaced one of them. He waved his hand at the table.

'Help yourself to tea, Miss Ana.'

She hesitated, unsure if it was a trick. Eventually she took one of the bottles and drank from it, relieved to at last rinse the taste of vomit from her mouth. The man waved the guards away. They walked out into the clearing and smoked by one of the cruisers.

'Beautiful, is it not?' said the man. He swung an arm at the view. 'I always enjoy it here. Miles from anywhere.' He took a drag and flicked ash onto the tray. 'Impossible to be found.' His grin revealed a row of nicotine-stained teeth.

Ana stared blankly at the horizon. Somewhere in the jungle a monkey called out.

'My name is Hartanto,' said the man. 'On behalf of the Indonesian Government, I apologise for your treatment last night. It was no way to treat a guest.'

'I'm a prisoner, not a guest.'

He leaned back and smiled. 'Well now, you are a spy.'

'I could never be a spy,' she said.

Smoke leaked from his nostrils as he chuckled to himself. 'Very good,' he said. 'Yet you convinced Inspector Rachmann to reveal state secrets, did you not?' The smile disappeared and he leaned towards her. 'That is espionage, Miss Ana. A crime in your country as well as mine.'

'It was journalism.'

'Journalism…' He stubbed his cigarette. 'Journalists pursue truth through noble means!' He pointed a skeletal finger at her. 'But not you. You exploit people. You exploited Rachmann.'

She shook her head. He retrieved another cigarette and lit it, almost unconsciously.

'Rachmann's weakness was his ideals,' he continued, 'his desire for justice. You used it to manipulate him, indifferent to the cost as long as you got what you wanted.' He took two short puffs to ensure the smoke was lit. 'Yes, Miss Ana, you are a spy.'

'Call me whatever you want,' she said. 'In a courtroom.'

Grey smoke puffed from his nose and mouth as he laughed. 'I am not here to charge you, Miss Ana. The truth is you are a victim.'

She frowned.

'This Jonah used you, did he not? The same way you used Rachmann.' He scratched his lip with his spare hand. 'Do you even know his real name?'

'I don't know what you're talking about.'

'It is no secret he is an intelligence officer, Miss Ana. He is declared to us and enjoys diplomatic privileges in this country. Privileges he has exploited to cause great harm.'

She folded her arms. 'That's nothing to do with me.'

'It hurts, doesn't it? To have trusted him, and to know it was all a trick so you would do his bidding.'

'I did everything for myself.'

Hartanto's expression changed. 'You can lie to yourself, Ana. But do not lie to me.'

'It's not a lie. The government had been manipulating Islamist groups. I wanted to know the truth.'

'You didn't care about the truth when you played your trick on the officer in Sofifi. You didn't care about the truth when you convinced Rachmann you had obtained a classified file when in fact you had not.' He leaned across the table. 'And yet, truth is your weakness, isn't it, Ana?' He leaned back and put another cigarette to his lips. 'Jonah and I are both trained to see it. He promised you would find it and it has ended badly for you.' He sparked his lighter. 'And for him.'

She sat up. 'What have you done to him?'

'Me?' He blew out smoke. 'Nothing. But he is wanted by many people and does not have much time.' He leaned towards her again. 'You can help him by helping me. You can help yourself.'

'I don't know where he is.'

'That is not important. He will find you, and when he does, we will know.'

She stared at her hands. Her nails were blackened with filth.

'You will be free, Ana.'

'I will be under surveillance.'

'For your own protection, of course, and for ours.'

'And if I refuse?'

'Then I will not be able to tell the prosecutor you assisted with our enquiries. And I will not be able to save Jonah's life.'

'You're not giving me a choice.'

The corner of his mouth raised slightly, and his eyes narrowed.

'We all live at the mercy of our choices, Miss Ana. It was your choices that put you in this position. It is your choice whether you escape from it.'

He shouted something at the guards. One of them ran up to the house and disappeared inside. He returned a minute later with Ana's backpack.

'I need your answer,' said Hartanto. 'Then you will be free to go.'

Her bag was empty except for a pre-purchased mobile phone with her SIM card taped to the packaging. She was wary enough of surveillance to presume Hartanto had rigged it to report all calls and texts along with her location. This was the trap he'd set, she presumed, but it gave her an idea.

'Okay,' she said.

Hartanto smiled and clicked his fingers. The two guards chucked their cigarettes and came for her.

33

They let her remove the hood once they reached the highway. It took another hour to reach the port at Sofifi. One of the guards opened her door and she stepped into the mid-afternoon humidity. They escorted her to the dock. Waves lapped at the bow of a small motorboat.

'Silahkan,' said one of the guards. Please. The helmsman took her backpack and helped her on board. The guard followed and sat down to face her.

'Go,' he said.

A black SUV awaited her at Bastiong port. Her guards helped her in, then left to head back to the boat. The driver sped through backstreets and dropped her by a pharmacy a few hundred metres from her guesthouse, as if to remind her they knew where she lived.

'You go,' said the driver. Ana gripped the backpack and climbed out to face a Ternate that had lost its charm. Passers-by seemed disinterested; shopfronts and prayer calls were dimmer than she remembered. The painted houses were dilapidated, and the air lacked its spicy scent.

She closed her door and the SUV drove away. As she slung her bag and began to walk towards her room, a van pulled up across the street. She turned the corner onto the main street that led to the guesthouse. Ahead of her a man sat on his motorcycle that was parked on the curb. He watched her cross the road then went back to his phone. She looked the way she had come. Another man had his hands in the pockets of his leather jacket. He paused, looked away, then stepped into the pharmacy. There were more watchers near the guesthouse complex. When she passed by the reception office, her landlord looked at her apologetically. A woman in hijab sat in front of his desk, fanning herself with a magazine. Ana assumed her driver would be one of those assigned to watch her. That made seven.

Her room was dark and silent. She threw her backpack on the sofa and sat with her back to the door while her eyes adjusted. Out of the gloom emerged shapes and details she remembered, some out of place or in new orientations. The room had been cleaned, no doubt to cover the tracks of whoever had sifted it.

She had asked the landlord not to clean the bathroom, and he had complied. Her toiletry items were in the sink. A bottle lay on the floor and leaked shampoo into the drain. The toilet stank, and she realised someone had used it. After she flushed it, she stepped onto the seat and inspected the ceiling vent. A three-inch blonde hair hung from one corner, where she had left it. It gave her hope. She picked at the plastic cover and it came free, and when she reached in her fingertips grazed something plastic. She stepped on her toes to grip it, then pulled. The zip-lock bag came free in her hands, and she opened it to find one million rupiah, a mobile phone with a spare SIM card, and a flashdrive that contained a copy of all her work. She sat down and held it tight against her chest; *thanks be to God.*

Her relief turned to nausea at the thought of what she was about to do. She opened the toilet seat and leaned over the bowl. She dry-retched twice; on the third convulsion her stomach loosened and she vomited repeatedly until she could no longer hold her weight. She lay on the floor and concentrated on breathing until she could repeat her plan in her mind. It was the same plan she had rehearsed while they had driven her to Sofifi, and only a slight variation from the one she conceived in her cell. It calmed her. She was ready.

She turned on the mobile phone and sent an SMS to the phone Hartanto had given her:

Meet at Sofifi port. 8pm. Jonah

A moment later, it arrived on the Hartanto phone. She dismantled the burner and flushed the used SIM card. She replaced it with the spare, then showered, changed, and made sure the apartment looked like she would return. Then she turned off the lights, opened the door and stepped out into the Ternate evening.

A sea breeze swept up the darkened hillside. A vehicle started up somewhere behind her as she turned left onto the main street. Ahead of her, the man in the leather jacket threw away a cigarette. He watched her pass then followed her to the next intersection. The woman in hijab talked on her phone across the street, the ridge of scar tissue on her palate obvious as she spoke. She gestured in different directions, then looked away when she saw Ana. A truck announced its arrival with a loud wail of its brakes and cut the woman's line of sight. Ana turned right and walked quickly across the street, away from the woman, to enter a side street that led downhill.

At the next main street, she turned right and entered a Circle K to buy a bottle of water. Fifty metres away, a man in a white t-shirt crossed the street and placed a phone to his ear. Leather Jacket emerged from the side street and looked around. Eventually he entered the Circle K and walked to the toiletries aisle to make a phone call. Ana checked the street again but saw no other watchers. She left the Circle K and crossed the road to a waiting taxi. '*Pelabuhan* Bastiong,' she said.

The taxi driver said nothing and accelerated away. Through the rear window, Ana watched Leather Jacket run for an ojek while White Tee hailed a taxi travelling in the opposite direction. Two cars turned onto the road behind her. Her taxi took a right to head downhill again, but the cars continued on.

'Pak,' she said. 'How much to the port?'

He looked at her in the rear-view mirror, uncomprehending.

'Mau berapa?' she said.

He checked his mirrors while he did a sum in his head. *'Lima ribu.'* Fifty thousand.

'Too much,' she said, and pointed out the window. 'Turn here.'

He turned south to run parallel to the main thoroughfare that led to the port. The street was clear. The second taxi hadn't reached the intersection.

'Stop.'

He did as she asked. She gave him thirty thousand, enough to raise confusion. She wanted him to remember her and tell whoever asked about the foreign girl who haggled over a five-dollar fare to the port and disappeared. Together with the intercepted text message, she hoped it would convince her watchers to divert resources to Bastiong. She left Hartanto's phone in the door pocket and got out as the second taxi entered the street. She crossed behind it as it squealed to a halt. She walked onto the thoroughfare and hailed an angkot that was headed north. The angkot slowed and she climbed aboard. She caught her breath as it accelerated, only to slow again. Someone called out behind her. A man was running to catch up. It was White Tee. He ran to catch the angkot and climbed in.

He slumped down in a seat near the front and caught his breath. He winced as he pulled out a phone and dialled a number, making no attempt to hide the fact he was watching her as he shouted into it. Ana pretended not to notice. She stared out the window and worked out a plan.

The sunlight had faded by the time they reached the angkot terminal at Ikan Bakar, a sea of floodlights, shopping malls and street seafood vendors that gave it the name. Ana disembarked and walked directly to a two-storey market building next to the terminal. White Tee followed ten metres behind and shouted into his phone.

She skirted past a stairway and into a doorway lit by fluorescent light. She gave herself five minutes before the others arrived.

A passageway led through a long row of Islamic clothing stalls. She entered the third stall on the right and browsed a rack of headscarves. White Tee appeared at the entrance to the hall and looked around. A group of Muslim women pushed past him and into the hallway.

'How much?' said Ana. She handed the salesgirl a green scarf.

'One hundred, mbak.'

Ana surprised her and gave her the cash. She wrapped the scarf around her head and stepped to the hall. Halfway along was an emergency exit door that led back to the angkot terminal. White Tee was ten metres from her. A group of girls laughed as they stepped out of another stall and into his path. She seized her moment and walked. She kept her head bowed as she navigated throngs of animated shoppers and haggard sales staff. Someone shouted further along the hallway. She reached the emergency door, looked up and froze.

Hijab Lady's bright orange headscarf stood out among the greens and greys that filled the hall. She watched Ana from the far entrance, eyes wide, unflinching with the movement of the crowd. Ana turned as White Tee emerged from a stall. He clocked her, then Hijab Lady, and reached for his phone. Hijab Lady brought a phone to her ear and began to move. White Tee stepped into a stall which had a view of the corridor. Ana faced her options: she could return to the apartment, stash her escape kit and hope to go back to being a prisoner, but they had Jonah's message, and once they recovered the phone from the taxi they would know she had either tried to escape or failed to follow through on her agreement. Run or not, Hartanto's deal would be off, and her life would amount to a mouldy cell.

So she would run.

A fire hydrant was mounted opposite the emergency door. Next to it was a small panel that read 'Emergency Break Glass' in

Indonesian and English. White Tee watched her. Hijab Lady was ten metres away. Ana took a breath and willed herself across the hall. Three steps – two. The panel was in reach. She reached out and pressed.

Nothing.

'Sana!' shouted a woman. It must have been Hijab Lady.

Ana looked down at the panel; the glass hadn't broken. She gripped her phone. White Tee stepped out from behind a rack of tunics. Ana struck the panel with the phone. Still nothing.

Commotion behind her. Commands to move. She swung the phone again and the glass cracked. Her phone fell, then, for a second, nothing happened.

Then everything happened at once.

A thousand alarms erupted in chorus with frantic screams and shouts from the women around her. Water burst from lines of pipes along the ceiling and drenched everything in sight. Shoppers and staff scrambled and slipped on the soaked floor. Ana dived for her phone and crawled between a gap of evacuees for the emergency exit. Someone pushed past her and fell. She followed the torrent of water and screaming women along the corridor, through a panel door and into the night air. Locals gathered among the angkots and she ran for them in search of cover. White Tee emerged from the emergency exit and looked around. A blur of orange flashed amongst a group of women who ran from the far exit. Sirens wailed in the distance. White Tee shouted to someone and Ana realised the other watchers would have by now reached the market. She adjusted her headscarf and walked south, head down but eyes up, leaving a trail of water behind her. There was no turning back now. She would escape, or she would rot.

She pushed through crowds of onlookers and headed for the walls of Fort Oranje that loomed over the next street. Fire trucks fought to pass jammed traffic. She crouched as she ran through a gap between buses into a shaded alcove by the enormous walls of the fort, sucking in air as she watched the line of cars. No-one followed. People meandered along the footpath from either direction; she checked each of them, but they were focused on the cacophony of sirens and alarms to the east. She had to keep moving. She tightened the scarf and ran south.

A narrow lane followed the southern wall of the fort. Two men smoked and laughed by a row of motorcycles at the far end. She stopped by a plane tree and checked her cash. She gripped a hundred-thousand rupiah note and started towards the two ojek riders. Only then did she see Leather Jacket.

He approached from the north, phone to his ear but not speaking, his eyes darting left and right across the scene. Ana hid behind the tree under shadow from the streetlight as he turned towards her. He was ten metres from her, eyes still scanning. She held the phone tight. Five metres now. The phone came away from his ear and disappeared. He stopped at the next tree along. She took a shallow breath and held it. Her pulse rang in her ears. Leather Jacket stood motionless for a time, and she checked behind her; one hundred metres to the next street and any chance of losing him in a crowd. With all her effort she took a controlled, silent breath, only to hear a sigh, but it wasn't her own. He'd found her. His boot crunched on gravel, and she tensed – this was it. But the next step was further away, as was the one after that. She stole a glance and saw him walk in the direction he'd come, followed by a thin stream of urine that drained from the base of the tree. She exhaled and steadied herself while she caught her breath. She was clear.

For now.

She ran to the boys and asked for an ojek. They looked at her wide-eyed before giggling to each other. Ana held out the cash and they fell silent. One of them composed himself, chucked his cigarette, and gestured to the motorcycle. *'Ke mana, mbak?'* he said. Ana checked for Leather Jacket, then showed the boy an address on her phone. He took it and studied the map while a taxi crept along the street, its light doused. Ana moved her face from view and kept watch on the street. The taxi passed without stopping and disappeared. The boy returned the phone, started the motorcycle and she climbed on.

They rode north, then uphill. Ana checked for signs of a tail but saw only a blur of headlights that petered out as they climbed higher. The boy found the address without difficulty, a grand old church with a wide lookout over the strait. She paid him off and continued on foot to a set of traffic lights. An internet café on the opposite corner promised deluxe food and cheap rates. She waited for a gap in traffic and walked towards it. A siren blared nearby. A car sped up for an amber light. She reached the sidewalk. A motorcycle rounded the corner and the passenger laughed. Three more paces, hand on the door. She pulled with resignation; if anyone had followed her here, so be it. The door opened and she stepped into a sanctuary of bright halogen, cigarette smoke and monitor glare. The attendant stared at her, and she realised she was still drenched from the market.

'Satu jam,' she said to him. One hour.

'Seratus ribu,' he said. One hundred thousand.

She took the cash from her pocket and handed him two fifties.

He looked out at the computers. *'Duabelas,'* he said. Twelve.

It was in the first row, in clear site of the front desk.

'Delapan-belas,' she said. Eighteen. She forced a smile.

He frowned, then wrote down a password.

'Makasih,' she said.

She caught a breath. The internet cafe was arranged in four rows of high-walled desks. In the far corner, three teenage boys giggled at something on one of the screens. Number eighteen was halfway along the second row, close to a door that read 'kamar kecil' – restroom – in scrawled handwriting. She sat down and typed in the code, and the computer unlocked to a standard Windows screen with icons for several dozen apps and games. A small window in the top-right corner counted down from sixty minutes.

She inserted the thumb drive and opened the familiar list of documents. One was a half-completed article she had written before she departed for Sofifi, the other her notes from Sabo. The last file was the video of the Sabo beheading.

Someone moaned behind her as she opened the draft article. The boys laughed, and she realised they were watching porn. She took a breath and began to type.

Despite her discomfort, the words flowed. She cleaned up her paragraphs on Sayeed's interview and documented what she knew of the extremist uprising in Sabo, then described the video of the beheading and the details she could remember from her interview with Rachmann. With twenty minutes to go she added the final details: facts she wasn't supposed to know, let alone disclose. Secrets that would turn the sectarian conflicts of North Maluku on their head and reveal to the world the folly of domestic oppression.

Noise at the door.

Two people had entered the cafe. She peeked over the partition to see a man and woman in their twenties she hadn't seen before. They said something to the receptionist, then looked out over the computers. Ana dipped her head. The boys were chatting. She saved her article to the thumb drive and removed it, ready to run for the bathrooms and what she hoped was an exit. The couple discussed prices with the attendant and she relaxed. If they were looking for a foreigner, he would have given her away by now. The woman said a cheery *'Nanti saja'* – later – and walked out. Ana checked the clock as soon as the door closed. Fourteen minutes.

Write.

She completed the final sentence with five minutes to go. She opened the internet browser and navigated to Gmail to create a new account, which she registered with the phone number of the spare SIM card. She wrote to Tanner and explained what she'd written and what to expect in the next forty-eight hours, then attached the article along with the video. When the timer was at thirty seconds, she pressed 'Send' and waited. The timer ran out. The boys behind her cheered. They had started playing FIFA; one of them had scored a goal.

She returned to the church and savoured the view over Ternate. The city's lights glimmered below her, returned to brilliance in spite of her ordeal while Sofifi and Sidangoli twinkled on the horizon under the black ridges that marked the Halmahera coast. But the view was lost, blurred by a film of tears as the torment of her ordeal overcame her. She sobbed into her hands, anxious not to draw attention, convinced her life would never again be the same, even if she had done what she knew was right. Eventually the convulsions of her chest settled. She was still alive; she was still free. All that was left now was to escape. She retrieved her burner phone and tried to turn it on, but her fingers slipped off the glass. She wiped them on her shirt and got the phone to flicker into life. The light of its screen seemed brighter than the sun as she opened the contacts list.

There was only one number.

34

The Toyota SUV crept along the darkened street. Ana waited behind the low wall of a vacant lot as the headlights swept over her and came to a halt in front of a shuttered workshop. A bead of light appeared at the driver's seat, and her phone vibrated in her pocket.

She walked up to the passenger door and knocked on the glass. The driver's face was lit up by the glow of his phone and she saw he was Caucasian. The door unlocked.

She opened it. 'Liam Ellis?'

He glanced at her, then along the street. 'Get in.'

She climbed in and closed the door. 'Drive. Please.'

Liam stared at her. His eyes were sunken into the plump flesh of his face, rendered pale by the light of his phone. Three days' growth lined his jaw and neck. The car smelt of body odour. He shut down the phone and placed it in the centre console.

'They'll find us here,' she said.

'Who, exactly?'

'The people working for Hartanto.'

Liam opened his mouth as if to say something, then frowned. He released the park brake and moved off. He drove downhill then turned south onto a major street. Ana watched the parked vehicles either side.

'Want to tell me what's going on?' said Liam. He slowed for a traffic light. It turned green as he reached it, and they continued.

'I was arrested.'

He glanced at her.

'I was meeting a source in Tobelo. They got both of us.' A fire engine crossed their path at the intersection ahead, lights blaring. It was headed uphill. 'They took my passport, laptop, everything. Threatened to charge me with spying.'

Liam drove without haste. He glanced at her, then focused on the road. 'You don't look under arrest.'

'They let me go.'

He squinted, then slowed to make a turn. A kaki lima sauntered across the road in front of them. Liam swore as he swerved to avoid it.

'You don't believe me,' she said.

'You said they accused you of spying.' The engine growled as Liam accelerated. 'Why would they release you?'

'They wanted my help to find Jonah.'

'Jonah?'

'I know it's not his real name.'

Liam sucked a breath through his teeth.

'Hartanto wanted to use me as bait, but I ran.' She braced for a pothole. 'Jonah told me I could trust you.'

They reached the main highway that ran north to south through the city. Only hours earlier, Ana had travelled this same road in the angkot under White Tee's gaze, but now it felt like a previous life. Liam turned right and parked by a shuttered travel agent.

'Why are you stopping?'

Two scooters cruised by. An angkot rang its bell as it passed in the opposite direction. 'There'll still be taxis along here,' he said.

'Police too, you arsehole.'

'Go home, Ana.'

'What home?' she shouted. 'A prison cell?'

Liam lifted a hand and scratched the stubble under his chin.

'Look, Ana, I don't know who Jonah is or what he told you, but I don't do…' he waved his hand around, 'this. I'm just a consular officer.'

'I know what you are, Liam.'

He turned to face her. 'You don't know shit,' he said, 'so save it. All I can do is make sure you receive fair treatment from the authorities and get access to competent representation. Apart from that, I'm no use to you, whatever you think you know.'

Ana stared at him and he looked away. A streetlight cast over his shoulders and left his face in shadow. A man crossed the road in the distance. She watched him turn onto the footpath and walk towards them.

'It's true, you know.' The man's face came into view as he approached. When he was twenty metres away, he turned down an alley. 'I was spying,' she said. Her voice was shaking. 'For Jonah.'

Liam turned to face her. He brought his hand to his mouth and cleared his throat.

'He came to see me a few days ago,' Ana continued. 'He explained the Indonesians were cutting some deal with the Islamists and he wanted to stop it.'

Liam shifted in his seat.

'Does that mean something to you, Liam?'

He clicked his tongue. 'What did it have to do with you?'

'He needed me to prove it. The police provided security for the negotiations, and my source, the one they arrested, was high up in POLDA.'

He let out a frustrated sigh and rubbed his nose. 'When did he come to see you?'

'Tuesday.'

'Two nights ago?'

'Two nights ago.'

He took a long breath, like he was calming himself. 'And did your source prove it?'

'Yeah,' she said. 'He showed me police reports of security

operations that matched the dates and places Jonah had given me. Then we were arrested.'

'Those reports would have been classified.'

She shrugged.

'You were stupid to go through with that.'

She stared out the window. He was right.

'You can see why I need your help,' she said. 'They'll arrest me if they find me. I won't stand a chance.'

Liam drummed his fingers on the wheel. Ana checked the time. It had been more than three hours since she fled her apartment. Most of Ternate would be on alert by now, and it would be impossible to get off the island.

'I guess you won't,' he said. He swore under his breath and started the SUV.

'Where are we going?' she said.

He pulled onto the road and accelerated.

'The only place you'll be safe.'

The apartment complex was built on a high ridge overlooking southern Ternate and lit by yellow floodlights. Liam parked and led Ana up several flights of stairs to a balcony that looked over Tidore. Ana took in the view while he unlocked the front door.

'Quick,' he said.

She followed him into a grand lounge room. Lights came on to reveal a high ceiling over an oversized open-plan kitchen. A television hung from a wall in front of a triple-set of plush sofas arranged around a wide coffee table. Liam left her and disappeared into a small hallway next to the dining area. Above a ten-seater dining table was a landscape of the Sydney skyline that stretched across the wall. Beyond was another balcony with a view of the Ternate lights.

Liam came back a few minutes later and pointed at a bedroom. 'You can sleep in there.' He gestured around the apartment. 'Bathroom's here, kitchen if you need anything.'

'Thanks,' she said. She entered the bedroom and sat on the remade bed. The linen smelled musty.

He held out his hand. 'Phone.'

She gave it to him.

'No calls, internet, anything. Anyone comes to the door, let me answer it. Don't go outside or look through the windows. You're not here.'

'Okay.'

'Get some sleep,' he said. 'I need to make a call.'

CANBERRA

'What the fuck do I do?' said Ellis.

Gibson sat down at the dining table. The clock on the microwave read one-thirty, but he knew it was slow. 'Calm down, Liam,' he said. 'Do the Indonesians know you have her?'

'It won't take them long. I need her out of here.'

'It's a diplomatic property. They can't get in there, even if they find her.'

'Let me call the embassy. Maybe they can send someone—'

'Don't call anyone,' said Gibson. 'Sit tight, stay calm. Let me deal with this.'

'Okay.'

Gibson rang off and rubbed his forehead. He dialled a number and got voicemail.

'It's Andy. Call me when you get this.'

He didn't need another flap. Carter's disappearance had already consumed the service and taken a chainsaw to its relations with BIN. If the Indonesians discovered ASIS was exploiting diplomatic privilege to protect Kovacevic, relations between the two countries would be set back years.

He was about to go back to bed when the phone rang.

'Thanks for calling back so late,' said Gibson.

'Nothing better to do,' said the DDG. 'Talk to me.'

'The girl is in our custody. She was investigating Indonesian negotiations with Islamist groups and got caught, then made a run for it. It could go loud.'

'I understand,' said the DDG. He seemed unfazed, despite hearing what might represent the largest crisis for ASIS in a generation.

'You knew.'

Of course he knew. The DDG was always a step ahead, and Gibson was forever catching up.

'*The Age* called DFAT tonight seeking comment,' said the DDG. 'Looks like she put it all to paper.'

Gibson ran his fingers through his hair and swore. 'Did they hint at what they know?'

'More than we do,' said the DDG. 'I guess we'll find out tomorrow morning.'

'And until then?'

'Get some sleep. Nothing we can do, and you need it.'

Gibson returned to bed. An arm found its way across his stomach and began a slow crawl upwards, tugging at his chest hair before coming to rest on his cheek.

'Anything wrong?' said Scarlett.

Plenty was wrong, not least his capitulation to his urges. Since the divorce, Gibson had lived a life of carefully cultivated celibacy designed to prevent any further trauma. Now he was sharing a bed again with a workmate who was barely half his age and due to fly out in a month's time. If anything, developments in Ternate were a relief. They would give him something else to agonise over.

'Everything's fine,' he said. He kissed her hand. 'Go back to sleep.'

He sure as hell wouldn't.

TERNATE

They came at three a.m.

Ana had been dozing, wrestling with the prospect of probable trial and imprisonment; of not recognising Melbourne when she finally returned. Now she lay motionless, scared to breathe. Blue and red lights flashed behind the window blind.

They knocked again and Liam called out. He padded across the living room and opened the front door. Low voices. Liam spoke, then another man said something in broken English. The door closed and there was silence.

She crept to the window and peeked through the curtain. Two police cars were parked on the street. More lights flashed further along, out of view. A policeman looked up at the apartment and she backed away, careful not to reveal movement. She put on a t-shirt and jeans and walked slowly to the living room. She found Liam in a singlet and boxer shorts.

He gave her a weary look. He looked shattered.

'How do they know I'm here?' she whispered.

'They don't,' he said. Liam sat on the sofa and rubbed his hands up his face. 'But it's an obvious place to check.'

Doors slammed outside and a car drove off. She sat next to him.

'Thank you for this,' she said. 'This isn't your mess.'

He groaned with fatigue. He stared at her with a pair of bloodshot eyes.

'He told me to do it,' he said. 'So I did.'

She reached out and touched his hand.

'Me too.'

35

Legu Gam celebrations had been at their climax the night Jonah had returned.

Ana had been awake, unable to sleep for the noise. Street music and excited chants filled her guesthouse as locals celebrated the birthday of the late sultan, one of countless ceremonies carried out during the festival. Somewhere nearby, a drum struck out of time with the music. It banged again and she realised someone was at the front door.

She rolled out of bed and tread softly to the sitting room. Another two bangs, harder this time. Despite her fear, she knew it was him. She unlatched the door and let Jonah inside. He shut it behind him and examined the apartment.

'Has anyone come to see you?' he said.

'Should they have?'

He moved to the sofa and sat down.

'No.'

Ana studied him. He wore the same cotton shirt and cargo pants he had worn the last time he had been here, muddied now, and torn at the cuffs. Brown stains by his waist and across his shoulders suggested violence.

'Did you find Sayeed?' she said.

Jonah coughed and looked around the room.

Ana's heart sank.

'I'm sorry,' he said.

The music became louder as the festival reached a crescendo. She took a chair from her desk and sat down, head in hands. Questions filled her mind but only one seemed to matter.

'How?'

Jonah's gaze fixed on hers. A lock of hair traced a long curve along the side of his face. 'No-one could have saved him.'

Her cheeks were wet. Suddenly Ana felt responsible for everything that had happened. Everything that would happen. She lowered her hands.

'Then why are you here, Jonah?'

Jonah sat forward, elbows resting on his knees. 'To seek your help.'

Outside, the music changed key and slowed.

'Why would I help you? You haven't helped me.'

'Ana—'

'You just told me my source is dead!' she shouted. 'The source you forced me to reveal so that *you* could protect him.'

Her voice echoed off the sitting room walls and mixed with the drumbeats from the street. Jonah matched her gaze but said nothing – there was nothing more to say. She ran her hands through her hair and stared at the floor. A teardrop fell from her nose and drained into a gap between the tiles.

'You need to go,' she said. She looked up. 'Now. Go.'

He remained still.

She stood up and pointed at the door. 'Go!'

He stared at her, and she realised how immovable he was.

'Fine,' she said. She walked to the kitchen counter and collected her backpack. She threw her phone inside and checked her purse for cash. She felt for the internal pocket and confirmed her passport was inside. Her Lonely Planet guide lay alongside. She thumbed through it looking for hotels or other places to stay. It was late, and most places would be booked out due to the festival, but she had better chances there than staying here. The airline ticket offices would open at nine, and she could be on a flight to Jakarta, or Makassar, or anywhere by mid—

'You were right about Kao and Tobelo.'

—afternoon, assuming she wanted to leave. It was impossible to know. She was tired, exhausted, and isolated; right now, she just wanted to go home and get away from everything. From North Maluku, from violence, from the man in her living room who—

Ana cut the thought. Her hand was wrapped tensely around the bag. She forced herself to let go and count to ten, then turned to face Jonah. 'Right how?'

He spoke to the empty space before him. 'Right that they were evidence of a realignment in North Maluku,' he said. 'A change of guard.'

Outside, the music died down, as if to listen.

'Until recently, we had kept the Islamists busy with one another,' he continued. 'A beating here, a theft there, an occasional burnt mosque, all to keep them at each other's throats. That way, they wouldn't become a threat.'

She shook her head and scoffed. 'You have to be joking,' she said. 'People died, Jonah.'

'I know.' Jonah turned to look at her. A bead of sweat coursed the contour of his cheek. 'Seventeen over six years. Each with a name, a hometown, a family. I know, because one way or another, I was a part of why they died.' The bead reached his jaw, held for a moment, and fell. 'But an insurgency would have killed thousands, Ana. Seventeen lives was a small price to pay for control.'

She looked at the ceiling in disbelief. 'Control,' she said under her breath, inaudible over the sound of drums and chants. Two pieces of a puzzle come together in her mind.

'Then along came Islamic State,' she said. She looked down at him. 'And now you can't *control* them anymore.'

Jonah leaned against the sofa back and nodded, ever-so-slightly.

Eventually, he gestured to the chair. Ana decided she wasn't leaving – not anymore – and returned to it.

'He's Indonesian,' he said once she had sat down. He held a thumb to his nose and cleared a nostril. 'Goes by the alias El-Akhtar. Made a reputation for himself in Syria before he returned. Now, with the way the world's going, he has the local Islamists under a spell.' He tucked a stray lock of hair behind his ear. 'Of course, the Indonesians are too spooked to confront him, so they're trying to negotiate a peace deal with his deputy. A man named Maqsood.'

She knew the name. 'Barpemis.'

'Barpemis,' he repeated. 'They think Maqsood has enough influence with El-Akhtar to contain him.'

Ana reclined on the chair. 'Good for them,' she said. 'If it brings peace.'

Jonah shifted forward. He was shaking his head, and for the first time she noticed his left eye was bloodshot.

'El-Akhtar wants no peace, Ana. This is a man humiliated by defeat in Syria and determined to claim North Maluku for Islamic State. The killings will continue, and tyranny will sweep over this place the same way it did in Iraq and Mindanao. No-one – not Maqsood, not the Indonesian Government – will be able to stop him, and in a few months there will be a new extremist enclave in Australia's backyard. Uncontrolled, uncontrollable, and determined to spread terror wherever it can.'

The drumbeats were now so intense they rattled the windows. Ana's head pounded as she recalled the image of the wind-blown IS flag, draped above the site of future horror, as it lapped at the façade of a Sabo mosque like a coming tide. Suddenly the drums eased and gave way to a whistling melody of Indonesian flutes.

'Why are you telling me this?' she said.

'Because you can prove the government was negotiating with Maqsood.'

Ana shifted on her seat and shook her head. 'Even if I thought that was a good idea,' she said, 'this is nothing to do with me.'

'Isn't it?'

She frowned at him. 'No!'

Jonah grasped her hands, tight enough that she could feel his pulse.

'I know you cared about Sayeed,' he said, 'and so you should.' His eyes were sorrowful, kind. His voice was mellow. 'It was Sayeed who'd discovered that the Indonesians were in contact with Maqsood and wanted to stop it. Maqsood's sympathies lie with Al-Qaeda, not IS, so Sayeed contacted you hoping that if the world knew there was an IS offshoot growing in North Maluku, the Indonesians would be forced to abandon their support for Maqsood.'

The strike of a snare drum outside made her jump.

'Of course, a beheading video would only have scared the Indonesians into more concessions,' he continued. 'Meanwhile, El-Akhtar would grow stronger until eventually he sought independence, at which point the government would have no choice but to send in the military. The only way to prevent a bloodbath is to scuttle the negotiations themselves. I can do that, but only with your help.'

He released her. Her hands fell on her lap, but she held his gaze.

'We're all sorry for the lives that have been lost, Ana. But think about those that would suffer under an Islamic State insurrection here. Think about the threat to the rest of the country if North Maluku falls. Think about home, and tell me you won't do everything you can to protect it.'

Ana looked at her hands. They were red and white from where he had gripped them and soaked in a film of sweat and tears. The parade outside drifted into the distance.

'If I were to help you,' she said eventually, 'what could I do?'

The apartment had fallen silent.

'Sayeed was able to trace Maqsood to his meetings with the government,' said Jonah. 'He knew where they took place, and when. But he couldn't get close enough to prove who was involved.'

'Why not?'

'Because the meetings were guarded by police.'

Another piece of the puzzle fell into place.

'You want me to contact Rachmann,' she said.

'Yes.'

She shook her head. 'I don't see how he can help.'

'Listen to me,' he said. 'Police escort is a big deal. It means reports, shift schedules, vehicle bookings, all recorded in files somewhere. Rachmann can get them for you; he might even have been involved. It doesn't matter. What matters is that he can prove the Indonesian government has betrayed the people of North Maluku.'

'You're asking me to spy for you.'

He leaned towards her and placed a hand on her knee. 'You said you were searching for truth. Now you can find it.'

Ana looked into his eyes. They were determined, forceful. She had watched him place the rabbit in the hat and wave his wand, and yet, despite everything she knew, she could not resist the spell.

'And what if I do?' she said. 'I'm a journalist.'

For the first time that evening, he had smiled.

'Exactly.'

The slam of the front door jolted Ana awake. She shielded her eyes from sunlight that poured in through the narrow gaps in the blinds as she fumbled for her phone. Then she remembered Liam had taken it.

Liam stood at the kitchen counter with his back to her. Beside him were two cups and a newspaper. He pressed a button on a coffee machine and it began to grind.

'How do you like it?' he said. There was something harsh in the tone of his voice.

'I don't,' she said. 'What's going on?'

He gestured at the newspaper. 'See for yourself.'

A copy of *The Age* lay on the counter. There was nothing

remarkable about it except for the words *'Indonesia Facilitating IS Revival',* her name and three paragraphs of text above a note that said, 'Continued on page 4'.

She held her breath in shock. The coffee machine whined as it leaked black fluid into a cup.

Liam turned to her, cup in hand. 'Made us all look like fools, didn't you? No mean feat.' He swirled the coffee and took a sip. 'My bosses say I should congratulate you. If it were up to me, I'd send you packing.'

She took a step forward. 'Really, Liam?' She waved an arm at the sunlit apartment. 'You think I want this? Stuck in some castle while police barricade the gates, never to know when I might leave?'

'Shit lifestyle choice,' said Liam. He took another sip. 'But plenty have made it to get famous. Now you have.'

'I did it for Jonah!'

He laughed. 'People do all sorts of things for him because they think they are doing it for themselves. You're no different.'

'Fuck you. Did you even read the article?'

'Every word.'

'Then explain how I knew about Maqsood's meetings in Kusuri.'

He put his cup on the counter.

Ana rested her hands on the counter. 'Like I said, Jonah wanted to stop the negotiations.'

'Seems unlikely,' he said. 'He knows the Indonesians aren't afraid of their own media.'

'So you're saying I betrayed him?'

He shrugged.

Ana shook her head, exasperated, and sat on one of the sofas. A cloud moved overhead, and the apartment darkened.

'Where is he, then?' she said. 'He's sure as fuck not here.'

Liam cocked his head and blinked.

'He comes to me in the night to tell me all about Maqsood meeting government agents in Kusuri and sends me away to tap my source, an assignment that probably put my source in jail and almost did the same for me, and yet, when I make my heroic return, he's not even here to receive the proof. Does that not seem odd to you?'

He downed the last of his cup and turned away from her. He reached for the machine and started another pour.

'He didn't even tell *you* what he was up to.' Ana stood up and returned to the counter. 'Surely, if his aim was to find out what my source knew, he'd have someone here to hear it. Someone like you, perhaps. But they're not, *Liam,* because that wasn't what he wanted. What he wanted was for me to prove Indonesia was negotiating with extremists, then let the world know.'

The machine rattled and squealed as the cup filled. Once it had finished, Liam turned and leaned on the counter.

'You know I'm right, don't you?'

His head was dipped, eyes on the *Age*. Eventually he raised it, then dipped again. He repeated the movement until it became a nod.

'Thank you,' she said.

He lifted the cup and drained it in one go.

Ana looked around the apartment. Generic paintings hung from most of the walls. Two bookshelves framed the television, lined with trinkets from across Indonesia and books on travel, photography and mountaineering. She picked up a book on avian zoology and thumbed through the pages. Each one contained photos of rare Indonesian bird species, no fewer than ten tagged with the copyright mark of Jonah Somerville.

She put the book down and said, 'This is his apartment, isn't it?'

Liam looked around the cavernous space. 'Yeah.'

'Were you friends?' she said.

Liam watched her, warily. 'Jonah doesn't have friends,' he said. 'He has assets.'

So that's what she was to him, then. An 'asset'.

She must have made a face. 'Don't take it personally,' said Liam, 'it's just how he is. Family breakup, teenage years on the mean streets, if he wasn't getting smacked around by his dad. You don't get through that by seeing the best in people. He brings out the worst, then makes it useful.'

She watched Liam for a while. He made another coffee, like it was a compulsion, and stood blankly, swirling the cup. Like he needed to be somewhere but couldn't admit it.

'Is he in trouble?' she said finally.

He studied her. 'You looking for another story?'

She held eye contact. His eyes fell.

'Yeah, he's in trouble,' he said. 'A lot of it.'

CANBERRA

'Do we believe her?' said the DDG.

'Not a chance,' said the Director of Operations. 'Throw her to the wolves. Jordan trusted her and she sold him out.'

For once, Neill seemed to agree with her. 'And the rest of us. The Indonesians will never work with us again after this.'

'I get it,' said the DDG, waving a hand to cut Neill off. 'Cat's out of the bag, public panicking, government demanding action, all of it, but IS's incursion was never going to stay secret for long, was it. I asked about the girl. Andy?'

The eyes of the room fell on Gibson.

He cleared his throat. 'I think we should give her some benefit of the doubt,' he said. 'If she's telling the truth then she's a hell of an agent, frankly.'

Neill's eyes fell into his teacup. Ops squinted at something out the window.

The DDG smiled and spoke at Legal. 'What are our options?'

Legal adjusted his tie and cleared his throat. 'Unfortunately, it will be difficult for the Indonesians to give her up under these circumstances,' he said. 'They can't enter the apartment, but they can arrest her the moment she leaves for any reason, such as a fire drill, harassment, noise, or anything that puts her off living there. Then there's the possibility of her situation going public.'

'Not much time, then,' said Ops.

The room fell silent. Kovacevic had publicly accused the Indonesian Government of abetting terrorism, and the Australians – ASIS, no less – were protecting her as a fugitive. It would be scandal upon scandal.

The DDG held his face in his hands and inhaled.

'Terry?' said Neill.

The DDG's hands fell on his lap. 'Let her stay,' he said. 'For now. I'll speak with the minister and figure something out.' His gaze turned to Gibson. 'Until then, no more *fucking* news stories.'

TOBELO

Forty-eight hours had passed by the time Kuwat, the courier Raf had forced from early retirement, made contact. Discipline had been no issue. Kopassus was the tip of the Indonesian spear, trained to withstand boredom as much as pain, but the anticipation of action ate at them. Then Raf reported Maqsood had called for a meeting, and tension became motion as Sugianto's men readied to move.

Sugianto peered at Raf's message. 'Your man's in a hurry.'

The message was a set of GPS coordinates and a time: 2030. No date was given, which meant tonight.

'Maqsood follows the news, just like every other Islamist,' said Carter. 'He knows if he waits long, he'll end up like Nadeer.'

The captain shrugged. 'Not such a bad outcome.'

'It is if we lose El-Akhtar.' Carter handed the phone back. 'Maqsood's our best option to find him.'

The captain nodded, then called for his men to ready up.

36

Sugianto was at the wheel of the Hilux. Carter rode shotgun, and three troopers, Benny, Darmo and Putro, each hand-picked by Sugianto, rode on the rear tray along with two holdalls of M4s, explosives and spare ammunition. All were silent, kitted up for war in camouflage fatigues and body armour, their faces painted black. They drove at a steady pace along the unsealed track that led to the target village. When he reached sight of houses, Sugianto doused the headlights, rendering the vehicle black in the moonless night. He turned right at the first intersection and parked in a grassed courtyard surrounded with houses.

Wawan, Sugianto's second-in-charge, appeared at a door to one of the houses dressed in civilian clothes while the troopers dismounted and unloaded their kit. Sugianto entered the house first, followed by Carter and the swift and silent movements of the Kopassus team. The holdalls went on the floor of a darkened sitting room that was bare except for a rotted rocking chair in one corner. One of the troopers gave Wawan a set of body armour while the others prepared their weapons and loadouts for the operation. Carter left them to it and looked out the main window. Ahead was the high wall of the target compound, above which only the iron roof was visible. Sugianto appeared alongside.

'We're ready.'

Carter inspected the rest of the street and the neighbouring houses. 'Time to go.'

Sugianto's bulk had loomed over the map that was held to the table with bulldog clips and scrawled with the coordinates Maqsood had provided. His right forefinger wrinkled the paper as he tapped it. 'Yaro,' he said. 'Fishing village on the southern edge of Lake Paca, an hour out of Tobelo. One access road in from the main highway, another that leads west into the mountains. By water you can pretty much disappear. No wonder Maqsood chose it.'

'Which one is his safehouse?' said Carter.

Sugianto slapped a Google Maps printout on the table, then pointed to a blurred grey rectangle. 'The address puts the target site here, not far from the lake.'

Carter picked up the printout. 'Any of your guys know the place?'

Sugianto clicked his tongue. 'Jihadi heartland, bos. Got no friends there.'

Carter dropped the piece of paper. It glided across the map and onto the floor. 'Now what?'

'Wawan will go in first to find an observation point and keep an eye out for your mate. We keep numbers to a minimum until he's in place.'

'And the rest of us?'

Sugianto pointed to a jungle clearing near the main road into town. 'Two minutes away, max, covering the main road in and out of town. Can't do shit about the western route.' He stood up straight. 'When – *if* – Maqsood arrives, Wawan will keep tabs on the situation in town. Then it's up to you.' He folded his arms and added, 'Assuming he's alone, otherwise we get the fuck out.'

Carter looked him in the eye. 'He'll be alone. He's got fewer friends now than you do.'

Sugianto grunted.

◆

Wawan had brought his motorcycle to a stop and looked north. The sunbaked street ran for a hundred and fifty metres, slightly downhill, lined by trees and old weatherboard houses. At the far end was a lakeside restaurant, beyond which he could see the mountain peaks of the northern shore. The street was almost empty. Wawan crossed and parked at a warung that had been built into an empty shipping container. Two women emerged, both in their twenties, all but their faces covered by hijab. Wawan smiled at them as he sat down. They gave him an appraising glance and disappeared.

He ordered an iced tea and spent the next twenty minutes observing the road. No-one followed him into town. The owner of the warung paid him no attention and played with his phone in the corner. Wawan drained his glass, typed out a message to Sugianto, then paid up and left.

He rode south, then west, until he reached another road that led to the lake. Ahead of him was the western road to the mountains. After one hundred metres, it disappeared into jungle. He rode north and parked under the shade of a row of plane trees. Ahead of him, on the left-hand side of the road, the roof of a two-storey structure was visible behind a three-metre-high concrete wall. To his right was a bedsit for rent. A skinny, sun-beaten man shovelled gravel into a wheelbarrow halfway along a side street. Two women rode past on a motorcycle. There was no activity in the vicinity of the compound.

No-one paid any attention as Wawan parked the motorcycle and set off north on foot. He crossed the street to reach the compound wall, then stopped as if to send a text message. There was no-one nearby. He checked surrounding windows for movement but saw nothing behind the dark glass. Halfway along the wall was the driveway gate to the complex. He kept the phone in his left hand as he walked and set it to camera mode. The gate was solid iron. As he passed it, he held his left arm out and stretched. When he reached the far corner of the wall, he checked his take: ten photos of the gate and the lock, three of them blurry. It would be enough.

He ate by the lakeside. The town was still quiet, and he was certain no-one had taken an interest in him. He sent the images of the gate to Sugianto and paid up. Three men in tunics arrived as he got up to leave. They watched Wawan warily as he smiled and pushed past them. They muttered to themselves as he exited the café and headed west. He paused when he reached jungle, but the men hadn't followed.

The forested track was pitted with ruts and holes, seemingly barely used. After fifty metres, Wawan stepped off and picked his way through the undergrowth to a clearing. Ahead of him was a row of low-set houses and, behind them, the high wall of the target compound.

The clearing was littered with refuse and the rusted shell of an old truck. He walked swiftly to the wall. There were no security cameras, and the neighbouring houses seemed empty. On the rear wall of the compound, facing towards the jungle hillside, was another solid iron gate. He took photos of the hinges and lock. There was no way to see inside.

Three steel drums lay in a nearby backyard. He checked he was clear and leapt the fence. The barrels were empty. He hoisted one across his shoulders and threw it into the clearing. He waited five minutes; there was no reaction.

Wawan steadied the barrel at the base of the compound wall and climbed up. He lowered himself to a squat, then, careful to maintain balance, jumped to reach the top. The concrete crumbled in his fingers and the barrel toppled. He looked left and right, but there was no-one in the clearing. Then, with all his strength, he pulled himself up to look over.

The house was two levels, built of breezeblocks, with no cameras or obvious signs of security. The windows were covered in dust that made it impossible to see inside. The house took up most of the walled space, with only a narrow gap to the wall on each side. On one side was an empty garbage bin. He dropped to the ground and continued south along a line of trees. He reached a small laneway between two houses that led to the main road. To his half-left was the bedsit and his motorcycle, still untouched. He took a room at the bedsit, sent his report to Sugianto, then set up his camera to wait for Maqsood.

Benny held at the corner by the main street and took a firing position on the compound. Darmo waited until Benny was set, checked the street and crossed, rifle up, to take his own position on the opposite side. *'Set.'*

Wawan and Putro moved across the darkened street. Sugianto waited until they had disappeared into the shadow on the far side, then turned to Carter and whispered, 'Now.'

Carter followed the captain across the street, loaded pistol in hand. Sugianto led him into a niche in the fence line in front of an abandoned house. Carter crouched against the fence to see the street. The town was quiet except for the sound of the breeze coming off the lake and the humming cicadas. Benny crossed the street and covered south.

The compound wall was fifty metres north. *'Moving,'* whispered Darmo over the radio. Putro followed him, both men close against the fence until they disappeared into the front yard of the final house in the row. *'Clear,'* said Putro.

Sugianto tapped Carter on the shoulder and they moved in pursuit. Wawan and Benny followed without a word.

The wall loomed ahead of them. 'Push up,' said Sugianto.

Darmo nodded. He moved up the wall then turned right to head for the corner. Putro followed him while Sugianto and Carter took cover against the wall. Benny and Wawan moved to the rear gate.

Sugianto looked at Carter. 'You ready?'

Carter nodded.

Sugianto reached for his radio and clicked the push-to-talk.

There was a noise somewhere south.

A starter motor.

Sugianto released the radio.

The sound of the engine grew. It was on the other side of town, headed towards them.

The troopers backed away from the street. Carter checked the Glock. Wawan and Benny were focused on the rear of the compound.

'Lights.'

Headlights lit a corner of a house south of them before a van appeared. It turned north onto the street and headed towards the compound.

'This your guy?' said Sugianto.

Carter ignored him. The van crept closer. Darmo and Putro followed its movement with their rifles. It was twenty metres away, ten. It wasn't slowing. The barrels swept in unison as it passed. Putro stepped out from the wall to clear his line of fire, then stepped back behind cover. The van was gone.

'Visual?' said Sugianto.

The radio clicked. *'A local,'* said Darmo.

Sugianto let out a long breath and looked at Carter. Carter nodded.

Sugianto made a check of his men, then reached for the push-to-talk.

Click.

'It doesn't feel right,' Sugianto had said. He sat on a wooden chair and inspected his fingernails. 'No-one has been in that house for a long time. No recent traffic on the driveway, no signs of life. Fuck knows what's inside.'

'Makes sense if it's a safehouse,' said Carter. He held up Wawan's photo of the front gate, taken on his scouting patrol. 'Where's Wawan?'

'Holed up in a rental flat to watch for Maqsood's arrival.' Sugianto leaned forward. 'Hasn't seen jack shit, bos.'

'He won't if Maqsood's already inside.'

The Kopassus man studied him. 'So what are you gonna do?'

'Wait,' said Carter. 'If he makes the meeting, we grab him and extract. Otherwise, we go in.'

'You don't know he's there.'

Carter placed his hands on the table and peered at Sugianto. 'Something is. And Maqsood wants us to find it.'

'Move,' said Sugianto.

Both pairs of troopers disappeared behind the walls. Carter moved up to the corner. Sugianto stayed behind him to cover south. The wind had picked up, but the street was quiet.

Darmo had taken a firing position to cover north. Benny was crouched behind him, in the niche of the main gate. He dropped his carry bag and pulled out a line of explosive. He kneaded it into the gap between the iron gates so that it would cut the iron bar, then connected the detonator and trigger box. He stepped behind the concrete wall. *'Set.'*

Sugianto shifted his weight.

Wawan's voice crackled over the radio: *'Set.'* Both gates were rigged to explode.

Sugianto took in a sharp breath and clicked the push-to-talk. *'Move in.'*

The wind settled. For a moment, there was silence.

It was nine-thirty. Maqsood was an hour late.

'No sign of movement,' said Sugianto.

Carter sat in the passenger seat of the Hilux. Through the treeline, he could barely see the road that led into Yaro.

'Bring me the phone,' said Carter.

Sugianto looked at him, then climbed out and spoke to one of the troopers. He returned a moment later and handed the burner to Carter. 'You sure about this?' he said.

Calling entailed some risk, since it could compromise Maqsood. But it was too late for that. If Maqsood was under surveillance or duress, there was nothing more Carter could do for him.

He dialled. The call went to automated voicemail.

Carter hung up. 'We go in.'

Sugianto shook his head. 'We've been here before, Carter. It nearly got you killed.'

Carter turned on him. 'It's different this time. He's on the run, Sugi, from faceless enemies we set upon him.'

Sugianto clicked his tongue. 'My men aren't equipped for a raid like this, Pak. I agreed to help you find El-Akhtar, not put my men in danger.'

Carter held the captain's gaze. 'Suit yourself.' He climbed out of the Hilux and retrieved his backpack from the rear tray.

Sugianto followed him. 'Where are you going?'

'Someone has to get inside that house.'

Benny stepped in Carter's way.

'I can't let you do that,' said Sugianto.

Carter turned to face the captain. 'You don't have a choice.'

Sugianto squinted.

'Remember, Sugi, you've aided and abetted a fugitive. Pretty serious crime. Enough to end a man's career.'

Sugianto sighed. 'You're an arsehole, Carter.' He turned to his troopers. 'Kit up,' he ordered.

'We leave in five minutes.'

Two thumps from the explosive charges echoed off the walls.

'Go,' said Sugianto. Carter crouched and ran. Darmo and Benny disappeared into a small cloud of dust where the gate had been.

'Push left,' said Darmo over the radio.

'Eyes on rear door,' said Wawan. The second team was inside the compound.

A starter motor sounded in the distance. Carter was three metres from the gate.

'Front door locked,' said Benny.

Carter reached the gate and looked inside. The house stood tall ahead of him. The windows were blacked out. Benny stood to one side of Darmo, who was picking the lock of the front door. Sugianto crouched alongside Carter, weapon facing to the street.

'Two's inside,' said Wawan.

Darmo put away his toolkit. Benny stepped back from the door and raised his rifle to provide cover. *'One is entering.'*

Darmo opened the door. Benny checked, then moved inside. A second later, both troopers had disappeared.

Carter prepared to move in.

'Wait,' said Sugianto.

'Sitting room clear,' whispered one of the troopers.

The street was still empty, but the wind had dropped. Two engines were audible now from the east.

'First floor clear.'

'Stairs.'

Sugianto moved to the other side of the gate and covered south. Carter moved inside the compound wall and looked out.

'Bedroom,' said a trooper. *'Check left.'*

The engines grew louder, but there was no sign of light anywhere in the town.

Sugianto checked his watch and shook his head.

'Clear.'

There was a burst of static in Carter's earpiece.

'What is that?'

'Could be weapons.'

The vehicles were somewhere south of town.

'Check the documents,' said a trooper. *'Two, take the master bedroom.'*

'Copy.'

Carter shifted so he could look south. The vehicles had stopped out of sight. Something moved to his left. Carter looked north but saw nothing.

'In, going left,' said one of the troopers. *'Clear.'*

'Wait, there's something here.'

Sugianto looked at Carter, then reached for his radio. *'Expedite.'*

'Stand by.'

The vehicles were on the move again. Sugianto shifted to get a better view of the road.

Static, then: *'...the wires lead there.'*

Carter heard a door slam to the north.

Sugianto grabbed his radio again. *'What is taking so—'*

'Bomb! Go!'

Sugianto looked up at the house, then at Carter. Suddenly his face lit up in headlights.

'Get out!'

Sugianto pulled Carter behind him and raised his rifle. Carter scrambled for cover. The vehicles accelerated. Sugianto braced his shoulder against the compound wall and aimed.

Then night became day.

The blast obliterated the top floor of the building and propelled Carter into the street. The shock of the blast reverberated throughout his limp body and echoed off the surrounding structures. Apart from the ringing of his ears, the world fell silent. His nostrils filled with the stench of cordite and burnt flesh.

He lifted his head as the sound of engines cut through the hiss. The Glock lay two metres ahead of him. Beyond, two discs of light approached along the road. He pushed towards the pistol with his legs. The lights became headlights that became a van. All he heard was ringing in his ears.

Something moved to his right. Sugianto was on his feet, leaning against what was left of the wall.

Gunfire burst from the side of the van. Sugianto raised his rifle and fired a three-round burst as a bullet struck the wall near his head. The van closed to within twenty metres, then swerved. Sugianto continued to fire as it mounted the opposite curb and struck a tree. Sugianto fired again. The gunner fell from the side door onto the ground.

Men were shouting from the north.

Sugianto braced the rifle on his thigh and reloaded. His left arm hung limp by his side. A second vehicle appeared.

Sugianto dragged his right leg as he turned north to open fire. The blood that poured from his neck glistened under the muzzle flash of the rifle. The *pop-pop-pop* reverberated across the street.

Carter dived and crawled for the Glock. His feet slipped on the gravel as gunfire erupted from the north. He looked up as Sugianto's head snapped back and its contents exploded over the white-painted wall. A half-second later another round struck him in the chest and propelled his broken body backwards to leave him sitting against the remains of the wall, much like Yoyok had, as his life drained onto the pavement.

The shouting was closer. Carter pushed forward again. The Glock was close now. His fingertips brushed the cold metal as they got to him.

He made a final lunge as the pistol was kicked away. The next kick struck his ribs.

He coiled into the foetal position as more blows landed. A vehicle pulled up and an attacker shouted something in Arabic. Someone punched his thigh and pulled his ankles. His legs were pulled straight as he was dragged along the ground. He rolled onto his back and saw five men tower over him. One of them spat on Carter's face. An engine idled close by. One of the men shouted again and the others lifted Carter. He reached up with his arms to break their grip and dropped to the ground. The next kick struck him in the kidney, and when he arched his back, one of them grabbed his hair and lifted his head. The others took him under his arms and lifted his legs. They threw him onto a metal tray. He tried to move away while two of them climbed on board and tied his hands and ankles. He held his breath for another strike, but it never came.

'Go!' shouted one of the men who had tied him.

Carter lay face down. As the ute started moving, he rolled onto his back, only to feel the sole of a boot on his shoulder and the hot muzzle of a rifle at his neck. He could see over the edge of the tray. They were headed north, through Tobelo. The city faded and he felt a cool breeze off the sea before they finally stopped. They had arrived at a village.

The men shouted at one another. More voices joined them from nearby. The tailgate was lowered and hands gripped his ankles. Carter clenched his jaw.

They pulled him off the ute by his feet. He landed face first onto gravel and rolled. A man stood over him, an AK-47 draped over his chest and a cigarette in his mouth. 'Take him inside,' shouted the man. Two men dragged him by the ankles and up a set of steps. Carter's head struck each one as they took him inside into a small, windowless room. Above him was a single lightbulb that hung from the ceiling on its cord. A metre from it was a butcher's hook suspended from a metal rung that was bolted to the ceiling. One of the men lifted him and cut the metal tape from his wrists.

'Stand up,' said the man with the AK.

Carter's mouth was full of blood and dirt. 'N—no.'

The AK struck him in the chest. He screamed.

'Stand up,' the man repeated.

Carter tried to stand and fell against the wall. A guard grabbed him by the wrists and retied them in front of him.

'Shokran,' said AK.

The guard pulled Carter's arms into the air. The other bearhugged him from behind and lifted him. The rope was looped over the hook, then he was released. There they left him, suspended from the ceiling, the light bulb alight only centimetres from his face. He cried out, but there was no answer. His toes scraped the ground as he tried and failed to lift his weight off his wrists. First his hands went numb, then his arms. Finally his head slumped forward, and he passed out.

37

CANBERRA

The Australian Signals Directorate picked up the first social-media reports within hours of the blast. Most of government was notified immediately, including ASIS. The duty officer had called Gibson straight away and by the time he was at his desk at five a.m, the intelligence community had filed their initial reports.

Cellular traffic showed a burst of activity in a region south-west of Tobelo, which corroborated evidence that initial tweets about the event were posted by locals of a town called Yaro, a fishing village at the south end of a large jungle lake and at the centre of Barpemis heartland. A bombing represented ANVIL's worst fears: a new threshold of sectarian violence and a point of no return.

The video changed all that. It was posted at eight-fifteen a.m. Australian time by a Yaro local whom Scarlett couldn't link to any Islamist groups. This was no propaganda video, only the survey of the devastation of a man's hometown. The video started inside the compound of a shattered building and panned to show a collapsed wall. The video taker's voice wavered as he described nearby cars with their windows blown out. Flames flickered from the charred van across the street. The camera followed someone into the structure and stopped by the body of an Indonesian soldier who lay where the front door had been, then the guide said there were more inside. The camera adjusted to the light and revealed four more soldiers in pieces near the staircase, half-buried by debris. The cameraman asked who they were but got no answer. Whoever they were, Gibson thought, they knew it was coming. The cameraman returned to the street through wreckage and clusters of shell-shocked bystanders. A group had gathered near the outside of the wall and parted as he approached.

The slumped body was framed by blood splatter across what remained of the wall. Gibson recognised Sugianto immediately. The friendly eyes, now separated by an entry wound, stared resolutely at a target on the ground by his feet. Four gunshot wounds in his chest caught the morning sunlight. Others, in his legs and left arm, drained blood onto the pavement.

Gibson paused the video to remember his comrade, now slain in pursuit of the terror he had fought against for so long. Then, in that moment of grief, the significance of the bullet wounds became clear: whoever had murdered Sugianto's team had waited for them. Gibson wiped his eyes and forced himself to watch the rest of the video. A woman entered the frame and said something while she held a bandage to her head, but Gibson's powers of interpretation had left him, and her words left only soft impressions on him until the only sound left in his tiny, windowless office was his own sobbing.

'You look like you need something stronger,' said Scarlett.

Gibson took a sip of burnt long black. 'This'll have to do.'

'Maybe some news will help.' She took a guest chair. 'Two things,' she said. 'The Defence Attaché just called. His counterpart confirmed the raid wasn't sanctioned. Sugianto's team was supposedly on training exercises. Since Tuesday.'

'That's when Jordan went off grid.'

'Mm-hmm.'

'What else?'

Scarlett lifted the folder in her lap and opened it on the desk. 'Satellite imagery of the target site from two days ago. DDG pulled some strings.'

Gibson peered at the printouts.

'The large white rectangle left and up from centre is the blast site,' said Scarlett. 'A house surrounded by a boundary wall. Matches up with the video.'

Behind the printout was a document. Gibson couldn't be bothered to read it. 'What does the report say?'

'They've looked at photos of the site over the past four weeks. No vehicles, laundry out to dry, nothing. My guess is a safehouse.'

'Rigged to blow?'

She shrugged. 'Depends on what was inside.'

Gibson rubbed his face. His thoughts went to the blood-stained wall.

'Not Sugianto,' he said.

'Pardon?'

'Sugianto was never in a hurry. He'd know everything about the house before going in: who owned it, who built it, who paid the bills. He'd have had eyes on it for days to watch who came, went, or walked past. These guys had shooters placed in waiting, which tells me Sugianto's boys rushed it. They were tipped off and felt like they had to move quickly.'

'It's the sort of thing Jordan would do.'

She'd said it innocently, as if reminiscing, but when he looked at her, she turned apologetic.

'Sorry, I didn't—'

'It's okay.'

He brought up the video taken in Yaro then scrolled to the last few minutes and the woman with the head injury. She spoke in a thick North Maluku accent that was difficult to make out.

Scarlett leaned in. 'What's she saying?'

'She was there when the bomb went off,' he said. 'She was knocked out by the blast but woke up when the shooting started.

They came in two vans. One of them was left burning on the street. Sugianto must have destroyed it.'

Scarlett watched him. 'Then the second one got him.'

'Yeah, they got him.' He shook his head, frustrated with himself for not having paid attention. 'Then they took the survivor.'

The options were limited. All agencies of Australian intelligence were tasked to divert whatever resources they had to North Maluku and begin a full sweep of mobile, satellite and radio traffic, but Gibson knew whoever had Carter would likely use encrypted messaging apps that would take too long to break. ASIS needed assets in place, but the loss of ANVIL meant they were blind. Ellis had been warned off contacting Anas or anyone else close to Hartanto. 'The Indonesians might not know Carter's missing,' said Security. 'We can't trust Anas not to tip off his boss.'

'We may not have a choice,' said Neill. 'We'll never find who took him without BIN support.'

Gibson had tried calling Hartanto earlier under the cover of expressing condolences for the Kopassus deaths. 'Unfortunately, he's not taking our calls.'

'Why should he?' said Ops. 'He doesn't need us anymore.'

It was obvious why not. Australian intelligence, decimated in North Maluku, was desperate just to save its own, let alone capable of performing its core mission of providing options and insight to government. It was only cold comfort that they weren't prepared to leave Carter behind.

The DDG crossed his legs and formed a steeple with his hands. Neill examined his teacup. Security scribbled something on a plain white pad.

'So where does that leave us?' said the DDG.

'We could offer a trade,' said Legal. 'Hand over Ana Kovacevic in return for Indonesia's assistance to locate and repatriate Mister Carter.'

The room stopped.

'She's a felon, after all,' said Legal. 'We have a duty of care to our employee.'

'Jesus Christ, Barron,' said the DDG. 'Did four years of law school turn you into a heartless bastard or were you born that way?'

Legal shrugged like it was a fair question.

'We damn well won't do anything of the sort.' The DDG stood up to signal the meeting was over. The LT shuffled out of their seats. Gibson stood and moved his chair back to its original position by the desk.

'Andy.'

Gibson stopped and waited for the group to file out. The DDG stood behind his desk and gestured to one of the seats opposite.

Gibson sat down. The DDG stared at him, as if unsure how to approach what he was about to say. Gibson thought of Scarlett, then of his shame. It was a helpful affair, if unnecessary, but it did nothing for him to be called out on it by the operational head of ASIS, especially at a time like this.

'Did you ever buy Nadeer's claim?' said the DDG.

Gibson was still ruminating on his imminent dismissal. 'Come again?'

'His claim about El-Akhtar's camp.' The DDG waved a hand. 'Somewhere up past Galela.'

Gibson thought back to Nadeer's interrogation and his revelation of El-Akhtar's identity. The reports at the time suggested there was no basis for any camps where Nadeer claimed, and with the events that followed, no-one took it further. 'It seemed like a desperate guess,' he said. 'The sort of thing someone would say to impress an interrogator.'

'Hm.' The DDG opened his safe and removed a purple folder marked *TOP SECRET // AUSTEO // CAULDRON.* Satellite intelligence for Indonesia. He placed it on the desk in front of Gibson and said, 'Have a look.'

Gibson squeezed the bridge of his nose and adjusted his glasses. The summary announced indications of likely encampments in the region of Saluta, a coastal village on the eastern shore of the peninsula at the northernmost tip of Halmahera.

The DDG spoke while Gibson scanned the pages. 'Had to perform all sorts of favours to convince these bastards to look at Yaro,' he said. 'So I figured, if I was to sell my soul to get a look south of the South China Sea, I might as well check out the rest of the neighbourhood.'

Gibson flipped through colourised prints of satellite photographs that had been taken in infra-red, visible and ultra-violet light.

'And I'm happy to say it was worth it,' the DDG continued.

Rows of tents were plainly visible amongst the foliage south of the village, where a flat region extended inland and showed signs of earthworks, drainage and communal farming. It was a training camp.

'How did we miss this the first time?' said Gibson.

'Probably wasn't there.' The DDG folded his arms. 'The latrines were only dug a week ago. El-Akhtar's settling in.'

Gibson looked at the photographs one more time and handed the file back. 'I guess we should pass it on to Jakarta.'

The DDG collected the file and returned it to the safe. 'Not if our man is there.'

'You think El-Akhtar has Jordan.'

The DDG sat down and drummed his fingers on the table. 'I'm certain.'

Gibson waited for an explanation. The drumming stopped.

'You know,' said the DDG, 'it always bothered me that Jordan would want to reveal BIN's negotiations with Maqsood.'

Gibson hummed agreement. It had played on his mind as well. 'Perhaps Kovacevic made it all up.'

The DDG stood up and walked to the window. 'She couldn't have,' he said. It was a fine Canberra day, blue sky, crisp, elm trees swaying in the breeze. 'She didn't know about Maqsood's connection to El-Akhtar, yet she wrote about it.' He shook his head. 'And even if she did know, why name Maqsood publicly?

No-one knows or cares who he is. She could have simply revealed IS's enclave and raked it in, and instead she invited retaliation.'

Gibson realised he was right. Revealing Maqsood had made no impression on the Australian audience; he was insignificant. All that had mattered was the black flag.

The DDG turned and stood behind his chair. 'Then I discovered the answer.'

Gibson raised an eyebrow.

The DDG was smiling. 'You on social media, Andy?'

Gibson shook his head and made a face. 'I'm not even sure I could spell it.'

'Quite alright. I've heard your social life isn't too bad lately anyway.'

Scarlett again. Another pang of shame.

'Every extremist faction with a name uses it,' the DDG continued. 'Especially Islamic State. Always did, still do.' He brushed something off his shoulder. 'One of the analysts ran a report for me, and sure enough, not long after Kovacevic's article hit paper, every Islamic extremist from here to Raqqa had commented on it. Almost unanimously, El-Akhtar comes out in bad shape. But notably'—his hands fell to the desk—'Maqsood comes out worse. Sellout, dog, traitor, pick your name.'

He leaned over the desk. 'So you can see El-Akhtar's problem. He's supposed to hate government, not let his number two climb into bed with a bunch of spooks. Hard to be credible as a fanatic with that sort of nonsense going on.' He pushed back and folded his arms. 'What we forget is how much these guys are driven by ego. The desire to outdo the other guy. This was a significant blow to El-Akhtar's prestige, if you could call it that.'

Gibson swept his fingers through his hair. It was all suddenly so obvious. 'Jordan wanted to compromise Maqsood,' he said.

'You got it.' The DDG sat down and slapped his thighs. 'And so what does our boy Maqsood do?' He held out an upturned palm. 'Well, Carter's counting on him calling for help, isn't he. Meanwhile,

El-Akhtar's worried Maqsood will run off to the Indonesians, even though, now that Maqsood's exposed, Hartanto wouldn't piss on him at this point. Maqsood surprises them both and offers Jordan's head as a dowry to his boss. He sets up a meeting with Jordan and tells El-Akhtar all about it. El-Akhtar's experienced, of course – he expects Jordan to show up with friends, so he brings a few of his own. A couple of bangs later, he's got our man.'

Gibson could think of no better theory. He shook his head and swore at himself. 'Impetuous bastard.'

'Don't blame Jordan for this.' The DDG leaned forward on the desk. 'He was always straining at the leash. Always taking it on himself to find a way. God knows we encouraged him, did we not? And now, you and I can have this conversation.' He looked over Gibson's shoulder at the frosted glass that separated his office from the main floor. 'Frankly, more of us should follow his example.'

But Gibson did blame Carter. More good men were dead for what he had done, and now his own life was at the end of a knife.

'Suppose Carter is in Saluta,' said Gibson, 'what then? The Indonesians won't help us.'

'Course they won't,' said the DDG. 'They'll string us out for concessions then turn Kovacevic into an international scandal. Besides, what's to say they wouldn't fuck up a rescue, even if they tried?' The DDG looked him in the eye. 'We need them both out of there before Hartanto finds Jordan. Get them out ourselves if we have to.'

'I don't see how,' said Gibson. 'It would take months to move operatives in and develop the sort of assets we'd need. Jordan might have days, at most, and if El-Akhtar doesn't kill him, Hartanto will.'

'Which is why we need eyes on *now.*'

Gibson frowned. Something in the way the DDG spoke indicated his next move. Gibson hadn't thought of it until now. It was unthinkable.

'You want to send in 4 Squadron.'

4 Squadron, Special Air Service Regiment, was the military

element tasked specifically to support ASIS activities worldwide: the experts in irregular warfare, personal protection, and hard-to-reach places.

The DDG nodded. 'Someone to keep an eye on things while we work out our options.'

'Has the minister approved this?'

'Naturally.'

Gibson frowned. 'Why would she take that risk?'

The DDG's trademark smirk appeared, and Gibson knew. For weeks, secret chatter along the halls of government had signalled thc pressure the minister was under. 'I didn't give her a choice,' said the DDG, and turned to look out the window. 'She had backed the Indonesians. They won't do anything about IS, so she's exposed. This was the only lever she had left to pull.'

'Does she know about Jordan?'

The DDG turned and studied Gibson. He took a step forward and leaned on the back of his chair.

'Australian spies don't look so good getting their heads chopped off,' said the DDG. 'Or on trial in a foreign country, for that matter. This way, she can say she took action. Better incompetent than impotent, for some. She can play that line however she damn-well wants.'

'And what happens to him if we succeed?'

The DDG held eye contact, but his focus drifted, as if staring at the horizon. He brought his hands down.

'For now, let's focus on getting him home.'

Gibson squeezed the bridge of his nose – knowing, accepting how it was to be. So unlike Carter for his fate to hinge on the self-interest of others. 'Okay,' he said. He glanced up at the DDG, who was leaned back on his chair, the fingers of each hand interleaved under his chin.

'Tell me you if you have a better idea,' said the DDG.

Gibson didn't have one, so he said nothing.

'Good,' said the DDG. 'We fly to Swan Island tomorrow.'

Gibson nodded, said his thanks, and walked slowly to his office while his mind processed the significance of what ASIS was now undertaking: a quasi-military operation on Indonesian soil, supposedly a noble mission to save Jordan Carter's life but in fact an act of political expediency. He got to his office, sat down, and dwelled on the potential consequences. He was sure they would dwarf whatever debts ASIS had already run up in the aftermath of ANVIL, to the point where there was no point worrying about it. He'd been given a chance to save Carter's life and it was up to him now to execute. So he did what he had come to do a lot more frequently over the past week:

He called Scarlett.

38

TERNATE

A simulated dial tone played while the softphone app routed to her mother's mobile in Melbourne's south-east suburbs. It was late to call, but Ana had few options. Liam had cut off all communications and had only relented after she pleaded that even prisoners could phone family. The dial tone halted and gave way to a background din of Russian opera, then, 'Hello?'

'Mama.'

There was a scratching sound, then the swing of a door. The opera quietened.

'Where are you, mileni?'

Ana couldn't tell her. The laptop connection was encrypted, but Liam had warned her not to discuss or confirm her location in case of eavesdroppers at her mother's end. It seemed ridiculous, but so did everything right now.

'Don't be worried, Mum.'

'How can I not? The papers say you are missing.'

Ana pulled at her hair, anxious at what was being said about her and what her friends and family might think. 'I'm okay,' she said. 'I'm just… working on a story.'

'You do not have to lie to me, my love.'

Ana leaned against the bed head and sobbed. 'I'm sorry, Mama.'

'Oh, Ana,' said her mother. 'You never listen. Now you're in so much trouble I—' Her voice cracked.

Ana looked around the blandly furnished bedroom. How had it come to this, and where would it end? Her mother was right: she had pushed too far, and she had only herself to blame. She didn't even know if it had accomplished anything.

'I did it for Dad,' she said. 'I wanted…' She took a breath to hold the emotion at bay. 'I thought that if I achieved something it would make up for things.' She could hold it back no more: the pent-up pain of every wasted night with her drunk father, her disgust when he woke her, breath reeking of alcohol, his tears when he found the words so hard and she found them so easy, that could have been tears of joy instead of remorse for his failures. She sobbed into the phone, then the sobs became wails, and she fell onto the mattress, face buried in the pillow.

'You cannot blame yourself for your father.'

Ana barely heard her. She felt the wetness on her face and pulled the pillow away. The tension in her chest lifted and the breaths became smooth again. She rolled over and stared at the ceiling fan.

'Everything I did was for him,' she said. 'I wanted to prove he hadn't failed.'

'Oh, mileni,' said her mother. 'Your father didn't die of failure.'

'He did, Mama. He came to Australia to make something of his life, and for nothing. Every day I saw the frustration in his face, the anguish at having to work another day carrying timber and cement for men who would never respect him. He hated it, Mama – he hated himself. He wished he'd never left Croatia.'

For a while there was silence on the line. Eventually her mother cleared her throat, and Ana realised she'd been crying.

'Did your father ever speak of a town called Stupni Do?'

Ana wiped her cheek. She knew Stupni Do as the site of a massacre during the Bosnian war, but Dad had never spoken about that.

'I don't remember.'

There was a rustling sound. Ana pictured her mother on the back porch, looking out over the back yard. The swing set was long gone, and the lawn, now turfed, was always mowed.

'He was in Vareš when the army came,' said her mother. 'He was a Croat, of course, so he was safe, but he hated them. They were drunk; they beat innocent people; they were an embarrassment. Then they went to Stupni Do.'

In spite of her family background, Ana had never explored the history of the Balkan conflict. That her father had been close to it compounded her sense of shame.

'Your father knew there were lots of Bosnians there and was afraid what the soldiers would do. So he followed them, but was held up by checkpoints. It took him two days to break through, and when he got there, it was too late.'

Her mother exhaled loudly into the phone.

'They could not be saved,' she said. 'The town was destroyed; the air smelled of burnt meat. He went inside one of the houses. The bodies were still smouldering, except for one.'

Ana was shaking. She held her fingertips to her face.

'She was no older than three or four.' Ana's mother's voice cracked, and she paused to compose herself. 'The fire hadn't reached the corner of the room where she lay facing the others. She looked peaceful, from a distance. But he knew from her eyes that she had watched the soldiers pour the petrol and light the match; watched her family burn while she suffocated all alone.'

Ana's understanding of her world, her father, her purpose, tumbled into new darkness. Her father's alcoholism, revulsion to pork, his cynicism, suddenly appeared anew. His pain was not born of ambition; it was trauma. A trauma inflicted by the world he'd sought to mend, in his own way, just as she had. Just as Jonah had.

'I never knew,' she said. 'I'm so sorry.'

'*Shh,* do not be sorry,' said her mother. 'He never wanted for you to know.' Her mother's voice was composed now, sober, but suddenly distant. Ana was falling away from her, into a cave of guilt beneath her newfound comprehension of her father, of Jonah, of Rachmann. Her mother's voice returned to her, and she was cold once again, alone in a dark bedroom: the prison of her own making.

'He never wanted you to know what evil there was in this world, Ana, what people were capable of doing to one another. He never wanted you to think that if you sacrificed yourself, it would make a difference. If he were still with us,' she said, 'he would tell you it wasn't worth it.'

A hand gripped her shoulder and shook her.

'Ana, wake up.'

Liam stood over her in the darkness.

'What's going on?' she said.

'Pack your things. There's not much time.'

He left the room.

Ana rubbed her eyes and looked at the bedside. Four a.m. She dressed and looked for her bag.

Liam returned five minutes later. 'Let's go.'

She followed him to the sitting room. A single lamp was on and she tripped over a dining chair. 'Tell me what's going on,' she said.

'All I know is we have half an hour,' he whispered. He checked his watch. 'Twenty-two minutes.'

He reached the front door, opened it, and checked outside. 'Now.'

'Where are we going?' she said.

'Quiet,' he said. He led her onto the balcony. Ternate glistened below them, dozing in the half light. She looked for police, or guards, but saw no-one. A taxi was parked in the carpark, lights out.

Liam led her down the stairs but turned away from the garage. As they reached the taxi a large Indonesian man got out and Ana recoiled.

Liam turned to her. 'Get in,' he whispered.

She threw her travel case into the back seat and climbed in. Another man sat in front. He turned to her.

'Raf?' she said.

He held a finger to his mouth, his tattoos barely visible in the glow of the dash. 'Floor,' he said.

Liam helped her lay in the foot well. He climbed in and placed his feet on the floor behind her. Jaja gave her a pillow, then climbed into the driver's seat.

They drove in silence along empty streets until they reached the sea. Jaja stopped after fifteen minutes to check for surveillance. When he was satisfied, he continued on, repeating the manoeuvre several times before they parked up. Daylight had begun to break and filled the cabin with red light.

'Out,' said Raf.

They helped her climb out of the foot well. The sun burned her eyes and she rummaged through her pack for sunglasses while a morning prayer call rang out from a nearby mosque. The stench of seawater and oil hung in the morning air. They were at a disused dock on the southern tip of Ternate. The conic peak of Maitara loomed to Ana's left, in the background was Tidore. To her right, something in the sky caught a vanguard ray of sunlight before disappearing.

'The warehouse,' said Liam.

Jaja unlocked a padlock on a roller door and heaved it open. Beyond was a long, iron warehouse that held disused truck engines, fuel drums, and machinery. A green jeep was parked at the far end. There was a sound in the distance, carried across the breeze. It grew louder and Ana realised it was an aeroplane.

'Thank you, gentlemen,' said Liam. He shook Raf and Jaja's hands.

Liam touched Ana's shoulder and ushered her inside.

Ana looked back. The two men stood there, silent under the dawn, Raf's mohawk flapping in the breeze, Jaja solid as a gigantic rock. Raf smiled and said, 'We keep you safe,' and they returned to the taxi. Ana watched them, unsure how to respond and incapable of expressing her gratitude.

Liam shut the door. Oil had spilled across the floor from a rusted drum and forced Ana to hold a cloth over her mouth. They walked past the jeep and through a door that led to an office for some kind of export-import company. The plane was close now, then the engine cut. They stepped outside as a white seaplane bounced across the waves into view.

'Your ride home,' said Liam. 'Courtesy of the Australian Government. Always gets five stars, but, well, that's classified.'

The plane slowed and rocked over the light morning swell. It stopped by the end of a long wooden pier and four men climbed out dressed in hiking clothes and boots. One of them opened a float and handed out large rucksacks. They repeated the process on the other float, then carried the bags, two to a man, along the docks and into the office building.

'Come,' said Liam.

She followed him onto the jetty. There were two pilots on board; both looked Australian. One of them watched the docks behind them while the other greeted Ellis.

Ellis helped Ana on board and fastened her seat belt. The pilot placed her bag in the float compartment.

'Where will they take me?'

'Home,' he said, 'but there'll be a few stops along the way. Some might not be scheduled, so be patient. You'll be home in a few days. Here, you'll need this.'

He took something from his pocket and handed it to her. It was an emergency passport in her name.

'Don't show it to any Indonesians, obviously.'

She stared at it and said, 'Thank you.'

He smiled. She hadn't seen him smile before. 'And, uh, if you could keep all this to yourself,' he waved to the dock warehouse and the plane, 'that would be helpful.'

She pocketed the passport. 'I suppose it'd be thanks.'

The pilot waited for the door to close and started the engine. She waved to Liam as they floated out from the dock. He waved back, then walked up the jetty and disappeared. As the plane took off, she looked back at Ternate one last time, as if in hope of a sign from Jonah that he was there, that he was okay. Whatever sacrifice he had made, and whatever deeds he had committed, she just hoped they were the right ones, and that they were worth something.

The four men counted ammunition, explosives and radios. One of them stopped what he was doing to greet Ellis. He was Carter's height, broad shouldered but narrow at the waist, like a rower. A trimmed red beard framed a kind-looking face of serene self-confidence.

'Sergeant Harding?' said Ellis.

'Dean.' Harding shook Ellis's hand. 'You got the vehicle?'

'Next door.'

Ellis looked past Harding. The other three men paid no attention as they repacked their kit.

Harding's hand was outstretched. Ellis fumbled for the key to the jeep and handed it to him. 'Anything else you need?'

'Nah, don't think so,' said Harding. He grinned.

They finished re-packing kit and moved everything into the warehouse. Ellis watched idly as they stowed the bags in the rear hold of the jeep and climbed on board. There was not a hint of tension or concern among them, and he had to remind himself they were SAS troopers and not a group of adventure hikers splashing cash on a remote jungle holiday. He knew he shouldn't ask but couldn't help himself: 'What are you guys doing here?'

One of the men gave Ellis a sideways glance.

'Did no-one tell you?' said Harding.

'No.'

Harding winked. 'Just a little camping trip.'

Ellis opened the roller door and Harding started the jeep. Ellis waved as they drove out, but they ignored him.

39

The steel bolts squealed as the door was unlocked. Carter swung half-conscious from the hook, numb from the blood loss in his arms. In his delirium, he hummed along to a call to Fajr prayer. It was morning.

The soldiers cut him from the hook. Carter's numb body collapsed on the floor as they walked out again. He moaned as the blood returned to his arms, then his hands, and when the stinging subsided, he began to feel them again. The soldiers left behind a guard dressed in a long tunic over combat fatigues. His narrow face was framed by the tendrils of a beard. He stared unblinkingly at Carter as he placed a plastic bowl in front of Carter's face.

'Makan.' Eat.

Carter placed his face in the bowl and ate. It was boiled rice in broth, tasteless and overcooked. Most of it spilled on the floor before Carter passed out. When he came to, the guard was staring at him, eyes sympathetic and pitiful. There was a shout from outside.

Bootsteps approached in the passageway. The guard backed away as two men entered the room. One of them held a piece of hessian material in his hand. Carter locked eyes with his guard until the hood was placed over his head.

'Take him,' said one of the men.

They dragged him out by the rope tied to his ankles. Carter groaned as he was dragged across the concrete floor of the passageway and onto gravel. Sunlight filled the hessian hood.

The men stopped. Carter took a breath.

Hands reached underneath his arms and lifted him up. Another man lifted his legs and he was thrown onto the metal tray of a truck. Two men climbed on after him and one of them shouted, 'Drive!' The truck started and began to move. A boot was placed on Carter's back.

They drove for half an hour. Every rut and pothole pounded Carter's face into the tray. They slowed and made a series of turns. Outlines of buildings were visible through the hessian. They were near the sea. A nearby minaret sounded off the *Dhuhur* prayer.

Noon.

They carried him from the vehicle. The minaret grew louder, then faded as he was taken into a building. The hood was removed to reveal a washroom. Water was thrown in his face and he fell. The men washed his face, hands and feet while he lay soaked on the concrete floor. The hood was replaced, and he was taken to another room where they tied his wrists and ankles to a chair. There he sat, hunched and shivering over the backrest, while water dripped on the floor beneath him. Metal scraped over the floor. Someone moved behind him and removed the hood.

The workshop was dark, lit only by a narrow window high on the wall over Carter's right shoulder. Carter strained to focus. A man stood over a workbench and scraped the curved blade of a scimitar over a sharpening stone, each scrape echoing off the breezeblock walls.

The man turned and stepped into the light. The hair and beard were longer, but the eyes retained the intensity of the seven-year-old mugshot. El-Akhtar held the blade up to the light and ran a finger along its edge, then turned it over to inspect the other side. The two men stared at each other until a guard stepped forward and placed a chair between them. A corner of El-Akhtar's mouth upturned into a grin as he sat down.

'Alhamdulillah,' he said.

The guard retreated to the doorway. El-Akhtar's eyes flicked away only briefly as he brought his sword up to Carter's ear and traced the line of his jaw. When the point of the blade reached Carter's chin, he pointed the sword upwards, and pushed.

Carter groaned as the sharpened tip cut into the flesh behind his jawbone. He strained his neck to follow the blade as El-Akhtar pushed the sword one way, then the other, to inspect his face. The blade returned to the centre. Blood trickled down Carter's neck and onto his chest. El-Akhtar's tongue glided over the top of his bottom lip, then flicked in retreat, like a serpent.

'There was a lieutenant that carried this blade in Raqqa,' said El-Akhtar. His voice was a clear baritone that belied his slight features. His eyes, red with fatigue, flicked across Carter's face with admiration as he talked.

Carter shivered with the pain and exertion.

'I fought for him during the liberation, then the occupation. He was a leader of men, this lieutenant, a gift to the caliphate. His men would have followed him into hell itself, had he commanded them, and the people of Raqqa feared him.'

Carter strained to breathe through his blocked nose.

'He carried this blade wherever he went. Kept it sharp at all times. It was a symbol of the might of *Da'esh* and the righteousness of Shariah law. A reminder to all sinners they would be punished without mercy. The sword represented justice. Thanks to the blade, and to Allah, there was peace.'

He lowered the sword. Carter's head fell forward and he gasped for air. El-Akhtar wiped the blood from the cutting edge with his fingertips.

'But the lieutenant was corrupt, of course, like so many others that are bent and twisted by power. Even Allah's guidance was lost to him. He became a philanderer. He took bribes. He smuggled wine.'

Carter's eyes followed the scimitar as it sliced the air in front of his face.

'But he still held this blade, and his men still feared him. Even if they no longer loved him.'

El-Akhtar lay the sword across his lap. Carter's breathing became shallow.

'There was a boy, no more than four,' continued El-Akhtar. His voice echoed in the workshop. 'He was accused of stealing bread from one of the merchants in our sector and brought to the lieutenant to face justice. Just a boy.' He lifted a hand to indicate height. 'It was for me to hold his arm. The boy was brought to me and I held him there. When he struggled, I gripped tighter. When he cried, I silenced him.' He stared coldly at Carter. 'He had no comprehension of what was happening, but this was not important. It was divine justice; Allah's love.'

Carter stared back. His head raised and lowered with his laboured breathing.

'The lieutenant swung the scimitar.' El-Akhtar's voice rose to a shout. 'His aim was perfect, but when he struck the boy'—he grabbed his arm midway between wrist and elbow—'the arm was not severed.' El-Akhtar raised the sword and made a cutting motion. Carter flinched. 'He swung again and again, but he could not penetrate the bone. This very blade.' He held it up for Carter to see. 'The lieutenant had failed to keep it sharp, just as his soul had become dull during those long months in Raqqa.'

El-Akhtar let out a long sigh. He stroked his beard and leaned towards Carter. Carter's rasps were the only sounds in the room.

'And yet, the boy was no thief.' El-Akhtar's cheek twitched. 'His only crime was to be the son of a rival of the merchant who accused him. The merchant had learned of the lieutenant's debauchery and threatened to reveal it unless the boy was maimed. All this to punish the father.' He hissed the words. 'This innocent boy suffered for the petty obsessions of infidels, nothing more. This was not justice, it was sin.' He held the blade up to Carter's face.

'Do you understand?'

Carter swallowed, then nodded.

'When I discovered this, I vowed to take revenge on this lieutenant.' He licked his top lip and spat on the floor. 'I offered to sharpen the blade. He was happy for the favour, so self-content he could not see his own foolishness. To give power away so easily! I spent a day and night sharpening this sword, and when I was done, I returned to him. He was drunk, and it was quiet. I held the blade up as if to give it to him'—he held the scimitar to Carter's neck—'and then slaughtered him with it.'

He thrust the blade past Carter's ear. Carter exhaled.

'Just as I will slaughter you, the infidel spy,'—he gripped Carter by the hair and held the blade at his throat—'for the innocent Muslims who suffered for your corruption, your manipulation, your desire for control.' El-Akhtar's voice rose to a shout. 'For the shattered wrists of North Maluku that you hack at, mercilessly, unjustly, to condemn it to eternal misery!' He lowered his voice. '*Alhamdulillah,* I have stopped you,' he said. 'I took the blade of your spies, your agents and your threats, and turned it against you and the infidels that support you.' He released Carter's head. 'My brothers will do the same to yours across the world, street by street, mountain by mountain, nation by nation, until the fires of Islam have expelled your crusaders, just as they did in Iraq, and Syria, and Afghanistan, and as they will in Jerusalem, New York, and Sydney. You cannot stop us.' He spat in Carter's face. 'You are king no more.'

Carter's head fell forward. A pool of blood had formed at his feet, expanded by drips of blood that fell from his wrists.

'And yet,' said El-Akhtar, 'the lieutenant remained dangerous, even in death.' His voice was calm and low. 'There were many who had followed his path to betray the caliphate. It took months to find them all.' He licked his top lip again. 'That was my mistake: to not force him to reveal those he had corrupted before killing him.' He cocked his head and placed the tip of the sword on Carter's nose.

'He would have told me anything at the point of his own sword. Just as you will.'

Carter braced as El-Akhtar stood up and moved behind him. The room was quiet apart from Carter's shivered breathing.

'Tell me who else works for you,' said El-Akhtar.

Carter sucked in a breath, then shook his head.

El-Akhtar gripped Carter's hair and pulled. He thrust the blade into the back of Carter's neck.

'Give me their names.'

Carter gasped.

El-Akhtar pushed the blade deeper.

Carter's body convulsed against El-Akhtar's weight. 'I—'

'Tell me!'

Carter choked. 'There are no others.'

El-Akhtar breathed heavily in Carter's ear. Blood pooled on the blade at Carter's neck.

'Who told you about the house in Yaro?'

Carter let out a noise. It could have been a cough, or a laugh.

'Tell me who it was!' El-Akhtar shouted.

Carter convulsed with pain and suffocation. El-Akhtar withdrew the sword and returned to his chair. Blood ran down Carter's back.

'This will not end until you tell me.'

Carter caught his breath while relief swept over him, not only from exertion but for newfound clarity. All the cards lay before him now, face up to the devastating glare of his failure. He could see every hand.

'You've been tricked, Zaid.' He coughed blood. 'Maqsood deceived us both.'

El-Akhtar snorted air and held the blade up to Carter's face. 'You may be fooled easily,' he said, 'but I am not.'

Carter choked down more blood. 'It was me who discovered Maqsood had shopped you to Hartanto, not the girl,' he said. 'She blew open the negotiations on my instruction and left them both exposed. I offered Maqsood a deal thinking I could turn him, but he led me to the safehouse knowing you would have it guarded.' His body shivered with cold. 'I thought he'd betrayed me so that you would forgive him.'

El-Akhtar twitched his cheek.

'But now I know he never told you I was coming,' said Carter. 'Which means the trap wasn't for me'—Carter sucked air through his teeth—'It was for you.'

El-Akhtar locked eyes with Carter and let out a deep growl.

'Now Hartanto has to destroy you to get at me,' said Carter, 'and when he does, Maqsood will live on to inherit the kingdom you built for him. *His* kingdom.' A bead of blood navigated Carter's face and pooled on his top lip. 'Maqsood let you subdue his rivals, root out my agents and pacify the Indonesians while he planned his strike. Now, he has his opportunity.' The blood leaked into his mouth and he spat it. 'That's why he led me there.'

El-Akhtar's eyes shifted to something beyond Carter's shoulder. He was still for a time, then his eyes returned to Carter to reveal fury. Then he stood up, lifted his knee, and let out a piercing scream.

The boot impacted Carter's chest and propelled him backwards. The room filled with white light as Carter's head struck concrete. When it faded, El-Akhtar was on top of him.

Carter cried out. El-Akhtar rolled him face down and placed his knee between his shoulder blades. He lifted Carter's head, sucked in a breath, and smashed it, face first, into the concrete. He lifted Carter again and said, 'This is not the end.' He thrust Carter's face down once more and stood up. The pressure on Carter's chest dissipated. Blood drained from his face.

El-Akhtar shouted something. The room lit up as the door opened. Carter lay still and choked for air until El-Akhtar's men arrived and lifted him. Carter coughed up blood.

The men hooded him and carried him back to his cell. The fearful and weary face of his guard was the first thing he saw when they removed the hood. The guard stared at him, shocked and scared, until Carter fell unconscious.

40

Each SAS man took a two-hour shift while the others slept. They drove without haste on the busy roads, taking no chances despite the urgency of the task. They reached Tobelo in the mid-afternoon, then continued north to Galela, where they turned west across the highlands to a dirt track that snaked along the west coast of the northern tip of Halmahera.

They parked the jeep in a small clearing just before sunset. They left behind jerry cans, maps, and false passports – evidence for anyone interested that they were a group of New Zealander hikers who would soon return – and rigged the jeep so they would know if anyone interfered with it. The rest of the kit they took with them: hiking packs filled with food, water, radios, night vision gear, ammunition, grenades, and personal weapons. They kitted up once they were out of sight of the road, and once night fell, began the fourteen-kilometre patrol to Saluta.

By four a.m they had found an overwatch point with a clear view south over the entire town. Coastline ran along Saluta's eastern flank, and to the south, a wide plain dotted with green tents led to a river inlet a mile away. Prayer calls rang from a mosque and the villagers began to wake. The team counted and recorded them through their night optics as they searched for a sign of Jordan Carter.

◆

Carter was woken by gunfire. Rhythmic pulses echoed through the cell, interrupted only by the shouts of instructors and the crash of waves on a nearby shore. The gunfire faded and gave way to footsteps. The door opened to reveal his guard, wide-eyed as though watching an exotic animal in a cage, an AK-47 in one hand, the hessian hood in the other. Eventually he stepped into the cell and placed the hood over Carter's head.

'Berdiri,' he said. Stand.

The guard led Carter outside at gunpoint. The town was silent now but for the sound of waves rolling upon the shore. Rubbish smoke mixed with the sea breeze inside Carter's hood. The guard pressed the barrel into his back and pushed him towards the sunlight. Waves lapped at Carter's feet, then his knees. 'Stop,' said the guard. His voice was fractured and uncertain. He shouted at Carter to get down. Carter dropped to his knees. The guard placed a hand on his neck and pressed him into the surf. Carter resisted, then a wave crashed into his face. *'Cuci!'* shouted the guard. Wash. Carter fought to keep his head above water as salt burned the wounds on his face and neck. Another wave struck him, and for a moment he was submerged. He thrashed in search of air. He gasped as the guard lifted him by the collar and pushed him up the beach. When he reached dry sand, he fell and landed on his back, sucking for air through the wet hessian, then rolled on his side to cough up seawater. His tongue and throat ached. The guard shouted at him to get up.

'Think it's him?' said Harding.

Robbo adjusted something on his rangefinder. 'Can't be sure thanks to the hood. Height and build match our guy.'

Harding focused his rifle optic on the southern corner of the town. The hooded man walked slowly up the sand and into a clearing framed by two outbuildings, south and west. A rubbish fire burned behind one of them. Beyond was jungle that led to the camps.

The hooded man fell to his knees.

'Air,' said Carter.

'Get up!'

Carter spluttered into the hood. Seawater and stomach acid burned his throat. His nose was blocked with blood.

'Please,' said the guard. 'Get up.'

Carter was still. He choked on the hessian.

For a moment, apart from the crashing of the waves, there was almost silence. Someone in the distance shouted. A motorcycle sped off somewhere to the west.

The guard stepped forward and gripped the hood. The hood came off to reveal two outbuildings and a barrel fire. To Carter's right was a small town. The pinnacle of a mosque was framed by a line of mountains that ran along the northern edge of the village as far as the sea. Carter fell forward and looked to the east. Fishing boats were landing north of the village. Land was visible on the horizon beyond them, which he knew must be Morotai.

A man appeared from one of the outbuildings and shouted at the guard.

'Enough,' said the guard, and replaced the hood.

SWAN ISLAND, VICTORIA, AUSTRALIA

The Officer Commanding of 4 Squadron, a stolid, red-headed major, stood at the front of the command centre of the Swan Island Army Base, a purpose-built facility for support of clandestine military operations worldwide, and pointed his laser pointer at a satellite image of Saluta.

'They're holding him here,' said the major. He waved the laser pointer over the southern end of town. 'To the south are the camps and the firing range. We've seen a dozen trainees so far, there could be more. They prayed, then they took turns shooting.'

'That means weapons,' said Gibson.

'That means weapons.'

Gibson rubbed his eyes. He and the DDG had flown by government jet to Avalon airport the previous evening and arrived at Swan Island after midnight. Fatigue seemed not to bother the DDG, who watched intently from the far end of the conference table.

'What are the options?' said Gibson.

The major glanced at the DDG before he spoke. 'Militarily, we'd need to send in a full troop. Best bet is a high-altitude parachute drop into the sea, then swim or boat in before dawn. We'd need twenty-four hours.'

'He could be dead in a fraction of that,' said Gibson.

'Either way, no-one will sign off on it,' said the DDG. He peered at the major. 'There must be something your lot can do.'

'If the Indonesians won't help, the only way would be to catch them by surprise and overwhelm them. If they move Carter for any reason and head north, we might be able to ambush them at a choke point here.' The laser pointer hovered around a hairpin bend in the coast road, a kilometre north-east of the town.

'With four men?' said Gibson.

'It's Harding's call,' said the officer. 'But if it can be done, we'll get it done.'

41

Carter sat against the wall of his cell in a pool of red-tinted water. He shivered with cold. Salt burned his throat and the wounds on his neck where the sword had sliced the skin. His guard muttered to himself in the corridor, and it soothed him.

'What's your name?' said Carter.

The muttering stopped. Carter repeated the question.

'I am not supposed to tell you.'

The muttering restarted. A pitter-patter of prayer.

'My name is Jordan,' said Carter. 'Did they tell you that?'

The guard shifted posture. 'They say you are a spy.' His voice was hesitant.

'It's true, I'm a spy.' Carter wiped blood from his lip. 'And my name is Jordan.'

'You came here to kill the imam.'

'Yes.'

'The imam will kill you.'

'Yes.'

'Are you afraid?'

Carter rested his head against the wall. 'Yes,' he said. 'Aren't you?'

The guard took a long breath. 'Is it true what you said?' he whispered. 'Did Abu Maqsood really betray us?'

Carter forced himself up and shuffled to the doorway. He could see the guard's shoulder through the gap.

'Tell me your name first.'

The guard hesitated before he put his face to the door. 'My name is Hasan.'

Carter's head fell and a tear fell to his lip. *Hasan.* His mind raced with images of his dead agent, strapped to a chair in a Tobelo suburb, broken and beaten in service to Carter. He'd been afraid, but Carter had compelled him to go anyway.

'Mister?'

Carter wiped his face. 'Yes, Maqsood betrayed you.'

'I do not understand.' There was urgency in the voice. 'He said he loved us.'

'Sometimes people sacrifice the people they love.'

He couldn't shake the image of Hasan. The warmth of Yoyok's blood on his hands. The stench of cordite over Sugianto's corpse.

'Why?'

For the greater good, thought Carter. To accomplish what was necessary. For self-interest.

'Because some people don't know what it means.'

Hasan was silent. One of the fishing boats powered out to sea as water dripped from the ceiling. Carter found himself in the shed of his childhood, where he hid from his father whenever he went berserk. Then, as now, he couldn't hide from his shame.

'Do you miss your family, Hasan?'

Hasan sniffed. 'Yes.'

'When will you see them again?'

'I don't know,' said Hasan. 'When I have finished my training, maybe, if the imam does not need me.'

A car horn sounded somewhere in the distance.

'When will you finish?'

Hasan whispered to himself. 'Three weeks.'

A voice called out, indistinct over the sound of waves.

'What does he train you for?'

The voice was too quiet to be the mosque. He caught a repeated call of *'Allahu akbar'* but nothing more.

'He teaches us to become martyrs.'

Carter sucked a sharp breath through his teeth. For a time, the only sound was the echo of his own breathing. 'Will you do it?' he said eventually.

Hasan hesitated. His voice carried a rasp. *'Inshallah.'*

The distant voice grew louder. Carter shifted himself closer to the door.

'Are there others?'

Hasan was whispering to himself again. 'Yes,' he said quietly. 'But they have gone.'

'Gone where?'

'To hide until called. Then, by God's will, strike the crusaders.'

The chatter continued. Carter inched closer to the gap in the door.

'When will they be called?'

Brakes squealed outside. Hasan shifted slightly.

'When, Hasan?'

'Wait.'

Hasan walked along the corridor and opened a door. The corridor filled with light and the sound of distant chanting. Someone shouted from the clearing outside. Hasan shouted something back and was admonished. When he returned, he unlocked Carter's cell door.

Carter backed away as Hasan entered. 'What's that noise?' he said.

Bootsteps sounded on the gravel outside.

Hasan adjusted the AK across his back and unfolded the hood. 'Please.'

'What's the noise, Hasan?'

The footsteps entered the corridor. Two men. The chants had grown louder, more energetic.

'The people have come to see,' said Hasan.

'See what?'

The men appeared in the door. They wore combat fatigues and heavy boots. Grenades and magazines were slung across their camouflage vests. One of them had long, matted hair that trailed from his taqiyah and blended with his beard. The other's head was shaved.

Carter pushed away from the door. One of the men snatched the hood and shoved Hasan against the wall. The other pushed Carter's legs aside and pulled him by his hair until he was face down. Carter groaned as the heavy placed his knee in his back and stretched the hood over his head.

The knee was removed. Hands pushed between his arms and ribs.

'Hasan!' shouted Carter.

They dragged him from the cell and the hood filled with light.

The growing crowd chanted to the calls of the loudspeaker. Harding kept watch on the coastal road where a bus emerged from the treeline and crossed the bridge. One of Harding's observers radioed sightings of scooters and lorries arriving from the north. The bus reached town and parked off road. Fifteen passengers climbed out and walked to those gathered at a complex of buildings that surrounded a square dirt courtyard.

'They're taking him into the village.' Robbo's rangefinder was trained on the Carter compound.

Harding sighted Carter through his scope. Two men dragged him past the four-wheel drive and along the driveway, then disappeared behind a building. Harding refocused on the mosque where another crowd had formed. The voice on the loudspeaker changed rhythm. The crowd began to spread out along the street.

'Bastards,' said Robbo.

Harding reached for his push-to-talk.

The SAS major relayed Harding's report.

Gibson hung his head. 'They're going to execute him,' he said.

'Do or die, major,' said the DDG. 'Must be something your boys can do. Take out the executioner, scatter the crowd?'

The SAS man was unmoved. 'Anything we do now will get our men killed,' he said. 'I'm sorry, gentlemen.'

'We're all sorry,' said the DDG.

The chants became jeers. Crowds moved in to shout at Carter, then backed away from his captors. A shadow moved in front of him. He lifted his feet as a reflex, but they were numb; he only knew they were still attached from the sound they made across the ruts and stones. The shadow made a retching noise and he felt cold fluid land on the side of his face. A stone struck his back, then the guards dragged him around a turn. The shouting grew louder. The loudspeaker grew louder still. They turned into another street and El-Akhtar's voice rose.

'In the name of Allah, the most gracious, the most merciful.'

The crowd closed around them. They beat his back and legs with sticks. Someone slapped his face and he groaned. The guards shouted for people to move out of the way.

'All the praise and thanks be to Allah, the lord of the world.'

Blood drained into his eye. The hood darkened as more onlookers crowded in. Something struck his ribs and they exploded in pain. He screamed and fell to the ground. The guards lifted him and shouted at the crowd to back away.

'The most gracious, the most merciful. Master of the day of judgement.'

The hood filled with light as the crowd parted. El-Akhtar was metres away. Carter was brought before a rectangular structure.

'You we worship, and you we ask for help.'

Carter's kneecap struck a step. His shout was drowned out by El-Akhtar.

'Guide us to the straight way.'

They reached the top of the platform. El-Akhtar was visible through the hood as he gesticulated. The sun glinted off the scimitar.

'The way of those on whom you have bestowed your grace…'

El-Akhtar's voice rose again.

'...not of those who earned your anger, nor of those who went astray!'

Carter let out a grunt as a guard gripped the hood and pulled back. The hessian tore his skin where the blood had dried. Sunlight blinded him. A young man in Islamic robes and a combat vest moved in front of them to reposition a camera. Only El-Akhtar's voice cut through the noise of the crowd.

'I show you now this spy,' he shouted. *'This evildoer and enemy of all muslims in every place.'*

The crowd jeered. El-Akhtar lifted the point of the blade to Carter's ear. Carter's vision blurred. He blinked.

El-Akhtar continued his calls. *'You have given Allah your faith and me your servitude. In return, I promise you protection from the infidels.'*

Something caught Carter's peripheral vision. A hand gripped his hair and turned his head towards the crowd.

'And under that protection you will live free. Free from evil, and free to worship. Free citizens of an independent Islamic State of North Maluku!'

The crowd shouted their approval. Carter watched to the west. The movement returned, like a stone skipping across the hilltops, followed by another. El-Akhtar paused for breath. The movement disappeared below the horizon.

Carter gasped as El-Akhtar gripped him by the hair and placed the cold blade against his neck. The cold gave way to the warmth of his blood. His breaths shortened to sharp pulses in his chest. El-Akhtar released his head and lifted the loudspeaker.

'There is no God but Allah,' he cried.

The crowd repeated the verse, but the shouts were muted. A distant pulse reverberated across the air.

'Muhammad is the messenger of Allah!'

The loudspeaker fell. El-Akhtar gripped Carter's head. Carter closed his eyes as the blade pressed into his neck. His breath stopped. The sound of blood pulsed through his ears.

Someone called out from the crowd. Carter opened his eyes to see confusion and panic. El-Akhtar hesitated. The pulsing sound grew louder.

'Helikopter!'

El-Akhtar withdrew the blade. Carter slumped forward. Shouts became screams and the crowd began to shift. Carter turned his head as helicopters descended the western ridgeline.

El-Akhtar shouted into the loudspeaker: *'Shoot them!'*

The square erupted with gunfire as El-Akhtar's soldiers engaged the incoming helicopters. Screaming onlookers ran in all directions in search of safety. El-Akhtar shouted something. Someone grasped Carter and pulled him from the platform.

'Take him,' shouted a soldier. Muzzle blasts and rotor noise resounded from all directions. Then another voice called to them, louder this time and from the air, to command them to cease fire and surrender their weapons. A soldier rolled Carter onto his stomach and hooded him.

Gibson stared helplessly at the screen. It had been inevitable the Indonesians would find El-Akhtar, but no-one expected them to arrive so soon and with enough knowledge to stage an attack. They'd been informed.

'There's nothing we can do,' said the major. 'Our best option is to let the Raider battalion rescue him once they've cleared the village.'

'They don't even know he's there,' said the DDG.

Gibson saw now that Maqsood had played them all. 'They know he's there,' he said. 'It's why they've come.'

Sparks pinged off the hull of the first Mi-17 as it came to a hover over a field west of the village. It turned lethargically before a minigun on its starboard side opened up on the jungle camps to the south. The second passed over the camp then north to land at a clearing where the north-bound road met the sea. Gunfire erupted from buildings east of the mosque and it aborted the approach.

The third helicopter, a Bell 412, orbited the town and broadcast commands to those below.

The first heli settled to a hover twenty feet above ground. Raiders rappelled from the rear hatch under fire from the village. Harding counted twenty soldiers out before the helicopter rose again and returned fire on the camps. There were too many civilians to fire on the village.

'Scalpel, Blackhat.'

Harding barely heard the call over the gunfire. He reached for the push-to-talk. 'Send it, Blackhat.'

The second Mi-17 had pushed south. It landed on the firing range and more Raiders ran out. Muzzle flashes appeared near the encampments and one of the Raiders fell.

The 412 swooped over his position as a radio message arrived.

'Fucking hell,' he said. *Click.* 'Say again.'

'Can you retrieve the package?'

Raiders moved building-to-building from the western edge of the village. A troop carrier shrouded in green canvas appeared from a structure near the coast and started moving up the road in their direction.

Harding shouted at Robbo. 'You got eyes on Carter?'

The southern Raiders were pinned down. Their chopper slowed above and behind them as its minigun opened fire.

'Centre of town. They're moving him south.'

Two men dragged the lifeless body by the arms. One of them signalled to a boy who moved ahead, weapon up. Ahead of them was the road where the truck had been. The western Raiders were held back by militants. The southern group advanced again under cover of the heli.

'Fuck, look,' said Robbo. 'By the mosque.'

A man clad in white had emerged from an alley. He was unremarkable except that he ran in the direction of the assaulting Raiders and carried unusual bulk around his torso. The Raiders spotted him, and within moments the ground by his feet erupted under gunfire. He persevered until he seemed to trip, fall, and roll. One of his arms reached for the sky, and half a second later, he exploded.

'Jesus,' said Robbo. A cloud of white smoke ascended from the centre of town.

'Scalpel, can you retrieve the package?'

Harding got eyes on Carter. His captors had sheltered from the bomb blast but were on the move again. West of them, Raiders fired volleys at unseen militants as they pushed further into town. There was no way to get close.

He clicked his radio. 'Blackhat, neg—'

He cut the transmission as the truck reappeared and rolled to a stop. The boy opened the rear tray and the soldiers loaded Carter on board. The 412 circled above and called for the vehicles to surrender.

'Scalpel, say again.'

Four militants trained their fire west while the others climbed onto the lorry. They fired another volley as the truck departed east, then ran to follow it. Others climbed into the four-wheel drive. There was only one way out of the village. The 412 made a sharp turn north to follow it. There was nowhere for it to land; it would have to intercept them at the next town, six kilometres away.

That would do.

Harding pressed transmit. 'Affirmative, Blackhat. In pursuit.'

Carter felt every rut and crevasse of the village roads. He bit down on a piece of hessian to blunt the shock. The truck turned north and his head struck someone's boot.

Something pinged off the tray of the truck, then the cabin.

Reports of AK fire filled the rear hold as the gunmen engaged a target behind them. Carter pushed away from the shock of the muzzle blasts. Someone held him down. He cried out but heard nothing over the gunfire.

One of the men bashed on the cabin. 'Drive faster!' The driver shouted something back. A helicopter flew overhead. Another bomb went off in the distance.

The truck turned right and the road surface smoothed. The sound of rotors faded to leave the sound of the truck engine and exerted breathing.

'Where did they go?' said a soldier.

One of them rapped on the cab of the truck. 'Faster!'

The truck accelerated. The rotors grew louder. The helicopter loudspeaker shouted to stop the vehicle.

'Can you hit them?' said one of the men.

Carter heard weeping.

One of the soldiers stepped over Carter and shouted at whoever was crying. The sobbing didn't stop. The helicopter issued another command.

The soldier fired a burst of three rounds followed by another seven, then held the trigger and screamed. When his magazine was depleted, the noise of the helicopter was gone.

'Did you kill them?'

'I don't know.'

One of the men laughed. 'You killed them!'

The men cheered.

The truck reached the crest of a hill and the engine cut.

One of the men banged on the cabin. 'Hey, keep going!'

Someone laughed. The truck began to slow.

'Dog!'

The truck hit something and dipped. Carter's head hit the front of the tray as someone fell on him. The engine stalled.

A door slammed shut in the distance, followed by a burst of gunfire.

Carter rolled away to get air. The breathing next to him was strained and short.

There was movement in the cab. Someone climbed out and shot at something. A second man opened the other door and fired a burst. 'Get out, get out!' shouted one of the soldiers.

The four-wheel drive idled somewhere nearby. Reports rang out from both vehicles. Boots thumped along the tray. One pair landed on the ground and the air cracked. The others hesitated.

'Where did he go?'

'Someone shot him!'

The breathing next to Carter became shallow. There were three loud cracks near the truck followed by deep thuds from the hillside. The smell of urine filled the rear hold of the troop carrier. Another burst of AK fire rang out.

'Shoot back. Do it!'

Hesitation. 'What about the bulè?'

'Forget him. Go!'

The gunmen jumped out and opened fire. One of the men screamed as he fired, his voice cut by another shockwave. His body landed next to the truck. Another soldier called out from across the road and fired. More cracks of gunfire. The thuds were louder now, and closer.

The soldier crawled away from Carter.

'Don't go, Hasan.'

Another burst rang out. A bullet rang off the truck chassis. A fighter let out a scream and writhed on the ground by the cab.

'They will kill us.' Hasan's cowering silhouette was visible through the hessian.

'They won't,' said Carter. 'They've come for me. You'll live if you surrender.'

'My brothers need me.'

'Your family needs you,' said Carter. 'You can see them again.'

'How?'

'Because it's over.'

Someone shouted from the hillside.

'Release me,' said Carter. 'Please.'

Hasan shuffled back to him and removed the hood. His bloodshot eyes peered out from his wet face. His pants were dark where he had urinated. He pointed his rifle at Carter.

Carter raised his hands. 'I won't hurt you.'

'Liar.' Hasan shivered. 'You are a spy.'

A soldier fired from near the side of the truck. There weren't many of them left.

'I told the truth about Maqsood,' said Carter.

Hasan blinked. He was still taking short, rapid breaths, like he had sprinted up a long hill. He looked at Carter's bindings, then at the road behind him.

He kneeled down and reached for his knife. Carter's hands came free. There was another shout in the distance, then movement outside.

Carter grabbed Hasan. 'Get down.'

The remaining militant opened fire on the hillside. The returning cracks were punctuated with the sound of lead impacting flesh. The body fell and the head slapped the side of the truck.

Hasan wept into Carter's chest. Carter reached for the AK. Hasan hesitated before releasing it. Carter's free arm wrapped across Hasan's chest, then up to his neck.

He squeezed.

Hasan's boots pounded across the metal tray as he convulsed. Carter braced himself against the side of the truck.

'Where are the bombers, Hasan?'

'I—' Hasan clawed at Carter's arm and gasped for breath. '—not—'

Carter held firm. 'Tell me.'

'Please,' whispered Hasan.

The scene had fallen silent, leaving only the sound of Hasan's desperate breathing and the slowing kicks of his feet. The gunfire had stopped; El-Akhtar's men lay dead or dying outside. They had been wiped out the same way Sugianto and his troopers had been, another band of victims to follow Hasan and Yoyok. The image of their slain bodies struck like a bullet.

Carter released his grip. Hasan fell away and sucked for air. Carter sat up and collected the AK.

He started for the tailgate. A bony hand gripped his arm and pulled him back.

'It is too late to stop them,' said Hasan. He took a strained breath. 'It is Allah's will.'

Carter released the boy's grip and held him by the shoulder.

'Wait here until they come for you,' he said. Beating helicopter blades droned in the distance. 'They will let you go home. Don't be afraid.'

Hasan's eyes shone up at him from the darkness.

'I don't want to die, Mister.'

Carter pushed himself to the edge of the tray and turned to face him.

'No-one else has to die.'

They took cover at the treeline and surveyed the road. The four-wheel drive had come to rest in a ditch, one dead militant either side, the driver dead. A fourth man remained inside, obscured by the shattered windscreen. Twenty metres further up, the troop carrier had wedged its front-right wheel in a gully. Five bodies lay next to it. The sixth lay on the opposite side of the road by the escarpment.

The sound of rotors loomed to the north.

'Move,' said Harding.

The four troopers moved swiftly along the road, rifles up, eyes and ears in search of movement. Robbo trained his rifle on the four-wheel drive as one of the troopers pushed up on it. He opened the rear passenger door and gave the signal to move in. Harding approached to find El-Akhtar's body slumped in the back seat, head hanging at an angle from where a bullet had struck him in the neck. Harding lifted the head and photographed it as the others moved up on the truck.

Two troopers held, one either side of the truck cab. The rotors were louder. The gunfire from the town had eased. Harding and Robbo crept along the left side of the truck, heads below the level of the tray. Harding reached the rear of the truck and heard weeping.

On his signal, Robbo walked in a wide arc to cover into the tray. When he was in position, he nodded.

Harding stood up and aimed his weapon into the truck. It took a second for his eyes to adjust to the gloom.

Movement.

He ducked behind the tailgate and swore under his breath. Robbo, rifle at the ready, shook his head. The helicopter crossed the road somewhere to the north and faded again. Harding stood up again, took a breath and looked inside.

The boy could not have been more than seventeen. He lay in a foetal position at the front of the tray, hands in front of his legs and unarmed. Harding climbed into the tray and went to him, the cabin filled with the sound of the boy's muttering and the stench of piss and cordite.

'Hey,' said Harding. *'Sudah aman.'* It's safe now.

The boy stared at him.

'Anda terluka?' said Harding. Are you hurt?

No response. Harding checked the boy over and found no injuries.

'Orang Australi ke mana?' Where did the Australian go?

Tears fell from the boy's eyes, wide and white in the gloom. The muttering stopped; his lips quivered as he tried to speak.

Harding gripped him and repeated his question. *'Orang Australi ke mana?'*

'Maqsood'—the boy wheezed—*'ngkhianatin kami.'*

Confused, Harding held him closer. *'Bilang lagi,'* he said. Say again.

The boy closed his eyes as the pulse of the rotors rose again. Soldiers shouted in the distance. Harding left the boy and climbed from the tray as the helicopter crossed in search of a landing point. There was no sign of Carter. In the distance, columns of smoke rose over the village. A fishing boat drifted fifty metres from the coastline, oblivious to the chaos on shore. The helicopter crossed again to begin an approach somewhere north. Harding watched it descend behind the trees and checked his watch. They were out of time. He turned to his men and, with a nod of his head, signalled to withdraw.

42

DARWIN

The corporal pointed her hand through a doorway and said, 'Wait here, please.'

Ana stepped into a conference room with a large window that offered a view across the aerodrome to Darwin airport.

'For how long?' said Ana.

The corporal reached for the door handle. 'Someone will be with you in a moment.'

The door closed softly to leave Ana in silence. She was tired of waiting, even if she was relieved to be on home soil. She took a chair by the window and watched a Boeing 737 spool up at the end of the runway.

It had taken four days to reach Darwin. The seaplane had flown multiple legs to reach Wetar island off the northern coast of East Timor, a flight that took most of the day. After midnight, she had been ushered onto a rusted fishing boat that continued south before handing her over to an East Timorese trawler somewhere north of Baucau. It was after six p.m. when they reached Dili, where she was met by an Australian woman who introduced herself as Justine from the Embassy and checked her into the Timor Plaza Hotel. 'Stay in your room until I come for you,' said Justine. 'Don't speak to anyone, and no calls or internet.' Ana spent the next two days alone with a streaming subscription and endless thoughts of spies, jihadists and home. Justine returned and took her to the airport for the flight to Darwin, a chartered jet that taxied away from Darwin's main terminal and parked at a hangar on the air force base.

Footsteps and lowered voices arrived in the hall. Ana sat upright as the door opened and two suited men walked in. The first, with slicked black hair, purple bowtie and large gold rings on each finger, introduced himself as Barron. The other was tieless and wore an easy smile. 'Andy,' he said as he rounded the table and shook her hand. 'Pleasure.'

Barron sat opposite her and twisted a gold ring around his finger. 'How were your travels, Ms Kovacevic?'

'What do you want?' she said.

Andy suppressed a smirk and sat down.

Barron cleared his throat. 'We would like to ask you some questions.'

Ana crossed her arms.

He removed a manila folder from a briefcase and opened it on the conference table. 'Perhaps first we could address the, uh, formalities.' He pushed the folder across to her and raked a hand through his hair.

She opened it to find a multi-page non-disclosure agreement stamped with the logo of the Australian Secret Intelligence Service.

'I'm not signing this,' she said. 'I want to go home.'

'Ms Kovacevic—'

'You can't hold me here, and the longer you do, the worse it will be for you.'

'Really now,' said Barron. 'There is no need for that.'

She pushed the folder back to him. Barron stared at it.

'You are free to go, of course, Ana,' said Andy. He rested his elbow on the table and smiled gently. 'We only hoped to have a conversation about Jonah before you did so.'

Ana studied him: the wavy grey hair, the thin-rimmed glasses that framed kind eyes. His was a handsome face, earnest and unthreatening. The kind that made you want to help.

'What about him?'

He glanced at Barron and shifted forward. 'How well did you know Jonah?' he said.

'Enough to trust him.'

Andy smiled again. 'He trusted you, too,' he said. 'We would like to support him, if you'll help us.'

'What's happened to him?'

Andy's smile turned apologetic. He pushed the form back to her.

She opened the folder and read the agreement again. It promised the full weight of the law if she revealed anything about her involvement with the Australian Government, especially anything to do with the intelligence services, but was otherwise lightweight, and probably unenforceable. Either way, there was nothing to censor her reporting on North Maluku.

She signed it with a pen that was clipped to the folder and handed it back to Barron. He countersigned and returned the folder to his briefcase.

'Thank you,' he said.

She slumped in her chair. 'Now what?'

Andy stood up and gestured to the door. 'Shall we take a walk?'

CANBERRA

The clear Canberra sky had turned a deeper shade of blue in the late afternoon. The birch trees had shed the last of their foliage to leave the city colourless. Inside the DDG's office, the air conditioning belched cold air as if determined to match the outside autumn chill. Gibson felt the cold but did nothing about it. Exhausted, he slumped on one of the guest chairs, tie half-undone, and stared out the window while he came to terms with himself. Not even the slamming door broke his reverie.

'So, how was it?' said the DDG. He strode through the office in a set of grey, skin-tight gym clothes. He wiped his hair with a towel which he threw over the back of his chair. He turned to face the room, hands on hips.

'Fine,' said Gibson, but it was only half-true. The honourable inspector-general and her staff had grilled him for the better part of six hours on ASIS's activities in North Maluku. No detail was spared scrutiny, from the time Operation ANVIL had been conceived to the events of the past weeks that had culminated in its unceremonious termination and the failed attempt to rescue a service operative. Gibson had played dead for his interrogators and now felt deader for it. He had contemplated ANVIL's justification ever since the riots in Kao, yet when called to explain ASIS's activities and judgements, not least his own, Gibson could point only to ministerial signoffs and risk assessments and present a bureaucratically unsatisfying rejoinder that ultimately, despite the costs, they had succeeded in defeating IS in the province. His only triumph had been to give Carter a fighting defence – even though the officer's actions were, in every legal sense, indefensible – by pointing to the lack of facts on the ground: there were no living witnesses to Carter's actions in the lead up to his capture, and given he was missing-in-action, these were arguable grounds to reserve judgement until he was found and brought in front of the panel. The inspector-general had seemed content with this, but whether for the sake of natural justice or just her preference for live prey, Gibson couldn't tell. Either way, such pleas would soon wither in front of what was to come: more hearings, adverse findings, puerile finger-pointing – the depressing self-flagellation of the Australian government bureaucracy. Gibson wasn't one to shirk accountability and he was honourable enough to own his mistakes, but endless investigations and enquiries would only—

'Andy.'

Gibson rubbed fatigue from his eyes and looked up. The DDG, standing over his throne, wore a look somewhere between concern and impatience.

'Cheer up, would you?' said the DDG. 'We won.'

'I'm not sure how.'

The DDG smirked. 'Come now.' He opened his safe to produce a bottle of scotch whiskey and two glasses. 'This is the business we're in, Andy. It's messy.' The seal of the bottle cracked in his hand as he unscrewed the top. 'El-Akhtar's dead, and *we*'—he gestured to himself and Gibson with his spare hand while he poured—'got him.' He closed the bottle and handed one of the glasses to Gibson. 'And to cap it off, an Islamic State insurrection in North Maluku has been averted. *Alhamdulillah,* as they say. Job well done.' He tipped his glass. 'Cheers.'

Gibson clinked his glass against the DDG's but felt none of the mirth. 'I'm glad you see the positive,' he said. 'From here, it looks like we rolled out the red carpet for Maqsood.'

'Well,' said the DDG, 'perhaps we did.' He sunk his scotch in one go and let out a satisfied *Ah* as he put his glass down. 'Not ideal, but the simple fact is that Maqsood's a lot better than any of the others, wouldn't you say? You would know.'

'He played us, Terry. All of us. And now he's got control of every Islamist faction in the province. This is what we all feared when we set up ANVIL.'

The DDG studied him. 'Sure,' he said. 'But look at it from the Indonesians' perspective. Maqsood may be a hardliner, but there's never been clear evidence of his involvement in terrorism. Moreover, whilst they missed out on taking El-Akhtar for themselves, in their eyes, Maqsood was the one who gave him up and that puts him back on Hartanto's birthday card list. The groups were already united thanks to El-Akhtar, so they'd be right to fear someone else stepping into the vacuum. Someone they don't control.'

And there was the key word, Gibson thought. *Control.* The genius of ANVIL had been knowing that control of people like Maqsood was illusory. The only way was to deceive them into controlling themselves.

Gibson swirled his scotch. The fluid left a brown film on the glass before draining, helplessly, back to the bottom.

'What does ASIS plan to do?'

'We have permission to leave Liam in place. Under strict conditions, of course. You know I had a lot of time for Jordan, but those days are over; unless we see a clear threat, the Australian Government doesn't want to be involved.' He let out an exaggerated sigh. 'We can sit and watch, but we have to leave this to the Indonesians.'

Gibson kept staring at his glass. It wasn't the outcome he'd feared most; Ellis in Ternate at least provided options. He lifted his glass and recoiled as the scotch scalded his throat.

'And what about Jordan?'

The DDG brought his hands to a steeple in front of his face.

'Harding says he saw him at the camp, but also says there was no way he got out of that truck unsighted.' He shrugged. 'Maybe he was never there; maybe Hartanto got him. We may never know.'

'That can't be the end of it.'

The DDG stood up and took Gibson's glass. 'Perhaps not.' He returned the bottle and both glasses to the safe. 'Kovacevic arrives tomorrow. And fuck me, with the paperwork that took, I should have left her in Dili.' He closed the safe with a clang. 'She was the last person we know other than Liam to see Jordan alive. You may as well fly to Darwin and find out what she knows.'

'Thanks, Terry.' Gibson stood up to leave.

'But that's as far as we go.'

Gibson nodded and approached the door.

'And I mean what I said, Andy.'

Gibson paused and turned to face the DDG.

'Be proud,' said the DDG. He stood over his desk and stared at Gibson. 'There was nothing more we could possibly do.'

Gibson wasn't so sure, but he said his thanks, shut the door and walked back to his office certain of one thing: whatever ASIS told itself, nothing was finished in North Maluku.

TERNATE

Seven rapid slams on the front door. A pause, then another five.

Ellis stumbled out of bed and searched for the light switch. Four more slams. The light came on and he pulled on a t-shirt and a pair of jeans. The pounding continued. *Fuck's sake.*

Two police officers stood at the front door looking pissed off. It was six a.m, so fair enough.

'We come in,' said one of them.

'Get lost,' said Ellis.

The other officer stood upright and stuck his chest out.

'I said get lost.'

They held eye contact until Hartanto appeared.

He marched towards Ellis along the balcony. Anas followed in his shadow with a briefcase and avoided Ellis's eye contact. The police moved out of the way.

'*Selamat pagi,* Pak Ellis,' said Hartanto.

'You know me, H-man. I don't speak Indonesian.'

'It means get the fuck out of the way.' Hartanto snapped his fingers and Anas handed him a piece of paper. Hartanto gave it to Ellis and smiled.

'Mister Jordan Carter has been declared *Persona Non Grata,*' said Hartanto. 'This is a copy of the letter to your minister revoking his diplomatic privileges with immediate effect.'

'Cool,' said Ellis. He gave Hartanto a laconic grin. 'Have you told Jordan?'

Hartanto stared at him with an amused look on his face. Anas handed him another page, still avoiding eye contact with Ellis.

Hartanto checked it and held it out for the Australian. 'Here is your minister's consent to search Mister Carter's residential premises. Not that we need it. Step aside, please.'

Ellis made a show of reading every word out loud. When he was finished, he stepped to one side and waved the officers through. Anas watched on from the balcony. Hartanto stood in the entryway and gazed at the ceiling.

'Nice place,' said Hartanto. 'You must be a housekeeper.'

'Something like that.'

The officers returned, half out of breath. *'Tidak ada, Pak.'* Not here.

'You're good at it.' Hartanto smiled. 'I wonder how you got her out?'

'No idea what you're talking about.' Ellis flashed a grin.

Anas glanced at Ellis, then Hartanto, before turning to look at the view.

'You should show more respect, Mister Ellis.' Hartanto stepped in so that their faces were inches apart. 'For too long your service treated us like fools. If it were up to you, there would be war in North Maluku. Now, thanks to me, there is peace, security and prosperity for these people.'

'Only as long as you give Maqsood what he wants,' said Ellis. 'One day you won't be able to, and by then he'll be too strong to stop.'

Hartanto examined Ellis's face. 'Easy for you to say, but there are no Australian lives on the line, are there?' He raised a finger at the Australian's chest. 'You should mind your own business, young man.'

Anas turned to face them and folded his arms. This time, he stared knowingly at Ellis.

Ellis smiled. 'Sorry, H-man. I get paid not to do that.'

CANBERRA

The air was bitter cold in the dark of morning. Scarlett lay in Gibson's arms while they listened to the whine of an old fan heater at the foot of the bed.

'You should relax,' said Scarlett. 'I post out soon. You'll miss this when I'm gone.'

Gibson stroked hair from her face while his mind retraced the previous day's debriefs. 'Everyone has the right to disappear,' he said.

She looked up at him. 'You don't really believe that.'

He kissed her forehead. 'No. But I wish it were true.'

Scarlett pushed herself up onto her elbows and frowned at him.

'Let him go,' she said. 'Jordan will show up when he decides to, just like you trained him to. Worrying about him won't help anyone.'

He supposed she was right, assuming Carter was still alive, but Gibson wouldn't stop until he knew for sure. He rubbed a lock of her hair between his fingertips, and the room suddenly filled with high-pitched noise.

'Oh, already?' said Scarlett. She rolled off him.

Gibson grabbed his phone and muted the alarm. 'Early flight,' he said. He kissed her. 'She lands soon.'

DARWIN

They stepped into typical Darwin day and followed a footpath along an empty street. Andy opened another button on his collar and rolled his sleeves.

'Jonah's missing,' said Andy. He paused while a large military plane taxied from a hangar a hundred metres away. 'The Indonesians don't have him, or at least they aren't saying so. Unlikely the militants do. You were one of the last people he spoke to who's still alive.'

Ana felt a chill through the tropical heat. 'What happened?'

Andy sighed. 'He acted outside the rules and got caught up in things.' He stopped and faced her. 'I'm sure you know what I mean.'

She nodded solemnly. 'What do you want to know?'

They stepped off the footpath to a barbecue gazebo in the middle of a lawn. They sat down and Andy fanned himself.

'Did he say anything about his intentions, contacts, how to reach him, anything like that?'

She thought back to the last time she had seen Jonah while the Legu Gam celebrations paraded along the street outside her guesthouse. During her escape, she had relived the memory until it was distorted and inconsistent, but it seemed clear to her now that Jonah never intended to see her again.

'No,' she said. A group of air force personnel walked by. 'But I sensed he felt let down by you. Like he'd been abandoned.'

'Held back, certainly.' Andy squinted at something across the airfield. 'Obviously, we did what we could for him.'

'I wouldn't know anything about that.' She looked at Andy. 'I don't even know his real name.'

He smiled sadly. 'Jordan,' he said. 'Jonah's a work name.'

She repeated the name to herself. 'And the photography?'

'All cover. Helped that he was good at it.' Andy's stare shifted to the horizon.

Ana followed his gaze across the airfield. There was nothing.

'I'm sorry I can't be more help,' she said. 'I can tell he meant a lot to you.'

He forced a grin. 'Quite alright,' he said. 'You did him proud.'

She wondered if she had, and whether any of it had been worthwhile. She admitted to herself she had done Jonah's bidding, despite what he stood for, and had done so willingly. He stood on the side of secrecy, manipulation and deception – tools he used for what he believed were noble outcomes, but the collateral damage of which she could not ignore. She thought about what had befallen him and whether he would care what he had put her through before her mind turned to Sayeed, to Rachmann and all the other anonymous victims of his work, only visible to her as tips of icebergs above an impenetrable ocean of secrets and lies.

'Was it worth it?' she said.

Andy turned to face her.

'The deception, the violence, the sacrifice,' she continued. 'Did you and your spies actually think you could solve the problems of North Maluku?'

He watched an airliner as it approached on final. Something hardened in his stare.

'I'm not here to make the world a better place,' he said. 'I'm here to serve this country's interests, whatever and wherever they may be.' Puffs of smoke lifted from the runway as the aircraft touched down. 'But I wonder, Ana: have you ever asked yourself the same question?'

Ana had contemplated the question countless times in the past ninety-six hours, all-the-while haunted by her mother's admonishment for the futility of her sacrifice and her guilt for Inspector Rachmann. She looked away as if to hide the fact, and in the shimmering haze of the aerodrome saw the surface of the lake where her father had taught her to fish as a young girl. Her most vivid memory of that time had been the way he stood at the bow of the tiny boat like the hero he was to her, jaw set hard against the wind, and how, as he stared resolutely at the distant horizon, the darkened skin around his eyes creased tight in lines of deep black. All this time, she had believed it was for the glare.

She turned back to Andy and said, 'I only wanted to find truth.'

In truth, she had found herself.

Bevan G. Roberts grew up in Canberra, Australia surrounded by technology, the military, and government. During a career in and around the departments of defence and foreign affairs, Bevan worked for a time at the Australian embassy in Indonesia, an experience that opened his eyes to Asia and inspired his first novel, *Kingdom of Spies.*

Bevan lives in Brisbane, Australia, with his wife and two amazing boys.

www.bevangroberts.com.au
@bevangroberts
#kingdomofspies

CPSIA information can be obtained
at www.ICGtesting.com
Printed in the USA
BVHW070952230822
645281BV00008B/451

9 780645 446999